BY TIMOTHY ZAHN

STAR WARS

STAR WARS: Choices of One
STAR WARS: Allegiance
STAR WARS: Outbound Flight
STAR WARS: Survivor's Quest
STAR WARS: Vision of the Future
STAR WARS: Specter of the Past
STAR WARS: The Last Command
STAR WARS: Dark Force Rising
STAR WARS: Heir to the Empire

ALSO

Cobra Alliance
The Judas Solution
Conquerors' Legacy
Conquerors' Heritage
Conquerors' Pride
Cobra Bargain
Cobra Strike
The Backlash Mission
Cobra
The Blackcollar

CHOICES OF ONE

STAR WARS

CHOICES OF ONE

Timothy Zahn

DEL REY BALLANTINE BOOKS
NEW YORK

Published in the United States by Del Rey, an imprint of The Random House Publishing Group, a division of Random House, Inc., New York.

DEL REY is a registered trademark and the Del Rey colophon is a trademark of Random House, Inc.

This book contains an excerpt from *Star Wars: Riptide* by Paul S. Kemp. This excerpt has been set for this edition only and may not reflect the final content of the forthcoming edition.

ISBN 978-0-345-51125-6

Printed in the United States of America on acid-free paper

www.starwars.com
www.delreybooks.com

2 4 6 8 9 7 5 3 1

First Edition

For Mom,
who never doubted that this whole
writing gig would work out someday

THE STAR WARS NOVELS TIMELINE

OLD REPUBLIC
5000–33 YEARS BEFORE
STAR WARS: A New Hope

Lost Tribe of the Sith*
Precipice
Skyborn
Paragon
Savior
Purgatory
Sentinel

3650 *YEARS BEFORE STAR WARS: A New Hope*

The Old Republic: Deceived
Lost Tribe of the Sith*
Pantheon
Secrets

Red Harvest

The Old Republic: Fatal Alliance

1032 *YEARS BEFORE STAR WARS: A New Hope*

Knight Errant

Darth Bane: Path of Destruction
Darth Bane: Rule of Two
Darth Bane: Dynasty of Evil

RISE OF THE EMPIRE
33–0 YEARS BEFORE
STAR WARS: A New Hope

Darth Maul: Saboteur*
Cloak of Deception
Darth Maul: Shadow Hunter

---

32 *YEARS BEFORE STAR WARS: A New Hope*

> ***STAR WARS:* EPISODE I**
> **THE PHANTOM MENACE**

Rogue Planet
Outbound Flight
The Approaching Storm

---

22 *YEARS BEFORE STAR WARS: A New Hope*

> ***STAR WARS:* EPISODE II**
> **ATTACK OF THE CLONES**

22–19 *YEARS BEFORE STAR WARS: A New Hope*

The Clone Wars
The Clone Wars: Wild Space
The Clone Wars: No Prisoners

Clone Wars Gambit
Stealth
Siege

Republic Commando
Hard Contact
Triple Zero
True Colors
Order 66

Shatterpoint
The Cestus Deception
The Hive*
MedStar I: Battle Surgeons
MedStar II: Jedi Healer
Jedi Trial
Yoda: Dark Rendezvous
Labyrinth of Evil

---

19 *YEARS BEFORE STAR WARS: A New Hope*

> ***STAR WARS:* EPISODE III**
> **REVENGE OF THE SITH**

Dark Lord: The Rise of Darth Vader
Imperial Commando 501st

Coruscant Nights
Jedi Twilight
Street of Shadows
Patterns of Force

The Han Solo Trilogy
The Paradise Snare
The Hutt Gambit
Rebel Dawn

The Adventures of Lando Calrissian
The Force Unleashed
The Han Solo Adventures
Death Troopers
The Force Unleashed II

*An eBook novella
**Forthcoming

REBELLION
0–5 YEARS AFTER
STAR WARS: A New Hope

Death Star
Shadow Games

0

| **STAR WARS: EPISODE IV** |
| **A NEW HOPE** |

Tales from the Mos Eisley Cantina
Tales from the Empire
Tales from the New Republic
Allegiance
Choices of One
Galaxies: The Ruins of Dantooine
Splinter of the Mind's Eye

3 *YEARS AFTER STAR WARS: A New Hope*

| **STAR WARS: EPISODE V** |
| **THE EMPIRE STRIKES BACK** |

Tales of the Bounty Hunters
Shadows of the Empire

4 *YEARS AFTER STAR WARS: A New Hope*

| **STAR WARS: EPISODE VI** |
| **RETURN OF THE JEDI** |

Tales from Jabba's Palace

The Bounty Hunter Wars
  The Mandalorian Armor
  Slave Ship
  Hard Merchandise

The Truce at Bakura
Luke Skywalker and the Shadows of
  Mindor

 NEW REPUBLIC
5–25 YEARS AFTER
STAR WARS: A New Hope

X-Wing
  Rogue Squadron
  Wedge's Gamble
  The Krytos Trap
  The Bacta War
  Wraith Squadron
  Iron Fist
  Solo Command

The Courtship of Princess Leia
A Forest Apart*
Tatooine Ghost

The Thrawn Trilogy
  Heir to the Empire
  Dark Force Rising
  The Last Command

X-Wing: Isard's Revenge

The Jedi Academy Trilogy
  Jedi Search
  Dark Apprentice
  Champions of the Force

I, Jedi
Children of the Jedi
Darksaber
Planet of Twilight
X-Wing: Starfighters of Adumar
The Crystal Star

The Black Fleet Crisis Trilogy
  Before the Storm
  Shield of Lies
  Tyrant's Test

The New Rebellion

The Corellian Trilogy
  Ambush at Corellia
  Assault at Selonia
  Showdown at Centerpoint

The Hand of Thrawn Duology
  Specter of the Past
  Vision of the Future

Fool's Bargain*
Survivor's Quest

*An eBook novella
**Forthcoming

THE STAR WARS NOVELS TIMELINE

NEW JEDI ORDER
25–40 YEARS AFTER
STAR WARS: A New Hope

Boba Fett: A Practical Man*

The New Jedi Order
Vector Prime
Dark Tide I: Onslaught
Dark Tide II: Ruin
Agents of Chaos I: Hero's Trial
Agents of Chaos II: Jedi Eclipse
Balance Point
Recovery*
Edge of Victory I: Conquest
Edge of Victory II: Rebirth
Star by Star
Dark Journey
Enemy Lines I: Rebel Dream
Enemy Lines II: Rebel Stand
Traitor
Destiny's Way
Ylesia*
Force Heretic I: Remnant
Force Heretic II: Refugee
Force Heretic III: Reunion
The Final Prophecy
The Unifying Force

35 *YEARS AFTER STAR WARS: A New Hope*

The Dark Nest Trilogy
The Joiner King
The Unseen Queen
The Swarm War

LEGACY
40+ YEARS AFTER
STAR WARS: A New Hope

Legacy of the Force
Betrayal
Bloodlines
Tempest
Exile
Sacrifice
Inferno
Fury
Revelation
Invincible

Crosscurrent
Riptide

Millennium Falcon

43 *YEARS AFTER STAR WARS: A New Hope*

Fate of the Jedi
Outcast
Omen
Abyss
Backlash
Allies
Vortex
Conviction
Ascension**
Apocalypse**

*An eBook novella
**Forthcoming

DRAMATIS PERSONAE

AIREN CRACKEN; Rebel leader (human male)

BIDOR FERROUZ; Imperial governor of Poln (human male)

CARLIST RIEEKAN; Rebel leader (human male)

DARRIC LaRONE; stormtrooper (human male)

GILAD PELLAEON; senior bridge officer, *Chimaera* (human male)

JOAK QUILLER; stormtrooper (human male)

HAN SOLO; captain, *Millennium Falcon* (human male)

KORLO BRIGHTWATER; stormtrooper (human male)

LEIA ORGANA; Rebel leader (human female)

LUKE SKYWALKER; Rebel (human male)

MARA JADE; Emperor's agent (human female)

NUSO ESVA; warlord (nonhuman male)

SABERAN MARCROSS; stormtrooper (human male)

TAXTRO GRAVE; stormtrooper (human male)

THRAWN; Imperial officer (Chiss male)

VAANTAAR; refugee (Troukree male)

VESTIN AXLON; Rebel leader (human male)

A long time ago in a galaxy far, far away. . . .

CHOICES OF ONE

The choices of one shape the futures of all.
　　　　　　　　　　　—Jedi saying

CHAPTER ONE

T HE LAST HYPERSPACE JUMP HAD BEEN A TRICKY ONE, STARTING AS IT did in one minor star system barely on the charts and ending in another even more obscure one. But the ISD *Chimaera*'s officers and crew were the finest in the galaxy, and as Commander Gilad Pellaeon looked over the repeater display he confirmed that they'd made the jump precisely.

He strode down the command walkway, gazing at the *Chimaera*'s long prow, wondering what in space they were doing here. The *Chimaera* was an Imperial Star Destroyer, a kilometer and a half of heavy armor and awesome weaponry, the very symbol and expression of Imperial power and authority. Even the arrogant anarchists of the Rebellion hesitated before going up against ships like this.

So with that same Rebellion boiling ever more loudly and violently across the Empire, with Lord Vader himself tasked with tracking down and destroying their leadership, what in the name of Imperial Center was the *Chimaera* doing on passenger transport duty?

"This is insane," Captain Calo Drusan muttered as he came up beside Pellaeon. "What in the *galaxy* is Command thinking of?"

"It does seem a bit odd," Pellaeon said diplomatically. "But I'm sure they have their reasons."

Drusan snorted. "If you believe that, you're a fool. Imperial Center has gone top-heavy with politicians, professional flatterers, and incompetents.

Reason and intelligence went down the garbage chutes a long time ago." He gestured at the starlit sky in front of them. "My guess is that someone's just trying to impress everyone with his ability to move fleet units around."

"Could be, sir," Pellaeon said, a small shiver running up his back. In general, Drusan was right about the way the Imperial court was going, though even a ship's captain shouldn't be discussing such things out loud.

In this case, however, Drusan was wrong . . . because this particular order hadn't come from some flunky at Imperial Center. That was how it had looked, and how it was clearly intended to look.

Unlike the captain, though, Pellaeon hadn't taken the order at face value, but had taken the time to run a backtrack. While it had indeed come through proper channels from Imperial Center, it hadn't originated there. It had, in fact, come from an undisclosed location in the Outer Rim.

According to the top-secret dispatches Drusan had shared with his senior officers, that was where Grand Admiral Zaarin was right now, quietly touring the edge of Imperial space aboard the ISD *Predominant*.

Which strongly implied that the *Chimaera*'s orders had come from the Grand Admiral himself.

"Incoming ship, Captain," the sensor officer called from the starboard crew pit. "Just jumped into the system. Sensors read it as a *Kazellis*-class light freighter."

Drusan whistled softly. "A Kazellis," he commented. "That's a rare bird—they stopped making those years ago. We have an ID yet?"

"Yes, sir," the comm officer called from the portside crew pit. "Code response confirms it's the *Salaban's Hope*."

Pellaeon cocked an eyebrow. Not only had their mysterious passenger arrived, but he'd arrived within minutes of the *Chimaera*'s own appearance. Either he had a highly developed sense of timing, or he was remarkably lucky.

"Vector?" Drusan asked.

"Directly starboard," the sensor officer called. "Range, eighty kilometers."

Not only practically on top of the *Chimaera* in time, but in position, as well. Pellaeon's estimation of the freighter's pilot went up another couple of notches.

Of course, not everyone saw it that way. "Kriffing fool," Drusan grunted. "What's he trying to do, run us down?"

Pellaeon took a few steps forward and peered out the starboard viewport. Sure enough, the glow of a sublight drive was just barely visible out there against the background stars.

Except that the glow *shouldn't* have been visible. Not at that distance. Not unless the pilot was hauling his sublights for all they were worth, and then some.

And the only reason someone would do that . . .

"Captain, I recommend we go to full alert," Pellaeon said urgently, turning back to Drusan. "That ship's running from something."

For a moment Drusan didn't reply, his eyes flicking past Pellaeon's shoulder to the approaching freighter. With an effort, Pellaeon forced himself to remain silent, letting his captain work through the logic in his own unhurried, methodical way.

Finally, to his relief, Drusan stirred. "Full alert," the captain called. "And reconfirm that identity code. Just in case he's not running *from* anyone, but is thinking of ramming us."

Pellaeon turned back to the viewport, hoping he'd been able to keep his bewilderment from showing before the captain could see it. Did Drusan honestly believe anyone would be stupid enough *and* suicidal enough to try such an insane stunt? Even the lunatics of the Rebellion knew better than that. Still, as long as Drusan's paranoid assumption got the shields up and the turbolasers charging—

"Incoming!" the sensor officer snapped. "Six unidentified ships jumping in, bearing in sweep-cluster pattern behind the *Salaban's Hope*."

"Come about," Drusan said, his voice taking on an edge of eagerness. The captain loved it when he had a chance to fire the *Chimaera*'s turbolasers at something. "All turbolasers to full power."

Pellaeon grimaced. As usual, Drusan was following standard combat procedure.

Only in this case, standard procedure wasn't going to work. By the time the *Chimaera* was ready to fire, the attackers would have caught up with the *Salaban's Hope* and be swarming it.

But if the *Chimaera* threw power to its sublight engines and headed straight toward the freighter, they might scare off the attackers, or at least give them a moment of pause. Closing the distance would also mean getting to the turbolasers' effective range a little sooner. "Captain, if I may suggest—"

"No, you may not, Commander," Drusan cut him off calmly. "This is no time for your fancy theories of combat."

"Captain, the *Salaban's Hope* is hailing us," the comm officer called. "Lord Odo requests your immediate attention."

Pellaeon frowned. *Lord Odo* was the sort of name that belonged in the Imperial court, not way out here in the Outer Rim. What would a member of the court be doing this far from Imperial Center?

"Put him through," Drusan ordered.

"Yes, sir." There was a click—

"Captain Drusan, this is Lord Odo," a melodious voice said from the bridge speaker. "As you may have noted, I've come under attack."

"I have indeed, Lord Odo," Drusan said. "We're charging the turbolaser batteries now."

"Excellent," Odo said. "In the meantime, may I request you shunt all other available power to the tractor beams and pull—"

"Not a good idea, my lord," Drusan warned. "At this range, a full-power tractor beam could severely damage your hull."

"That you shunt all power to the tractor beams," Odo repeated, a sudden edge to his voice, "and pull the two endmost attackers toward you."

"And if we breach—" Belatedly, Drusan broke off. "Oh. Yes. Yes, I understand. Ensign Caln, tractors on the two endmost raiders—lock up, and reel in."

Pellaeon turned back to the viewport, a lump in his throat. The engine flares of the attacking ships were visible now, blazing against the stars as they drove hard on the *Salaban's Hope*'s stern. Drusan had been right about the dangers of full-power tractor beams at this range. Clearly, that was what Odo was hoping for, that the *Chimaera*'s tractors would be strong enough to crack or even shatter the raiders' hulls.

But if the attackers' ships were stronger than Odo thought, all the maneuver would accomplish would be to pull two of the raiders forward into close-fire range faster and easier than they could manage on their own.

At which point the *Salaban's Hope* would have enemy lasers behind it *and* on both flanks, and it was unlikely that it would have enough shield capacity to handle all three. Hissing softly between his teeth, Pellaeon watched.

Abruptly, the two pursuing ships on the ends began corkscrewing violently, their drive trails spinning like children's windsparklers. "Tractors engaged," the tractor officer called. "Attackers locked and coming toward us."

"Any signs of hull fractures?" Drusan asked.

"Nothing registering, sir," the sensor officer reported.

"Acknowledged," Drusan said. "So much for that," he added to Pellaeon.

"Well, at least they can't fire on the *Salaban's Hope*," Pellaeon pointed out. "Not with that helix yaw."

"Difficult to get a stable targeting lock that way," Drusan agreed reluctantly. "But not impossible."

And then, suddenly, Pellaeon got it. Odo wasn't just hoping the *Chimaera*'s tractors would tear the attacking ships apart. He was letting the Imperials pull the raiders up alongside him, banking on the helix yaw to interfere with their own firing long enough—

He was still working through the logic when the *Salaban's Hope*'s lasers flashed to either side, blasting the two tractored raiders to scrap.

And as the expanding clouds of debris twisted free of the tractors' grip, they naturally and inevitably fell backward past the still-accelerating *Salaban's Hope*, and directly into the paths of the four raiders still chasing it.

"Captain, turbolasers online," the weapons officer reported.

"Target the remaining attackers." Drusan snorted. "That is, if there's anything there still worth targeting. And alert the hangar bay duty officer that he has a ship coming in."

He looked at Pellaeon. "If this Lord Odo is a member of the Imperial court," he murmured, "at least he's a competent one."

"Yes, sir," Pellaeon said. "Shall I take over here while you go down to welcome him?"

Drusan made a face. "Fortunately, I'm too busy cleaning up this mess to bother with visitors," he said. "You go. Get him aboard, get him settled—you know the routine. Tell him I'll be down to greet him as soon as we've made the jump to lightspeed."

"Yes, sir," Pellaeon said. "Maybe I can get him to tell us where exactly that encrypted course setting we were sent is taking us."

"Don't count on it, Commander," Drusan said. "The Imperial court loves its secrets as much as anyone else." He waved a hand. "Dismissed."

Pellaeon had never before had the dubious honor of welcoming an actual member of the Imperial court aboard his ship. But he'd heard all the stories about the nobles' arrogance, their love of all things rare and expensive, and their colorful and sycophantic entourages.

Lord Odo proved to be a surprise. The first person to emerge into the hangar bay from the docking tunnel was an old, frail-looking human dressed not in lush and expensive colors but in plain, drab pilot's garb. The second was another human—Pellaeon assumed he was human, anyway—dressed in a gray-and-burgundy hooded robe, black gloves, boots, and cloak, and the black metal full-face mask of a pantomime-mute actor.

There was no third person. If Odo had an entourage, he'd apparently left it behind.

Pellaeon waited, just to be sure, until the pilot signaled for the boarding hatch to be sealed. As it closed with a thump, he stepped forward. "Lord Odo," he said, bowing at the waist and hoping fervently that the visitor would forgive any unintentional lapses in proper court etiquette. "I'm Commander Gilad Pellaeon, third bridge officer of the Imperial Star Destroyer *Chimaera*. Captain Drusan asked me to greet you, and to inform you that he'll pay his own respects as soon as his duties on the bridge permit."

"Thank you, Commander," Odo said in the same melodious voice Pellaeon had heard on the bridge, now muffled slightly by the mask. There was no mouth opening, Pellaeon noted, nor were there even any eye slits. Either Odo could somehow see right through the metal, or else there was a compact heads-up display built into the inside. "Are we on our way?"

"Yes, sir," Pellaeon said, glancing at the nearest readout panel just to make sure. "I believe the encrypted course data that arrived with your boarding authorization said it would be a ten-standard-hour journey."

"Correct," Odo confirmed. "I trust you'll forgive my appearance. My reason for this visit must remain private and my identity unrevealed."

"No explanation necessary, sir," Pellaeon hastened to assure him. "I understand how things are done in the Imperial court."

"Do you, now," Odo said. "Excellent. Perhaps later you can instruct me on its more subtle aspects."

Pellaeon felt a frown crease his forehead. Was Odo merely having a joke at a lowly fleet officer's expense? Or did he really *not* know the nuances of Imperial court procedure and behavior?

In which case, he was obviously not a member of the court. So who *was* he?

"I trust you have quarters prepared for us," Odo continued. "The journey was long and fraught with danger." The masked and hooded head inclined slightly. "Speaking of which, may I also thank you for your assistance against those raiders."

"Our pleasure, my lord," Pellaeon said, wondering for a split second if he should point out that the main tactical thrust of the engagement had in fact been Odo's.

Probably not. It wouldn't do for the Imperial fleet to admit that a visiting civilian had come up with a better combat plan than they had. "And yes, quarters have been arranged just off the hangar bay for you and your pilot." He looked at the pilot and raised his eyebrows. "Your name?"

The pilot looked at Odo, as if seeking permission to speak. Odo made no move, and after a moment the pilot looked back at Pellaeon. "Call me Sorro," he said. His voice was as old and tired as the rest of him.

"Honored to meet you," Pellaeon said, turning back to Odo. "If you'll follow me, my lord, I'll escort you to your quarters."

Exactly nine and three-quarter standard hours later, even though it wasn't his watch, Pellaeon made sure to be on the *Chimaera*'s bridge.

It was a waste of effort. The Star Destroyer emerged on the dark side of a completely unremarkable world, with an unremarkable yellow sun peeking over the planet's horizon and an unremarkable starscape all around them.

"And we aren't likely to see anything else, either," Drusan growled. "We have orders to hold position right here until Lord Odo returns."

"There he goes," Pellaeon said, pointing at the glow of the *Salaban's*

Hope's drive as the freighter emerged from beneath the *Chimaera*'s long prow. The freighter headed toward the planetary horizon ahead, its image fogging briefly as it circled past the edge of atmosphere, and then vanished.

"What do you think about that mask of his?"

With an effort, Pellaeon dragged his mind away from the mystery of where they were to the mystery of who Odo was. "He definitely doesn't want anyone knowing who he is," he said.

"Who *or* what," Drusan said. "I had Environmental Services do a scan of the air outflow from his quarters. I thought—"

"You *what?*" Pellaeon interrupted, aghast. "Sir, the orders made it clear we weren't to question, interfere, or intrude upon Lord Odo's activities."

"Which I haven't," Drusan said. "Keeping tabs on my ship's systems is part of my job."

"But—"

"Besides which, it didn't work," Drusan said sourly. "There are fifty different species biomarkers coming off him, at least eight of which the computer can't even identify."

"Probably coming from his mask," Pellaeon murmured, remembering now the sets of parallel slits set into the mask's curved cheekbone areas. "I assumed the cheek slits were merely decorative."

"Apparently, they're stocked with biomarkers," Drusan said. "Clever little flimp, isn't he? Still, whatever the reason for his visit, it should be over soon and we'll be able to take him and his ship back where we found them."

"Unless he wants us to take him elsewhere," Pellaeon pointed out.

"What does he need us for?" Drusan countered. "He's got a ship and a pilot. Let him go on his own." He exhaled noisily. "Well, there's no point standing around waiting for him. I'm heading back to my quarters. I suggest you do likewise, Commander."

"Yes, sir," Pellaeon said. Giving the planetary horizon one final look, he followed Drusan back down the command walkway.

———

"Well?" the Emperor asked.

For a moment Senior Captain Thrawn didn't answer, merely continued to gaze out the viewport at the forested landscape stretched out below. "An interesting situation," the blue-skinned Chiss said at last.

Seated at the helm of his freighter, Jorj Car'das kept his gaze straight ahead at the moon's horizon, wishing fervently that he was still in his self-imposed exile from the rest of the universe. Thrawn clearly didn't need him here. The Emperor clearly didn't want him here.

But Thrawn had quietly insisted. Why, Car'das didn't know. Maybe Thrawn felt he owed Car'das. Maybe he thought he was doing Car'das a favor by bringing him back into contact with the high and mighty this way.

Car'das also didn't know why the Emperor hadn't chosen to make an issue of his presence aboard. Maybe he regarded Thrawn highly enough to forgive the other's little quirks. Maybe he was just amused by Car'das's obvious discomfort.

Car'das didn't know. Nor did he really care. About anything.

"First of all, the multifrequency force field you have set up should be more than adequate to protect the construction site," Thrawn said, gesturing past Car'das's shoulder at the huge half-finished sphere floating above the moon's surface. "I trust the generator has redundant energy sources, plus an umbrella shield to protect it from orbital attack?"

"It does," the Emperor confirmed. "There are also a number of fully crewed garrisons in the forest around the generator."

"Has the moon any inhabitants?"

"Primitives only," the Emperor said contemptuously.

"In that case multiple garrisons are an inefficient use of resources," Thrawn said. "I would recommend burning off the forest for a hundred kilometers around the generator and putting a small mechanized force of AT-ATs and juggernaut heavy assault vehicles under the umbrella shield. Add in point support from three or four wing-clusters of hoverscouts, and the rest of the troops and equipment could be reassigned to trouble spots elsewhere in the Empire."

"So you would suggest I make the generator completely unassailable?" Palpatine asked.

"I assumed that was the intent." Thrawn paused, and Car'das glanced back in time to see the captain's glowing eyes narrow. "Unless, of course, you're setting a trap."

"Of course," the Emperor said calmly. "You of all my officers should understand the usefulness of a well-laid trap."

"Indeed," Thrawn agreed. "One final recommendation: don't dismiss too quickly those natives you mentioned. Even primitives can sometimes be used to deadly effect."

"They will not be a problem," the Emperor said, dismissing the natives with a small wave of his hand. "They don't like strangers. *Any* strangers."

"I leave that to your judgment," Thrawn said.

"Yes," Palpatine said flatly. "And now, I sense you have a request to make. Speak."

"Thank you, Your Highness," Thrawn said. If he was surprised or discomfited by the Emperor's casual reading of his mind, it didn't show in his voice. "It concerns a warlord named Nuso Esva who has become a serious power in the Unknown Regions."

Palpatine gave a small snort. "I wonder sometimes if you focus too much of your attention in those far reaches, Captain."

"It was you who authorized me to make such surveys," Thrawn reminded him. "And properly so. The Rebellion is a threat, but hardly the most serious one facing the Empire."

"In *your* opinion."

"Yes," Thrawn said.

There was a short pause. "Continue," the Emperor said.

"Warlord Nuso Esva has become one of those threats," Thrawn said. "He possesses an unusually strong spacegoing navy, along with many slave and tributary worlds stretching into Wild Space and to the edge of the Empire. I believe he is even now planning to extend his influence into Imperial space."

"An alien, I presume," Palpatine said, his voice dripping with disgust. "Can he be bought?"

"Not bought, bargained with, or allied with," Thrawn said. "I've sent several communiqués to him suggesting each of those options. He's turned down all of them."

"And what makes you think he wishes to extend his reach into my Empire?"

"He's begun a campaign against some of the worlds at the edge of the territories I've pacified," Thrawn said. "His usual pattern is to use hit-and-fade tactics on shipping, or attempt to bribe or otherwise suborn the officials on those worlds."

"All of whom are also aliens," Palpatine said with a sniff. "I've warned you before that such beings cannot be molded into any sort of permanent political structure. The history of the Republic proves that."

"Perhaps," Thrawn said. "The point is that Nuso Esva is using these raids to pin down my forces, and the only targets I can see that are worth such efforts are in Imperial space. Obviously, this cannot be tolerated."

"Then deal with him," the Emperor said flatly.

"I intend to," Thrawn said. "The difficulty is that my forces are already overextended and overcommitted. In order to deal a crushing blow I'll need a minimum of six more Star Destroyers."

Out of the corner of his eye, Car'das saw the Emperor's eyes narrow. "Do you seriously believe I have six Star Destroyers to spare, Captain Thrawn?"

"I wouldn't ask if it wasn't important," Thrawn said evenly. "It's not just the border sectors that are at risk, either. There are indications he may also be making overtures to the Rebellion."

"Then perhaps you should speak to Lord Vader," the Emperor said. "The Rebellion is his special interest. Perhaps *he* can give you the Star Destroyers you require."

"An excellent suggestion, Your Highness," Thrawn said, inclining his head. "I may do just that."

"It would be interesting to hear what the two of you have to say to each other." The Emperor gestured. "We're finished here, pilot. Return us to the *Predominant*."

"Yes, Your Highness," Car'das said. Getting a firm grip on the yoke, he put the ship into a smooth curve and headed for the Star Destroyer orbiting in the near distance behind them, wondering distantly if Thrawn realized what he was getting himself into. Sitting here with the Emperor and a silent pair of Imperial Guards behind him was bad enough.

But Vader was even worse. Ever since Yavin, every report Car'das had picked up had indicated that the appropriately titled Dark Lord of the Sith had grown a whole lot darker. The thought of asking him for *any-*

thing, let alone six Star Destroyers, was something Car'das's mind wasn't up to.

It hadn't always been that way. Once, Car'das had been head of an organization that had spanned the galaxy, a network of smugglers and information brokers who had serviced everyone from the Hutts to the highest levels of the Imperial court. Car'das himself had been to the edge of Chiss space with Thrawn, back before the Clone Wars had savaged the Republic. He'd worked with the young commander, watching as he defeated forces far larger than his own. Later, as Car'das's organization grew, he'd had many occasions to speak directly with some of the most powerful men in Palpatine's new Empire. In those days, standing before Darth Vader would have been little more than an unusually interesting day.

But that had been before Car'das's nearly fatal encounter long ago with that Dark Jedi. Before his subsequent illness and weakness and impending death. Before his abrupt decision to abandon his organization and leave it helpless before the infighting that was probably tearing it apart at this very moment.

Before he'd given up—on everything.

Still, even with his past burned behind him and his future lying bleak and formless in front of him, Car'das could feel an unexpected and unwelcome flicker of old curiosity stirring inside him.

It really *would* be interesting to hear what Thrawn and Vader had to say to each other.

Pellaeon had returned to his quarters, and had been asleep for nearly six hours when he was awakened by the insistent buzz of his intercom. Rolling over, he tapped the key. "Pellaeon."

"This is the captain." Drusan's voice was practically quivering with suppressed emotion. "Report to the bridge immediately."

The rest of the senior bridge officers were already assembled across from the aft bridge turbolift when Pellaeon arrived. He eased his way through toward the front, noting uneasily that the group also included all the off-duty engine room officers and the senior commanders of the *Chimaera*'s TIE fighter, trooper, and stormtrooper contingents. Whatever was going on, it was big.

He found Drusan waiting stiffly beside one of the consoles. Beside the captain, standing silent and still, was Lord Odo.

"Now that we're all assembled," Drusan said, his eyes flicking to Pellaeon, "I have an announcement. We've been selected for the honor"—he leaned on the word just a bit too hard—"of acting as Lord Odo's personal transport on a special assignment."

His lip twitched. "As part of that assignment, Lord Odo will be in ultimate command of the *Chimaera*," he continued. "I trust all of you will respect his position and give him your full measures of skill, effort, and obedience. Questions?"

The first officer, Senior Commander Grondarle, cleared his throat. "May I ask the nature of this assignment?" he asked.

"It's important," Odo told him evenly. "For now, that's all you need to know."

There was a brief, awkward silence. "Have you orders for us, my lord?" Drusan asked at last.

Odo's hand came up from beneath his cloak, a data card in his gloved fingers. "Here's our new course," he said, offering the card to Drusan. "Our first stop will be the Wroona system."

"And what exactly is at Wroona?" Grondarle asked.

"Commander," Drusan said warningly.

"That's all right, Captain," Odo said. "There's some specialized equipment that I'll need to fulfill our mission. The equipment is at Wroona. As it won't come to us, we shall have to go to it."

Grondarle's eyes narrowed. But he knew better than to rise to the bait. Better officers than him, Pellaeon knew, had been shunted to nowhere stations for reacting to the sarcasm of superiors. "Yes, sir," he said.

"Take this to navigation," Drusan said, handing Grondarle the data card. "Get us moving as soon as the course is loaded."

"Yes, sir." Taking the card, Grondarle strode through the pathway that opened up for him and headed through the archway into the main bridge.

"The rest of you, as you were," Drusan continued, looking around the group. "The watch change is coming up. Don't miss it."

He looked at Odo. "Our new commander," he added, "wouldn't like it."

———

Pellaeon was back in his quarters by the time the *Chimaera* made the jump to lightspeed. There was, he judged, enough time for him to grab another two hours of sleep before his next shift.

But sleep wouldn't come.

Lord Odo wasn't human. That much was pretty well guaranteed by the extraordinary means he'd taken to disguise himself, with the mask and the confusing mix of biomarkers. Pellaeon himself didn't have anything against aliens, and in fact had known and worked with quite a few whom he'd greatly respected.

But the Emperor wasn't like that. His opinion of aliens was well known, and while he was willing enough to make alliances with aliens when it served his purposes, there were virtually none in the senior positions of the court or the military. The only exception Pellaeon knew of was Senior Captain Thrawn, and even he was frequently sent away into the Unknown Regions to get him off Imperial Center for a while.

So who was Odo? That was the question that kept chasing itself around Pellaeon's brain. Who was Odo, and what was this mission that was important enough to take the *Chimaera* off patrol duty and put it under an alien's command?

Pellaeon didn't know, and it was clear that Odo himself wasn't going to tell them.

But maybe there was another way. The Empire, after all, was the greatest repository of information the universe had ever known. Maybe Odo had left a trail somewhere that could be followed.

Getting up, Pellaeon put on a robe and went to his desk. He turned on the computer and keyed the intercom for the duty security officer. "This is Commander Pellaeon," he said when the officer answered. "Where are Lord Odo and his pilot?"

"Lord Odo is on the bridge," the officer replied. "Sorro is in their shared quarters."

"When was Sorro last out?"

"One moment . . . it appears that when they returned from their planetary excursion, he went to the bay officers' mess while Lord Odo went to the bridge."

"Lord Odo doesn't eat on the bridge, does he?"

"He hasn't so far," the officer said. "Sorro typically brings food back to their quarters for him."

"Any particular types of food?"

"There've only been three meals, so I can't make any generalizations," the officer said. "But so far it's been a different menu each time. Would you like a list?"

"Yes, send it to me," Pellaeon said. A person's taste in food and drink could be useful clues in establishing his identity. "And set up a standing order to inform me whenever Sorro leaves his quarters. I presume Captain Drusan has already told you to keep track of them both?"

"Yes, sir, he has."

"Good. Carry on."

Pellaeon keyed off the intercom, and for a moment he gazed off into space. Then, settling himself in his chair, he began punching computer keys. Somewhere on his way to gaining the Empire's trust, *someone* had to have crossed official paths with Odo, Sorro, or the *Salaban's Hope*.

Wherever and whenever that was, Pellaeon was going to find it.

CHAPTER TWO

T HE CRAWL SPACE UNDER THE MINING OPERATIONS COMPLEX HAD BEEN tricky to find. It had been even trickier to get into, and it had been trickier still to find the right junction box.

But it had been worth it, Han Solo decided with satisfaction as he poked his probe around the tangle of wires. Even with the dirt and the heat.

Even with the company.

"Han?" Luke Skywalker murmured from behind him—for at least the fifth time. "How's it going?"

"It'd go faster if I didn't have to keep stopping to answer your questions," Han growled, easing a group of wires aside with his probe. The kid was good enough in a fight, but he had a bad habit of talking too much when he was nervous.

"Right," Luke said. "Sorry."

Han grunted, blowing a drop of sweat off the tip of his nose as he pushed his way past another knot of wires. Why Imperials couldn't keep their wiring nice and neat and easy to track through was beyond him. Not a Hutt's curse worth of pride in their work.

Still, if the workers had had any pride, they probably wouldn't have put a nice convenient junction box down here beneath the complex's reactor heat exchanger where anyone with half a brain could get to it. In which case he and Luke would have had to do this the hard way.

"I just wanted to remind you that I'm ready whenever you are," Luke said.

"Great," Han said. "I'll let you know." There it was: the junction he was looking for. Keeping the other wires out of the way with his probe, he maneuvered his jumper clip into the gap. A little delicate maneuvering, a little gentle touch . . .

And without even a spark, he had it sealed.

"Also, Leia just called," Luke continued. "She said we're pushing the timing here—"

"All done," Han said, easing the probe back out of the box.

"Great," Luke said.

And with a sudden *snap-hiss*, the blue-white blade of his lightsaber flared into the narrow crawl space.

"Hey—*watch* it!" Han snapped, flinching back from the blade hovering way too close over his head and arm. "I said it's *done*."

For a moment the hum and blaze of the lightsaber continued to fill Han's ears and eyes. Then, to his relief, the kid finally closed it down. "I thought I was supposed to take care of the alarm and lock once you found the right junction," he said, an edge of not-quite accusation in his voice.

"Sure, if you don't mind everyone knowing someone with a lightsaber was messing around down here," Han said.

"Maybe they'll blame Vader."

"Funny," Han grunted. "A lot of people have seen you running around with that thing, you know. And not just Rebels. Anyway, it's done—I hotwired around it."

"Oh," Luke said, and as Han's eyes recovered from the lightsaber's glare he saw an uncertain frown on the kid's face. "So why am I here?"

"Maybe Leia didn't think I should be out at night without supervision." Han pulled out his comlink and flicked it on. "This is Solo," he said, identifying himself. "You're clear."

"Right," Princess Leia Organa's voice came back, the word sharply clipped, her tone no-nonsense and business-like.

But Han could read beneath the tone. Whatever she said, whatever she did, she was crazy about him.

He was pretty sure, anyway.

"Now what?" Luke asked.

"We get out of here," Han said, stuffing his tools back in their pouch and closing the junction box cover. "I just hope whatever they want in there is worth all this."

"I hope so, too," Luke said. "We really need a new base."

Han frowned. "They're looking for a new *base*?" He nodded upward toward the building above them. "In *there*?"

"Yes," Luke said, sounding surprised. "Didn't Leia tell you? It's a mining clearinghouse, with records of all the major mining operations in this part of the Empire."

"I know what it is," Han said patiently. "I thought we were looking for some bulk cruisers or ore carriers we could grab."

"That's the cover, sure," Luke said. "But that's just to leave a false trail. The real plan is to download a bunch of locations where mining operations were started but abandoned. Leia thinks that—"

"Yeah, I know what she thinks," Han growled, wiping irritably at the sweat on his forehead. "A place with no mining usually means there's nothing else worth grabbing, either, which means no one wants the place."

"That's what she said," Luke confirmed. "Sorry—I thought you knew."

"I guess not." Han jerked a thumb back along the crawl space. "Go on, get moving."

The trek back down the crawl space was just as long, hot, and dirty as the inward trip had been. Finally, they reached the access point. "Too bad Chewie was too big to fit in the tunnel," Luke commented, grunting as he pushed up the access cover and maneuvered it off the opening, letting in a rush of cool night air. "If he'd come with us instead of Leia—"

"Quiet," Han interrupted, pushing up beside him and listening hard. Somewhere in the near distance he could hear the whine of an approaching landspeeder. "Out of the way—out of the way."

"What is it?" Luke asked, pressing himself against the side of the tunnel to let Han past.

"Security patrol," Han said, easing his head up out of the opening. The narrow alleyway they were in was about two hundred meters long, squeezed in between two windowless walls and lit by half a dozen pole-mounted glow panels spaced along the sides of the buildings. The distant whine was getting louder, which meant the security patrol was getting closer.

The crucial question was, was it heading *toward* the building Leia and the others should be leaving right about now? Or was it headed *away* from them?

There was no way to know. But this was no time for taking chances. "Give me your lightsaber," he said, pulling himself out through the opening.

"What?" Luke said. "But—"

"Give it to me and then get out of there," Han snapped. "We need to make a distraction."

Reluctantly, Luke unclipped the lightsaber and held it up. Han snatched it out of his hand and ran to the nearest of the light poles, peering at the lightsaber's grip. If he remembered right, the activation switch was right *there* . . .

With its usual *snap-hiss*, the blue-white blade appeared. Gripping the weapon with both hands, making sure to keep the blade pointed away from him, Han braked to a halt by the pole. If this was a standard design, the power conduit should run right up through the center. Setting the tip of the blade against the housing, he gave it a firm push.

And with a small flash of yellow-white, the glow panel above him went dark.

"What are you *doing*?" Luke gasped.

"Getting their attention," Han told him, glancing back over his shoulder. The landspeeder still wasn't visible, but it was getting louder. "Come on," he added, heading away from the sound at a quick jog.

"First close that down and give it back to me," Luke said, running beside him at a cautious distance. "You're going to get one of us killed."

"I got it under control," Han assured him.

"Now," Luke said firmly, starting to reach out a hand and then apparently thinking better of it. "Come on."

Han rolled his eyes and shut off the weapon. "Fine—you do the next one."

"Okay," Luke said taking the lightsaber and sprinting toward the next light post.

He had reached it, and had just ignited the weapon when the security landspeeder swung into view at the other end of the alleyway. "Han!" Luke bit out.

"Yeah, I see them," Han growled, snatching out his blaster. "Get that light out."

His answer was another brief sizzle as the glow panel overhead went dark. The landspeeder had meanwhile turned into the alleyway, and in the glow of the remaining light panels Han could see there were four men in the vehicle. Lifting his blaster, he carefully lined up the muzzle on the landspeeder's front left edge and fired.

With a gratifying crackle of metal and plasteel, the landspeeder dropped onto its side. There was a brief earsplitting screech as the vehicle's edge scraped against the permacrete, and then all four passengers were dumped out as the landspeeder made a hard left and slammed nose-first into the building on that side.

"Go!" Han ordered Luke, turning and sprinting toward the other end of the alleyway. If they could get out before the men back there pulled themselves together and called it in, they should be able to get back to Leia and the airspeeder before reinforcements arrived.

They'd made it halfway to the far end of the alleyway when another landspeeder blew into sight directly ahead of them. It wobbled slightly and then braked to a halt across the opening, blocking their escape.

"Han?" Luke called.

"Yeah, yeah," Han said, skidding to a halt and wondering what they were going to do this time. Hitting the forward power coupler like he had with the other landspeeder wouldn't do any good now that the thing was already stopped and its occupants were climbing out. There was no cover anywhere nearby, and no way out.

Unless Luke could cut a new door for them with his lightsaber. "Luke—"

"No, *behind* us," Luke cut in.

Han twisted around. Their airspeeder had appeared behind them, burning through the alley with its stabilizer wingtips running bare centimeters from the walls. Hanging half out one of the side doors, his hairy arms stretched down toward them, was Chewie.

"Get ready, kid," Han said. Spinning back around toward the security men forming up behind their landspeeder, he fired off a few shots to keep them occupied and then stuck his left arm straight up into the air. This was probably going to hurt.

An instant later Chewie's hand closed around his forearm and yanked him straight up off the permacrete.

There was a muffled yelp from Luke as he was similarly grabbed. Clenching his teeth, squinting his eyes against the sudden windstorm in his face, Han fired off a couple more wild shots at the security guards. The airspeeder swung over the guards and the landspeeder and Han felt himself swing to the side as the pilot made a sharp left around the side of the building. Fumbling his blaster back into its holster, he squeezed his eyes shut, wondering if Leia was going to make them ride like this all the way back to the rendezvous point.

Then, abruptly, his body swung forward as the pilot slowed, his stomach lurching as they dropped back to the ground. His feet touched permacrete—

"Get in!" Leia snapped as Chewie let go of his arm.

Ten seconds later they were back in the air, now with Luke and Han safely inside. "What in space was *that* all about?" Leia demanded as Han rubbed his shoulder.

"I heard a security patrol," Han told her. "I thought it'd be a good idea if they didn't know about the evening's company."

"So naturally you start waving blasters around." She transferred her glare to Luke. "*And* lightsabers."

"You're missing the point, sweetheart," Han said calmly. "Okay, so they know we were in the alley. But thanks to us, they *don't* know which building you were in."

Leia opened her mouth . . . closed it again as she apparently got where he was going. Knowing which of the complex's buildings the intruders had invaded would considerably narrow security's search for what they'd been up to. "There are still only four buildings whose alarms you could shut off from that alleyway," she said stubbornly.

"And they don't know which of the four it was," Han repeated patiently. "*And* they didn't get to see which door you came out of, either."

Leia's face darkened. She'd lost this one, and she knew it. If security had spotted the team leaving, it would have not only told them which building to focus on, but also given them a clue as to which *part* of the building they'd been in. This way, they would have to search everything.

"That's okay—you don't have to thank me," Han said into the stiff silence. "Luke and I are part of the team."

He looked at Luke, but the kid was keeping exceptionally still and quiet. For that matter, so were all the others.

He looked back at Leia, to find that she'd turned away from him and was staring out the side window. And was also being still and quiet.

The trip back to the rendezvous point was a *lot* longer than the inward trip had been.

At least General Carlist Rieekan was happy. Not that Han would have cared much if he hadn't been. "Excellent work, Princess," the general said, nodding to her and sweeping his eyes approvingly around the rest of the group gathered at the table. "Well done, all of you. With Vader breathing down our necks, we desperately need to carve ourselves a little breathing space. Hopefully, one of the planets on this list will fit the bill."

He picked up the handful of data cards, fingering them as if they were some kind of anti-Vader Jedi magic. "That's all for now," he said. "Your individual commanders will have your next assignments. Princess Leia, Skywalker, I'd like you to stay behind a moment. The rest of you, dismissed."

There was a general scraping of chairs and feet as the team left the table and headed for the door. All, of course, except Leia and Luke.

And Han.

Leia seemed to be the first one besides Rieekan to notice that Han was making no move to leave. She gave him a puzzled look, then a frown, and finally a glare. It was on the glare that Luke also noticed Han's lack of movement, though all he did was look puzzled. Chewie gave him one of those what-are-you-doing-now sort of looks, but left without saying anything.

Rieekan, predictably, didn't react at all. He waited until everyone else had left before speaking. "Is there a problem, Solo?" he asked calmly.

"I'm here for the extra meeting," Han told him, just as calmly. "I thought I was part of the team."

Rieekan nodded. "And you are."

"So let's get on with it," Han said, folding his arms across his chest.

For a moment Rieekan eyed him in silence. Then, gesturing Han toward a door at one side of the conference room, he stood up. "Will you two excuse me a moment?" he said. "Solo and I need a word in private."

Han had been on the receiving end of enough reprimands during his time in the fleet to know that this one was likely to be a Class A windstorm. But to his surprise, Rieekan merely let the door slide shut behind them and raised his eyebrows. "All right," he said. "Let's hear it."

A straight-up question, Han decided, deserved a straight-up answer. "I wasn't told what the real mission tonight was," he said. "I didn't *not* understand. I was deliberately not told."

"Would knowing we were looking for a new base have made a difference in how you handled your part of the job?"

"*My* part, probably not," Han conceded. "But it could have made a big difference in Leia's. I know something about mining operations, and there are a few tips I could have given her."

"Such as?"

"Such as to stay clear of anything that smells of Hutt," Han said. "And I don't just mean places with *Hutt* in the name. There are at least fifteen different covers and shells they like to use."

"That's good to know," Rieekan said, nodding. "Maybe you can help the analysts sift through the data once it's been compiled."

"That's not the point," Han growled. "If I'm going to be part of this Rebellion thing, I need to be kept up to speed with what's going on."

"You think that, do you?" Rieekan asked.

"We just agreed I'm part of the group," Han countered. "What do I have to do? Become an officer?"

Rieekan looked him straight in the eye. "Basically, yes."

Han stared at him. The question had been one-third rhetorical and two-thirds sarcastic. Rieekan's response had been neither. "You're kidding."

"Not at all," Rieekan said. "You were in the fleet—you know how this works. The upper ranks get the data and the authority to make decisions. The lower ranks get just enough of both to do their assigned tasks."

"Fine," Han growled. "So how do I get the big rank bars?"

"You know how that part works, too," Rieekan said. "To be a leader you have to lead."

Han snorted. "Now you're flying in circles."

"Not really," Rieekan said. "Lower ranks get limited data and authority, like I said. But they also have limited responsibility. Leaders don't have the luxury of passing the blame elsewhere."

"I've led teams before," Han reminded him. "That Shelkonwa thing, for one. Luke and Chewie and me did pretty good on that one."

"And you've done well on teams with Princess Leia, too," Rieekan agreed. "But all those people are friends, or at least associates. People you know and trust. They're not a group of soldiers or pilots whose strengths and weaknesses you don't know and can't compensate for. Soldiers you have to order into a battle, knowing full well that some of them—maybe even most of them—are going to die."

Han felt his stomach tighten. "Yeah. That's the hard part, isn't it?"

"It's the worst part of all," Rieekan agreed quietly. "There's an old saying—I don't know where it comes from. Jedi, probably. It goes like this: 'The choices of one shape the futures of all.' Ever heard that before?"

"Everyone's got a version of that one," Han said. "Doesn't mean a lot."

"My point is that true leaders are fully and constantly aware of that fact," Rieekan said. "They understand the possible consequences of their decisions, and are willing to bear that weight." He cocked an eyebrow. "The question is whether that's a step you're willing to take."

"So you're saying you want me to be an officer *and* a leader?" Han asked.

To his mild surprise, Rieekan not only didn't take offense but even chuckled. "Point taken," he conceded. "I've known a few officers who weren't leaders. And some leaders who weren't officers."

For no particular reason Han's mind flashed to those five rogue stormtroopers who'd helped him and Luke get Leia off Shelkonwa. The head of that group, LaRone, had definitely been one of those rankless leaders. "So what now?" he asked.

Rieekan shrugged. "You go off and think about it," he said. "Because I want you to be *very* sure you're ready before you make the commitment."

Han nodded. "Fair enough."

"Good," Rieekan said. "In the meantime, it occurs to me that there may be a part you can play in the mission I was going to discuss with Princess Leia and Skywalker. You're welcome to sit in and make comments and suggestions." He gestured. "Shall we go?"

Luke and Leia were still sitting quietly when Han and Rieekan returned to the main conference room. A third person had also joined the group: a grim-faced man probably twenty years older than Rieekan, with the broad shoulders and chest of a former rink fighter and what looked like a permanent downturn to the corners of his mouth.

Who had, maybe not coincidentally, taken the chair Han had been sitting in earlier.

"Ah — Master Axlon." Rieekan greeted the newcomer with a polite nod. "Thank you for joining us."

"My apologies on my tardiness," Axlon said, nodding in turn. "My meeting with Mon Mothma ran longer than anticipated."

"That's all right," Rieekan assured him. "May I present Master Skywalker and Captain Solo. Princess Leia you already know, of course. This is Vestin Axlon, former governor of Logarra District on Alderaan."

Han grimaced. An Alderaanian. No wonder the man had a permanent sour on. "Pleased to meet you, Governor," he said.

"It's *Master* Axlon now, Captain Solo," Axlon corrected darkly, his mouth turning down a little more. "*Alderaan.* You *did* hear about Alderaan, didn't you?"

"Yeah, I heard about it," Han said, annoyed despite himself. "Matter of fact, I was the first one on the scene after Tarkin hit the place."

Leia stirred in her seat. "Han," she murmured warningly.

"That's all right, Your Highness," Axlon said, a ghost of a smile briefly turning his mouth upward again. "Yes, I remember now where I heard your name, Captain. My apologies. We owe you a great debt."

"Don't worry about it," Han said. At least *someone* appreciated him.

"If you'll take a seat, Solo?" Rieekan said, gesturing to the chair beside Axlon.

"Sure," Han said, pulling out the chair beside Leia and taking that one instead. "What's going on?"

"Actually, we're not sure," Rieekan said, resuming his seat at the head of the table. "It's either a great opportunity or an extremely obvious trap. Master Axlon?"

Axlon cleared his throat. "A few days ago I received a communiqué from Governor Bidor Ferrouz of Candoras sector," he said. "I'm sure a seasoned traveler like Captain Solo knows all about Candoras, but for the rest of you it's an Outer Rim region that edges into Wild Space and sort of trails off into the Unknown Regions. Under the Republic it was considered something of a bulwark against potential threats from both those areas. Under the Empire—" He made a face. "It's apparently considered expendable."

"Since Governor Ferrouz's communiqué arrived we've been working our usual information sources, trying to learn everything we can about the situation out there," Rieekan said, touching a key on his control board. The table's holodisplay lit up, showing a portion of the Outer Rim and a small, ragged-edged sector bordering on the blank area of Unknown Space. "As Master Axlon indicated, Candoras is far from the mainstream of Imperial life and commerce, with a sector fleet consisting of four antiquated Dreadnoughts and some smaller ships, and limited resources of all sorts."

"Unfortunately, they also seem to have an alien warlord named Nuso Esva edging his way along their border," Axlon said grimly. "According to our sources, Nuso Esva has already conquered a number of systems in the Unknown Regions and is thinking about adding some Imperial territory to his collection. Candoras, apparently, is number one on his list."

"So what does this have to do with us?" Han asked.

"What it has to do with us, Captain," Axlon said heavily, "is that Governor Ferrouz is offering a very intriguing deal: a full-fledged base for the Alliance, complete with logistical support, docking facilities, and one of the finest natural supply depots in the galaxy—"

"Wait a minute," Luke interrupted, his eyes wide. "He's offering us a *base*? Not just an anchorage or hiding place, but an actual *base*?"

"That's what he says," Rieekan said. He manipulated the controls, and the holo zoomed in on a single star and then on a double planet circling that star. "This is the Poln system, Candoras's capital. Poln Major, the larger world, is the actual seat of government. The smaller world, Poln

Minor, used to be a center of mining and manufacturing, and while its significance has decreased over the years it still has a fair role in both areas. That's where he proposes we establish our base. I've already confirmed that the system has enough ship traffic to disguise our own movements."

"Poln Minor also has a network of deep caverns and abandoned mining hubs," Axlon said. "Some of them are being used as storehouses, but others are empty and would be ideal for caching our own equipment." He gestured. "That's what I meant by a natural supply depot. A few of the caverns are just under the surface, but others are deep enough to be completely hidden from any external scan."

"Sounds ideal," Leia said. "What does Governor Ferrouz want for all this generosity?"

"According to the communiqué, nothing," Axlon said. "He assures us we'll be safe, protected by his sector fleet, and more than welcome. He also hints that he's planning to secede from the Empire in the near future and throw his official support to the Alliance."

Han snorted. "Like we haven't heard *that* one before."

"Granted," Axlon conceded. "And no one's saying that we necessarily believe him. The point is that we've been offered a base where, if nothing else, we'll have plenty of warning before a major attack."

"The question is, a major attack by whom?" Leia asked. "I assume it's obvious to everyone that Ferrouz is angling to have Alliance firepower on hand to bolster his defenses if this Nuso Esva character tries to move against him."

"Or like you said, it could be a straight-out trap," Luke said. "The minute we settle in, fifty Star Destroyers show up and we're caught like womp rats."

"That's certainly a possibility," Axlon agreed. "But it may surprise you to hear that I think the odds of that are fairly small. Our sources say Ferrouz petitioned the fleet for more warships about four months ago and no one even bothered to respond to his request. All indications are that Imperial Center has largely forgotten Candoras even exists."

"Besides, if they wanted to lay a trap for us, there are more likely places to do it," Leia commented. "Someplace with a decent sector fleet, for starters. Getting a strike force to Candoras would mean shifting and retasking a lot of ships. That would take a lot of time and effort, and be pretty obvious to our spies."

"So instead we move in and get hit by Nuso Esva," Han said. "Not sure I see how that gains us anything."

Axlon turned a scowl toward him. "Captain—"

"It gains us in two ways," Rieekan interrupted. "First, if the presence of an Alliance force makes Nuso Esva reconsider his invasion plans, that risk goes completely away. Second, if Nuso Esva *does* attack, our forces may be able to help Ferrouz beat him back."

"Since when did we start doing the Imperial fleet's job for them?" Han asked.

"Since the ultimate goal of the Rebellion is to free the galaxy," Rieekan said with an air of strained patience. "It wouldn't be much of a victory if we overthrew one tyrant only to have him replaced by another."

"Is Nuso Esva *that* powerful?" Luke asked.

"We have no idea how powerful he is," Axlon said. "All we know is that Governor Ferrouz is clearly concerned."

"Let's talk about Ferrouz for a moment," Leia said. "What do we know about him?"

"Ten years ago he was considered an up-and-coming young politician, one of the brightest to have come out of Imperial Center over the past decade," Axlon said. "He's young, barely into his forties, with a wife and a six-year-old daughter. He's also apparently an excellent administrator." He shrugged. "Unfortunately, that's all we know."

"Which is why someone has to go out to Poln Major and actually meet the man," Rieekan said. "Mon Mothma and I think a small group could slip in without any difficulty—"

"*Wait* a second," Han interrupted. "You're sending Leia into danger *again*?"

"As it happens, no," Rieekan said calmly. "Master Axlon has volunteered for the negotiator's position."

Han looked at Axlon, feeling the unpleasant sensation of the deck dropping out from under him. "Oh," he said lamely.

"The original plan was to fly him to Poln Major in one of our transports," Rieekan continued. "But I'm thinking now that you and the *Millennium Falcon* would be even better."

"That's not a bad idea," Axlon said, eyeing Han thoughtfully. "With the deterioration of Poln Minor's mining infrastructure over the past few years, a lot of smugglers and other criminal types have taken over significant parts of the planet. You would fit right in."

Han grimaced. Didn't the Alliance know *any* other smugglers they could use for these things? He opened his mouth to point that out—

And only then did he spot the look on Rieekan's face. A cool, measuring, judging look.

"Sounds wonderful," Han growled. "When do we leave?"

Rieekan turned to Axlon. "Master Axlon?"

"I'd like one last brief talk with Mon Mothma to clarify a couple of our negotiating boundaries," Axlon said. "After that I'll be ready to go."

"Fine," Han said, standing up. "I'll go find Chewie and see what it'll take to get the *Falcon* ready." He headed away, slapping Luke's shoulder lightly in passing as he headed for the door. "See you, kid."

He ignored Leia completely. Not that she probably noticed.

The meeting had ended, and Luke was heading down the corridor when he heard a voice from behind call his name. He turned to find Axlon hurrying toward him. "A word, if I may?" the older man said.

"Sure," Luke said, frowning. He wasn't very good yet at sensing moods and emotions through the Force, but even with his limited skills Axlon had struck him as an odd mixture of icy calm and burning passion. "Is there something you need?"

"As a matter of fact, there is," Axlon said as he trotted to a halt. "I want you to go to Poln Major with me."

"I appreciate the invitation," Luke said. "But you heard General Rieekan back there. I'm on first-wave fighter duty."

"Which would be a complete waste of your talents," Axlon scoffed. "The Alliance has any number of men and women who can fly transport escort." He lifted a finger. "But it has only *one* Jedi."

"I'm hardly a Jedi," Luke said. "Not yet."

"But you're the closest we've got," Axlon persisted. "That makes you someone I very much want beside me when I sit down to talk with Governor Ferrouz. Not for defense, but for psychological insight."

"If you want insight, you'd do better to take someone like Admiral Ackbar," Luke said. "Even Leia's better than I am."

"Both of whom are busy with assignments of their own," Axlon said firmly. "Don't worry, I've already talked to General Rieekan about this— that's why I stayed behind just now. He said that if you're willing, you can go with me."

Luke pursed his lips. Though he would never have said so aloud, he'd been less than enthusiastic about having to stay behind and put together an escort for the first Alliance forces into Poln Major. Especially when Han and Leia had been given much more interesting assignments. Going in with Axlon would definitely be a step up. "If the general's game, I guess I am, too," he said.

"Excellent," Axlon said. "One more thing. I want you to come into Poln Major independently of Captain Solo and me. A wild card, as it were, in case Ferrouz's offer isn't what it seems."

"Oh," Luke said, his growing excitement taking an unpleasant power drop. Even with the *Falcon*'s many quirks, he always enjoyed flying aboard her, especially when she was working well and Han was in a correspondingly good mood. And Chewie was good company. "So I'll be coming in one of the Alliance's other freighters?"

"No, no," Axlon said. "You'd be coming in one of our Z-95 Headhunters."

"A Z-95?" Luke echoed, feeling his eyes widen. "Isn't that a little obvious?"

"Not at all," Axlon assured him. "Z-95s are a common enough sight in that part of the galaxy. A couple hours' work to get rid of the Alliance markings, swap out the ID transponder for one with a copy of the safe-conduct code that Governor Ferrouz gave us, load the hyperdrive course, and you'll be all set."

"I suppose," Luke said, his enthusiasm dropping another few points. Alliance Z-95s had perfectly capable hyperdrives, and even though they weren't equipped with astromech droids they could comfortably hold the settings for a trip to and from the Poln system.

On the other hand, X-wings weren't exactly designed with long-range travel in mind, and Z-95 cockpits were even more cramped. "If you really think that's necessary."

"It is," Axlon said firmly. "So that's settled. Good. I don't know how long Captain Solo will take getting his ship ready, but I don't want you too far behind us."

"*Behind* you?" Luke said, frowning. "We're not even flying in convoy?"

Axlon shook his head. "As I said, Z-95s are common enough, but they're usually with private security firms that only fly escort for liners and other top-end ships." He considered. "Besides, it might be best if Captain Solo didn't know you were coming along. The more freedom of movement you have, the better."

Luke thought back to Han's reaction in the crawl space when he'd found out that Leia hadn't told him the true nature of their information raid. "That might not be a good idea," he warned. "Han likes to know what's going on."

"Captain Solo is a soldier," Axlon said, his tone cooling. "He gets to know what's necessary for his part of the mission. No less, no more."

"Sure, I understand," Luke said. "But in Han's case—"

"And we really don't have time to discuss it," Axlon interrupted. "I've alerted the mechanics to start removing the markings, but I imagine you'll want to supervise the ID swap-out procedure personally. Good luck, and I'll contact you once we're on Poln Major." Without waiting for a response, he gave Luke a brisk nod and walked away.

Luke watched him go, wincing. Despite its downsides, this was definitely a more exciting mission than the one he'd originally been given, and he was grateful to Axlon for getting it for him. But Han wasn't going to like being left in the dark twice in two missions. He was likely to not like it very loudly, and probably with a blaster close to hand.

And it occurred to Luke that Chewie wasn't *always* good company.

But Axlon was right. This was war, and they all had to do what they were told. Han would get over it.

He hoped.

CHAPTER THREE

T HE MAN WAS FAT, RED-FACED, AND SWEATING PROFUSELY. THE KIND OF sweating that could only come of having the muzzle of a small hold-out blaster a meter from one's face.

Mara Jade had often seen men in that kind of sweat. Far too often. "Judgment has been passed, Judge Lamos Chatoor," she said formally. "Have you any final words to say in your defense?"

"Only that your so-called judgment is insane," Chatoor ground out. "Because of a single dubious decision—*one* decision—after twenty years in the judicator's seat, you condemn me to *death*?"

Mara sighed. The sweating was common. The passionate and self-serving rationalizations were universal. "You haven't been listening," she said. "A single decision may have brought you to my attention, but it's hardly the reason for your sentence."

"Then what have I done wrong?" Chatoor asked, his voice half demanding, half pleading. "I've worked hard to dispense the Empire's justice to the best of my ability, in deeply trying circumstances that were not of my making. How can you hold an occasional lapse of judgment against me?"

He was stalling for time, Mara knew. But she was willing to oblige. Even when the evidence was clear and her mind was made up, she never entered into these things lightly. "We're not talking lapses of judgment," she said. "We're talking five years of systematic extortion, theft, and influence selling. You've made a second career of levying extra fines and declaring overline surcharges, then shunting the extra money to your friends and supporters."

"They were people in need," Chatoor insisted. "Is it wrong for a judge to have friends among such people?"

"It is when the so-called friendships are based solely on the exchange of money and favors," Mara said, a flicker of sensation stirring at the back of her mind. Two men were coming through the empty courtroom back there, making their stealthy way toward the chamber door behind her. "That's not friendship," she went on, subtly shifting her weight onto her left leg. "That's criminal collusion."

"But I've done nothing illegal," Chatoor persisted. "You can look at the records, speak to the people involved—"

And right in the middle of his sentence, the door behind Mara slammed open and a pair of blaster bolts exploded toward her back.

The shots never reached their intended target. Mara had already dropped her blaster, letting it fall with a clatter onto the judge's desk, and spun around, yanking out her lightsaber. The magenta blade *snap-hiss*ed into existence in front of her, deflecting those first two bolts into the walls.

Unfortunately for the gunmen, they continued firing. Mara sent their next bolts, one each, straight back into their own chests.

She waited until both men had crumpled lifelessly to the floor, just to be sure. Then she spun back around, tucking her elbows and twisting her lightsaber with her.

Just in time to halt Chatoor's desperate lunge across his desk as he tried to reach her dropped blaster.

For a long moment, she held the pose, the tip of her lightsaber blade almost touching Chatoor's throat, his own hand frozen bare centimeters from her blaster, his face white and contorted with fear and impotent rage. "For the record," Mara said at last, keeping her voice steady, "the innocent never try to shoot an Imperial agent in the back."

"You can't win," Chatoor bit out, his voice hoarse. "You can kill me— you can kill a hundred like me—but your precious Empire is still doomed. If the Rebels don't bring it down, it'll collapse from its own internal rot." His eyes bored into hers. "And then where will you be, my arrogant young

Imperial agent? Your power will be gone, your protectors dead or imprisoned. You already don't have any friends."

He turned over his outstretched hand so it was palm-upward. "But I can help you. *I* can be your friend. Spare my life—leave me in my position here—and I can create a refuge where you'll be safe when it all falls apart around you—"

With a flick of her wrists, Mara passed the lightsaber blade through his neck, silencing his voice forever.

For a moment she remained standing there, gazing at the body slumped over the desk where so many quiet deals had been made to defraud the Empire of its rightful assets and the Empire's citizens of their lives and liberty. "In the name of the Emperor," she said softly.

Shutting down her lightsaber, she retrieved her blaster and slid it back into its forearm sheath. Then, turning her back on yet another bit of freshly cleansed corruption, she left the chamber.

She passed fifteen more people on her way out of the courthouse. All of them stared at her, openly or furtively, as she strode past. None of them was foolish enough to try to stop her.

Her rented airspeeder was waiting unmolested where she'd left it three blocks away. Her transport, a heavily modified Sienar *Lambda*-class shuttle that she'd left on an out-of-the-way field two hundred kilometers north, was likewise.

She was sitting at the computer desk in her quarters, filling out her report, when she heard the familiar voice in her head. *My child?*

She smiled. *My lord,* she responded to the Emperor's silent call.

Your mission?

Complete, Mara said. *Justice has been done.*

Excellent, the Emperor said, and Mara could visualize his thin, satisfied smile.

She could also sense that he had a new assignment for her. *And now?* she asked.

Treason, the thought came, and she could feel his dark, brooding scowl. An image flashed into her mind, the picture of a surprisingly young Imperial governor. One allied with . . . Rebels?

Mara felt her lips twist. Like that ugly little affair with Governor

Choard on Shelkonwa three standard months ago. Didn't these high-ranking politicians ever learn? *His name?*

Ferrouz of Candoras sector, the Emperor told her. *Data sent.*

Mara looked over at the comm panel. The computer's download light was glowing a quiet blue. *Confirmed, my lord.*

Then go, the Emperor ordered. *But I warn you—this will not be easy.*

Mara had to smile at that one. Of course it wouldn't be easy. Easy tasks could be given to the military, or the heavy-handed thugs of the Imperial Security Bureau, or even Lord Vader and the *Executor's* massive firepower. The hard jobs, the subtle jobs—those were reserved for the Emperor's Hand. *I have confidence in my training,* she said.

Go, then, and dispense my justice.

I will, my lord, Mara promised.

Yes, the Emperor said, and once again Mara could see his smile. *We will speak again after. Farewell, my child.*

With that, the image of his smile faded, his voice went silent, and he was gone.

For a moment Mara sat motionless, holding on to that last glimpse of his face. On one level, Judge Chatoor's dying ploy had held a grain of truth. Mara really *didn't* have any friends.

But that was all right. She had her work, and she had the Emperor's approval and respect, and she had the sure knowledge that what she was doing was right. Friendship was a luxury, and something she could do without.

The last ray of the Emperor's presence faded away into the darkness of space. Taking a deep breath, Mara turned back to her computer and keyed for the download.

She skimmed the data first, catching all the high points. Then she read it more carefully, studying every detail that the Emperor had seen fit to send her. Then, just to make sure, she read it through again.

He was right. This wasn't going to be easy.

A rumbling in her stomach reminded her that she hadn't eaten since leaving for Judge Chatoor's court fifteen hours ago. Getting up from the computer, she went into the galley and pulled out a packet of ribenes with white-glaze.

If Ferrouz was planning to secede from the Empire, she reflected as she put the ribenes into the cooker, he was certainly going about it the right way. His sector fleet, while laughably small, had been dispersed to a number of different systems close to Poln, where it couldn't be taken out with a single blow but at the same time could respond quickly to any threat against the capital. He'd done the exact opposite with his sector's stormtrooper contingents, bringing most of them to Poln Major to bolster the defenses of his communications and the governor's palace itself.

Then there was the other half of the double planet, Poln Minor. Large enough to support only a marginal atmosphere, the place was honeycombed with mines, both working and abandoned, storehouses, maintenance centers, and large-scale work posts. If pressed hard enough, and if he could get across the gap separating the two worlds, Ferrouz could probably hold out there for years.

Certainly other unsavory people had done so. Poln Minor was reputed to be the home of hundreds of smugglers and other criminal types that years of sporadic Imperial efforts had failed to dislodge. Ferrouz might even have been in communication with some of those groups, opening up the possibility that he might bring them onto his side in a fight, or at least hide behind them should things go sour.

Poln Minor was also the key to any deal he might be making with the Rebel Alliance. A small army could hide within all those abandoned mines, along with a good-sized task force of small ships, ready to throw against whatever force the Emperor sent in response to Ferrouz's bid for independence. Between the Rebels and his own sector fleet, Ferrouz might be willing to gamble that he would be more trouble than he was worth, especially that far out on the Empire's periphery.

And finally, just to make things interesting, Poln Major had over the years also become home to dozens of different nonhuman species, many of them unknown groups who had apparently drifted in from Wild Space and the Unknown Regions and settled in and around the capital. The ISB section of Mara's report warned that some of those aliens might be mercenaries brought in by the governor. Even if that proved to be untrue, the mere presence of unknown aliens with unknown abilities and temperaments always added an extra layer of risk to a ground operation. Ferrouz was smart enough to know that and exploit it.

At least Mara now understood why the Emperor had chosen her for this mission. Someone had to slip into Poln Major, get to Ferrouz, and dispatch him before any of the defenses and responses could be triggered and launched. Ferrouz's probable successor, General Kauf Ularno, was about as unimaginative a military commander as could be imagined, but the ISB profiled him as stolidly loyal and certainly capable of taking back the capital and evicting whatever Rebels Ferrouz might have already brought in.

The cooker signaled, and Mara pulled out the tray and took it back to her desk. Setting it down beside the computer, she pulled up the map section of the report.

The first step, obviously, was to get to the Poln system. Her current ship was a capable enough transport, but arriving on Poln Major in an Imperial shuttle wouldn't be a very smart thing to do. Her *very* first step, therefore, would be to get herself a more inconspicuous ship.

Once she was on the ground, the next step would be to get into the governor's palace. Given all the extra stormtroopers Ferrouz had brought in, it might be handy for Mara to bring in a few of her own, for both reconnaissance and possible cover.

She felt her lip twist as she gnawed a bite of cream-glazed meat off the ribene bone. She'd worked with other Imperial forces over the years, of course, many times. But that didn't mean she'd ever really liked it. Commandeering temporary allies meant revealing at least part of her identity, even if it was just the fact that she was a vaguely defined Imperial agent. Such revelations automatically added to her vulnerability.

Worse, walking into a local garrison or fleet anchorage meant taking whatever they had available, whether good and competent or lazy and useless. Picking out random stormtroopers was an even shakier proposition these days, given Vader's habit of periodically combing through the ranks and transferring all the best and brightest into his personal 501st Legion.

On the other hand, there *was* a group of stormtroopers Mara had worked with before. A group that had proved itself capable, competent, and trustworthy. A group that even had its own shabby-looking transport.

The downside was that those particular stormtroopers were military deserters.

Taking another bite, Mara keyed for one of her private consolidation search files. Back on Shelkonwa, after that unpleasantness with Governor

Choard, she'd told LaRone and the other four stormtroopers to get off the planet and stay out of sight and out of trouble.

The first part of her order they'd obeyed. The rest they hadn't.

She ran her eyes down the list of little news tidbits that her search engine had gleaned from the Empire's vast information networks over the past three months. Here, a small-time warlord had disappeared, his control over a terrified countryside ended. There, commerce from a small farming and manufacturing colony suddenly resumed as a pirate nest went up in unexplained flames. Elsewhere, a regional administrator abruptly resigned his post and the increasingly distressed citizen petitions against him stopped arriving at the sector office.

Small injustices, of the sort that too often slipped through the cracks of the overextended government machinery. All of them corrected, usually overnight, always accompanied by rumors of a stormtrooper vanguard that had apparently proved that the Empire was finally taking the problem seriously.

And somewhere in the vicinity of every one of those incidents, buried unnoticed in the thick stacks of docking listings, had been a Suwantek TL-1800 transport. Always with a different ship's ID, of course. But always the same ship.

The self-named Hand of Judgment was alive and well and cutting a private fireline through the galaxy's criminals and petty tyrants.

Mara had been following the group's movements since Shelkonwa with decidedly mixed feelings. She'd looked into their story as to how and why they'd deserted their posts, and as far as she could tell it had more or less checked out, though a lot of the key evidence had been buried or destroyed by the ISB's cover-up specialists. She'd thought about bringing in LaRone and the others and getting them acquitted at a proper trial so that they could return to the Imperial service they'd been trained for and sworn to serve—the service that desperately needed men of their quality.

On the other hand, the ISB would be out for vengeance, and with the distractions inherent in Mara's job she knew she couldn't even guarantee a fair trial, let alone an acquittal. And she had to admit that LaRone and the others had found a niche for themselves in bringing Imperial justice to the galaxy on a more informal basis.

The long-term question of what to do with them was still without an answer. The short-term question, though, was much clearer.

They were going to Poln Major with her. Whether they liked it or not.

There was still the matter of finding them, of course. For that, Mara had her computer, its predictor capabilities, and her history of LaRone's recent movements.

More important, she had the Force.

She finished cleaning the meat off the last of the ribenes and set the tray aside. The last record she had of the Hand of Judgment placed them in the middle of a minor water dispute in Griren Province on the planet Hapor. Taking Hapor as a center point, she keyed for a summary of nearby citizen petitions, complaints, and backpocket police and military reports. A few minutes of consolidation on the computer's part, a few more minutes of reading on Mara's, and she had it narrowed to three likely possibilities.

Taking a deep breath, she stretched out to the Force.

She hadn't spent much time with the renegades, but that brief period had been hardened in the fire of combat against mutual enemies. Deep within her, Mara understood these men, had an indescribable yet solid sense of how they thought and acted. And as she gazed at the three possibilities, letting her mind focus in on those missions and the multidimensional images of the five stormtroopers, one of the listings slid inexorably to the foreground.

She had them.

She took another deep breath, allowing the focus of her mind to open up, letting in the gentle breezes from the transport's air system, the coldness of the control panel beneath her hand, the delicate leftover smell of the ribenes. Standing up, she headed to the cockpit and keyed in the start-up sequence. The minor world Elegasso, where a local election had been blatantly rigged, was the spot that logic and intuition told her would be LaRone's next target. The planet was a good distance away, but her ship had a better-than-average hyperdrive, and she should be able to get there within a day or two. It was unlikely that LaRone would be able to arrive, assess the situation, make a plan, and deal with the crooked politicians before then.

All she had to do was get to Elegasso, settle in, and wait. Sooner or later, whatever the Hand of Judgment was up to at the moment, they would find their way to her.

Daric LaRone's last thought just before the hail of blaster bolts blew the last bit of roof off his partial shelter was that this would be a really rotten place to die.

"LaRone!" someone shouted faintly through the static filling the headset of his stormtrooper helmet. Saberan Marcross, probably, though it was hard to identify voices through the partial comlink jamming the mercenary group out there was using. "You all right?"

"I'm still alive, if that's what you mean," LaRone shouted back. "What in space is the matter with these guys, anyway? Don't they know that stormtroopers always win?"

"Some people have to learn things the hard way," Taxtro Grave put in. "Can either of you see behind what's left of that fountain? I think that's where their heavy repeater is, but I can't get a clear shot."

Ignoring the blaster bolts steadily eating away at the pockmarked wall in front of him, LaRone popped his head up for a quick look. Sure enough, he could see the repeater peeking out from behind one of the slabs of broken stone. "I can see the muzzle, but that's all," he reported, ducking down again. "It's at the south end, between the fountain and that big broken slab."

"That should put the gunner in my field of fire," Marcross said. "Any chance you two can pull some of their blanket off me?"

"Believe me, I'm trying," LaRone assured him, wincing as an extra-large chunk of wall blew free and bounced off his armored shoulder. "The guys over here burn fire like they own a Tibanna mine."

"Same over here," Grave said. "This would be a really good time for either Brightwater or Quiller to make a dramatic entrance."

"You listening, you two?" LaRone called. "Brightwater? Quiller?"

His only answer was a fresh volley of fire from the mercs. The other two members of their little group must be out of comlink range.

Or else they were dead.

LaRone bared his teeth in a snarl, leaning around his shelter to fire off a few more shots. They weren't dead. They couldn't be. They were just taking their time about bringing in backup, that was all. Across to his left came a sudden crunching of masonry, and he heard Marcross grunt as part of his firing position came down on top of him. LaRone opened his mouth to call to him, to make sure he was okay.

He paused, his ears straining against the high-pitched blaster noise. Someone in the distance was screaming. Someone, or something. The scream grew louder . . .

And with as dramatic an entrance as LaRone could have hoped for, Brightwater and his Aratech 74-Z speeder bike roared into view over the ridge behind them, the bike's underslung blaster cannon spitting death and destruction at the mercenaries. The stream of fire that had been focused on LaRone faltered as some of the mercs flinched or else shifted their attention to this new threat—

There was the sudden thunderclap of a shattered Tibanna gas canister, and the whine of the repeater abruptly went silent. "Got him!" Marcross called. Overhead, Brightwater blew past, turning and jinking as he wove his screaming speeder bike in and out of the bursts of enemy fire. LaRone leaned out of his shelter again, shifting his BlasTech E-11 to full auto and raking the mercs' positions.

He was still trying to draw their fire away from Brightwater, and Brightwater himself was dangerously close to getting swatted straight out of the sky, when a bellowing roar hammered across the sounds of battle. LaRone looked to his left and saw their tricked-out Suwantek TL-1800 freighter rise into view above the ruins of the old city, its heavy laser cannons blazing across the morning sky as they hammered the enemy positions.

Abruptly the static vanished as the cannon fire found the comlink jammer. "Quiller, what've you got?" LaRone called, easing his head up for a better look.

"All the targets a growing boy could ever want," Joak Quiller returned tautly from the Suwantek. "Man, they really have a nest back there, don't they?"

"Like you wouldn't believe," LaRone agreed tightly. "Can you handle them?"

"Of course," Quiller said. "They're not exactly geared up for this kind of firepower. We should have gone this route in the first place."

LaRone grimaced. Except that bringing in the Suwantek would have instantly alerted the mercs that this wasn't just a standard stormtrooper unit with standard stormtrooper weapons and equipment. That was a conclusion LaRone had very much hoped to avoid drawing for them.

Which meant that he and the others now had no choice but to finish the job. Completely. "Just make sure it's done," he told Quiller grimly. "Make sure it's all done."

Either Quiller caught the sudden change in LaRone's tone or he'd already arrived at the same unpleasant conclusion on his own. "Understood," he said. "Keep your heads down."

Fortunately—LaRone supposed it was fortunate, anyway—this particular band of mercenaries didn't seem interested in survival if survival meant surrender. By the time LaRone and the others were finally able to leave their splintered cover points, all fifty mercs were dead.

And it was way past time to go.

A standard hour later, having hurried through an abbreviated round of thanks from the grateful farmers who now had their land and their lives back, the five stormtroopers were aboard the Suwantek and getting the blazes out of there.

"Well, that was fun," Quiller commented from the helm as the sky faded around them, turning from blue to dark blue to starlit black.

"Speak for yourself," Grave grunted as he applied a burn patch to his arm. His fifth, LaRone noted, and that was just the ones he could see. "That's one more set of armor down the disposal. My third in two months, if anyone's counting."

"That's because you insist on standing still while you line up your shots," Brightwater said. "I'm telling you, speeder bikes are the way to go."

"Yeah, and how's *your* armor holding up?" Grave countered pointedly.

"It's not parade-ground quality anymore," Brightwater conceded. "But it's still there."

"Barely," Grave said.

"Like everyone else's," Marcross said. "LaRone, we can't keep going this way. Our armor's being shot off us piece by piece, we're running out of Tibanna gas, grenades, and other supplies, and that admittedly impressive scream that was coming from Brightwater's speeder probably means something aboard is about to fail there, too."

"It's the accelerator pedal linkage," Brightwater said. "This'll be my third fix on the thing."

"And the other speeder bike isn't in any better shape, is it?" Marcross asked.

Brightwater shrugged. "A little. Not much. I might also mention that the stash of credits the ISB was kind enough to leave aboard this ship is likewise starting to run thin."

"Ditto for the stash of ship IDs," Quiller put in reluctantly. "We're burning through those like Hutt promises."

"Even if we weren't, all the fancy IDs in the galaxy aren't going to help us if enough people figure out the connection between us and this ship," Marcross added. "There aren't *that* many Suwanteks still flying around this part of the galaxy."

"I know," LaRone said, an ache in his heart that had nothing to do with the burns throbbing on his arms and chest. Ever since they'd left their posts aboard the Imperial Star Destroyer *Reprisal*—he still couldn't bring himself to use the word *deserted*, not even in his own mind—he and the others had been fighting their own private crusade against evil and corruption in this corner of the Empire.

The fact that they'd survived as long as they had was due partly to their own combat skills, but also in no small part to their good luck in having grabbed an Imperial Security Bureau covert ship on their way off the *Reprisal*. Thanks to the ISB's extensive weapons upgrades to the Suwantek and its hidden caches of equipment and money, they'd been able to take on injustice wherever they'd found it. Mercenaries, swoop gangs, pirate bases—none of them had been able to stop the Hand of Judgment.

But the others were right. The end was rapidly approaching. Once the supplies and money ran dry, they would be finished. They would have no choice but to do as that Imperial agent Jade had ordered them three months earlier back on Shelkonwa: stay out of sight, and out of trouble.

And their private war for justice would be over.

"None of which is to say we're ready to hit the escape pods quite yet,"

Quiller said into his thoughts. "We've still got at least five IDs we haven't used, and we can probably recycle some of the older ones that we haven't used for a while."

"That won't help with the armor," Marcross pointed out. "We've got, what, a couple of fresh sets each, and that's it?"

"Plus we still have the damaged ones," Brightwater said. "I don't know about yours, but I can probably cobble another set of scout armor out of the various bits and pieces."

"We can probably do the same," LaRone said. "But that's not really the point. The point is that, no matter how carefully we stretch our resources, we can definitely see the end ahead of us."

For a long moment, no one spoke. "It's been a good run," Grave offered at last. "I've got no regrets."

"Me, neither," Brightwater seconded. "We've helped a lot of hurting people over these past few months."

"A lot more, I daresay, than we did when we were official stormtroopers," Marcross murmured.

"Agreed," Quiller said. "So what's the plan, LaRone? We skip that stolen-election thing on Elegasso and start looking for someplace to go to ground?"

"I hate to pass up something that blatant," Grave murmured. "It's small enough, and they're mostly just armed politicians. We should be able to show up in armor and frighten them into backing off and calling a new election."

"Which they might steal again," Brightwater pointed out.

"I doubt it," Grave said. "There's something very persuasive about having a BlasTech E-11 stuck in your face while an Imperial stormtrooper warns you that he'll be watching your political ethics from now on."

"Which we won't be," Marcross pointed out. "But of course they won't know that."

"Grave's right," LaRone decided. "I think we can handle that one before we retire."

"What about that pottery thing I told you about?" Brightwater asked.

LaRone scratched his cheek. The pottery thing was a report one of the farmers back there had heard about from his cousin on another world. A small group of dirt-poor artisans had found a patch of exotic, one-of-a-kind clay and had finally started making a successful living by creating striking and marketable sculptures from it.

Or they had been until the local government had gotten wind of the operation and decided to take it over for their own profit. Since the bureaucrats didn't have a gram of artistic skill themselves, their solution had been to turn the genuine sculptors into slave labor.

LaRone knew nothing about art, and even less about sculpture. But he knew a lot about greed and oppression, and didn't much like either. Neither did his four comrades. "I don't see why we can't do both," he told Brightwater. "Pickerin's only a few hours from Elegasso, and it's more or less on the way."

"There's also a decent Imperial database on Pickerin," Quiller said, peering at his data display. "Maybe we can sneak in there after we break the sculptors loose and get some ideas of where we can . . . you know."

"Bury ourselves away from the universe?" Brightwater suggested.

"Something like that," LaRone conceded. "Quiller, go ahead and set course for Pickerin. If we're going out, we might as well go out with a bang."

The landing field they were directed to on Pickerin was about as small and isolated a place as LaRone had ever seen. Still, it was only a few kilometers from the town where the enslaved artisans were producing their statues under the guns of their oppressors. Quiller landed the Suwantek, keyed the systems into lockdown standby, and lowered the landing ramp for the customs officials and the usual brief questionnaire and collection of landing fees.

LaRone was waiting at the top of the ramp, their latest set of forged ship's documents in hand, when the ramp area erupted with a blast of cold, bitter-smelling gas.

"Cover!" LaRone snapped with his last breath, grabbing for his blaster as he dived for the ramp control.

He was unconscious before he reached it.

CHAPTER FOUR

LORD ODO'S PREVIOUS TIME AWAY FROM THE *CHIMAERA*, DURING HIS mysterious meeting at the unknown world, had lasted over five hours. His visit to Wroona lasted precisely one.

"Signal from Lord Odo, Commander," the comm officer announced. "The *Salaban's Hope* has reached docking position and is being tractored aboard. Lord Odo requests that we set a course for the Poln system in Candoras sector, and that we leave as soon as the freighter is secured aboard."

Pellaeon nodded. "Navigation?"

"Running the calculation now, sir," the nav officer confirmed. "It'll take a few minutes."

"Acknowledged," Pellaeon said. Turning, he walked back along the command walkway to the aft bridge and keyed the Poln system into the computer console there.

He was skimming through the summary when the turbolift door hissed open and Captain Drusan appeared. "Report?"

"Lord Odo is on his way back from Wroona, sir," Pellaeon told him. "We're to leave for the Candoras sector and the Poln system once he's aboard."

"Candoras?" Leaning over Pellaeon's shoulder, Drusan peered at the display. "What is there that anyone could find interesting?"

"I don't know, sir." Pellaeon gestured toward the screen. "I was hoping I might find a clue here. So far, though, nothing's jumping out at me."

Drusan grunted. "What about that computer search you've been doing?" he asked, lowering his voice. "Any luck?"

"Not yet, sir," Pellaeon said, wincing a little. He'd thought his search had been more discreet than that. "But I've only made it through the top three data tiers. There are at least four more to go, plus the obscure single-system ones that are already half legend."

"But that doesn't make sense," Drusan insisted. "Someone with *lord* attached to his name should be right there on the top tier. Yet you say he's not. So where exactly does his title come from?"

"Possibly one of the smaller systems," Pellaeon said. "Some of those are very big on titles and general pageantry."

"Maybe." Drusan lowered his voice still further. "What do you think of him, Commander? Do you think he can be trusted?"

"I hardly think my opinion matters, sir," Pellaeon said carefully. "Someone in authority clearly trusts him."

"Maybe," Drusan said again. "Well, I suppose we'll just have to see how matters unfold. Are the watch reports finished?"

"Yes, sir, I believe so."

"Good." Drusan turned and stalked through the archway into the main bridge.

Pellaeon was still trying to find something interesting in the Poln system when the turbolift door once again opened and the masked, robed figure of Lord Odo swept onto the bridge. "Commander Pellaeon," he said, greeting Pellaeon briefly as he turned to look down the command walkway at the stars still filling the viewport. "I gave orders to leave as soon as the *Salaban's Hope* was aboard."

"The delay was my decision, my lord," Drusan said, reappearing through the archway. "I wanted to make sure your errand had been successful before we left the region."

"It was," Odo assured him coolly.

"The equipment you required has been brought aboard?" Drusan persisted.

"It has," Odo said. "You will speak to the helm now."

Drusan seemed to draw himself up. "Helm?" he called. "Engage new course setting. Activate hyperdrive."

"Acknowledged," the faint call came back. Across the bridge, the stars exploded into starlines, and the *Chimaera* was on its way.

"Thank you." Deliberately, Odo walked over to the captain, stopping bare centimeters away from him. "The next time I give an order, Captain," he said, his voice low but curiously carrying, "I expect it to be carried out."

Drusan's lip twitched, but to his credit he stayed where he was instead of backing up. "Understood, my lord," he said.

For a long moment, Odo held his pose. Then he turned his mask to Pellaeon. "I believe your watch is over, Commander Pellaeon," he said. "You may go about your other activities."

Pellaeon looked at Drusan. Technically, only the captain had the authority to dismiss the senior bridge officer from his watch.

But Drusan had apparently had enough confrontation for one day. His head bobbed once and then jerked microscopically toward the turbolift. "Yes, my lord," Pellaeon said. Stepping a bit gingerly past the robed figure, he headed to the turbolift and escaped.

He was nearly to his quarters when his comlink signaled. "Commander, this is Lieutenant Tibbale, duty security officer," the caller identified himself. "As per your standing order, I wished to inform you that Lord Odo's pilot has left his quarters and is currently in the bay officers' mess."

"Thank you," Pellaeon said, and keyed off. Returning the comlink to its holder, he reset the turbolift's destination.

Odo had told him to go about his other activities. He'd never said those activities couldn't include a meal.

The *Chimaera's* various mess rooms always did a brisk business in the first hour after a watch change, but Sorro's civilian outfit made him stand out of the crowd. He was sitting alone at a two-person table against the rear bulkhead. Working his way through the crowd, Pellaeon reached his side. "Good day, Master Sorro," he said. "May I join you?"

Sorro looked up from his tray, and it seemed to Pellaeon that the lines around his eyes hardened a bit. "Commander Pellaeon, isn't it?" he asked, his voice neutral.

"Yes," Pellaeon confirmed. "May I join you?"

Sorro's eyes flicked to Pellaeon's empty hands, then back up to his face. "If you're looking for information about our mission, you'll have to ask Lord Odo. I'm just the pilot."

"And I'm just the third bridge officer," Pellaeon reminded him. "Mission coordination is Captain Drusan's job, not mine. I simply wanted to talk to you for a few moments."

Sorro shook his head. "Sorry. I'm not really in the mood for company."

He returned his attention to his food. Pellaeon stayed where he was, and after a few more bites Sorro looked up again. "Didn't you hear me?" he growled. "Go away."

"My ship, Master Sorro, not yours," Pellaeon reminded him. "What are you afraid of?"

"I didn't say I was afraid," Sorro countered. "I said I wasn't interested in company."

"Then you picked the wrong job," Pellaeon said. "Bringing an Imperial lord aboard an Imperial Star Destroyer guarantees you lots of company."

For another handful of seconds Sorro glared up at him. Pellaeon returned the gaze, not moving or speaking.

With a sigh, Sorro lowered his eyes. "It's said that patience is a virtue, Commander," he said, waving at the chair across from him. "So is persistence. What did you want to talk about?"

"Nothing mysterious or ominous, I assure you," Pellaeon said as he sat down. "I mostly wanted to inquire as to whether you and Lord Odo were being treated properly. Your quarters, for instance—are they satisfactory?"

"Lord Odo hasn't complained," Sorro said. "They're certainly no better or worse than one would expect to find aboard a warship."

"Hardly what you and his lordship are used to, though, I assume?" Pellaeon suggested.

Sorro looked down at his tray. "I've seen worse," he said. "I can't speak for his lordship."

"Ah," Pellaeon said. "My mistake. I was under the impression that you were Lord Odo's permanent pilot."

Sorro shook his head. "Nothing about my life is permanent anymore," he said in a low voice. "Nothing permanent. Nothing stable." He opened his right hand and gazed into the palm as if there was some clue or memory there that only he could see. "Nothing pleasant."

"I'm sorry," Pellaeon said. "So then Lord Odo merely brought you in for this particular job?"

Sorro's lip twisted. "You could say that." He gazed into his hand for another second, then closed it into a tired-looking fist. "Have you ever lost everything, Commander Pellaeon? No—stupid question. Of course you've never lost everything."

"Not everything, no," Pellaeon said. "But I've had my share of losses."

"What, promotions?" Sorro scoffed. "The last dessert cube in the mess line?"

"Battles," Pellaeon said evenly. "Subordinates. Comrades. Friends."

Sorro's throat tightened. "Yes, I suppose you have," he said, gesturing to Pellaeon's uniform. "But at least you have your priorities straight." He opened his hand and again gazed into it. "Not everyone does."

"No, they don't," Pellaeon agreed. "But it's never too late for a man to recognize his shortcomings and change them."

Sorro shook his head. "I wish that was true. But it isn't. Not always."

"Yes, it is," Pellaeon said firmly. "Where there's life, there's the hope of change."

Sorro snorted. "Please. Neat, clichéd phrases never solved anything."

"Not if they remain nothing but neat clichéd phrases," Pellaeon said. "They have to spark regret, resolve, and action."

Abruptly the mess room chatter around them vanished into a taut silence. Frowning, Pellaeon looked up.

Lord Odo was standing just inside the doorway, his masked face pointed at Pellaeon and Sorro.

"My lord," Sorro said hastily, starting to get to his feet.

Odo made a small gesture, and Sorro broke off the movement, sinking down again into his seat. "May I help you, Lord Odo?" Pellaeon asked, standing up.

"My quarters are being changed, Commander Pellaeon," Odo said. If he was annoyed to find one of the *Chimaera*'s officers having a private conversation with his pilot, it wasn't audible in his voice. "I wished Sorro's assistance."

"Of course, my lord," Sorro said, again starting to get up.

"But since he's in the middle of a meal," Odo continued smoothly, "perhaps *you* would assist me, Commander."

Pellaeon hesitated. Moving trunks and equipment was hardly something a senior officer should be doing. Odo surely knew that.

On the other hand, this might be Pellaeon's best chance of getting a look at the things Odo had brought aboard the *Chimaera*. Not to mention the chance to speak privately with Odo himself. "I would be honored, my lord," he said, stepping away from the table.

"Excellent," Odo said. His mask turned slightly. "When you're finished, Sorro, make your way to the bridge. They'll direct you to our new quarters."

Pellaeon waited until he and Odo were walking along the corridor before speaking again. "May I ask what the problem is with your quarters?"

"There's no problem," Odo assured him. "Now that we're en route to our final destination and will have no need for quick access to the *Salaban's Hope*, I wished to be closer to the bridge. Captain Drusan has therefore assigned us new quarters there."

Pellaeon felt his stomach tighten. The only quarters available near the bridge were for visiting dignitaries: sector governors, Grand Moffs, or special Imperial agents like Darth Vader. "I'm sure you'll find them more convenient," he murmured.

"Indeed," Odo said. "What do you think of him?"

Pellaeon frowned. "Who?"

"My pilot, of course," Odo said. "You *were* interrogating him, weren't you?"

"Not at all," Pellaeon said hastily. "Ironically enough, I'd been asking him if your quarters were satisfactory."

"Indeed," Odo said. "You may also have noticed Sorro's deep unhappiness."

"It was a bit hard to miss," Pellaeon conceded. "What exactly happened to him?"

"He didn't tell you?"

"Just vague hints," Pellaeon said. "He asked if I'd ever lost everything. What exactly did he lose?"

"As he said: everything." For a few steps Odo was silent. "Tell me, Commander. Have you ever heard the saying 'The choices of one shape the futures of all'?"

"Yes, I believe so," Pellaeon said. "Jedi, isn't it?"

"The Jedi may have stolen it," Odo said. "But it was originally from the *Song of Salaban*. The point is that each person's decisions affect everyone around him. Friends, family, business associates—even total strangers. You ask what happened to Sorro? That's what happened. He made bad decisions—many of them. In the process, he lost everything he held of value."

"I'm sorry," Pellaeon murmured. "What will he do now?"

"That's entirely up to him," Odo said. "I rather hope he decides to fight to get it back." He motioned toward his cabin's door. "In here."

Odo's original rooms were a set of junior officers' quarters, with two beds, a refresher station, and a few small pieces of furniture. The five travel cases the *Chimaera*'s crewers had brought across from the *Salaban's Hope* were already clustered together on a floating repulsor cart in the center of the room.

And in the middle of the group of bags were two new items: a pair of meter-long cylinders about fifteen centimeters across with long shoulder straps attached. The specialized equipment, apparently, that Odo had brought back from Wroona.

Stepping to the cart, Odo retrieved the cylinders from among the other bags. "You will guide the cart, Commander," he said, gesturing to the cart's control panel.

"As you wish, my lord," Pellaeon said as he keyed the cart off standby. "You can put those back if you wish," he added, nodding to the cylinders. "The cart can handle the entire load."

"I know that," Odo said, looping one strap around each of his shoulders. "Follow me."

The rest of the trip to the command section was made in silence. Most of the junior officers they passed seemed a bit startled at the sight of a senior bridge officer driving a cart, but none of them said anything. The crewers, in contrast, studiously ignored the odd procession as being none of their business.

One lone petty officer was brave enough or conscientious enough to offer his assistance, and though Odo turned him down, Pellaeon made sure to memorize the man's face and duty sector. The next promotions list would be opening soon for officer recommendations.

As Pellaeon had anticipated, Odo led them to the visiting-dignitary suite two corridors aft of the bridge. What Pellaeon hadn't expected was that Captain Drusan would be waiting there for them. "Lord Odo," the captain said, his eyes flashing oddly at Pellaeon as he bowed to Odo. "Thank you for your willingness to move your quarters. I'm sure you'll find these more than satisfactory."

"I'm certain I will, Captain," Odo said, looking around the room, his eyes lingering for a moment on the display and repeater board, which the occupant could use to monitor nearly all of the *Chimaera*'s systems. "Commander Pellaeon was kind enough to assist with the move."

"So I see," Drusan said, giving Pellaeon that same odd look. "I would have been happy to assign you a crewer instead."

"I was more than happy to offer my assistance," Pellaeon said.

"Yes," Drusan murmured, his gaze dropping from Pellaeon's face to the cluster of bags on the cart. "But I'm sure we can handle things from here. Dismissed."

"Yes, sir." Pellaeon inclined his head to Odo. "Lord Odo."

A minute later he was on the turbolift heading back toward officers' country. Now would normally be the time for a meal, some reading, and then sleep. But today the meal and sleep could wait. Suddenly his brain was churning with possibilities.

He still didn't know who or what Lord Odo was. But finally he had a fresh idea of where to look.

"Here we go," Han muttered, and pushed back the hyperdrive levers. In front of him, the mottled hyperspace sky flashed with starlines and then the stars of the Poln system.

For a minute he let the *Falcon* coast, heading generally inward as he studied the twin planets ahead. Even without their size difference it would have been easy to tell the two worlds apart. Poln Major was all shades of blue and green and white, with scattered clumps of glittering lights on the night side. Poln Minor was mostly browns and grays, with a bare handful of lights. Probably the entrances to the various spaceports, he decided, or else the markers of underground storage and maintenance facilities. And if Rieekan was right, the holes where a whole lot of smugglers, pirates, and other fringe types were hiding.

Beside him, Chewie rumbled. "Yeah, I see it," Han said sourly, eyeing the flashing lights of the Golan I Space Defense Station in high orbit over Poln Major. Rieekan had assured him that the Golan was mostly an empty shell these days, running with maybe 30 percent of its normal crew and rated firepower.

But even 30 percent of a Golan still left it as a serious obstacle for any Alliance forces trying to move in. On the other hand, if it could be taken intact, that same firepower would then be on the Alliance's side. He made a mental note to suggest that Axlon make the station one of his demands to Governor Ferrouz.

There was the sound of footsteps behind him.

"Are we there?" Axlon asked.

"Yeah," Han confirmed, setting his teeth firmly together. Four days of riding together in a cramped light freighter—four days of the man finding a way to get on every single one of Han's nerves—had left him with a powerful urge to open the hatch to clean air again. Or maybe just to find a convenient piece of vacuum and toss his passenger out into it.

Axlon was polite, but in a subtly superior way that even Her Worshipfulness Princess Leia couldn't match. He asked obvious and irritating questions, and continually gave the impression that Han should be happier about answering them. He was an avid but unskilled sabacc player, and every time he lost it was clear he thought Han had cheated. Even when he hadn't.

But worse even than all the surface irritants was what was simmering behind the man's eyes. There was a swirl of anger, tenacity, and nervousness back there, in a fluid and ever-changing combination that set Han's teeth on edge. He'd seen that kind of personality before, and it usually got the offender and his pals chased out of a cantina or off a world at a high rate of speed.

Or it got them all killed.

Chewie had noticed it, too, even though the big Wookiee was too polite to mention it. Still, when something bothered Chewie, Han had long
ago learned it was worth keeping an eye on.

Chewie rumbled again.

"What?" Han asked, snapping out of his reverie.

Chewie repeated the comment, this time pointing to the aft sensor
readout.

Han frowned. The Wookiee was right—there was a Z-95 back there,
about half a minute behind the *Falcon* and twenty degrees to starboard.

There were still plenty of Z-95s running around the galaxy, especially
out here at the edges where security services couldn't afford newer fighters, or didn't want to put the more expensive hardware at risk. And the ship
was definitely not showing Alliance markings.

But it was coming in on more or less the same vector as the *Falcon*,
though that twenty-degree spread meant the pilot was trying *not* to look
like he was coming in on that vector.

And something about the way the pilot was handling the fighter
strongly reminded Han of Luke.

Han felt his eyes narrow. Rieekan had told him that Luke was going to
be handling some of the follow-up fighter stuff. But Rieekan didn't exactly
have a spotless record as far as lying through his teeth was concerned. And
now that Han thought about it, he remembered that when he and Axlon
had said good-bye to Luke, the kid had been pretty vague about what he
was going to be doing for the next few weeks.

Chewie rumbled. "Yeah, yeah, I see him," Han said.

"See who?" Axlon asked, a little too quickly.

"Chewie was just wondering about the Golan out there," Han said, casually easing the *Falcon* to the right. If that really was Luke out there, he
wouldn't want Han getting close enough to get a clear look through the
canopy.

Sure enough, Han had barely begun to close the gap when the Z-95
started a drift of its own, heading the same direction and at the same speed
as the *Falcon*.

Muttering under his breath, Han drifted the *Falcon* back onto her original vector. This time the Z-95 didn't try to match the maneuver, but simply continued easing to starboard as if that had been the pilot's plan all along. Even Luke wasn't inexperienced enough at this sort of thing to look like he was trying to play follow-my-twist with the *Falcon*. Especially when he was obviously trying to keep his presence here a secret. Him, Rieekan, and everyone else.

Including Axlon? "So it's just the three of us, huh?" Han commented. "Three against a whole Imperial garrison?"

"Oh, please," Axlon scoffed. "It's hardly going to come to that. Don't you get it? Governor Ferrouz *wants* us here. He's not going to do anything to jeopardize this deal."

"Yeah," Han muttered. "Right."

CHAPTER FIVE

T HE THING THAT'S SO FUNNY ABOUT THIS," THE CHEERFUL-VOICED MAN commented into the darkness that surrounded LaRone, "is how easily you were caught."

LaRone didn't answer. He hadn't been answering, in fact, for the past three standard hours or so, the full length of time he and the others had been sitting here with binders on their wrists and blindfolds across their eyes. Partly because he didn't want to dignify the other man's ramblings. Mostly because there really was nothing he could say.

And because Cheerful was right. LaRone had walked right into the trap, his eyes open, his blaster still in its holster.

And now, much sooner than he'd anticipated, the Hand of Judgment's run really *was* all over. Their attackers had taken all five of them, and as far as LaRone could tell, they had done it without firing a single shot.

He still didn't know who these men were, whether they were mercenaries, Imperials, or just some local criminal gang. But it didn't really matter. LaRone and the others would either be killed outright or turned over to the Empire, which amounted to the same thing.

Whatever his motivation, whatever his plan, the man gloating at LaRone from across the room had every reason to be cheerful.

Still, LaRone was becoming increasingly puzzled by the fact that they'd been sitting here all this time with no attempts at questioning or torture other than having to listen to the man talk. Did he simply want them in pristine condition when he turned them over to the Imperial Security Bureau? The thought of that made LaRone's skin crawl.

Somewhere across the room behind Cheerful's voice, a door opened. "There you are," Cheerful said, sounding decidedly less cheerful now. "About time."

"Is this them?" a cold voice—male—demanded.

"Most of them," Cheerful confirmed. "I admit they're not much to look at—"

"Take those off," Cold Voice interrupted. "I want them to see me while I explain the realities of life to them."

"Not sure that's a good idea," Cheerful warned. "They may not look it, but I'll bet they'll get real talky once they get to the other end of their one-way ride."

"You may have things to hide, Doss," Cold Voice said. "I don't. I want to look them in the eye."

"Fine," Cheerful said with a sigh. "You're the boss. Kinker, Shippo— you heard the man."

There was a brief patter of footsteps, and a dull light blazed suddenly in LaRone's eyes as the blindfold was ripped off his face. For a moment he squinted against the light, and then his eyes adjusted.

They were in some kind of office, probably the customs building he'd seen from the Suwantek on their way in. The place was typical of this size landing field: small and somewhat decrepit, with a couple of scan tables, two desks, and walls that were lined with shelving and equipment cabi-nets. At least half of the shelving LaRone could see from his position was bare, and he suspected most of the cabinets were empty, as well.

Four men faced them from across the room. One, a large, evil-looking man with brown-and-white-striped hair, was sitting casually on one of the scan tables. Standing stiffly beside him was a somewhat older man in a dark business tunic and matching trousers. The other two men—Kinker and Shippo, LaRone assumed—stood off to the sides between them and LaRone, four blindfolds hanging loosely from their hands. At the far end of the room, a third guard lounged by the building's only visible door.

LaRone felt himself stiffen as a stray fact belatedly caught his attention. Kinker and Shippo were holding *four* blindfolds?

Trying to seem casual, he looked to either side of him. Marcross sat in the chair to his right, his hands shackled like LaRone's behind his back. To Marcross's right was Quiller; to LaRone's left was Grave.

Brightwater was nowhere to be seen.

"You're right, Doss, they really don't look like much," the businessman said in the same cold voice as he eyed the stormtroopers. "Do they have a leader?"

Beside LaRone, Marcross stirred. "That would be me," LaRone spoke up. "And you?"

"What, you don't even know my name?" the other retorted. "You came to this sector intent on overthrowing me, and you don't even know my *name*?"

"Of course we do," Marcross said calmly. "You're Bok Yost, recently elected to the post of chancellor in the Skemp District on Elegasso."

LaRone suppressed a grimace, embarrassment momentarily eclipsing his quiet dread of the future looming over them all. He should have recognized Yost right off, even if he wasn't wearing the official robes of office the way he'd been in all the holos they'd seen of the man.

"That's right," Yost said. "Recently and *legally* elected."

"I said you'd been elected," Marcross corrected mildly. "I didn't say it had been legal."

"I warned you about these jokers," Doss murmured. "Self-righteous clear down to the marrow."

"Yes, aren't they?" Yost said, his voice going even colder. "And I see that trying to explain the realities of life would be a waste of time."

"Realities, as in if you bribe someone enough, he'll go away?" LaRone suggested.

"Exactly," Yost said with a thin smile. "I *was* going to offer you a substantial sum of money to come over to my side. You're clearly highly competent—Doss's list of your accomplishments over the past few months makes that impressively clear. But I see now that such an offer would be a waste of time. I suppose the only question now is what we do with you. Doss?"

"Easiest part of all," Doss said, his voice all cheerful again. "All you have to do is whistle up the Pickerin garrison and hand them over to them. Did I forget to mention they're military deserters?"

"As a matter of fact, you did," Yost rumbled, eyeing LaRone with a new gleam in his eye. "I was wondering where they'd found stormtrooper gear to steal."

"Now you know," Doss said. "So get on your comlink and call the garrison."

Yost snorted. "Don't be ridiculous. I'm a government official now. I can't do that."

Doss threw the other a confused look. "Of course you can," he said. "You being an official will add a whole lot more weight to the charges—"

"And being an official," Yost cut in, "I can't accept rewards for the return of deserters."

Doss's frown cleared. "Ah. No, I guess you can't. I suppose you'll want half?"

"I want two-thirds," Yost corrected. "You and your men can have the rest."

"What, an entire third for us?" Doss said sarcastically. "Very generous of you."

"Don't be ungrateful," Yost admonished. "Don't forget that I'm the one who identified the threat and came up with this ridiculous pottery rumor for you to lure them in with. The fact of the matter is that I'm being more than generous. Especially since you'll also keep your very hefty fee."

For a moment the two men glared at each other. "For whatever it's worth," LaRone offered into the stiff silence, "whatever he's paying, Doss, we'll double it."

"Shut up," Doss growled. "Fine. A third of the reward plus our fee. And we get to keep their ship."

"Agreed." Yost looked over at LaRone. "Well. Let's bundle them aboard your ship and go wake up the Imperials."

"No need," a quiet voice said from somewhere to LaRone's right. "We're already awake."

LaRone twisted his head around toward the voice. A young woman was standing in the shadows by a bank of dusty storage lockers twenty meters away. Behind her, one of the locker doors hung open, as if she'd been hiding inside the whole time. She was wearing a peasant's tunic over baggy trousers and low boots, the rustic outfit topped off with a short hooded cloak. The hood was pulled low over her forehead, covering her hair and concealing the upper half of her face.

In impressive unison Doss's three guards snatched out their blasters.

"What's that supposed to mean?" Doss demanded as all three weapons swung to target the woman. "Who are you? What are you doing here?"

"You're Mikhtor Doss, aren't you?" the woman asked, taking another step toward Doss and Yost before coming to a halt. "I've read about you and your mercenaries." She cocked her head. "Or are you actually pirates? The reports are a bit vague."

"Who *is* this creature?" Yost demanded. "Doss, if this is some trick—"

"Shut it," Doss cut him off, his eyes on the woman. "Whatever rumors you've been listening to, it's all nonsense. We're a fully licensed paramilitary group, cleared by the sector governor himself."

"Which means nothing," the woman said calmly. "Especially in this sector, where the governor's office is long overdue for a cleaning."

"It's the times," Doss said philosophically. "What about you? Haven't you and your associates ever skidded across the line?"

The woman shook her head. "I have no associates. I work alone."

Doss clucked his tongue. "Wrong answer," he said. "Kill her."

The three guards raised their blasters and fired—

—and staggered and fell onto the dusty floor a second later as a brilliant lightsaber blade flashed into existence in front of the woman, catching all three blaster bolts and caroming them straight back at the shooters.

For a single heartbeat Doss goggled in disbelief at the sudden and unexpected carnage. Then, throwing himself backward over the edge of the scan table in a desperate bid for cover, he yanked out his blaster and fired.

He was still trying for the relative safety of the table's rear when his shot was ricocheted back at him, blowing off the side of his head. He disappeared over the edge of the table, his blaster dropping onto the table and clattering to the floor at Yost's feet.

And as the lightsaber blade settled down in front of the woman and the magenta glow bathed her shadowed face in soft light, LaRone felt his breath freeze in his throat.

This wasn't just a simple peasant woman, or even some important Imperial functionary or bounty hunter. This was the Imperial agent who called herself Jade.

This was the Emperor's Hand.

For a long moment, the only sound in the room was the hum of Jade's lightsaber. "Well?" she invited calmly, her eyes on Yost.

Yost's breath was coming in quick, shallow puffs. "I'm Chancellor Yost," he stammered. "Chancellor of—"

"Of Skemp District on Elegasso," Jade finished for him. "Yes, I know. I was there when you got the call from Doss."

Yost's tongue dabbed nervously at his lips. "I'm a duly elected government official," he insisted.

The lightsaber blade lifted. "Are you?" Jade asked pointedly.

Yost shot a furtive look at LaRone. "I . . . there may have been . . . some questions . . ." He trailed off.

"Let's try a different approach," Jade suggested. "Doss captured five men. Four are here. Where's the fifth?"

Yost looked at LaRone again. "Aboard their ship," he said. "Not Doss's ship—their ship. He said they needed to . . . persuade . . . the pilot to unlock the helm for them."

LaRone frowned. That one actually made a certain amount of sense.

Except that Brightwater wasn't their pilot. Quiller was, and Quiller was right here with the rest of them.

So why had they taken Brightwater?

"Good," Jade said briskly. With a sizzling hiss the lightsaber blade disappeared. "You've just bought yourself your life. Your ship is waiting at the other end of the field. You'll get aboard her, go home, and never mention this incident to anyone. *And* . . ."

Yost stared at her, looked at LaRone, back at Jade. "And?" he asked carefully.

Jade cocked her head. "If you have to ask, I may have to kill you after all."

Yost swallowed visibly. "There may have been some irregularities with the election," he conceded. "Perhaps it would be best if I called for a new one."

"A wise idea," Jade said. "You'll step down, of course, until the new results are in."

Yost's lips drew back in the beginnings of a snarl. But then his gaze dropped to the lightsaber hilt in her hand and the snarl faded away. "Of course."

"Good," Jade said briskly. "Then go."

That one, at least, Yost didn't have to hear twice. He rounded the end of the table and walked as quickly toward the door as he could without breaking into an actual run. "And remember," Jade called after him. "We *will* be watching."

The other didn't reply, turn around, or even slow his pace. The door opened at his approach, and he hurried out into the night.

"Well," Jade said briskly as she strode over to the four stormtroopers. "Everyone all right?"

"Yes, I think so," LaRone said, eyeing her uncomfortably. Now that the immediate crisis had passed, the question of what she was doing here was raising shivers across his back.

Because offhand, he couldn't think of any answer to that question that he was going to like.

"Good." Jade stepped around behind the row of chairs, and with a *snap-hiss* her lightsaber blade once again sent a glow of magenta light across the room. "Let's get you out of here and go get Brightwater, shall we?"

"If Yost wasn't lying about where they had him," Quiller warned.

"He wasn't." There was a slight tug at LaRone's wrists as the lightsaber sliced through his binders. "One of Doss's men told him all about Brightwater while they were heading over here from Yost's ship."

"You were close enough to hear them?" Grave asked, sounding puzzled.

"It wasn't very hard," Jade assured him. "I came in aboard Yost's ship."

"Aboard his *ship*?" Quiller echoed, sounding stunned.

"First rule of following someone," Jade said as she freed the others. "The simplest way is always to hitch a ride with him."

"That's the *easy* way?" Marcross asked.

"I said it was simple," Jade corrected. "I didn't say it was *easy*."

"Please don't take this wrong," LaRone said, massaging his sore wrists as he stood up, "but what are you doing here?"

"All in good time," Jade said as she stepped around in front of them.

Exactly, LaRone thought, like a field commander preparing to lead the troops. "First things first. Grab those blasters, and let's go find Brightwater."

Doss had left five men on duty in the Suwantek, plus two more busy at the task of interrogating Brightwater. All seven were caught by surprise at the sudden appearance of Jade and the four stormtroopers. All seven decided to make a fight of it.

All seven died quickly.

Though if LaRone had realized up front what they'd done to Brightwater, he might have been tempted to make their deaths last a little longer.

"About time," Brightwater said as LaRone and Quiller unstrapped him from the bed where the mercenaries had tied him. His voice was weak; his eyes were swollen half shut. "Who's that? Watch it—there's someone behind you."

"It's all right," Quiller assured him, his voice dark and grim as Grave popped open the medpac. "It's Jade. She came by to help."

"*Jade?*" Brightwater asked, making an effort to open his eyes a little wider. "What's—" He broke off into a coughing fit. "What's she doing here?"

"Helping get you out," LaRone told him. "Hold still, will you?"

"So much for your lucky coin," Grave commented as he loaded a hypo with a painkiller.

"Hey, I'm alive, aren't I?" Brightwater pointed out weakly.

"Lucky coin?" Jade asked as she peered into Brightwater's eyes and delicately touched his forehead. Some Force thing, LaRone guessed.

"A worthless old pre-Empire druggat he picked up a couple of months ago," Grave told her. "Some grateful farmer was trying to unload them on us. Brightwater's the only one who took one. You see the kind of luck the thing gets you."

"Like I said, I'm still alive," Brightwater said.

"So am I, and I don't have to lug around extra stuff," Grave countered as he injected the painkiller.

"This from a guy who carries around a T-28 sniper rifle for the fun of it," LaRone said. "How is he?"

"Like he says, he's alive," Jade said. "But he's going to need a few days in a bacta tank. You have one aboard this ship?"

"A subminiature, yes," Marcross said grimly. "Our bacta supply's running low, but we should have enough for at least one more treatment."

"That's all right," Jade said. "I've got a tank and plenty of bacta aboard my ship back on Elegasso. Give me the helm lock code and I'll get us into the air."

"That's okay—I'll take us up," Quiller said. "Where on Elegasso are you?"

"Coskone Field, northern edge of Skemp City," Jade said. She frowned. "*You're* the pilot? Then why were they interrogating *him?*"

"Because they're mercenaries," Brightwater said. "That means they're stupid."

"And also because this idiot pushed past me into the cockpit when the gas started flooding in," Quiller said, giving Brightwater a final worried glower as he slipped past Jade. "They probably found him sitting in the pilot's seat when they got in," he added over his shoulder as he headed forward toward the cockpit.

LaRone nodded. He should have guessed it would be something like that. Quiller would have been just leaving the cockpit when the attack started, which would have been Doss's cue that he was the one to beat the lock code out of.

Only Brightwater had made sure he would be the one actually *in* the cockpit when their captors started looking around. "That true, Brightwater?" he asked.

"I was just looking for someplace soft to black out in," Brightwater protested. "You know how uncomfortable these decks are to fall on."

"Sure," LaRone said.

"Joking aside, that was a pretty stupid thing to do," Marcross said. "They could have crippled you."

"Hey, I fly speeder bikes for a living," Brightwater said, wincing as he tried to shrug. "Sitting-down work. I'm not the one who always has to be running around everywhere."

"Or they could have killed you," Grave said bluntly.

Brightwater tried the shrug again. "Better me than Quiller."

Marcross shook his head and turned to face Jade. "You going to ask, LaRone? Or should I?"

LaRone braced himself. "I will," he said. "I think 'all in good time' has arrived, Jade."

"So it has," Jade said. "Bottom line: I'm on a job that requires me to infiltrate a heavily guarded governor's residence. The governor in question has brought in a lot of his sector's stormtroopers to guard him. It occurred to me that a few unknown stormtroopers mixed in among a lot more unknown stormtroopers might be able to do some efficient recon and infiltration."

The room had suddenly gone quiet. Even Brightwater's labored breathing seemed subdued. "You're asking us to work for you," LaRone said.

Jade's eyebrows went up fractionally. "Did I say anything about *asking*?"

The room went even quieter. LaRone could feel the others' eyes on him as he gazed into Jade's unreadable expression. "Just because they don't know us doesn't mean we can pass without being challenged or identified," he said. "And if we're caught, we're dead."

"Not to worry," Jade assured him. "I have all the authority I need to get you out of any trouble you land in."

"Only if you're there at the right place and time," Marcross said. "It doesn't sound like we're going to be running in the same circles you are."

"What's this governor supposed to have done?" Grave asked. "If it's not a big secret."

"We think he's trying to make a deal with the Rebellion," Jade said.

"Really," LaRone said, his mind flicking back to Governor Choard on Shelkonwa. "Is this your specialty now? Dealing with seditious governors?"

"My specialty is doing things quietly," Jade told him. "Any other concerns?"

Grave cleared his throat. "If this is a Rebel Alliance thing," he asked, "are we likely to find Lord Vader coming into play somewhere down the road?"

"I got Lord Vader off your backs once," Jade reminded him. "I can do it again if I have to."

Beneath LaRone's feet, the deck lurched slightly as Quiller got the Suwantek into the air. "Meanwhile, we need to get Brightwater into bacta as soon as possible," Jade went on as she stepped back into the doorway. "Does Quiller know about the hyperdrive kick setting?"

"I don't know," LaRone said. "What's a kick setting?"

"It's something ISB ships are sometimes equipped with," Jade said. "Engaging it jumps your hyperdrive speed about twenty percent."

"No, I don't think he knows about that," LaRone said, feeling his eyebrows rising on his forehead. After all these months, there were still secrets to this ship that he and the others hadn't found? "That could have been very handy on occasion."

"Often it's not, since it eats up fuel forty percent faster," Jade said. "In this case, I think the Empire can afford the extra expense." Her eyes shifted to Brightwater. "Take care of him. We're likely to need a good speeder scout on this mission." She stepped into the corridor and headed toward the cockpit.

Grave let out a quiet sigh. "Terrific," he muttered. "Doesn't this just cap off an already lovely day?"

LaRone grimaced. "It could be worse."

"Really?" Grave countered. "May I point out that Jade's wonderful secret credentials only get us out of trouble if the governor and his stormtroopers *haven't* gone over to the Rebels. If they have, she's got nothing."

"Except a lightsaber," Marcross reminded him.

"That's great for her," Grave said. "Not so great for us. *And* then there's Vader."

"Whom Jade can deal with," LaRone said.

"Who drags along the entire Five-oh-First everywhere he goes," Grave retorted. "You want to try explaining to one of *them* our current lack of operational IDs?"

"You want to tell Jade thanks, but we're turning down the job?" LaRone said sourly.

"LaRone?" Brightwater said weakly.

LaRone looked down in surprise. He'd assumed Brightwater was already fast asleep. "Yes?" he said.

"We're going out anyway," the injured man said. "We know that." He took a careful breath. "Let's go out with a bang."

"I agree," Marcross said quietly. "If we can keep a Rebel governor from dragging his whole sector into chaos, we'll have done more for order and justice than ten years of these little operations could accomplish."

"Besides which," Grave added, "it didn't sound like Jade was giving us a choice."

LaRone grimaced. But they were right. "I know," he said. "Okay. If this is going to be the Hand of Judgment's final mission, let's make it one for the legends."

"If there's anyone left to remember," Grave murmured.

"There will be." LaRone looked down at Brightwater again. "In the meantime, it's three hours to Elegasso. Let's get Brightwater to the medical bay and see what we can do for him until then."

CHAPTER SIX

ACCORDING TO THE INFORMATION HAN HAD BEEN ABLE TO DIG UP, Whitestone City, the capital of Poln Major and Candoras sector, was a vibrant, cosmopolitan sprawl with a dynamic business and light manufacturing community, exciting nightlife, and a robust citizenry of humans and dozens of alien species.

Maybe the rest of the city was like that. But as far as he could tell, the spaceport district looked more like Mos Eisley than any genteel "cosmopolitan sprawl."

Han had some decidedly mixed feelings about Mos Eisley. He'd been robbed more than once there, and even beaten up a couple of times. It was also one of Jabba the Hutt's main terminals for contraband, which meant there were always plenty of unpleasant and dangerous people wandering around. He'd had to shoot his share of troublemakers there, Greedo being only the latest of that crowd.

Mos Eisley was also where he'd fallen in with Luke and the late crazy Jedi Kenobi, which was how he'd met Leia and gotten tied in with the whole Rebel Alliance. Some days that fell on the good side of the ledger. Some days it didn't.

This was rapidly turning out to be one of the days when it didn't.

"I'll tell you one last time," Axlon said, leaning hard on the word *last*. "I don't need you out there holding my hand. I can navigate the city perfectly well on my own."

"Yeah, you're going to do great out here," Han said, eyeing the scruffy, furtive, and otherwise low-grade humans and aliens filling the streets outside their docking bay. "You going to walk all the way to the governor's palace, or what?"

"There's an airspeeder rental stand less than a kilometer away," Axlon said patiently.

"Fine," Han said. "We'll walk you over there. That's what you diplomatic people are big on, right? Compromise?"

"Solo—"

"And on the way," Han said, "we can stop by Luke's docking bay and bring him along."

Axlon drew back a little. "What are you talking about?" he asked cautiously.

Han sighed. Just because he and Chewie were smugglers, did people like Axlon *always* have to assume they were stupid? "We saw his Z-95 on the way in," he told Axlon as patiently as he could. "Not sure where he put down, but from the vector he was on I'd say he was somewhere between bays fifty-two and fifty-eight."

Axlon sighed. "It's fifty-six," he said reluctantly. "Blast it, Solo. You weren't supposed to know he was along."

"Yeah, I already figured out that part," Han growled. And he'd already decided he was going to have a *very* long talk with General Rieekan when they got back. "You want to stand here all day? Or do you want to go get him?"

Every spaceport Han had ever visited had its own unique set of sounds and smells, and Whitestone's was no exception. Unlike some places, though, a lot of the sounds seemed to be oddly residential, including the cries and noises of playing children, and most of the aromas seemed to be coming from cooking.

The reason for that was quickly evident. At their side of the port, at least, only about half the landing bays were actually in service. The rest had been taken over by locals and turned into slum quarters.

Or refugee camps. Two of the bays they passed seemed to have become home to beings of species that Han had never seen before. Various styles of booths had been set up around the entrances to each of those bays, and were being run by aliens offering everything from exotic foods to jewelry to brightly colored cloth and clothing.

And this was on Poln Major, Han thought glumly as he and the others maneuvered their way through the crowds. He could hardly wait to see what things were like on Poln Minor, the less reputable half of the double planet.

Luke was waiting outside his docking bay, looking around at the masses with the same expression Han had seen on the kid inside the Mos Eisley cantina. He spotted them as they came around the corner—or more likely he spotted Chewie towering over the crowd—and Han saw his expression change. Not much, but enough to know that the kid was surprised to see the two of them with Axlon.

Which meant it wasn't just Rieekan and Axlon who were playing this stupid game. Luke was in on it, too.

"Hey, Han," Luke greeted him hesitantly as the three of them came up to him. "Hey, Chewie. I thought—" He looked uncertainly at Axlon. "That you . . ."

"No, he wasn't supposed to know," Axlon said pointedly. "*You* were supposed to keep him from spotting you."

Luke winced. "Sorry."

"So we'll just have to make do," Axlon went on. He nodded to the bay entrance. "Any trouble?"

Luke shook his head. "Like you said, there are a lot of Z-95s around, and the special-pass ID you gave me worked just fine." He looked at Han. "You had one, too, right?"

"No, we were challenged and shot down an hour ago," Han growled. "So where's this airspeeder rental place?"

Axlon looked around them. "It should be right over—" He broke off, his eyes widening at something behind Han. "Watch out!" he snapped.

Han spun around, his hand dropping to the grip of his blaster. Walking toward them were three aliens, their eyes small and white-rimmed beneath heavy brow ridges, their skin a mix of dark green scales and similarly colored patches of fur. They were wearing cheap-looking sack clothing, mismatched, probably bought from one of the booths in the area.

And each of them was holding a long, exquisitely detailed, hook-tipped knife.

Behind him, Han heard the *snap-hiss* as Luke ignited his lightsaber. "Han?" Luke muttered tensely.

"Easy, kid," Han said, leaving his blaster right where it was in its holster. "Just relax."

The aliens weren't holding the knives in stabbing or throwing positions. The weapons were simply resting across their palms.

They weren't a gang looking for an easy score. They were a group of merchants hoping to sell their wares. And judging by their suddenly widened eyes, they were just as startled by Luke and his lightsaber as Axlon had been by them and their knives.

"Your pardon, noble friendlies," the lead alien said in heavily accented Basic as he and the other two came to an abrupt halt. "Such finely clothed and equipmented—" He stumbled over the word. "And equipped beings as yourselves must surely have a high interest in uniquely hand-forged carving tools."

"Not today," Han told him, eyeing the knife in the alien's outstretched hand. It was a pretty nifty-looking weapon, he had to admit. In close quarters, if you knew what you were doing, it would probably do as well as a blaster. Close quarters like, say, a crowded cantina with one of Jabba's trigger-happy bounty hunters sitting across the table.

But handy though the knife might be, Han knew better than to buy one. At least not here and now. The instant the other merchants and vendors in the area spotted credits changing hands, they would be on him like carrion flies, shoving cloth and furs and melons and everything else in his face, blathering their sales pitches in his ears as they tried to get him to buy something from them, too. Not exactly the way to start a supposedly low-key mission.

And speaking of low-key . . . "Luke, shut that thing off, will you?" he growled.

There was a sizzling hiss, and the lightsaber hum cut off. "Sorry," Luke said. "I thought—"

"Yeah, yeah, I know." The three aliens were still standing there, their hands outstretched hopefully. With one last look at the knives, Han turned away. "So once we get the airspeeder, where are we going?" he asked, putting one hand on Luke's shoulder and the other on Axlon's and pushing both of them in the direction of the airspeeder rental sign he could now see hovering over the street a couple of blocks away.

"Luke and I have a rendezvous with our new friend," Axlon said. "What you and Chewbacca do is entirely up to you."

"Great," Han said. "We'll come with you."

"Except that," Axlon said firmly.

"I don't know, Governor," Luke spoke up hesitantly. "As long as they know anyway—"

"We don't need them," Axlon cut him off. "They were only to provide transport. More than that, we don't *want* them."

Luke threw a furtive look at Han. "But—"

"It's okay," Han told him, feeling a twinge of guilt at his earlier unkind thoughts. Luke might have been dragged into this thing, but he wouldn't have been the one who decided to lock Han out of it. "I know when I'm not wanted. Just watch yourselves."

"We will," Axlon promised. "Come on, Skywalker." Tapping Luke's arm, he headed off through the milling crowd. Luke gave Han and Chewie one final look, then turned and followed.

Beside Han, Chewie rumbled a suggestion. "Forget it," Han growled. "You don't exactly blend into a crowd, you know. He'd spot us before we got within three blocks of wherever this meeting is."

He looked up. Beyond the wispy clouds, Poln Minor was a small, pale half circle floating against the blue sky. "So let him go play deal maker," he went on. "You and me are going to go see what kind of stuff our supposed new best friend has to offer."

He turned and headed back toward their docking bay, waving away the knife merchants as they started hopefully toward him again. "Or," he added, "whether this whole thing is nothing but a trap."

The Poln system was reportedly one of the closest inhabited double planetary systems in the Empire, with the two worlds separated by only fifty thousand kilometers. There were a fair number of ships traveling between them, though from the size of the corridors that had been zoned Han guessed that the traffic had once been more than twice what it was at the moment.

Still, Axlon had at least been right about the Poln system being able to handle Rebel traffic along with its own.

Axlon had been pretty closemouthed during the trip from the Rebel base, refusing to give Han so much as a hint as to what Governor Ferrouz might have already discussed with him or Mon Mothma. But Axlon liked his sleep as much as anyone, and the encryption he'd put on his datapad had turned out to be one of the ones Han had been given for use with his own Alliance reports. According to the notes tucked away on one of Axlon's data cards, the mines Ferrouz was offering were in Poln Minor's Seventh Octant. The safest and easiest access to that region was a series of tunnels leading out from the Yellowstrike Spaceport, the octant's largest landing site.

Which, to Han's way of thinking, automatically put Yellowstrike at the bottom of the list. The safe and easy routes, he'd learned a long time ago, were traveled mostly by the lazy, the unimaginative, and people who wore badges and carried stacks of wanted posts on their datapads.

Instead, he turned the *Falcon* toward one of the octant's smaller and less conspicuous ports.

Like everything else on Poln Minor, Quartzedge Port was built mostly underground. Its organization was also decidedly on the casual side, to the point where Han was simply instructed by the control center to choose any of the unoccupied landing bays he wanted. Picking one of the eight open pits at random, he maneuvered the *Falcon* into it. By the time he'd finished powering the engines down to standby, the dome had closed above him and the bay had been brought up from Poln Minor's marginal surface air pressure to the more comfortable standard level. Lowering the ramp, he headed outside with Chewie.

The bay, he'd noted on the way down, had a single exit door, probably leading into an air lock for the times when someone needed to get in while the dome was open. Lounging by the door were three men, all armed, all with the look of Mos Eisley troublemakers about them. Making sure his blaster was riding loose in its holster, Han headed over.

"Afternoon," one of them called genially, his greasy-looking hair and impressively scraggly mustache glinting in the light. His eyes flicked to Chewie, then back to Han. "Need your name and cargo."

"Name's Darth Vader," Han told him. "Got a flat-load of broken Imperial promises."

None of the three men so much as smiled. "Cute," Mustache grunted. "You want to try again?"

"Actually, my cargo bay's empty," Han told him. "We're here to try our luck at a little prospecting."

Given that every mine in this part of Poln Minor had been drained dry decades ago, that one should have gotten at least a cynical smile from them. But again, none of their expressions even cracked. "Yeah?" Mustache asked, his voice as expressionless as his face. "Heading anywhere in particular?"

Han shrugged. The most heavily marked part of Axlon's encrypted map had been something called the Anyat-en mining complex. "I thought we'd try the old Anyat-en area," he said, trying to watch all three of them at once.

And *that* one finally got him a reaction. It was small, just a twitch of cheek muscles from one of Mustache's buddies, a balding, unshaven man with dark eyes. But it was definitely there.

These weren't just random fringe cutthroats or smugglers. And they'd definitely heard of Anyat-en.

Mustache played it cool. "Anyat-en, huh?" he asked casually. "Yeah, I think I've heard of it. What's there that's still worth digging up?"

"Don't know yet," Han said, playing it just as cool. "But the place used to be all platinum, and platinum prices are up. I had some time on my hands, and figured it'd be worth a look."

"Could be," Mustache agreed. "Tell you what. Just because I like your face, we're going to let you go without paying the usual docking fee. But if you find anything, we'll take half on your way out. Fair enough?"

Han shrugged. "Make it a tenth and you've got a deal."

Baldy made a contemptuous sound in the back of his throat, but Mustache merely smiled. "We got three blasters. You've got one. Make it half."

"One blaster, plus one Wookiee," Han reminded him. "A tenth."

Mustache eyed Chewie. "A quarter."

"Fine," Han said. It was, he knew, a little ridiculous to be bargaining over profits he was never going to make. But there was still a chance Mustache and his pals thought he and Chewie were just innocent treasure hunters, and it would be out of character for him not to bargain.

"Good," Mustache said briskly. "Best of luck to you. There's a row of landspeeders just past the air lock—help yourself. Fact, we'll make it even easier. I think there are some shovels and pickaxes in one of the lockers across from them. Probably a little rusty, but they ought to do, 'specially seeing as you don't have any of your own."

"That's because we were just going to scope out the place this time around," Han improvised. "But as long as you're offering, sure, why not?"

"You're welcome," Mustache said drily. "You need a map?"

"No, thanks," Han said. "It's supposed to be about a hundred fifty kilometers straight down Corridor CC Four-Oh-Eight-Seven, right?"

"If you say so," Mustache said. "Have fun."

"And come back rich," Baldy added as Han and Chewie walked past them through the door.

The landspeeders and tools were right where Mustache had said. The shovels were indeed rusty and half broken, and the landspeeders weren't in much better shape. Han gave each of the vehicles a test rev, picked the one that sounded least like it was going to fall apart in the next two hours, and they headed out.

The tunnel Han had headed down was probably typical of the abandoned mine system. Most of the overhead glow panels were gone, though the emergency permlights set into the upper and lower walls every hundred meters or so were still running. Fortunately, the landspeeder had good headlights, which let Han avoid the various heaps of stone chips that littered the tunnel floor, residue from years of small rockfalls from the ceiling and walls. The air smelled thin and stale, and aside from the labored hum of their own landspeeder the whole place was eerily quiet.

Chewie rumbled a question into the hum. "Of course we're not going straight there," Han confirmed. "You saw how Mustache and his buddies reacted when I told them where we were going. They either know something, or think they do."

Chewie growled again.

"Sure, but just because someone knows we're coming doesn't mean they know where we're coming *from*," Han reminded him as he pulled out his datapad and the copy he'd made of Axlon's maps. "Here—see if you can find a back way into the caverns. Maybe we can at least surprise them a little."

The cantina where Axlon and Governor Ferrouz had arranged to meet was large, elaborately decorated, and—from what Luke could see of the menu—very expensive.

But they didn't have enough time to properly enjoy either the décor or the aromas wafting through the main room. A hard-faced thug type with eyes that seemed to be trying to cut straight through to the back of Luke's skull intercepted them at the door and led them through the main dining area to a private room more subtly decorated than the rest of the restaurant.

Sitting alone at the head of a long table, a steaming platter of small, off-white spheres in front of him and three more hard-faced men standing against the wall behind him, was Governor Ferrouz.

He rose to his feet as Luke and Axlon were ushered into the room. "Governor Axlon," Ferrouz said gravely. "It's an honor to meet you in person."

"The honor is mine, Governor Ferrouz," Axlon assured him. "May I present my associate, Master Luke Skywalker."

"Master Skywalker," Ferrouz said, a frown creasing his face as he nodded in greeting. "I believe I've heard your name before."

"He was at Yavin," Axlon said. "One of those who helped avenge the destruction of Alderaan."

Ferrouz's cheek twitched. "Of course," he murmured. "Please; sit down. I took the liberty of ordering some stuffed sharru mushrooms for us."

"Thank you," Axlon said, walking to the table and taking the seat at Ferrouz's right. "Have you ever had stuffed sharrus, Luke?"

"No," Luke said, feeling distinctly uncomfortable as he sat down beside

Axlon, trying not to look at the three expressionless bodyguards behind Ferrouz. "We didn't have them where I grew up."

"Well, you'll like them," Axlon said placidly, selecting one of the small spheres and taking a careful bite from one side. "Ah—a seafood stuffing, is it?"

"Yes," Ferrouz said. "Local shell-crayke from Burnish Bay. Shall we get to business?"

"By all means," Axlon said. He popped the remainder of the mushroom into his mouth and selected another one. "What I'd like first is a confirmation of the exact location you have in mind for our use, including which spaceports and other facilities will be available. I also wish to know what equipment and support you intend to supply, and who will be acting as liaison between us."

Ferrouz frowned, shooting a glance at Luke. "If you'll forgive me, Master Axlon, we could have done all that via comlink."

"I said that was for a start," Axlon reminded him. "At any rate, face-to-face meetings are always so much more rewarding. Wouldn't you agree, Luke?"

Luke suppressed a grimace. Here he was, doing his level best to vanish into the background, and meanwhile Axlon seemed to be doing *his* level best to drag him into the forefront of everyone's attention.

Could that be the real reason Axlon had brought him along? Did he simply want Luke to draw the attention of Ferrouz and his bodyguards away from Axlon so that—

With an effort, Luke forced himself to relax. So that Axlon could do what? Nothing, that was what. There was literally nothing the man could do with four pairs of suspicious eyes watching his every move.

No, Luke was surely here for the reason Axlon had first approached him: to see what his Jedi senses could get from Ferrouz. Taking a careful breath, listening with half an ear as the two men began throwing around names and numbers, he stretched out with the Force.

And felt his chest tighten. Normally, he could barely sense the emotions moving along beneath the surface of the people he was with. But Ferrouz wasn't like Leia or Han. His whole sense was practically screaming with emotion. All sorts of emotions: fear and anger, hopelessness and defiance, sadness and determination.

And betrayal. Especially betrayal.

But whose betrayal? Axlon's? Ferrouz's? Someone else's? Luke stretched out harder, focusing on the Force, trying to sift through the turbulence—

"Luke."

The sound of his name abruptly snapped him out of his concentration. He opened his mouth to acknowledge—

"—may want to come along as well," Axlon continued, and Luke realized that he was addressing Ferrouz, not talking to Luke himself. "I trust that will be acceptable?"

"If he wishes to accompany you," Ferrouz said, looking at Luke. Luke held the other's gaze, trying to reach out again with the Force.

But the moment had passed. The turbulence was still there, but Luke was too weak and inexperienced to get the connection back.

"Excellent," Axlon said. "At the palace, then, whenever we're able to get our team here to assess the Anyat-en facilities. Say, a week or so?"

"Whenever you're ready," Ferrouz said. "You have the pass I gave you?"

"Right here," Axlon said, tapping his tunic. "Thank you for your time, Governor." He lifted a finger. "One more thing," he went on. "I'd appreciate it if you could make sure all your people are out of the Anyat-en area, including the Yellowstrike and Quartzedge spaceports."

"That's already been done," Ferrouz said. "I had my people out of the area two days ago."

"Including customs officials?" Axlon asked.

"Including everyone," Ferrouz said tartly. "I just said that."

"So you did," Axlon said, ducking his head in apology. Tapping Luke on the arm, he stood up. "Thank you again, Governor. I'll be in touch."

They were outside the cantina, wending their way through the crowds toward their rented airspeeder, before Axlon spoke again. "What do you think?"

"About what?" Luke asked.

"The deal, of course," Axlon said, throwing an odd look at him. "The Anyat-en complex for our base and storage. The Saras-ev enclosed landing area for transport, loading, and unloading. All the rest of it. Weren't you paying attention?"

Luke shook his head. "I was trying to read Governor Ferrouz."

"Trying to *read* him?"

"Through the Force," Luke said, frowning. "Isn't that what you brought me along for?"

"Well, yes," Axlon said, stumbling a little on the words. "Yes, of course. I just didn't think you could . . . never mind. What did you find out?"

"Not much," Luke had to admit. "There's a lot of turmoil in him."

Axlon grunted. "Not surprising, under the circumstances."

"There was one thing, though, that I got very clearly," Luke continued. "It was a sense of betrayal."

Axlon stopped short. "Betrayal?"

"Yes," Luke said. He stopped, too, and turned to face the other.

And felt his muscles stiffen. The look on Axlon's face . . . "But it may not mean he's going to betray us," he hastened to add. "It could be he's feeling betrayed by the Empire. Or he's worried that some of his people might betray him."

"Yes," Axlon said, some of the sudden dark tension fading from his face. "Yes, that could certainly be it. The Imperial Security Bureau might very well have planted an agent or two within the palace to watch him. We'll need to be careful when we go there." Glancing around, as if suddenly concerned about eavesdroppers, he started walking again.

"What was that about, there at the end?" Luke asked, falling into step again beside him. "We're going to the palace?"

"*I* am," Axlon said. "Whether you go with me is up to you. Weren't you listening to *any* of it?"

"No, I already told you," Luke said. "I was—"

"You were using the Force," Axlon finished for him, an edge of exasperation in his voice. "Sometimes I wonder how the Jedi lasted as long as they did. Or how the *Republic* lasted with Jedi running the show."

Luke felt his face flush. How dare Axlon talk about the Jedi that way?

He took a deep breath, stretching out to the Force for calm the way Ben Kenobi had taught him. *There is no emotion; there is peace.* Anger was as much a trap as fear, Ben had warned.

Besides, Axlon was speaking out of ignorance, not animosity. It was up to Luke to show him what Jedi were, what they could be, and what they could do.

Once Luke figured all of that out himself, of course. If he ever did.

He sighed. In the all-too-short time he and Ben had had together, the old Jedi had taught him a great deal about the Force. But there was so much more he still had to learn.

Vader had taken Ben away from him, just as Vader's stormtroopers had taken his uncle and aunt. Like Alderaan, more scores that would someday need to be settled.

"Let's get back to the ship," Axlon said into his musings. "See if Solo's calmed down yet." He paused. "By the way. Do you think Ferrouz was telling the truth about having pulled all his people out of the Anyat-en area?"

Luke frowned. "I don't know," he said. "I'm not—I can't read thoughts that way. That's not how it works. Why do you ask?"

"No reason," Axlon murmured. "No reason at all."

CHAPTER SEVEN

CAPTAIN DRUSAN LOOKED UP FROM THE DATAPAD. "AN ARKANIAN," HE said flatly.

"I believe so, yes," Pellaeon said, trying to read the other's expression. But the mottled hyperspace sky flowing across the bridge viewport at the captain's back was throwing just enough shadow over his face to make that impossible. "His height and mass are well within the species range. The mask would cover the distinctive white eyes, and it would be child's play for an Arkanian to gather all those biomarkers—"

"Why Arkanian?" Drusan interrupted. "Why not someone from any of a dozen other species?"

"Because he quoted me a line from something called the *Song of Salaban*," Pellaeon said. "It's an ancient Arkanian legend about a man whose family and village were captured by an enemy force, who then force him to go on a quest of sacrifice to win their release."

"So Lord Odo studies ancient legends," Drusan said with a shrug. "Grand Admiral Zaarin has a passion for music. Senior Captain Thrawn is insane over art. I knew a colonel once who collected different versions of sabacc cards. There are eccentrics all across the galaxy."

"Perhaps, sir," Pellaeon said. "But there's more. On the assumption that Odo was, in fact, Arkanian, I checked the ISB's at-large criminal registry for that species. It turns out that there are five major Arkanian criminals currently unaccounted for. All five are wanted for medical atrocities, and any one of them would have both the ability and the arrogance to fake an order with an eye toward getting aboard the *Chimaera*."

Drusan shot a look over Pellaeon's shoulder—possibly checking to see whether any of the bridge crew was close enough to overhear them, but more likely making sure Lord Odo was still at the computer console in the aft bridge where he'd been when Pellaeon arrived a few minutes ago. "Are you suggesting that we have a monster aboard?"

"That is indeed my fear, sir," Pellaeon said. "Under the circumstances, I respectfully recommend that you exercise your rights under the Captain's Authority directives and find out exactly who and what Odo is. At the very least, we should take another look at his authorization to be aboard this ship."

Again, Drusan looked over Pellaeon's shoulder. "Very well, Commander," he said, lowering his voice. "I wasn't supposed to share this with you or anyone else aboard the *Chimaera*. But under the circumstances . . . Lord Odo's orders didn't come from Imperial Center."

Pellaeon nodded. "Yes, sir, I know."

Drusan seemed taken aback. "You *know*?"

"I backtracked the routing," Pellaeon explained, wondering uneasily if he shouldn't have said that. "I thought it prudent, given the unusual circumstances."

"I see," Drusan murmured. "And where exactly did that backtrack take you?"

"The order came from somewhere in the Outer Rim," Pellaeon said. "I wasn't able to locate it any more precisely." He hesitated. "My original thought was that perhaps Odo had been sent by Grand Admiral Zaarin, since he's reported to be somewhere in that general region. But I'm wondering now if Odo simply used an Outer Rim origination to make it *look* like the orders came from Zaarin."

Drusan hissed out a breath, and some of the stiffness seemed to leave his spine. "I'm impressed, Commander," he said. "I truly am. Not many officers, even senior officers, would have taken it upon themselves to follow this course in the first place. Even fewer would have stayed with it long enough to reach a conclusion."

He paused, and this time, despite the flowing hyperspace sky, Pellaeon could see the tight smile on the other's face. "Even more impressive, most of your conclusions were accurate," Drusan continued. "Lord Odo *is* Arkanian; and his orders *did* come from the *Predominant.*"

"Are you certain of that, sir?" Pellaeon asked carefully. He was treading on dangerous ground, he knew, pressing the same point over and over to a superior officer. "Orders *have* been faked before. Codes and encryptions *have* been stolen."

"True enough," Drusan agreed. "But the one communication no one can fake is a personal transmission from the Emperor himself."

Pellaeon felt his eyes widen. "The *Emperor?*"

Drusan chuckled. "Yes, that was my reaction, too," he said. "It seems that the Emperor has joined Zaarin in his quiet tour of the Outer Rim."

"And he contacted you? Directly?"

"*Very* directly," Drusan said, his smile turning into a grimace. Pellaeon winced in sympathy—conversations between the Emperor and his subordinates tended to be not very pleasant. "No, Commander," the captain continued quietly. "Whatever mysteries still hover around Lord Odo, rest assured that he and his mission have been sanctioned at the absolute highest level."

"Yes, sir," Pellaeon said, feeling a flush of embarrassment. He should have known that Drusan would have made sure Odo didn't pose any danger to the *Chimaera.* Especially since a threat to Drusan's ship would also be a threat to his career. "May I ask what his mission is?"

Drusan snorted. "Really, Commander. One confidential security breach isn't enough for you? You want me to commit a second, as well?"

Pellaeon winced again. "My apologies, sir."

"That's all right," Drusan said drily. "How can I complain about your persistence when I've just finished praising you for it?" He pursed his lips. "I'll tell you this much. Lord Odo has evidence of an agreement in progress between the Rebel Alliance and an alien warlord named Nuso Esva from the Unknown Regions. There's also a strong possibility that the agreement is being brokered by the Candoras sector's Governor Ferrouz himself. The Emperor has asked Lord Odo to look into it, and assigned the *Chimaera* to provide him transport and any support he may need."

"I see," Pellaeon said, feeling his stomach tighten. An Imperial governor, dabbling in treason? That was unheard of. "And he chose an Arkanian because Rebel spies wouldn't be as quick to track the movements of an outsider as they would someone from the fleet or Imperial court?"

"Yes," Drusan said, eyeing him closely. "Yes, exactly. Once again, Commander, your insights do you proud. None of this is to be repeated, of course. To anyone."

"Understood, sir," Pellaeon said. "Again, my apologies for pressing a matter that was none of my business."

"The safety of this ship, the fleet, and the Empire is the business of all Imperial officers," Drusan countered solemnly. "So are persistence and initiative. Well done, Commander. The fleet needs more officers like you."

"Thank you, sir."

Drusan gave a curt nod. "Dismissed."

Lord Odo was no longer at the computer console when Pellaeon retraced his path down the command walkway to the aft bridge. He signaled for the turbolift, wondering where the other had gotten to.

It was as Pellaeon was stepping into the turbolift car that an odd question suddenly struck him.

Arkanians had a reputation for arrogance, along with an attitude of racial superiority that even the Hutts would be hard-pressed to match. Most Arkanians that Pellaeon had met firmly believed that they could do anything any other species could do, and that they could do it better.

So why would one of them lower himself so far as to employ a human pilot to fly his ship for him?

For a brief moment, Pellaeon was tempted to go back to Drusan and ask. But then the door slid shut, and the car started toward Pellaeon's quarters and the soft bed he'd spent far too few hours in lately. And he'd pushed security protocol enough for one day.

Besides, there were still four days to the Poln system. There would be plenty of time for him to find an opportunity to put that question to the captain.

"You really should stop that," Thrawn commented from his seat at the computer console.

Car'das frowned. "Stop what?"

"You should stop pacing," Thrawn said. "It doesn't gain you anything."

Car'das grimaced. Lost in thought, he hadn't been aware that he *was* pacing. "It helps me think," he said. "I always pace when I'm trying to solve a problem."

"You never did before."

"Well, I do now," Car'das growled. "Is it a problem for you?"

"Not at all," Thrawn said, his glowing red eyes seeming to burn into Car'das's pale face. "Is this problem something I can help with?"

"No," Car'das told him shortly. He turned his back and started pacing again.

And abruptly stopped. With four days to Poln Major and whatever unknowns were waiting for them there, it was time he finally brought this into the open. "Yes, actually, there is," he said, turning around again. "You can tell me why we're here."

Thrawn tilted his head slightly. "Why *we're* here?" he asked.

"Fine," Car'das ground out. "Why *I'm* here. It makes no sense. I don't have access to information you might want, I'm rotten company, and you're at least as good a pilot as I am. Why didn't you just leave me where I was?"

Thrawn's blue-black eyebrows rose. "You mean on the run?" he asked pointedly.

Car'das took a careful breath, his lungs and chest aching with the expansion. "I'm dying, Thrawn," he said quietly. "I know I don't look it right now, but I am. I'm living on stims and patchworks, and that's not going to last much longer." He gestured vaguely toward the vast universe lying beyond the ship. "There's only one place in the galaxy where I was told I might be able to find a cure. Maybe I will. Maybe I won't. Maybe all I'll find is some answers. You blame me for trying to get there?"

"Of course not," Thrawn said. "What questions are you looking for answers to?"

Car'das sighed. "I don't even know that."

For a moment silence returned to the room. "Yet when I called, you came," Thrawn said. "If you were so eager to leave, why didn't you tell me all this before?"

"I don't know that, either," Car'das admitted. "Maybe I figured I owed you." He shook his head. "Maybe because this is my last chance to do something useful for the rest of the galaxy."

"You've done any number of useful things," Thrawn reminded him. "Including the saving of my life."

"Ancient history," Car'das said, his stomach tightening with shame and guilt. "For years I've done absolutely nothing except build up my smuggling organization. Not to help anyone, the way I used to send information to Imperial Center to help the government root out criminals and traitors. It was all just for my own aggrandizement and power." He shook his head. "I've wasted my life, Thrawn. These last years . . . I've wasted them all."

"Perhaps," Thrawn said, his voice quiet. "Yet the need to create is a drive that lies deep within each of us. We all strive to build empires, whether of stone or people or words. Empires we hope will survive us. In the end, though, each of us must necessarily leave our creations behind. All we can hope for is to also leave behind a worthy successor to continue our work. Or who can at least maintain it for a season."

"Perhaps," Car'das said. Thrawn was right, of course. He usually was. And Car'das had indeed left behind such a worthy successor, a trusted lieutenant named Talon Karrde.

The crucial question was whether Karrde would survive the seeds of chaos Car'das had also left behind.

But it was too late to worry about that now. The future of his organization was already in motion, and even if Car'das went back right now there would be no way for him to restore order.

But then, the future was always changing. All futures were.

"I notice, though, that you haven't answered my question," Car'das said. "*You're* here to protect the Empire from Warlord Nuso Esva. But why am *I* here?"

"Because my forces are busy in the Unknown Regions, tied down with the defense of my allies," Thrawn said. "Because I'm alone, and it's always useful to have an extra set of eyes or hands."

"But why me?" Car'das persisted. "You have the Emperor's ear. Why not a Royal Guard, or some brilliant junior fleet officer?" He snorted. "Why not Vader himself? If you could stand his company."

Thrawn smiled . . . and to Car'das's amazement, there was sadness in the other's normally calm expression. "Because," he said quietly, "you're the only one I trust."

Car'das stared at him, some of his own self-pity fading away into a fresh pool of shame. Thrawn had left everything: his home, his people, his prestige, his life. He'd dedicated himself to protecting the civilized parts of the galaxy against pirates, warlords, and distant, nameless nightmares that Car'das could barely even imagine.

And yet, in the end, all that work and sacrifice had come down to this. The greatest military mind of the age, with only a single, solitary, worthless man whom he could trust. "I'm sorry," he said quietly.

"No apology needed," Thrawn assured him. "I'm the one who should apologize. With luck, this should be over in two or three weeks, and then you can continue your journey." He tilted his head. "Or we could return to the *Executor* and I could release you now."

Car'das made a face. "Thanks, but I have no intention of turning you over to Vader's tender mercies. Aside from everything else, he has a reputation for capriciousness even the Hutts can't match. What if he suddenly decides to renege on your deal?"

"He won't," Thrawn assured him. "Impulsive or not, Lord Vader has a strong personal agenda, plus as much enlightened self-interest as anyone. I have no doubt he'll play the role I've assigned him."

Car'das shivered. A fleet captain talking openly about Darth Vader playing an assigned role was normally how first officers got sudden promotions. All the more reason not to leave the two of them together any longer than absolutely necessary. "I'm sure he will," he said. "I'm hungry. You want anything?"

"No, thank you," Thrawn said, his voice distant, his attention already back on the computer monitor.

Mentally, Car'das shook his head as he levered himself out of his seat. Blunt conversations like this were probably why Thrawn didn't have anyone else in the Empire he could trust. The fleet, like the Imperial court, thrived on evasion, politics, and smiling masks. Anything approaching openness was looked upon with suspicion.

Still, he had to admit as he headed down the corridor, maybe Thrawn's straightforward honesty wasn't such a bad thing. Certainly Car'das himself felt better than he had in weeks. Maybe even in months. He'd thought this trip was his last chance to do something fine and noble. Now he was sure of it.

He could only hope he would live long enough to see it through to the end.

The Seventh Octant's tunnel system was about as convoluted a noodle-bake as Han had ever seen. But Axlon's maps were good ones, and after a couple of hours of weaving back and forth, Han finally had them on course for the Anyat-en mining area again.

Only now, instead of coming in from the direction of the Quartzedge Port like a reasonable man might expect, he and Chewie were coming up on the complex from the direction of one of the other abandoned mining caverns. A direction no one would ever expect company to come from.

He hoped.

Five kilometers from the edge of the complex he shut down the land-speeder's headlights and slowed to a speed where they could navigate more or less safely by the faint illumination of the widely spaced permlights. A kilometer from the edge, he let the landspeeder coast to a stop.

For a minute they just sat quietly, letting their ears adjust to the absence of the repulsorlifts' hum. Then, in the distance, Han heard the faint mur-mur of voices.

A *lot* of voices.

He looked at Chewie. The Wookiee gave a low rumble of agreement.

"Right," Han said, drawing his blaster as he climbed out of the land-speeder. "Let's see what kind of trouble we're looking at."

According to Axlon's data, the Anyat-en complex consisted of eight ir-regularly shaped caverns that had been hollowed out of the rock as the veins and clumps of ore had been removed. Han and Chewie headed down the tunnel, passing a few small side caves along the way that had probably been designated as equipment or fuel storage. They walked care-fully, watching their footing, trying not to make too much noise on the rock chips that littered the ground.

They were within fifty meters of the nearest of the big caverns, and Han could see the flickering light of glow rods against the tunnel wall, when there was a sudden crunch of gravel directly behind them. "That's far enough," a quiet voice warned.

Han stopped, swallowing a curse. He'd checked the first few side caves as he and Chewie had passed, but since all of them had been empty he'd stopped bothering, instead focusing all his attention on the voices and lights ahead. Now that carelessness was going to cost him.

Or rather, it was going to cost the man behind them. From the sound of his voice, he was probably within Chewie's reach, and Han doubted anyone on Poln Minor had ever seen how fast a Wookiee could move. "Take it easy," he said soothingly, raising his blaster high above his head. If the guard was foolish enough to watch the weapon or, even better, stepped closer to take it from Han's hand . . .

"*Chewbacca?*" the guard asked. "That you?"

Blinking, Han turned to look behind him.

It wasn't a smuggler, or a pirate, or one of Governor Ferrouz's men. It was, in fact—

"Colonel Cracken?" Wedge Antilles called. "Colonel? Got a surprise for you."

The murmur of voices ahead abruptly stopped. A moment later the reflected light from all the glow rods grew brighter as a whole crowd headed toward the cavern entrance.

Grimacing, Han dropped his blaster into its holster. Wedge here; Colonel Airen Cracken here. The only thing that could possibly make it worse would be—

"Han!" Leia said, her voice and expression halfway between astonished and furious, in a way that only she could pull off. "What are *you* doing here?"

"Yes, I know we aren't supposed to move in until Axlon formally makes the deal," Leia said, keeping her voice low as she and Han walked into the cavern she and the others had just started examining. "And we haven't. We just thought it would be a good idea to have an advance team come in and look things over."

"Yeah," Han grunted. "Nice."

Leia took a deep breath, trying *very* hard not to be irritated. Han had been ordered to stay with Axlon on Poln Major. He shouldn't be here at all, let alone poking around and demanding explanations. Or acting like she and Cracken were doing anything wrong.

Especially since this unofficial sortie had been Axlon's idea in the first place. If their chief negotiator thought it was legitimate, Han of all people shouldn't be second-guessing him.

"At least now we know who those guys were at Quartzedge," Han said sourly. "They could have said something when we first came in."

Leia frowned. Quartzedge? Who had Cracken put at Quartzedge? She opened her mouth to ask—

"Hey!" someone called from across the cavern, his glow rod playing over a section of broken wall. "Colonel? Princess? You're going to want to see this."

Leia started across the chamber, wondering briefly if she should order Han to stay here.

But it was too late. With his longer stride, he was already ahead of her. Scowling, Leia hurried to catch up.

Han was nearly to the man with the glow rod—it was one of the techs, Leia saw now, a short, earnest type named Anselm—when Cracken caught up to Han, deftly slipped a shoulder in front of him, and got to the opening first.

Even in the faint light reflecting off the dark rock, Leia saw Cracken's eyes widen. "Well, well," he murmured. "What have we *here*?"

Han and Chewie were already at his side, peering in along the glow rod beam. Putting on a burst of fast-walk speed, Leia moved up beside them.

The hole, as she'd expected, opened into another dome-ceilinged cavern, its floor about a meter and a half higher than the one they were currently standing in. But unlike all the rest of the abandoned mines they'd explored, this one wasn't empty. It was, in fact, stocked with orderly rows of equipment.

And not just any equipment. *Military* equipment. She could see a rack of E-Web repeating blasters, another rack holding grenades plus a pair of Merr-Sonn grenade mortars, and, at the very edge of the light, what looked like a pair of outpost-style sensor beacons.

"Anselm?" Cracken prompted. "Analysis, please."

"Uh—" Anselm floundered, and Leia felt a flicker of sympathy for the man. He was mainly a ship tech who spent most of his time up to his elbows in partially disassembled starfighter engines. Cracken had brought him along to check on the suitability of their new caverns for ship repair bays, as well as to ride herd on the old, battered freighter Rieekan had picked to slip them into the Poln system.

Now, with a single stroke, Anselm's whole job description for this trip had abruptly been expanded. "Uh—" he tried again.

"I'll take a look," Han said, starting to step past Cracken.

"*I'll* take a look," Leia countered, grabbing his arm and yanking him to a halt. "For starters, you'll never get through that opening."

"No problem," Han said, drawing his blaster. "I'll just make it bigger."

"As you were, Solo," Cracken said coolly. "All right, Princess, you're on. Ten minutes, no more, and don't touch anything. Toksi, give her a boost."

Leia stepped to the hole and set her foot gingerly onto the cupped hands of one of Cracken's burliest men. Up close, she could see that the hole was smaller than it had looked from farther away, and was jagged-edged besides.

But there was no way she wasn't going to get through it. Not with Cracken and the rest of them watching. *Especially* not with Han watching. Wincing as the edges scraped across her jumpsuit and dug into the skin beneath, she eased her way up and through into the other chamber. Pulling out her glow rod, she switched it on.

The cavern wasn't very big, only about twenty meters across. But its limited floor space was astonishingly well stocked. Along with the equipment she'd already seen were more racks of weapons, Tibanna gas canisters, and enough gear to set up a small encampment or listening post.

There was another cavern opening off the far end, with the glint of metal showing faintly in the light of her glow rod. Giving the encampment gear a quick look as she passed, she headed across to the other cavern. This one was also loaded, having been turned into a fully equipped armorers' machine shop, complete with two portable fusion generators to run all the gear.

And in the next room . . .

She made it back to the broken wall five minutes after Cracken's ten-minute time limit was up, arriving to find one of the smaller Rebellion men—small, but not small enough—struggling mightily to slip through the opening to come look for her. She helped him back down, then followed him through.

"Well?" Cracken said, lowering his datapad as Toksi helped her to the floor.

"It's the sabacc pot," Leia told him. "We've got blasters, Tibanna gas, and an armorers' workshop. *And* beyond that, there's a whole cavern full of combat-modified T-47 airspeeders."

"You're kidding," Cracken said, his eyes widening. "How many?"

"Twelve," Leia said. "There's also a tunnel off one side wide enough to get them out, and one of the big conveyance tunnels down the way is big enough for one of our transports. And that's not the last of the caverns, either."

"You're right on that one," Cracken agreed, offering her his datapad. "Near as I can figure from these maps of Axlon's, that's the Lisath-re mining system through there."

Leia grimaced as she studied the tangled cavern layout. "Unfortunately, Lisath-re isn't part of our agreement with Ferrouz."

"Not yet," Cracken said. "But maybe we can change that. I want you to take one of the speeders back to Yellowstrike where you can get a clear comm signal and see if Axlon can throw an addendum onto the deal to get us those extra caverns."

Leia frowned. "You don't really think he'd give all this up, do you?"

"Depends on whether this stuff is actually his," he said. "Solo thinks it isn't, and I tend to agree with him."

Leia looked around. *That* was what she'd been missing, she realized suddenly, since her return from the other caverns: Han's loud voice and smirking face. "Where is he?"

"He and Chewbacca headed back to Quartzedge," Cracken told her, nodding back over his shoulder. "He said three men were hanging around the port on his way in. If they aren't Ferrouz's men, they may be sentries for whoever owns this equipment. Either way, we should probably have a good talk with them."

"Yes," Leia said mechanically, still looking around. Chewie had gone with him, of course. But that still left the odds three against two.

"Don't worry, I sent Erick and Flind with them," Cracken added. "They'll be okay."

"Of course they will," Leia said, feeling a small flush of embarrassment. Han was a big boy, and he could take care of himself. Not that she really cared that much one way or the other. "We need to find another way into those caverns," she said, taking Cracken's datapad from him. "Let's see what else our future benefactor may have left us."

They checked the *Falcon*'s landing bay, all the other bays they could get into, and the deserted customs office.

In the end, they found no one, and nothing.

"You sure you didn't just dream up these guys, Solo?" Flind asked as they headed back into the *Falcon*'s bay.

"Funny," Han said, scowling across the open space at his ship. She looked all right. Unfortunately, that didn't mean a whole lot. "I guess you two might as well start on the outside."

"Start what?" Flind asked suspiciously.

"Checking for trackers," Han said. "Me and Chewie'll take the inside."

"Solo—"

"Hang on and I'll get you a scanner," Han cut him off, keying the ramp.

"Forget it," Erick growled. "We've got work to do."

"Hey, no problem," Han said calmly. "I'll just give Cracken a call and tell him you don't want to be bothered sweeping Axlon's ambassadorial ship."

Erick snorted. "Ambassadorial *ship*?"

"You can't call him anyway," Flind said as Han headed up the ramp. "There's no baseline comm service between here and there, and the comlink relay isn't working."

"That's okay," Han said, opening the equipment locker beside the hatch and pulling out two EnhanceScan portable scanners. "I can call Rieekan instead. Or Mon Mothma. Here—catch."

He tossed the sensors down the ramp to the two glowering men. "Might as well start at the bow and stern," he told them as Chewie walked up the ramp and joined him. "Call me if you find anything—I'll want to see it before you take it off."

The two men looked at each other. Then, without a word, they stomped off in their assigned directions. "Here," Han said, pulling out the last EnhanceScan and handing it to Chewie. "Start with the engines. I'd better see if Axlon's missed us yet."

Sure enough, the comm was signaling no fewer than six waiting messages. All were from Axlon, with steadily increasing levels of irritation and anger. Han listened to all six, mostly for amusement, then keyed for Axlon's comlink.

"About time," the other growled after Han had identified himself. "Where have you *been*?"

"Working," Han said. "How about you?"

"We've got the preliminary agreement," Axlon said. "We'll be meeting again in a few days to hammer out any last-minute details. Skywalker says you left the spaceport?"

"I had some errands," Han said, eyeing the comm speaker thoughtfully. So Luke had had to tell Axlon that the *Falcon* was missing? Axlon hadn't spotted that himself? "Where's Luke now?"

"I don't know," Axlon said. "Back at his ship, I assume. I've taken a room at a hotel near the palace. No point in making a crosstown trip every time I want to talk to our friend."

"Makes sense," Han said. Especially when the Alliance was paying the bills. "You get one for Luke, too?"

"No," Axlon said, sounding puzzled. "I assumed he'd be making his own arrangements."

Han made a face. Or, more likely, now that Luke's cover was blown Axlon was expecting him to bunk aboard the *Falcon* with Han and Chewie. "You talked to Cracken yet?" he asked.

There was a short pause. "Cracken?" Axlon said cautiously.

"Colonel Airen Cracken," Han said, striving for patience. He was getting really tired of these games. "Him and Her Worshipfulness. You know: your former—"

"Yes, yes, I know who you mean," Axlon said stiffly. "The question is, why do *you* know?"

"Probably because I'm smarter than you think," Han told him. "Like

I was saying, you need to talk to Cracken. There's another cave system you'll want to put on the bargaining list."

"Another—oh," Axlon interrupted himself. "Fine. I'll talk to him as soon as I can. Anyway, I need to tell him he can bring in the official survey team. Where are you now?"

"Busy," Han said. "You need something, let me know. Otherwise, don't."

"Solo—"

With a flick of his finger, Han cut off the comm.

For a few minutes he stared out the cockpit canopy at the dull rock of the landing bay, listening to the indistinct voices of Flind and Erick wafting faintly up the boarding ramp and into the cockpit.

And tried to think. Because something about this whole thing didn't make sense.

He was still trying to figure it out when the comm beeped again. Scowling, he punched the activation key. If this was Axlon again . . . "Solo," he growled.

"It's Leia. Are you all right?"

"Sure," Han said. "Why?"

"Because you told us there were mysterious men hanging around the *Falcon*," she said, sounding a little miffed. "Remember?"

"Oh—right," Han said. "Well, they aren't now. They were gone by the time we got here."

"Really," Leia said. "That's strange."

"Yeah, I was thinking that, too," Han said. "If they were watching to see who's snooping around, why leave now? Especially since we said we were going to the Anyat-en mines, which was right next to that handy little weapons stash."

"Unless they didn't realize the cave wall had been broken through," Leia said, sounding doubtful.

"We were still going to that area," Han pointed out. "They should at least have waited for us to come back to see if we'd seen anything."

"They probably weren't expecting you back so soon," Leia pointed out. "Maybe they figured they had time to leave and come back later." She paused. "Or maybe they just wanted to get a look at your ship while you weren't there."

"Or maybe more than a look," Han said. "I've got Chewie and the other two looking for trackers."

"Good idea," Leia said. "Some of the techs might be better at that, though. You want me to send you a couple of them?"

"No, we can handle it," Han assured her. "Could also be that they were Ferrouz's people, and he pulled them off once he and Axlon had their deal."

"Not according to Axlon," Leia said. "I asked him that, and he told me Ferrouz said all his people were already out of the area."

"Unless he was lying," Han said sourly. "Speaking of Axlon, he said something about calling in a survey team. I thought you *were* the survey team."

"He means the real, official team waiting outside the system," Leia said. "Our job was just to take a quick look around. They're supposed to do a full examination and analysis of the caverns and figure out what we can do with them. Under the circumstances, though, we're going to need a slightly bigger party."

"To look over the stuff we found?"

"The stuff *we* found, yes," Leia corrected pointedly. "General Rieekan's putting together a full quartermaster's squad, along with a logistics support group to triage the equipment, plus a few transports for when we're ready to start taking stuff out."

"Hold it," Han said, frowning. "We're taking stuff out already? We don't even know who it belongs to yet."

"Hence, the triage," Leia said. "We'll want to grab the most vital equipment before whoever owns it notices."

"Yeah, well, that probably won't take too long," Han warned. "And if it's Ferrouz's stash, he's going be unhappy in a really loud way."

"Which is why Axlon will be broaching the subject of the Lisath-re mines with him as soon as he can," Leia said. "If there's no reaction, we can assume the equipment belongs to smugglers or pirates instead. I don't think there's any moral issue with stealing stolen property."

"I was thinking more about pirate gangs that pack almost as big a punch as the Imperials," Han growled. "I've run into some of them, and if that stuff is theirs, *they're* definitely going to have some issues."

"Don't worry, Rieekan will be sending a full escort with the team," Leia assured him. "A fighter wing at the very least. Possibly a couple of light cruisers along with them."

Han grimaced. "That should make Ferrouz happy."

"I'm sure he'll be delighted," Leia said. "Doesn't sound like you are, though."

"Not really, no," Han said. "But since when does that matter to anyone?"

There was a short pause. "It matters," Leia said, her voice carefully neutral. "Watch yourself, okay?"

"I always do, sweetheart," Han assured her. "You want me to stick around here for a while?"

"Thanks, but I think we can manage," Leia said, sounding suddenly frosty. Probably the sweetheart thing, Han guessed. "Go back to Poln Major. If something goes wrong, you're Axlon's only way out of there."

"Sure," Han said. "You need me, just call."

There was a click, and the comm cut off.

For a moment Han gazed down at the control board. Then, shaking his head, he keyed for a full diagnostic of the *Falcon*'s systems.

Mustache and his pals might have just have been scouting for easy targets. Or they may have wanted to keep tabs on where the *Falcon* went by installing a tracking device or two.

Or they may have decided they didn't want the *Falcon* going anywhere. Ever.

Chewie and Cracken's men were already looking for trackers. Han had better get busy and look for sabotage.

CHAPTER EIGHT

THERE HAD BEEN SOME SORT OF MELTDOWN WITH THE POLN MAJOR space traffic system, and the Suwantek had been stuck in a holding pattern for two hours waiting for a landing slot.

But everything had now been sorted out, and Quiller was finally bringing the freighter down toward the Whitestone City spaceport. "Any particular approach you'd like me to use?" he asked Jade as they came in low over the city. "There's enough slack in their lanes for me to wander a little to one side or the other if you want."

"Just hold to the center," she said, gazing out at the mosaic of buildings and streets below from LaRone's usual position in the copilot's seat. "We're too far from the palace to see anything useful, and there's no point in drawing attention to ourselves."

"Hold it," LaRone said, leaning over Jade's shoulder as something caught his eye. "Is that a stormtrooper station over there?"

"Where?"

"There," LaRone said. He pointed, his arm brushing Jade's hair as he did so. Fortunately, she didn't seem to notice. "That white octagon tucked in between bays thirty-five and thirty-six."

"Does look like one, doesn't it," Jade agreed. "It's not on the maps I was given. Interesting."

"Must be a recent add-on," Quiller said. "Maybe Ferrouz figured the spaceport wasn't secure enough and wanted to put more firepower at the scene."

"Or else it's not the spaceport itself but the environs he's concerned about," Marcross suggested from beside LaRone. "If that's not a slum down there, it's working very hard to become one."

"Either way, the station's worth checking out," LaRone said. "Watching how they handle shifts and patrol patterns should give us some idea of how they're organized, which should give us a better chance of slipping ourselves into the rotation."

"In case that's what you decide you want us to do," Marcross added.

"Sounds reasonable," Jade agreed. "No armor—we want to keep this low-profile."

"Understood," LaRone said. "Will you be coming with us?"

Jade shook her head. "I'll take one of the landspeeders and head over to the nicer part of town. See if Ferrouz has added any extra stormtrooper stations near the palace."

Fifteen minutes later they were down. Customs procedures consisted of a few questions, a perfunctory glance at each of their false IDs, and an equally perfunctory warning about not causing trouble. Plus a docking fee, of course, with enough extra padding around the usual rate that LaRone was pretty sure the inspector was using it to supplement his salary.

Under other circumstances, that kind of blatant graft would probably have caused him and the others to take a closer look at the customs system, with an eye toward seeing how far the corruption had spread. But with possible treason lurking in the governor's palace, customs fraud was pretty low on the priority list.

Jade already had her bag packed, and as soon as the customs man left she headed off in the nicer of the Suwantek's two landspeeders, weaving her way expertly through the crowds of pedestrians and the booths and ramshackle homes that lined most of the streets. LaRone and the others left the bay on foot and headed toward the stormtrooper station.

The streets were noisy, echoing with a dozen different languages as well as Basic, the latter ranging from almost cultured to badly mangled. There were many species represented, including at least two LaRone wasn't familiar with. Sales booths of all sorts lined the streets, adding cooking aromas and the additional noise of hawkers to the scene.

"And all this guy can think about is making deals with traitors," Grave muttered from LaRone's side as they passed a particularly squalid-looking homestead that seemed to have been built entirely from packing crates.

"Can't really blame the Rebellion for this," Brightwater murmured back. "At least not all of it. I've seen slums this bad on Coruscant."

"I wasn't blaming anyone but Ferrouz," Grave said. "If you accept the position of governor, part of your job is to make sure all your people have a decent shot at making something good out of their lives."

Quiller cleared his throat. "Speaking of the Rebellion," he said, "did anyone else notice the YT-1300 transport sitting in bay forty on our way in?"

LaRone eyed him, the back of his neck tingling. There were plenty of old YTs still kicking around the Empire. But the way Quiller had said that . . . "Solo's ship?"

"*Solo?*" Brightwater echoed. "*Here?*"

"Not sure," Quiller said. "We were too far away for a positive visual, and I didn't want to key in a cone scan, not with Jade sitting right there watching."

"Why not?" Marcross asked. "Solo's a Rebel. If he's here, that pretty well confirms that Ferrouz's a traitor."

"Hey, I don't even know that it *was* Solo," Quiller protested. "Even if it was, there could be all sorts of reasons why he's here that have nothing to do with Ferrouz."

"He's right," LaRone said firmly, jumping in before the argument could pick up any more momentum. They'd ended up working with Solo a few months back, along with his Wookiee copilot and the young would-be Jedi Luke Skywalker. Things had worked out well enough, but it wasn't an experience that LaRone was eager to repeat. And it probably wouldn't have been even if the three of them *weren't* Rebels. "Besides, passing judgment—of any sort—isn't our job. That's Jade's end of the deal."

"What if we actually spot Solo here?" Marcross asked. "Do we tell her about it?"

"I think we have to," Grave said. "Our job is support, and intel is part of that."

"I agree," LaRone said reluctantly. Just because he wouldn't want to work with Solo again didn't mean he wanted him handed over to the tender mercies of Imperial Security, either. "Though before we do, we should try to get his side of whatever's going on."

"Assuming he'll even talk to us," Brightwater pointed out. "Considering that we *are* Imperials again."

"Very unofficially," LaRone reminded him, frowning. Half a block ahead, the normal traffic flow had been interrupted by a knot of people standing and looking at something happening on the right-hand side of the street. Even as the five stormtroopers moved toward it, other passersby were stopping to join the onlookers.

Marcross had spotted it, too. "Some kind of street performance?" he suggested.

"Too quiet," Grave said. "I'm guessing we'll find a dead body or two over there."

"Or someone about to get that way," LaRone said, grimacing. Blasters weren't exactly uncommon out here, but in keeping with her low-profile plan, Jade had ordered them to stick with hold-out blasters, which were much easier to conceal than their standard BlasTech DH-17 sidearms.

Unfortunately, hold-out blasters were also a lot less powerful than the DH-17s, both in rate of fire and in total number of shots per Tibanna charge. If there was trouble up there, they could quickly find themselves at a dangerous firepower disadvantage.

There was nothing to do but give it a try. "Line-spread penetration," LaRone ordered, making sure his hold-out blaster was within easy reach. "Let's see what's going on."

They reached the edge of the crowd. LaRone picked a likely spot and started easing his way through the press, the other stormtroopers continuing on to make their own insertions at other places down the line where they would all be within covering positions of one another. LaRone reached the last line of onlookers, pried open a small gap between a Rodian and a Devaronian, and stepped to the inside of the circle.

Three meters in front of him were four aliens, burgundy-feathered beings of a species LaRone didn't recognize. Their faces, and the blasters gripped in their hands, were pointed toward three aliens sporting green scales and fur tufts, who were themselves standing behind three more of the feathered aliens, the whole crowd of them under the canopy of a rough, open-fronted store made of shipping crates and scrap metal.

LaRone's first thought was that the Greenies were hiding behind the Feathers. But then he spotted the knife in one of the Greenies' hands. Each of them had a knife, he saw now, wicked, hook-tipped weapons that they were holding firmly against the Feathers' throats.

The Greenies weren't hiding behind the Feathers. They were using them as living shields.

"I will pay back the price," one of the Greenies was saying as LaRone arrived. "But not at the point of a weapon."

"You will pay back, and double," snarled one of the armed Feathers facing him. On the last word he took a quick step to his left, probably hoping to shift position far enough to get a clear shot over his compatriot's shoulder. The Greenies turned in response, rotating their captive Feathers the necessary few degrees to keep them in the armed Feathers' lines of fire. The other armed Feathers tried stretching their line, but quickly retreated into their original clump as two more knife-wielding Greenies at the edges of the crowd silently warned them back.

"You will pay *triple*," the Feather spokesman bit out. "And a life each for any harmed by you."

"I will pay the price only," the Greenie said firmly. "And you will *not* harm our defenseless."

LaRone grimaced as he belatedly spotted the small group of Greenies crouched together in a close huddle in the shadow of the store behind the knife holders. Several of them appeared to be adults, though of a slightly smaller build and with fewer patches of green fur among the green scales. The rest were much smaller versions, clearly children.

A motion to LaRone's left caught his eye, and he looked over to see Marcross slip into view at the front of the far end of the crowd. The other three stormtroopers, he noted, were also standing by.

LaRone took a deep breath. "What seems to be the problem here?" he asked, taking a step toward the confrontation.

One of the armed Feathers turned to face him, his blaster swiveling to point at LaRone's chest. "Be gone, human," he ground out. "This concerns not you."

"Justice concerns everyone," LaRone said, keeping his hands motionless at his sides. There was a risk, he knew, that the alien would just shoot him and be done with it. But while the Feathers were clearly angry, they didn't seem crazy enough to open fire on perfect strangers in front of a hundred witnesses. "Did these people rob you?"

"He sold me a knife," the Feather spokesman growled over his shoulder, his eyes still on the Greenie spokesman. "The knife broke. I demand a proper return of the cost."

"Sounds reasonable enough," LaRone agreed, looking at the Greenies. "Do you refuse?"

"Our knives do not break under proper usage," the Greenie spokesman insisted. "If I am to return his cost, I must have the broken knife in return so that I may examine it and discover its flaws."

"Yet the knife *did* break," the Feather insisted. "His statement insults my honor and my word."

"He thus demands twice his cost," the Greenie added. "Such a burden we cannot afford to pay."

"I see." LaRone gestured to the Greenies' living-shield arrangement. "Tell me how this happened."

"They came in with weapons and loud demands," the Greenie said. "We feared for our defenseless."

"They demanded we leave without return of the cost," the Feather said.

"I asked that they sheathe their weapons while we spoke of the matter," the Greenie countered.

"They attacked us with their cursed knives."

"They threatened our defenseless."

"Yes, all right," LaRone said, raising his voice to be heard. He'd had to deal with this sort of thing any number of times back in his official days as a stormtrooper. With aliens, especially unknown aliens, it really could be as simple and straightforward as competing, horn-locked honors. "Enough. Show me the broken knife."

There was just the slightest pause. "I do not have it," the Feather said stiffly.

LaRone grimaced. Or, it could be that one of the two sides was trying to cheat the other. "Why not?" he asked. "Where is it?"

"It is not here," the Feather said, his anger level starting to ratchet up again. "When I have received twice the cost, I will return it. But not until the money is in my hand."

"Sorry, but it doesn't work that way," LaRone told him. "You give me the broken knife, and I'll have the merchant return the money you paid for it."

"*Double* the cost!"

LaRone shook his head. "It doesn't work that way, either."

The Feather snarled something in a clickety-sounding language. The one holding the blaster on LaRone took a step toward him, raising the weapon to point at LaRone's face. There was the short, sharp crack of a blaster—

With a warbling screech, the Feather lurched forward, his right leg collapsing beneath him as Grave's shot expertly grazed the outside of his knee joint. LaRone was ready, taking another quick step forward and twisting the blaster from the alien's suddenly slack grip. Turning it around into firing position, he leveled it at the other three armed Feathers. "Weapons down," he ordered.

The three Feathers started to turn, stopping abruptly as Grave sent a warning shot into the ground between them and LaRone. For a moment they froze, their blasters hanging halfway between LaRone and their original Greenie targets. Then the Feather spokesman clicked again, and all three slowly returned their blasters to their cross-chest holsters.

"Thank you," LaRone said. He turned his borrowed blaster onto the Greenies and their living shields. "Your turn. Weapons down."

The spokesman murmured something, and the Greenies released their grips on the Feathers. As the former hostages stepped hastily away, the knives similarly vanished into sheaths.

"Thank you," LaRone said, turning back to the Feathers. "Now. The broken knife, if you please."

"It is not here," the Feather growled. "I said that already."

"Yes, I forgot," LaRone said. "Fine. We can all go back to your place and get it." He lifted the blaster slightly. "You'll go under guard, of course, with your hands in binders. Just as a precaution."

Even without knowing the species and their facial expressions, LaRone had no doubt the glare the Feather sent him was one of pure hatred. But LaRone also had no doubt that someone who'd played the honor card as proudly as this one had would do anything to avoid being marched through crowded streets looking like a criminal. "It is here," he growled reluctantly, reaching into a side pocket in his tunic and pulling out a duplicate of the knives the Greenies had just sheathed.

Or rather, pulling it halfway out of the pocket. There he stopped, with only the hilt and half the blade showing.

Mentally, LaRone shook his head. Just as he'd suspected. "Thank you," he said, stepping forward past the Feather still squirming on the ground. He got a grip on the knife hilt, and as the Feather released it he pulled it the rest of the way out of the other's pocket.

As he did so, he took a casual step to his left, interposing his sleeve between the knife and the watching crowd. "Yes—I see," he said, nodding sagely at the perfectly intact blade as he lowered his arm to his side, concealing the knife between his sleeve and his thigh.

He turned to the Greenies. "I have the knife," he confirmed. "You will now return to him the cost."

For a moment the Greenie spokesman eyed him in silence. Then, also in silence, he stepped forward. Drawing some coins from a pouch at his waist, he handed them to the Feather.

"And now honor and justice are both satisfied," LaRone said. "All may go about their business."

He turned to look at the ring of onlookers. "*All* may go," he said firmly.

Slowly, as if disappointed that the show was over, the crowd began to break up. LaRone glanced over at the Feather whom Grave had shot, who had been helped to his feet and was leaning on one of his compatriots, then turned to the head Feather. "Don't come back," he warned quietly. "The Empire takes a very dim view of cheats and would-be thieves."

The Feather glared at him, his cheek feathers ruffling. "What is the Empire?" he spat.

"The Empire is the ground on which you're standing," LaRone told him. "More important, if you come back, the knife merchants will probably tell everyone else that you tried to cheat them."

The Feather's glare slipped, just a bit. "They may say so regardless."

"I'll encourage them not to," LaRone said.

The ruffled feathers smoothed out. "I stand in your debt," he muttered, almost too softly for LaRone to hear.

"You're welcome," LaRone told him. "You can repay the debt by leaving the merchant and his people alone."

The Feather drew himself up. "Our weapon?" he demanded, holding out his hand.

LaRone considered. Then, reversing his borrowed blaster, he handed it over. "Remember what I said."

"I am not likely to forget." The Feather made a sharp gesture to his companions and gave some more clickety orders. With baleful looks at LaRone, the whole group turned their backs on him in unison and stalked away.

Grave stepped to LaRone's side. "Well, that went well," he said drily. "You probably shouldn't have given him back his blaster."

"If they want trouble, one weapon's difference isn't likely to slow them down," LaRone said. "Besides, it's better to leave them completely in our debt."

"Yes, they strike me as a little like Yuzzem," Brightwater commented as he joined them. "Quick-tempered, but with a strict code of honor."

"That was my impression, too," LaRone agreed. "I tried to trade his debt to me for a promise to leave our knife makers alone. We'll see if it works."

"What debt?" Marcross asked as he and Quiller came up.

"This," LaRone said, showing them the unbroken knife. "Come on—let's return it to its proper owners."

The Greenies were still standing in a row in front of their defenseless, their hands ready on their sheathed knives as they watched the Feathers disappear into the pedestrian traffic. Behind them, though, the females and children had gotten to their feet and were starting hesitantly to return to their activities. "Thank you," the head Greenie said as the stormtroopers came up to them. "We are in your debt."

"No problem," LaRone assured him. "I'm glad we could help." He reversed the knife and extended the hilt toward him. "Here's your property."

The Greenie gave a wet-sounding snort as he saw the unbroken blade. "As I suspected," he said contemptuously. "You should have exposed his fraud for all to see."

"It's always a good idea to leave people with something more to lose," LaRone said as the other took the weapon.

"And his claims certainly aren't likely to damage your business," Brightwater added. "I've seen many blades in my travels, and yours is exceptionally well crafted."

"Your kindness is most welcome," the Greenie said. "I am Vaantaar, leader of this small group of Troukree. I stand in your debt."

"No problem," LaRone said. "I'm LaRone. These are Brightwater, Grave, Marcross, and Quiller."

"I don't think I've ever seen people of your sort before," Marcross said. "Where are you from?"

"There," Vaantaar said, gesturing toward the sky. "From the stars you call the Unknown Regions. We fled here, in hope, from the ravages of a terrible enemy." His small, white-rimmed eyes narrowed. "An enemy we fear may soon assail us here, as well."

LaRone frowned. Jade hadn't said anything about alien threats being part of this operation. "Who is this enemy?" he asked.

"They are a group of beings, some allies, some slaves," Vaantaar said. "They attack and destroy under the orders of an evil creature named Warlord Nuso Esva."

"What sort of being is he?" Marcross asked. "Is he one of the feathered people who were just here?"

"The Pineath?" Vaantaar's eyes flashed with contempt. "No, Nuso Esva is not Pineath. Though perhaps the Pineath have now joined him. They are the sort of foul-minded creatures he would use to his advantage. Especially here, in the mud and fear that is this world."

"Do you know anything else about him?" LaRone asked. "His species, or what he looks like?"

Vaantaar gave a furtive glance over his shoulder at the females and children. "I have seen only the dark challenge he sends before each of his attacks," he said in a low voice. "He is constructed similarly to you, but with his covering surface smooth and soft and shimmering like a rainbow."

"His covering?" Grave asked, tapping the back of his hand. "You mean his skin?"

"His skin, yes," Vaantaar said. "His head covering is arranged similarly to yours, but the tendrils are much longer and are pure black. His eyes are . . . I do not know the word. They are bright yellow, and give off many small reflections."

"Multifaceted, like an insect's?" Brightwater suggested. He pulled out his datapad and punched up a picture of a Noehon. "Like this?"

"Like, but unlike," Vaantaar said, nodding at the picture. "Nuso Esva's eyes are smaller, and lie nestled within the head like yours or mine, instead of being on the outside as this creature's are."

LaRone looked at the others. "Any of this sounding familiar?"

"Not to me," Brightwater said, putting the datapad back into his pocket.

"Me, neither," Grave said. "I would have said near-human until he mentioned the eyes. Now I'm not so sure."

"Of course, if he's from the Unknown Regions, it's not unreasonable that we've never run into his species before," Brightwater pointed out.

"True," LaRone said. "I was hoping he was someone from the Empire playing conquest games."

"Nuso Esva plays no games," Vaantaar said darkly. "He conquers, and he destroys."

"You said you were afraid he would be coming here," Quiller said. "Why here? Is there something in the Poln system of particular value?"

Vaantaar gave a whistling sigh. "What does any warlord find of value in new territory? He wishes only to conquer, to hold, and to exploit. That is all that matters to such beings."

He lowered his eyes. "He was preparing to conquer or destroy our own world when we fled," he said quietly. "To this day, we do not know which was its fate."

"Well, if he tries to show his face here, he's going to be in for a surprise," Quiller assured him. "I doubt he's got anything that could take on an Imperial Star Destroyer."

"I pray that you are correct," Vaantaar said. "I have seen his legacy of destruction. I do not wish to see more of it."

"Nor do any of the rest of us," LaRone told him. "Try not to worry." He gestured to the others. "In the meantime, we need to move along."

"Again, we are in your debt," Vaantaar said. He hesitated, balancing the knife LaRone had given him across the dog-like pads on parts of his palm and finger joints. Then, as if suddenly coming to a decision, he flipped the weapon around and held the hilt out toward LaRone. "In gratitude for your aid," he said.

"I'm honored," LaRone said. "But there's no need. Our honor and pleasure is in the helping of others."

"As our honor and pleasure is in paying our debts," Vaantaar said, still holding out the knife.

LaRone looked at Brightwater. The other was gazing unblinkingly at the knife. Practically salivating over it, in fact. "Then we accept with thanks," LaRone said, taking the weapon. Silently, one of the other Troukree stepped forward and handed LaRone a matching sheath of some sort of tooled leather. "Thank you again," LaRone said, sliding the knife into the sheath. It fit snugly, yet at the same time was surprisingly easy to draw. "Farewell, and take care."

He gestured, and the stormtroopers resumed their journey toward the stormtrooper station. "Here," LaRone said, handing the sheathed knife to Brightwater. "Early Transland Day present. Enjoy."

"Oh, I couldn't," Brightwater protested.

"Yes, he could," Quiller said drily. "Come on, buddy. Take it before your eyes fall out of their sockets."

"Well, if you insist," Brightwater said, taking it almost reverently and sliding it out of its sheath for another look.

"First an antique druggat, and now this," Grave said. "How come Brightwater gets all the good stuff?"

"It's my kind face and generous personality," Brightwater said, tucking the knife into his belt at the small of his back and pulling the edge of his tunic down over it.

"Yes, that must be it," Marcross agreed. "Any of you ever hear Jade mention this Nuso Esva character? Or any other threat in this area besides the Rebellion?"

"She didn't say anything to me," Grave said. "Brightwater? You were with her the longest."

"If you can call floating in her bacta tank being with her," Brightwater said. "And no, I didn't hear anything."

"But we'll hear plenty if we don't get some data on the stormtrooper station by tonight," LaRone warned. "Playtime over, gentlemen. Let's get back to work."

CHAPTER NINE

ONE OF THE FIRST DISCOVERIES OF POLN MAJOR'S ORIGINAL SETTLERS had been a long line of large mounds, one to two hundred meters tall, which when sliced open yielded rich lodes of a hard, white, crystalline stone that was both highly decorative and strong enough to build with. Decades later, when the double planet first joined the Old Republic, that bit of their early history had been honored by constructing the governor's palace out of that same white stone and setting it in front of and slightly beneath the last, partially mined mound, which at that time had marked the edge of Whitestone City.

The effect, visitors to the city all agreed, was striking. Some saw the gouged-out mound as an oddly shaped breaking wave of pure whitewater that had frozen in midair, its crest towering over the palace. Others, focusing on the view from straight on, saw it as a scaled-up version of the falling-star domes that were a prominent style of souvenir sold at virtually every tourist spot in the Empire.

Standing at the window of her sixth-floor room in the Hewntree Hotel, two blocks from the glittering white mound and palace, Mara wondered if Poln Major gift shops had such falling-star domes of the scene for sale. Almost certainly they did.

Taking one last trinn berry from the room's fruit bowl and popping it into her mouth, she went back to the chair she'd placed two meters back from the window and sat down. She'd had a falling-star dome once, she remembered. Most of her childhood was vague and shadowy, but she distinctly remembered the trouble she'd gotten into when she'd broken open the dome to find out what made the falling-star streaks when it was shaken.

Breaking into cheap plastic souvenir domes was easy. Breaking into Governor Ferrouz's palace was going to be considerably more difficult.

She switched on her special electrobinoculars and focused again on the palace. The wall that encircled most of the Empire's palaces had here been truncated into an arc, running from one edge of the mound cutout to the other. The mound itself took the place of the rest of the wall. The grounds enclosed by the mound and wall were more oval than circular, with the main open areas to the right and left of the palace. Mara couldn't see much of either area from her current vantage point, but from the Emperor's data she knew there were formal gardens on one side and an outdoor theater and small fragrance jungle on the other.

The mound itself rose a good fifty meters above the palace, and in fact the tip of the crest overhung the rear third of the building. Normally, that would suggest the possibility of a rappelling incursion. In this case, though, it was such an obvious approach that Ferrouz or his predecessors had taken special care to close it off. At least half of the unobtrusive wall-mounted lasers were aimed up and inward, their swivels blocked to keep them from firing down into the compound itself but more than capable of picking off someone dropping spider-like from a rappelling line.

Not that a potential infiltrator would find it easy to get into rappelling position in the first place. The mound's base was patrolled by scout troopers on speeder bikes, who flew regular patrols that covered all approaches to the rear and sides of the mound. Most of the time the speeder bikes stopped where the compound's wall met the mound and turned back to circle the other way, but occasionally a trooper would continue on, cutting close alongside the wall and swooping past the gate, then continuing around to the mound's other side. The sheer randomness of those extra circuits made it impossible to predict when an opening in the pattern would take place, which made getting to the mound, let alone climbing it, problematic at best.

The wall itself was just as bad. It was a good five meters tall, with six watchtowers spaced out along it, each of which was occupied by at least three guards at all times. The wall was set back about fifty meters from the major street that ran past the front of the palace and compound, sitting across a wide paved road spur that led from the street to the gate. Two pairs of guards stood at the gate, which was opened only when vehicles were entering or leaving. The outer part of the wall was patrolled by four pairs of stormtroopers, and Mara had no doubt there were more walking the inside perimeter as well. She hadn't yet seen the nighttime routine, but the security would undoubtedly be tightened as darkness fell across the city. More stormtroopers and armed patrollers moved among the shops and residence areas of the city sector nearest the palace, undoubtedly trained to spot signs of brewing trouble.

Mara had breached high-security walls before, either climbing them or using her lightsaber to cut through them. But such tricks usually required a guard corps that had been lulled by routine into negligence. The fact that Ferrouz was using stormtroopers to supplement the palace guard corps strongly implied that Mara would find no such negligence.

Which left only the gate itself.

She focused her electrobinoculars on it. The structure was as tall as the rest of the wall, decorated with intricate bas-reliefs highlighting some of Poln Major's historical events. To one side was a narrow personnel door, barely big enough for a fully armored stormtrooper to pass through and thus impossible for a gang or mob to effectively rush. From what little she could see as the outside guard was being changed, it looked like the door also included a weapon and energy-source scanner.

The four guards currently posted at the gate were dressed in an elaborate blue-and-red livery—probably, like the bas-reliefs, something from Poln Major's distant past. They weren't wearing any armor, but when the wind blew just right Mara could briefly see the slight bulges of blasters concealed beneath their capelets.

There were no outside controls for the gate. One of the guards had to call inside via comlink whenever a speeder truck or other vehicle came up requesting entrance. The oval shape of the compound meant that the gate was also the closest part of the wall to the palace, probably no more than fifty meters away from the main entrance.

Vehicles with proper authorization were allowed inside without any

fuss, but Mara could see as the gate closed that each was then stopped between the wall and the palace for a search. With her electrobinoculars'
audio capabilities, she'd also eavesdropped on the guards' orders to the inside gatekeepers, and it was clear that a system of rolling passwords was
in use.

Clearly, no one was getting in without a battalion of armored troops or
invitation from someone already inside. And a governor presumably engaged in treason was unlikely to throw his gate wide to visiting officials,
media personalities, art dealers, or dignitaries from minor worlds.

But he might open the gate to a criminal. Or at least, his guards might.

Returning her electrobinoculars to their case, Mara left her room and
headed downstairs. There was an open-air tapcaf she'd noted, across the
main street from the wall and a little way down from the gate itself.

Time for a little experiment.

The tapcaf was doing brisk business, but Mara was able to find a small
table to herself out on the patio facing the palace grounds. She ordered a
half flute of one of the local brandies and for a few minutes sipped it as she
watched the flow of humans and aliens along the walkway between her
and the street. She would have preferred to try this with another palace-
authorized vehicle in place, but for the first fifteen minutes no such vehicle came along.

She had just concluded that she was going to have to make do without
that added embellishment when a speeder truck with a baker's logo turned
onto the spur and headed in toward the gate.

Mara sat up straighter in her chair, her eyes flicking back and forth as
she looked for a likely target. Approaching from her right, in the lane closest to the spur, was an open-topped landspeeder with a teenage girl driving, the wind whipping through her hair. The vehicle flashed past Mara
and started to pass the spur.

Stretching out to the Force, Mara twisted the landspeeder's control
wheel hard over to the right.

The landspeeder spun onto the spur, weaving and bobbing with interrupted inertia as it made the turn. Even at her distance Mara could see the
girl's panic as she wrestled with her suddenly rogue vehicle, trying to turn
it off its new path. Mara kept a tight Force grip on the wheel, noting out of

the corner of her eye that the gate was just starting to open to admit the speeder truck. The teen, apparently only now spotting the truck directly in her path, abandoned her attempts to steer and stomped with all her weight on the brakes.

She just made it. The landspeeder bobbed to a stop bare centimeters away from the speeder truck's rear crash plate.

And as the gate hastily closed again in front of the truck, all four of the liveried guards arrowed in on the landspeeder, their concealed blasters drawn and pointed at the hapless girl.

The near accident and resulting drama had already caused traffic on the street to grind almost to a halt as drivers slowed down, craning their necks to see what was happening. Some of the tapcaf's patrons abandoned their drinks and stood up, the better to see over the creeping vehicles.

Mara didn't bother. She already knew how standard guard procedure worked, the normal routine of checking vehicle registration and personal ID. All she cared about was what the guards would do once the first-tier protocols had been completed.

She didn't have long to wait. Barely a minute after the guards arrived at the landspeeder, the teen was ordered out of the vehicle and marched over to the gate. The small side door had opened and a middle-aged man in a gray uniform was waiting there for her. They held a brief conversation, then the middle-aged man had another conversation on his comlink. A few minutes later two more gray-uniformed men emerged from the side door and headed over to the landspeeder. The liveried guards stayed with the teen, moving her a few meters away from the gate and door and standing her out of the way beside the wall. Peering over the still-sluggish traffic, Mara saw the two gray-suited guards move the landspeeder off the road and then pop open the engine compartment. A minute later, the gate finally opened again and the speeder truck was allowed through.

Mara nodded to herself. So a minor infraction, even a mysterious one, would only earn the perpetrator a talking-to outside the wall. It would presumably take a more serious threat to get hauled inside for more thorough questioning.

Fortunately, serious threats were one of Mara's specialties.

She finished her drink, left a pile of credits that included a generous tip, and headed off into the market section that extended several blocks away from the palace compound. In the center of the market section, tucked away between the cantinas and legal offices, was a small electronics store.

The salesclerk was a male Verpine, two meters of bipedal insectoid cheer and technological enthusiasm who would probably have described everything in the store in minute detail had Mara given him half a chance. Fortunately, she knew what she wanted, and ten minutes later she left with a child's model airspeeder and the toy's remote controller unit, plus a few other inexpensive electronic components. She returned to the hotel, spent a few minutes flying the airspeeder around the room to check it out, then set it aside and pulled out her comlink.

"Report," she ordered when LaRone answered.

"We've done a preliminary check," the stormtrooper told her. "Assuming this station runs on the same protocols and procedures as the palace contingent, I think we've got a pretty good handle on how to deal with them."

"Good," Mara said. "Get back to the ship, load your gear into the speeder truck, and get over here. I'll meet you at the Iceview Tapcaf across from the palace in two hours. I also want you to pull a record of all ships that have entered or left the system in the past three days."

"Acknowledged," LaRone said. "Any equipment in particular you want us to bring?"

"Everything you'll need for an incursion," Mara told him. "I'll give you the plan tonight after we eat.

"Tomorrow morning, we're going in."

The double planet drifting across the starfield ahead did not, in Pellaeon's opinion, have anything particularly noteworthy about it. Aside, of course, from the relative novelty of it being a double planet in the first place.

But apart from that there was nothing. The number of spaceships moving in and out was nothing like the traffic around Imperial Center or Corellia, neither in quantity nor in the size and sheer opulence of the vehicles involved. The power-grid map showed large areas of Poln Major still relatively undeveloped, and much of Poln Minor to be virtually uninhabited. The Golan I Defense Platform orbiting Poln Major was more than half deserted, with barely 30 percent of its weapons still powered. A single Dreadnought, the *Sarissa*, circled Poln Minor, and was even less functional than the Golan. All in all, the place was practically the definition of a galactic backplanet.

Which made it a perfect place for Rebels and alien warlords to meet in secret and seduce an Imperial governor from his sworn duty.

There was a footstep behind him, and Pellaeon turned to see Captain Drusan striding down the command walkway. "So that's the place," the captain rumbled as he came to a halt beside Pellaeon. "Not much to look at, is it?"

"No, sir, it isn't," Pellaeon agreed. "I wonder how long it's been since they've had a Star Destroyer pay a visit."

"If they've ever had one here at all," Drusan said. "A shame we can't give them more of a show. See those eight ships over there, the ones cutting across the *Sarissa*'s bow on their way into Poln Minor? What do you make of them?"

Pellaeon peered out the viewport, resisting the temptation to look at the tactical display or call for a comm-scan readout. Drusan obviously wanted to see what he could see by himself. "The three big ones are Gallofree Yards GR-75 transports," he said. "The other five are probably Corellian light freighters of some sort—I can't tell which model from this distance."

"Anything unusual about their formation?"

Pellaeon gave the rest of the traffic pattern a quick look for comparison. "Not really," he said. "There's still enough mining on Poln Minor for transports that size to make stops, both to bring in new equipment and supplies and to take out finished product."

"Reasonable enough," Drusan said. "What if I also told you that comm-scan reports all the ships are heavily armed? Heavily enough to be skirting the law, in fact."

"That would raise my suspicions enough to take a closer look," Pellaeon said. "But there are also a large number of smuggler and pirate gangs operating from this system. Even a legitimate operation would need to arm both its transports and its escort ships or risk attack and capture." He pointed. "And the fact that they're moving past the *Sarissa* instead of avoiding it implies that they are, in fact, legitimate."

"Yes, that's the crowning subtlety, isn't it," Drusan agreed grimly. "But in this case, appearances are deceiving. Lord Odo has informed me that those are, in fact, Rebel Alliance ships."

Pellaeon felt his throat tighten. If the Rebels had brought in that much carrying capacity, they must be expecting to obtain a great deal of matériel from their coming deal with Nuso Esva. Matériel, or soldiers.

And the fact that the *Sarissa* was letting them skim right past its turbo-lasers was a strong indication that Odo was also right about Governor Ferrouz being involved. "Do we take them now, sir?" he asked Drusan. "Or do we wait to see if they bring in more?"

"Neither," Drusan said. "Lord Odo has something else in mind. We'll take a leisurely pass by Poln Minor, as if we just dropped out of hyperspace to recalibrate our course, and then head out." He paused. "Into the Unknown Regions."

Pellaeon felt his mouth drop open. "The *Unknown Regions*?"

"Don't worry, we won't be going very deep," Drusan assured him. "Only a few hours. And we have full nav data for the route we'll be taking. Perfectly safe."

Pellaeon grimaced. Perfectly safe . . . except for all the possible dangers out there, from pirates, mercenaries, and aliens like Nuso Esva. "May I ask the nature of our mission?"

"Lord Odo was a bit vague on that point," Drusan conceded. "I gather we're going to be delivering a bit of a surprise to one of Nuso Esva's attack squadrons."

"Ah," Pellaeon murmured. "By ourselves?"

"We're an Imperial Star Destroyer, Commander Pellaeon," Drusan said, his voice darkening. "We don't need anyone's help to bring the Empire's strength and order to bear. On *anyone*."

"Yes, sir," Pellaeon said, ducking his head. "My apologies."

"Yes," Drusan said. "And we'll hardly be alone. Senior Captain Thrawn and the *Admonitor* are also out there, and Lord Odo assures me we'll be joining with them somewhere along the way."

"And Senior Captain Thrawn is no doubt aware of our imminent arrival?"

"*Someone's* certainly aware," Drusan said. "If not Thrawn, then who?"

Pellaeon nodded. He'd also seen the reports from Security about Odo's use of the *Chimaera's* HoloNet transmitter to send messages to someone in either Wild Space or the Unknown Regions. "Who indeed?" he agreed.

Which still left them traveling into an unknown situation, going up against an unknown enemy with unknown resources. Only now they would have the dubious assistance of another Star Destroyer and a small flotilla of smaller warships, under the command of an alien officer who was apparently so poor at the fleet's political games that he kept getting kicked off Imperial Center and booted out into the Unknown Regions.

All of it on the orders of someone whose full plans they still didn't know.

Still, it was the Emperor himself who had given Odo his orders. Presumably, he knew what he was doing.

"Helm?" Drusan called, interrupting Pellaeon's thoughts.

"Sir?" the helm officer answered briskly.

"Complete our observation arc past Poln Minor, then take us out," Drusan ordered. "Course as per Lord Odo's data card."

"Yes, sir."

Drusan smiled tightly at Pellaeon. "Cheer up, Commander," he said. "We're going hunting."

Car'das looked up from the sensor display. "They're Rebel transports, all right," he confirmed. "And those armed Corellian freighters are their escort."

Thrawn nodded. "How well armed are they?"

Car'das snorted. "I'm sure they're doing their best. Knowing Rebels, they'll probably put up a decent fight."

"Yes," Thrawn said. "Let's hope they don't simply compute the odds and slink away."

Car'das shrugged noncommittally. Thrawn didn't think much of the Rebels, he knew. More than that, his study of the Republic had given him a dim view of any governing body that relied on the consensus of dozens of species, each of which had its own way of thinking about the universe and one another. In Thrawn's view, a strong, unified government was the only way the galaxy would survive against the shadowy alien threat moving across the galaxy. A threat that had already touched Chiss space and would someday reach the Empire.

Car'das understood Thrawn's thinking on the subject, and on one level he could certainly agree. While Thrawn had been pushing against governmental inertia in the Chiss Ascendancy, Car'das had lived through the chaotic middle of the Separatist movement and the Clone Wars. He'd seen the damage a hundred species with a hundred private agendas could do.

On the other hand, only a fool could believe that the Empire under Palpatine was doing a better job in the unity department than the Republic had.

"So what's next?" he asked, mostly to change the subject.

"I need to contact my agent on Poln Major," Thrawn said. "Once I've had his report, we'll be ready to leave."

"To the Unknown Regions," Car'das said, grimacing. For him, the Unknown Regions didn't exactly hold fond memories.

"Yes," Thrawn said. "Nuso Esva will certainly be there. We need to be, too."

"To make sure his game fails?"

"On the contrary," Thrawn said softly. "To make sure it succeeds."

The Poln Minor atmosphere was thin, dank, and—especially at night—cold. Very cold. Leia had never really liked cold all that much, and as she stood on the rocky ground of Poln Minor's surface she could practically feel ice forming on her eyebrows.

But at the moment, the cold was the farthest thing from her mind.

The Star Destroyer was leaving.

"You sure?" Cracken asked from beside her.

"Very sure," Leia said, pressing her electrobinoculars to her eyes and trying not to accidentally nudge her breath mask. "It's pulling away—there it goes." She lowered the electrobinoculars. "It just made the jump to hyperspace."

Cracken heaved a sigh. "That," he said, "was way too close."

Leia nodded soberly. Any agreements Axlon had made with Governor Ferrouz would hardly be honored by other Imperials. And the unexpected arrival of a Star Destroyer, even for a brief time, was definitely a cause for concern. "I wonder if someone suspects something."

"I'm sure *somebody* does," Cracken said, still gazing out at the stars. "Ferrouz can't possibly have hidden this deal from everyone. The real question is whether that someone has managed to get Imperial Center's attention."

"With a corrupt governor at the center of it, I'd say that's likely," Leia said. "I wonder if we should take what we've got and get out while we can."

Cracken scratched his cheek. "I don't know," he said. "We haven't even gotten all the cold-weather gear together, let alone all those nice T-47s. I'd hate to leave all that behind for no reason."

"If it *is* for no reason," Leia warned. Still, if Imperial Center had any serious suspicions, that Star Destroyer should at least have stayed long enough to do some spot checks. Maybe it really *had* just been passing through. "Axlon's supposed to meet Ferrouz tomorrow morning. Maybe he can find out what that was all about."

"I'll call and have him put that on the agenda," Cracken said. "Meanwhile, it might be a good idea to bring in more firepower. At least enough to hold off any attack while we get the transports out."

Leia winced. The idea of putting even more of the Alliance's precious ships at risk here than they already had sent warning shivers through her. But Cracken was right. Losing the Gallofree transports, let alone the goods that were being loaded aboard them, would be a devastating blow to the Alliance's ability to move people and equipment around the Empire. "All right, but nothing too obvious," she said. "No cruisers or frigates."

"I'll keep it down to X-wings and maybe a couple of gunships," Cracken promised. "I just wish I knew how well armed the Dreadnought and Golan are. The way Imperial Center prioritizes things, I'm guessing both are being held together by hopes and curses. But there's no way to know for sure unless one of them actually opens fire on us."

"Which we really don't want happening," Leia agreed. An odd idea flicked across her mind. "Do you know where Han is?"

"Solo? I assume he's back on Poln Major." Cracken raised his eyebrows. "Where you sent him three days ago."

"With Han, getting an order isn't necessarily a guarantee of compliance," Leia pointed out. "I was just thinking that some of the smugglers who hang out here must have gone head-to-head with either the *Sarissa* or the *Golan* over the years. Maybe we should bring Han back and see if he can sound out the locals for us."

"You want him *here* when Axlon's about to go into the palace?" Cracken asked, frowning at her over his breath mask. "I thought you wanted him nearby in case Axlon needed a quick extraction."

"If Ferrouz hasn't pulled a double cross by now, I doubt he's going to," Leia said. "Besides, it's not like Han is exactly in position for a quick rescue anyway. He's out at the spaceport, while Axlon's all the way across town in one of the hotels near the palace."

"I'll bet Solo's thrilled to death with that arrangement," Cracken said drily.

"I've seen him happier," Leia conceded.

"Not sure I ever have," Cracken said with a grunt. "But no, talking to the locals makes sense. You want me to give him his new orders?"

"No, that's all right," Leia said reluctantly. Han had been a master at punching her switches almost since their first meeting aboard the Death Star, and he'd only gotten better at it over the past few months. But irritating though that might personally be for her, she'd also noted that he took orders from her better than he did from Rieekan or anyone else. Not well, but better. "I'll tell him."

"Mm."

She looked over. "What?" she demanded.

"Solo's certainly got the capability," he said. "He's proved that time and again. The question is whether he's got the will."

Leia shook her head. "That's entirely up to him."

"Is it?" Cracken countered. "I've noticed that you have an unusual level of influence over him. Even more than Skywalker does. If you pressed him, it might be enough to tip the balance."

Leia grimaced behind her breath mask. "You really want that to be his reason for becoming a full part of the Alliance? My pressure on him?"

"This is war, Princess," Cracken said bluntly. "I've taken in deserters, fringe criminals, scoundrels, general all-around scum—" He grimaced. "—even former politicians. I mean to win this thing, by whatever means and with whatever levers I have to use to do it." He gestured to her. "If you're not . . ." He left the sentence unfinished.

"We'll win, Colonel," Leia said. "But not by manipulating people. Certainly not the good ones."

"I admire your idealism," he said. "I hope it doesn't backfire on you."

Leia turned away, her eyes filling with sudden tears. Idealism was what had gotten her involved with the Rebel Alliance in the first place. It had cost her her reputation, her status, and her seat in the Senate.

It had also cost her her home, her father, and nearly everything else she'd ever held dear. "We'd better get back," she said over her shoulder. "You need to call Axlon. And I need to call Han."

There wasn't much floor space in the *Falcon* where a person could get a proper angry stomp going. But Han did his best, with the result that both Luke and Chewie were already looking up as he came around the corner from the cockpit tunnel.

"What's happened?" Luke asked anxiously.

"What else?" Han growled, stomping a little more as he crossed over to where the two of them were sitting at the game board. "Or maybe I should say *who* else?"

Luke winced. "Leia?"

"Like I said, who else?" Han said, dropping onto the wraparound couch beside Chewie. "Doesn't the Alliance know *any* other smugglers beside me?"

Chewie rumbled a suggestion.

"Come on—the rest of them can't be *that* untrustworthy," Han argued.

"Rieekan wouldn't keep them around if they were. I think Her Worshipful-ness just likes throwing things like this in our lap."

"What things?" Luke asked.

"They want me to go back to Poln Minor and mingle with the other riffraff," Han told him. "See what I can find out about the weapons readi-ness of the Golan and that Dreadnought out there."

"I thought Ferrouz was on our side," Luke said, frowning. "Why do we care about that?"

Chewie warbled a question.

"No, there's no sign of Nuso Esva's fleet," Han told him. "If the guy even has one. At least nothing Leia told me about."

"So why do we care about the Golan and *Sarissa*?" Luke persisted.

"How should I know?" Han growled. There wasn't any point in worry-ing the kid about the Star Destroyer that had just passed through the Poln system. Especially not since it had already left. "You know Cracken. He's not happy if he doesn't see at least three threats coming at him from differ-ent directions."

"I guess," Luke said, not sounding all that convinced.

Mentally, Han shook his head. His lying technique must be slipping. "But you know the military," he said, standing up. "Even Rebel militaries. Show up and do what you're told."

"I suppose," Luke said, standing up, too.

"That's okay—go ahead and finish your game," Han said, waving him back. "I'll take us out."

"Actually, I can't go," Luke said, looking pained. "Axlon called me while you were talking to Leia. He's going into the palace tomorrow some-time to talk to Ferrouz and wants me standing by in case of trouble."

Han frowned, the Star Destroyer visit again flashing to mind. "He's more paranoid even than Cracken," he said. "Tell him you've got better things to do than sit around and play nursedroid for him."

"Sorry," Luke said. "I can't."

Han grimaced. "Yeah, I know. Show up and do what you're told. So where are you going to spend the night? In your Z-95?"

"Luckily, no," Luke said. "There's a hotel about a block from where Axlon's staying. He said he'd booked me a room there."

"A cheaper place than his?"

"Probably," Luke said. "I was going to finish the game first, but if you need to leave, I'll just grab my things and get going."

"Yeah," Han said. "Well . . . watch yourself, okay?"

A brief frown creased Luke's forehead. But he just nodded. "You, too," he said, and headed over to the bunk where his small bag was stowed.

Han looked back at Chewie; the big Wookiee was gazing knowingly at him. Han shook his head microscopically—they would discuss it after the kid left. Chewie nodded and busied himself with closing down the game. Then, heaving himself off the couch, he warbled a farewell to Luke and headed for the cockpit.

Ten minutes later, with the *Falcon* prepped and cleared, they headed out.

And finally, Chewie asked what was going on.

"I don't know," Han told him. "But strange stuff's starting to happen. I don't think this is going to work out as neatly as Axlon thought it would."

Chewie muttered something under his breath.

"Nope," Han agreed. "It never does, does it?"

With a sigh, Mara set her datapad on the desk.

So that was it. A grand total of thirty Rebel ships had landed on Poln Major and Poln Minor over the past three days, including twelve today alone, everything from Z-95 Headhunters and thinly disguised T-65 X-wings all the way up to good-sized GR-75 transports. None of them had even been challenged, let alone stopped or boarded.

And the orders to let them pass unexamined had come directly from the governor's palace.

The Emperor's information had been correct. Governor Ferrouz was a traitor.

Mara stepped over to the window, a haze of sadness settling across her mood. Bidor Ferrouz had been one of the best career politicians to come out of Imperial Center in the past ten years, the sort of person Mara always thought about when she heard whisperings from the galaxy's citizens about the oppressions visited on them by the Empire. With men like

Ferrouz in power, she always argued to herself, whatever evils might have found their way into Palpatine's grand vision of unity and peace would sooner or later be rooted out.

How could a man like Ferrouz fall so far and so quickly? It was incredible. And yet, somehow, it had happened.

Or had it?

Mara raised her eyes from the palace to the dome of white rock behind it, glittering faintly in the lights of the city. She hadn't proved Ferrouz's guilt. Not yet. All she'd proved was that someone high up in the palace was cooperating with the Rebels. The most likely candidate was Ferrouz, but it could also be General Ularno, the defense department's Captain Greterine, or conceivably even one of Ferrouz's three senior staffers.

No, Mara couldn't be absolutely sure Ferrouz was the traitor until she'd gotten into the palace's own records. And she couldn't do that until she was inside.

Which would happen tomorrow.

She gave the palace one final look, then opaqued the window and started to undress. She would go to bed now and get a good night's sleep. She would pretend that Ferrouz was still loyal, and this was some serious misreading of the evidence on her part. Tomorrow, once she proved his treason beyond a glimmer of doubt, she would do her job.

And the Empire would be a better place for it.

CHAPTER TEN

I T WAS ONE OF THE TRUISMS OF THE SPACEFARING LIFE THAT SPACEPORTS seldom slept, and the farther they were from the local sun the less sleep they got.

In general, Han had pretty much found that to be the case. He'd also added one more observational rule: When the spaceport was a long way from law and order and respectable people, it got even less sleep. Or none at all.

All of which meant that Poln Minor's Dankcamp Village, half a kilometer underground and peopled almost entirely by smugglers, mercenaries, wanted criminals, and the people who served them, would probably be up all night. Certainly it hadn't shown any signs of slowing down during the three hours since he and Chewie had arrived in town, or during the half hour since they'd parked themselves at a table in this particular cantina and ordered yet another round of drinks.

From one of the cantina's three entrances across the room came a burst of boisterous laughter. Han looked over as a group of men with identically cut beards, plus a Rodian with an obviously fake one, strode into the room, all of them laughing over some joke. That joke possibly being the Rodian's beard.

A distinct possibility; but Han's brief flicker of hope faded as they came all the way into the room and he got a good look at their sidearms. Most of them were carrying simple sporting blasters, with a couple of old Clone Wars–era DC-15s thrown in. Smugglers, or maybe a skimper or swoop gang. Scowling, he turned back to his drink.

Chewie rumbled a question.

"Because they're smugglers, not mercs," Han told him patiently. "And because asking questions gets you noticed. We don't want to be noticed until we're ready to get the answers we want, and then throttle-burn it out of here. That means we have to wait until we find some mercs, who will know what happens if you run a *big* armed ship past the Golan and the *Sarissa.*"

Chewie growled again.

"How should I know?" Han growled back. "Okay, okay—if we don't spot someone in ten more minutes we'll try that place we saw down the tunnel. If there's nothing there, we'll go find some other town."

The big Wookiee muttered under his breath.

"Hey, don't blame me," Han protested. "This was you-know-who's idea."

"What sort of someone are you looking for?" a voice from Han's right asked in Durese.

Han looked up. A Duros was standing there, a military-grade BlasTech DH-17 belted at his side. Finally. "The sort who knows how things work around here," Han told him. "You a local, or just passing through?"

The Duros smiled, his small mouth curling just slightly upward at the corners. "You don't remember me, do you?"

The skin on the back of Han's neck began to tingle. His Durese was pretty good, but he was only fair at reading Duros' facial expressions. This one was either amused or really, really angry. "Should I?" he asked cautiously.

"I worked for Jabba the Hutt a long season ago," the Duros said. "You are Solo, are you not?"

Chewie rumbled warningly.

"Be of calm mind," the Duros said hastily, holding both hands up to the Wookiee. "I have no longer a connection to the Hutt cartels, and have no interest in seeking the bounty I hear rests on your shoulders."

Han grimaced. Even way out here, Jabba had managed to get the word out. Terrific. "But others may not be so picky?" he suggested.

The Duros' eyes glittered. "Be of calm mind," he said again. "Many here have barely even heard of the Hutts, let alone have thoughts or compassion for them." He cocked his head. "I, for one, find inspiration in finding others who have successfully slipped from Jabba's grasp."

"Glad to hear it," Han said. "In that case, maybe you can help me. You're flying with mercs now, right?"

The Duros shook his head. "A mercenary's life is not for you, Solo," he said firmly. "Not unless you've learned better how to take orders."

"Not a lot," Han conceded. "What I was looking for—"

"But there is easier money to be made this night," the Duros continued. "Do you know how to mount and calibrate Caldorf VII interceptor missiles?"

Han felt his back stiffen. Caldorf VIIs were medium-range heavy missiles, usually mounted on capital ships. The Alliance had a bunch of them, mostly on escort frigates and a few of their gunships. "Sure," he said. "I can mount 'em up, anyway," he amended. "I've got a buddy who knows how to calibrate them. What's up?"

"An unusual person has been scouring the city for knowledgeable workers who will accept payment and not speak afterward of what they've seen," the Duros said. "I can point him out if he comes in, if you choose." He cocked his head again. "For, say, two hundred?"

Han leaned back in his seat. "Seems kind of steep," he said.

"The price would of course include my personal recommendation of your skills and discretion."

"Your recommendation carries that kind of weight?" Han asked.

"Several of my group have been already hired," the Duros said. "But we leave tonight, and our experts depart with us. I assure you, the payment for the work will far exceed your payment to me."

"So you'll be taking off right past the Dreadnought and Golan, huh?" Han asked. "That's not a problem for you?"

The Duros waved a hand. "Neither is a threat," he said. "Do you wish me to point out the employer if he arrives?"

Han looked across the crowded cantina. "Tell you what," he said. "For *five* hundred, how about you go find him and bring him here?"

The Duros eyed him. "*Five* hundred?"

"That's right," Han said, digging out a hundred in high-denomination coins and handing them over. "Here's the upfront. Bring him here, and you'll get the rest."

"Very well."

The Duros started to turn away. Han caught his arm. "Of course," he added, "if you try pulling some scam like bringing in one of your buddies to con me with a dip line, you'll answer to Chewie."

Chewie rumbled, his voice even deeper than usual. "There will be no game," the Duros promised. "I already have Jabba watching the skies for me. I have no interest in you doing so, as well."

"Good," Han said. "Hurry back."

The Duros nodded and headed briskly across the room toward the door. As he walked out into the large cavern that contained the bulk of the village, Han saw him pull out a comlink.

Chewie gave a contemptuous snort.

"Of course he's just going to call around to his buddies until they find the guy for me," Han said, pulling out his own comlink. "No one works any harder for their money than they have to. But it still buys us some time."

At this hour, he expected Leia to be sound asleep. But if she was, it didn't show in her voice. "You have something?" she asked.

"Yeah, but not exactly what you're looking for," Han said. "Do we have anyone here who can calibrate Caldorf VII interceptors?"

There was a short pause. "Caldorf VIIs?"

"Yes or no?" Han growled. "I've been offered a job mounting them, but I need someone who can calibrate the things, too."

"Yes, we have someone," Leia said. "Who's this job for?"

"No idea," Han said. "But I figure you could probably undersling a Caldorf VII on an airspeeder without too much refitting."

"You mean like the T-47s we found in the cavern?" Leia said doubt-fully. "I don't know. They're not really designed for that sort of thing."

"Well, somebody's trying to load them on *something*," Han said. "If it's those T-47s, this might be our chance to find out who owns them."

"I suppose," Leia agreed. "Where are you?"

"Capperling's Cantina in Dankcamp Village," Han told her. "You need directions?"

"We can find it," Leia said. "How soon do you need someone?"

"Five minutes ago," Han said. "No way to know how long it'll take for my friend to find his contact and get back here."

"You have a *friend* here?"

"You going to talk, or you going to get your tech over here?" Han growled. "We don't have time for this."

"Expert's on the way," Leia assured him. "I'm more interested in this so-called friend you conveniently found."

"He's more like a passing acquaintance," Han said. "He's a Duros who used to work for Jabba's cartel, same as me."

"Really," Leia said suspiciously. "Small universe."

"Big cartel," Han said. "And if *I* were hiding out from Jabba, this is the kind of place where I'd do it, too."

"What if he's planning to turn you in for the bounty?"

"Then he wouldn't have bothered offering me a job," Han said. "No, I think his plan is to help me make a big enough stack of money that I can keep running. The more I'm out there drawing Jabba's attention, the less Jabba will be looking for him."

"Maybe," Leia said, still sounding suspicious. "All right, wait there."

Han clicked off the comlink, rolling his eyes. Wait here. Like he had anything else to do. "Chewie, go check out that other room back there, will you?" he said, nodding toward an archway that led off the side of the main bar. "If the Duros is thinking about pulling an ambush, that's where they'll get everyone organized."

Chewie warbled a question.

"Sure, if you're still thirsty," Han told him, experimentally swishing his own half-full cup. "Picking up another bottle will give you a better excuse to go over to the bar anyway. Just get whatever you want for yourself—I'm still okay here."

Nodding acknowledgment, Chewie got up and started weaving his way through the tables toward the archway side of the bar. Han watched him for a minute, then looked over at the door where the Duros had disappeared. Coming up with the four hundred he still owed would be a little tricky. Maybe the Duros would accept a little less, or maybe Han could get an advance from this mysterious employer. There was a brush of air as someone stepped over to his table—

And to Han's stunned disbelief, Leia dropped into the chair beside him. "That fast enough?" she asked.

It took Han two tries to get his mouth working. "What are *you* doing here?"

"We were checking out the conveyance tunnel that runs along the southern edge of town," she explained. "The ones designed to accommodate ore freighters. We wanted to confirm that they're big enough for our transports to use. That could be handy when it comes time to—"

"What are you doing *here*?" Han interrupted as patiently as he could. "In this cantina? In that seat?"

"You wanted someone who can calibrate missiles," Leia said. "Here I am."

"Uh-uh," Han said firmly. "No."

"It's me or no one," Leia said, just as firmly. "I'm the only one within half an hour of here who can do it." Her eyes flicked over Han's shoulder. "And if that's your Duros, it looks like I'm just in time."

Swallowing a curse, Han turned around in his chair.

It was the Duros, all right, along with a human and a robed and hooded alien. The alien was humanoid, with black hair and yellow insectoid eyes peeking out from the hood. Even with most of the alien's face in shadow, Han could see that his skin shimmered with color as he moved, like the rainbow haze from a spray of water.

Han shifted his eyes to the human . . . and felt his heart seize up.

Because it wasn't just any human. It was Baldy, one of the two men who'd been with Mustache at the Quartzedge Port when Han and Chewie first landed on Poln Minor.

Han still didn't know who those men were, or who they were working for. But given that he'd told them he was going to the Anyat-en mines, it was a good bet they knew he and Chewie were with the Alliance.

It was an even better bet that whoever they were working for wouldn't want the Alliance knowing about that private stash of weaponry and T-47 airspeeders.

And depending on how badly they didn't want the Alliance knowing that, they might open fire right here and now. Baldy's eyes swept the room and came to a sudden halt, aimed like turbolasers at the bar.

At the big, shaggy, crowd-towering form of Chewie.

"Get ready to duck," Han ordered Leia quietly, slipping his hand casually under the table and getting a grip on his blaster. The minute the Wookiee started back to their table, Baldy would track his vector and spot Han.

Briefly, Han wondered if there might be time to get Chewie on the comlink, or otherwise wave him off. But there wasn't, and either activity would probably just draw Baldy's attention to him that much faster. He looked sideways at the bar, wishing fleetingly that Chewie had some of that Force stuff Luke had.

But to Han's surprise, he found that Chewie wasn't looking back at him. Instead, he was looking at Baldy and his friends. For a couple of seconds he and Baldy seemed to lock eyes. Then, as the bartender set a bottle on the bar in front of him, Chewie turned his back on the three by the door. He gestured, and the bartender pulled two mugs from beneath the bar and set them beside the bottle. Chewie gave Baldy one final look over his shoulder, then picked up the bottle and mugs.

Only he didn't head back to Han's table. Instead, he lumbered through the archway and disappeared into the back room.

"What's he doing?" Leia murmured.

"Saving our skins," Han murmured back, watching Baldy out of the corner of his eye. Baldy was murmuring urgently to the yellow-eyed alien, his hand on his holstered blaster, his eyes on the archway where Chewie had disappeared. The alien said something in return. Baldy nodded and headed after the Wookiee, his hand still on his blaster. The alien turned and murmured something to the Duros, who nodded and gestured toward Han.

None of the byplay had been lost on Leia. "Han?" she asked tensely.

"Just play it casual," Han told her as the Duros and alien headed toward them.

"What about Chewie?"

"He can take care of himself," Han said shortly. "Sit there and be quiet. I'll do the talking."

Normally, he knew, she would have found something snide to say to an order like that. But she remained silent. Han watched the two aliens coming toward them, also keeping an eye on Baldy as he disappeared through the archway.

Three seconds later the Duros and alien sat down at their table. "I greet you," the Duros said, gesturing to Han. "This is my friend—"

"Call me Shrike," Han interrupted. "This is Payne. I hear you need some weapons work done."

"Which of you is the expert he spoke of?" the alien said. His voice was as shimmery as his skin, with clipped edges to each of his words.

"We work together," Han said. "I load, she calibrates."

"*If* the pay is good enough," Leia added.

"I pay for speed and expertise," the alien said, focusing on her. "You can calibrate Caldorf VII and Regginis Mol interceptor missiles?"

Han felt his throat tighten. It was a trap, a trick question a real weapons programmer would spot in an instant. He should have expected something like this, and warned Leia about it.

Fortunately, she was already on top of it. "Caldorfs, yes," she said. "Good luck finding anyone who can do Regginis Mols."

"Why?" the alien asked.

"Because they stopped making those twenty years ago," Leia said. "That was a Clone Wars–era weapon. Not a very good one, either."

The alien relaxed, just slightly. "My mistake," he said. "I pay two hundred per missile mounted and calibrated. Do you wish the job?"

"Yes," Han said. "Where and when? And what do we call you?"

"Call me Ranquiv," the alien said. "We leave at once."

Beside him, Han felt Leia stir. "I'll need to stop at my room and get a few things first," she said.

"I have all you'll need," Ranquiv said. "We leave at once. Or you don't leave at all."

Han looked at Leia. Her mouth was tight, but she nodded. "Fine," he said, looking back at Ranquiv. "You've got yourself a deal."

"There is also the matter of my fee," the Duros reminded him.

"Right." Han jerked a thumb at him. "He gets another four hundred," he told Leia. "Pay him, will you?" Without waiting for a reply, he stood up. "Ready when you are."

"My transport awaits," Ranquiv said. "It will be a six-hour trip. Come."

Han felt his eyes narrow. "Six *hours?*"

"You have agreed," Ranquiv said, his shimmering voice going suddenly dark. "You may not refuse now."

"And would do so at your own risk," the Duros added warningly. "Other armed beings would come quickly at Ranquiv's order."

Han grimaced. And the first one who would answer that call would probably be Baldy, charging in from the other room. The minute he recognized Han . . . "Fine," he growled. "This just better be worth it."

Han had assumed that Ranquiv's transport would be a spacegoing vehicle, at which point six hours from Dankcamp Village could be on the far side of Poln Minor or nearly anywhere on Poln Major. But the vehicle instead turned out to be a thirty-seat speeder bus, in as bad a shape as all the rest of the machinery seemed to be down here. The bus was nearly full, but Han and Leia managed to find a pair of seats together.

They'd barely settled into them when the bus took off, maneuvering through the dim lights of the half dozen caverns that made up the city and heading out into one of the wide, main tunnels.

It was quickly clear that it wasn't going to be a particularly pleasant journey. The bus was old, the paint was peeling off the walls, and it smelled. There was also some malfunction in the left repulsorlifts' regulator circuit, and every few seconds the vehicle gave a little lurching dip to the side.

But with the rumble of the repulsorlifts filling the bus, he and Leia finally had a chance to confer in private.

"Han, what have you gotten us into?" Leia demanded, her eyes flashing ominously. "We're not heading for the Anyat-en region—even in this thing, that's less than two hours from here."

"Yeah, I know," Han conceded. "But this whole business still seems pretty shady."

"If you want to investigate shady businesses, go join CorSec," Leia said tartly. "We should have backed out."

"Oh, yeah, that would've worked," Han growled. "You know that guy Chewie decoyed away? He was one of the ones who hit us up at the Quartzedge Port three days ago. The ones who weren't there when we went back. The ones who know we're Alliance."

"Oh," Leia said in a slightly more civil tone.

"Right, *oh*," Han mimicked. "If he'd spotted us pretending to be guns for hire, Ranquiv would probably have called in all those guns the Duros promised he had waiting to jump."

"That could still happen if his friend gets away from Chewie," Leia pointed out.

"He won't," Han promised. "Not a chance. Not from Chewie."

"I hope you're right," Leia said. "Let me see if I've got this straight. You and I are headed for an unknown location, up to a thousand kilometers away, to load missiles for an unknown alien with an unknown purpose, with no one in the Alliance knowing where we are. That about cover it?"

Han thought it over. Put that way, he admitted, it sounded worse than it probably was. "Yeah, I suppose," he agreed. "Why, is that a problem?"

She gave him a single glare and then turned to gaze out the window at the utterly uninteresting rock wall flowing past outside.

Casually, Han looked around. The other passengers seemed about evenly split between hardened fringe types and young, earnest, hungry-looking kids who probably figured they could do anything with computers and were desperate to earn some money. Grimacing, he settled back into his seat. He could try to watch their route in the hope that he could find his way back if he needed to. But unless this was a real straight route, six hours of zigzagging was going to be nearly impossible to memorize or even track on his datapad.

Besides, Leia was probably planning to try that anyway. She was the senior command staff here, after all. That kind of planning was her job.

Han's job, as low-level order follower, was merely to keep up his strength and stamina for whenever senior command staff decided to issue him some orders.

Leaning back in his seat, he drew his blaster and slipped it inside his vest, folding his arms across it so that no one could accidentally walk off with it.

It would be all right. He would make sure of that. If only because Her Highness would never let him hear the end of it otherwise.

Closing his eyes, he settled down to try to get some sleep.

———————

"Slow down, Chewie," Luke said as the rumbles and roars poured from his comlink. "I can hardly understand you."

There was a short pause as Chewie took a deep breath. Then the rumbles resumed, only marginally slower.

But it was slow enough, this time, for Luke to get all of it.

"Okay, calm down," he told the Wookiee, trying to think. Han and Leia gone, no idea where they'd disappeared to, no idea even whether Chewie had gotten to the mysterious fake smuggler before he could clue in the Duros and the unknown alien as to who Han really was. "First things first. What did you do with the guy you clobbered?"

Chewie's answer was short and succinct. "Okay," Luke said. "You'd better call Leia—sorry; better call Cracken—and have him send someone to get him out of the dumpster. They might be able to question him and find out where they took Han and Leia after he comes to."

Chewie growled an acknowledgment, then another question.

"Yes, absolutely I'll come up and help," Luke promised. Though what he could do to find Han and Leia that Cracken's people couldn't do on their own, he couldn't imagine. "You call Cracken, and I'll let Axlon know I'm heading up."

He keyed off and punched in Axlon's code. The ambassador had made it clear that he wanted Luke near the palace today, but under the circumstances he would surely be willing to modify his plans.

To Luke's surprise, he wasn't.

"But it's an emergency," Luke protested. "Han and Leia have disappeared, and we don't know what kind of danger they might be in. They need me there."

"And I need you here," Axlon said flatly. "More than Cracken does."

Luke felt a tingling run through him. There was something in the man's voice . . . "Is something about to happen?" he asked carefully.

Axlon hesitated. "I don't know all the details," he said. "But I think the governor's life is in danger. Serious, immediate danger."

"Does he know?" Luke asked. "I mean, shouldn't you be telling him instead of me?"

"I've tried," Axlon said. "But he's determined to go ahead with our agreement, and says he won't hide from shadows."

Luke grimaced. Leia was like that, too. A prime target for Imperial agents, yet she always refused to stay behind and keep a low profile when there was work to be done. "Do we know anything about who it is he's not hiding from?"

"Nothing solid," Axlon said. "But it's rumored that the agent's weapon of choice is a lightsaber. In fact, I can tell you now that that's the main reason I wanted you to come here with me. The only weapon that can block a lightsaber, after all, is another lightsaber."

Luke felt his mouth drop open. Was Axlon seriously suggesting what Luke thought he was suggesting? "You *do* realize I'm not a Jedi, right?" he said carefully. "Ben barely got me started on lightsaber combat. I'm not ready to take on anyone who knows what they're doing."

"It won't come to that," Axlon assured him. "You have to understand the psychology of the situation. In general, no one carries a weapon like that unless they know how to use it. Therefore, just having you and your lightsaber in sight near the palace gate will force the agent to assume you *do* know how to fight with it, and to wonder what kind of obstacle you might be. That will force her to rethink her plan—"

"*Her* plan?" Luke asked. "The agent is a woman?"

"So I hear," Axlon said. "As I was saying, she'll have to rethink her plan, and anything that buys time is to our advantage."

Unless the agent decided to test Luke's skill before she went to the bother of changing those plans, Luke thought, grimacing.

Still, the Force was with Luke. Wasn't it?

"I'll call Cracken and tell him that we're sticking with the original plan," Axlon went on. "You just settle down and get some sleep. I want you outside, in the vicinity of the palace gate, at ten o'clock sharp tomorrow morning. Understood?"

"Understood," Luke said with a sigh. He'd already told Chewie he didn't think he could do anything to help. Chewie hadn't listened. There didn't seem much point in telling Axlon the same thing.

"Good lad," Axlon said. "Now go get some sleep." He paused, and Luke could almost see the other's tight smile. "Tomorrow, Master Skywalker, you will see the Rebellion start on the path to victory. I guarantee it."

CHAPTER ELEVEN

THE EARLY-MORNING TRAFFIC RUSH HAD FADED INTO THE STEADY BUT not road-jamming level that LaRone had seen the previous day when he and the others had first arrived in the palace area. Now, three blocks away from the palace gate, he and Marcross waited for Jade to make her move.

LaRone didn't know how Marcross felt. But personally, he felt like an idiot. An idiot standing at the center of an optical sight's cross-lines.

The full-length hooded robes he and Marcross were wearing weren't going to work. They just weren't. Never mind that robes like these were worn by lower-class workers, farmers, and traders all across the galaxy, and that he'd seen at least five other people wearing similar outfits in the past half hour. Never mind that the robes reached to the ground and the sleeves draped past his fingertips, completely covering the stormtrooper armor he and Marcross were wearing underneath them.

The problem was that their armor was *way* too bulky to pass as human physique. Even worse, every time Marcross moved, LaRone could see the brief but obvious impressions of the various armor sections pressing against the cloth. LaRone knew he was undoubtedly showing off the same impressions himself.

Jade, naturally, hadn't had the slightest qualm about throwing them to the battle dogs this way. She'd assured them that the general population never noticed things like that, especially not in a neighborhood they were already intimately familiar with. They would travel blindly on their respective errands without seeing anything beyond where their feet were striking the ground.

She had a point, LaRone supposed. But the common people weren't the population segment he was worried about. Whitestone City's citizens might ignore their environment, but he doubted the patrollers and roving stormtrooper teams would be so inattentive.

Particularly, say, those two stormtroopers who were even now coming toward them down the quiet side street where Jade had ordered them to wait.

Beside him, Marcross murmured something under his breath.

"Just stay cool," LaRone advised quietly, feeling the sweat breaking out on his skin as he tried not to stare at the approaching Imperials. "And don't move," he added. "Moving accentuates your outline."

"Like that's going to help," Marcross muttered. "Where *is* she, anyway?"

"She'll be here," LaRone assured him.

Unless, of course, Jade's *real* plan was simply to set up him and Marcross to be captured. A pair of stormtrooper deserters might easily make enough of a diversionary fuss to let her slip into the palace undetected.

Twenty meters in front of the approaching stormtroopers, a hooded figure emerged from a narrow alley, moving with the careful fragility of extreme old age. The person started to turn to the right, caught sight of the stormtroopers—

And abruptly turned and fled back into the alley, at a considerably enhanced rate of speed.

The stormtroopers, LaRone reflected, were only human. The very sight of fugitive behavior was like throwing raw meat to a rancor. "Halt!" one of them called in his mechanically filtered vocoder voice as both of them took off after the figure. They disappeared into the alley, their BlasTech E-11s lowered into hip-firing position.

LaRone turned to Marcross. "Should we give her a minute?" he asked.

Marcross wrinkled his nose. "She'll probably be mad if we show up late," he pointed out.

"Right," LaRone said, nodding. "Let's go."

They found the two stormtroopers sprawled on the ground near the middle of the alley, more or less out of sight from either end. Jade had pushed back her hood and was crouched over one of them, her hands spread on either side of his faceplate as she gazed intently into his eyepieces.

"Dead?" LaRone asked as he and Marcross came up to her.

"Sonic," she said, her voice sounding distant as she focused on the task at hand. "Delivered up under the helmet rim. They'll be all right in a couple of hours."

LaRone nodded. Jade was ruthless enough with the traitors she was sent to deal with, but he'd seen her go out of her way to keep the innocent and the loyal out of her line of fire. "Get busy on the other one's ID," she added.

Marcross was already kneeling beside the second unconscious stormtrooper, his removal tool slipped under the man's left shoulder piece. The white-on-white trooper ID marks were nearly undetectable to normal eyesight, even at close range, but were easily visible to another stormtrooper's vision enhancements.

Along with its other covert equipment, the Suwantek had included several false shoulder IDs. Up to now, though, LaRone had always opted for the team to use unmarked shoulder pieces instead. It had seemed preferable to risk the awkwardness of having to explain how their IDs had worn off to facing the instant suspicion of showing up with the markings of a unit that happened to be in an entirely different part of the galaxy.

Here, given Jade's plan, they had no choice but to wear IDs.

Luckily, they also knew which IDs to use.

Marcross had just finished detaching the shoulder piece when Jade gave a sharp nod. "Got it," she said. Shifting her hands to the sides of the stormtrooper's helmet, she started to ease it off over his head. "Marcross?"

"Clear," Marcross said, lifting up the detached shoulder piece as he moved over to the stormtrooper Jade had just unhelmeted. Handing the shoulder piece to LaRone, he knelt down and started working on the other trooper's shoulder. As he worked, LaRone pulled Marcross's robe open and started fastening the new ID in place, watching Jade out of the corner of his eye as she moved to the trooper Marcross had just finished with.

Along with the shoulder IDs, the other half of a successful masquerade was getting onto the palace comlink grid. And that was far and away the trickier half. Stormtrooper helmets included a tongue switch, which had to be tripped before removing the helmet. Otherwise, the comlink would instantly scramble both the frequency rotation sequence and the encryption suite, leaving it all but useless.

For most would-be infiltrators, that was an insurmountable hurdle. But not for Jade. She had the Force, and she knew exactly where the tongue switch was located. A bit of telekinesis, a delicate tweaking of the switch, and the helmet could be removed with its comm system intact.

Two minutes later, with both helmets removed and both shoulder pieces in place, LaRone and Marcross were ready to go. "Double-check the helmets," Jade ordered as she handed them over. "Make sure I got it right."

Marcross nodded and slid the helmet over his head. A few seconds of listening to the palace security chatter was all it took. "Yes, we're in," he confirmed, locking the helmet securely to his collar. "But it doesn't sound like we're on the same system as the gate guards."

"Shouldn't be a problem—you'll be talking to them in person anyway," Jade reminded him, giving each of their shoulder pieces a final check. "Put these two in that storeroom over there to sleep off the sonic—I've already sliced the lock for you. Then plug in your private frequency and make sure Brightwater and the others are in position in case we need a fast breakout. Which of you has it?"

"I do," Marcross said, reaching behind him and tapping the cylindrical thermal detonator at the small of his back. It was slightly but noticeably longer than the standard stormtrooper version, which in LaRone's opinion made it as much a potential threat to them as their robe-covered armor had been earlier.

As usual, Jade had waved away his fears, contending that the same familiarity that kept citizens from noting anything subtly different on familiar streets would likewise keep stormtroopers from noticing subtle differences on their even more familiar armor.

She'd been right about the robe. LaRone hoped she was right about the thermal detonator pack, too.

"Good," Jade said, handing a small, flat disk to LaRone. "Here's the sonic. If you need to use it, remember that you need to slip it up beneath the helmet rim, double-circle-side inward, and squeeze the edge."

"Right," LaRone said. She'd gone through this twice with them all the previous night, but it never hurt to double- and triple-check with unfamiliar weapons.

"When will we know when to move?" Marcross asked.

"Just keep listening," Jade said, opening her brown robe the rest of the way to reveal a loose blue-and-silver ankle-length dress underneath. "Trust me, you'll know. And don't be late."

She went over to the side of the alley, dropping the robe and picking up a small bag lying among the bits of garbage there. With the bag tucked under her arm, she strode briskly away.

"What do you think?" Marcross asked quietly.

LaRone grimaced behind his faceplate. "So far she's been right about everything," he said.

Marcross grunted. "Let's just hope we're in a position to collect the pieces if she starts not being right. Come on, let's get these guys out of sight."

Landspeeder theft was a serious business in the Empire, particularly out here on the edges where vehicles—especially decent ones—were scarcer than on the older and more populous worlds. One of the results was that theft protection systems, while less sophisticated than those on Imperial Center, were employed much more consistently.

Not that security systems of any sort made much of a difference to Mara Jade.

She had already walked through the neighborhood earlier that morning and found what she needed: an open-topped landspeeder like the one the teenager had been driving yesterday, conveniently parked along a quiet side street. Mara had it unlocked and started in thirty seconds, and drove off to her chosen insertion point a kilometer from the palace gate. Setting the landspeeder on idle, she pulled a wide-brimmed hat from her bag, unfolded it, and put it on, stuffing most of her red-gold hair inside.

The bag's other item, the controller to the toy airspeeder, went onto the passenger seat, with the empty bag laid casually over it.

The next phase of the plan, unfortunately, wasn't under her direct control. She had to wait for another open-topped vehicle to come by, traveling in the proper direction, with a driver and no other passengers who might slant the witness reports.

But the Force was with her. Five minutes after settling down she spotted the perfect vehicle approaching from behind: a low-backed speeder truck with an open cab. She waited until it passed, then pulled smoothly into the traffic flow directly behind it.

Ahead, the spur leading to the palace gate was coming up fast. Stretching out in the Force, Mara got a grip on the speeder truck's wheel. As the truck reached the spur, she wrenched the wheel hard over, sending the truck careening onto the short road heading for the gate. A second later, as she also reached the spur, she spun her own wheel and headed in after him.

The truck driver managed to overcome his stunned surprise at his vehicle's erratic behavior and brake before he hit the gate. He had barely enough time to heave a sigh of relief when Mara slammed full-tilt into his rear crash plate, the impact lurching the truck another three meters forward.

Yesterday's landspeeder incident had been a perplexing but isolated event. Today's, though, made it part of a pattern, and Mara knew how security forces were trained to react to patterns. She'd barely shut down her engine when she and the trucker were both swarmed by guards, both the livery-wearing group and a dozen stormtroopers who streamed briskly out through the personnel door by the main gate.

One of the liveried guards got to Mara first. "Hands in the air," he ordered, his blaster steady on her chest as he jogged up to the side of her stolen speeder.

"I didn't do this," Mara protested as she raised her hands. "My wheel just *turned*. All by itself."

"Sure it did," the guard growled, gesturing with his free hand. "Come on—out."

A minute later Mara was standing beside the landspeeder, her hands still raised, watching yet more stormtroopers emerge from the palace compound. The speeder truck driver was also standing beside his vehicle, a similar crowd of security personnel gathered around him as he stuttered the same story Mara had already given her group.

"I tell you, this wasn't my fault," Mara went on, watching the liveried guard's face as his helmet comlink murmured into his ear. There was a slight hardening of his expression. "Look, I'm late for a very important meeting," she added, starting to edge along the side of the vehicle. "You can keep my speeder and check it for yourself—I'll come back for it later."

"Stay where you are!" the guard snapped, taking a long step to cut off her escape. "You're not the registered owner of this vehicle."

"Yes, thank you, I know that," Mara said in a tone of exaggerated patience. "It belongs to my friend Carolle. Go ahead and call her—she'll tell you she let me borrow it."

"*There* she is," a flat stormtrooper vocoder voice came from the right.

Mara turned. LaRone and Marcross were marching toward her clump of guards, their gait and postures stiff and determined. "Hold that woman— we saw her shoplifting from an electronics store."

"An *electronics* store?" the guard echoed, frowning as he shifted his gaze from Mara to the landspeeder itself.

"That's ridiculous," Mara insisted, mentally crossing her fingers as she watched the guard's eyes move methodically around the passenger compartment. If necessary, LaRone or Marcross could perform the next step, but it would be better if an official palace security man figured it out on his own. "He's lying. I've never stolen a thing in my life."

"Quiet," the guard ordered as his eyes fell on the crumpled bag lying casually on the front passenger seat. "Watch her," he ordered the stormtroopers, and walked around the rear of the landspeeder to the passenger side. Carefully, he lifted the bag, revealing the controller for the toy airspeeder Mara had bought yesterday. "What's this?" he asked.

"How should I know?" Mara countered. "I told you, I borrowed it from my friend."

"Uh-huh." The guard picked up the controller and turned it over in his hand, studying the controls and peering suspiciously at the extra electronic components Mara had attached randomly to the top and sides. He set his fingers on the controls, glancing quickly at Mara to see her reaction. Mara kept her face expressionless, stretching out with the Force. Tentatively, the guard moved one of the controls.

And in perfect sync, Mara twitched the speeder truck's control wheel.

The guard's head jerked hard toward the truck. So did the truck driver's and several of the troopers guarding him. "I didn't do that," the driver protested frantically.

"*I* did," Mara's guard called to them, holding up the controller and pointing to Mara. "Binders. Now."

One of the stormtroopers stepped forward, pulling a set of binders from one of his utility pouches. "And hobble her," the guard added. "This one's something special."

A moment later Mara's hands were shackled in front of her and her ankles were fastened together by twenty centimeters of chain. "You two: take her to interrogation," the guard said, pointing at two of the palace stormtroopers. "And take this to the lab," he added, handing the controller to one of the other stormtroopers.

"We'll take her," LaRone offered, taking a step forward.

"They'll do it," the guard said. "You're on patrol."

"*Our* arrest," LaRone said firmly. "*We'll* take her in."

The guard glared at him. But he'd probably had enough experience with stormtroopers to know that they were just as ambitious as any other military professionals. Denying them the chance to add a glowing entry to their service record would make him a couple of enemies, and no one wanted that. "Fine—you can go along," he growled. "But I won't be answerable to your commander if you get in trouble for being off your patrol."

They set off toward the gate, the palace stormtroopers walking in front of Mara, LaRone and Marcross walking behind her. It was a slightly awkward processional, given the hobble's limitation on Mara's usually longer stride. But by the time they reached the gate and shifted to single file to get through the door, she'd accustomed herself to the new rhythm.

She hadn't been able to see into the grounds yesterday, but she'd assumed at the time that Ferrouz would have doubled or tripled the standard palace guard. Now, as she and her escort headed down the walkway, she discovered that, if anything, she'd underestimated the governor's level of caution. There were at least thirty stormtroopers patrolling the area, including several pairs of the speeder scouts that she'd also seen guarding the approaches to the white-stone mound towering over the palace.

It was just as well, Mara reflected, that she hadn't tried to get in by simply breaching the wall.

The main palace doors were large and elaborate, with the same decorative pattern that she'd seen on the entry gate. But suspected spies and saboteurs apparently weren't given such elegant treatment. Her stormtrooper escort instead angled off toward a smaller side door, half hidden among a stand of sculpted bushes. As they approached, the door opened and three men stepped outside to meet them, all three wearing the gray uniforms Mara had seen yesterday. The oldest of the three, who Mara could now see was wearing a major's insignia, was the middle-aged man who'd come out of the courtyard during yesterday's incident to interrogate the teenager.

"As you were," the major said as Mara and her escort came up to him. "We'll take it from here."

"We have to make a report," LaRone said firmly.

"Then go make it," the major said, his eyes narrowing as he studied Mara. "I remember you. You were at the tapcaf across the street yesterday when that other landspeeder tried to crash the gate."

"I have no idea what you're talking about," Mara said stiffly.

"Of course not," the major said, looking back at the stormtroopers. "I said you were dismissed. Return to your assigned duties."

"Sir—" LaRone began.

"Take her," the major ordered, gesturing to his two men as he turned his back on the stormtroopers.

Mara half turned toward LaRone, inclined her head microscopically toward the bushes clustered around them. Then, as the two gray-suited guards took her upper arms, she let them guide her to the open door. The major stepped aside to let them pass and then followed, sealing the door behind them with a data-card–sized passkey.

The palace floor plans that the Emperor had sent Mara hadn't included any listing of interrogation rooms or holding cells—hardly surprising, given that such facilities weren't supposed to exist in high-level governmental residences. It was usually up to each individual local ruler to make whatever quiet and strictly unofficial arrangements he chose in that area.

Mara had seen many such facilities over the years, ranging from deep, terrifying dungeons to light, airy containment rooms designed to lull prisoners into a relaxed sense of false hope. But such minor details apart, the one thing all interrogation specialists had in common was the desire to keep their activities as secret and unobserved as possible.

This one was no exception. The hallway Mara found herself in was short, unoccupied, and without any doors at all lining the sides. Besides the door they'd entered by, there was only a single turbolift door twenty meters away at the hallway's far end. It was the perfect place for a prisoner to disappear, possibly never to be heard from again.

It was also the perfect place for that same prisoner to make her escape.

Mara let them walk her halfway down the hall, giving the palace stormtroopers outside plenty of time to start back to their posts and hopefully be out of earshot of anything that happened in here. Then, looking down at the binders on her wrists, she used the Force to pop them free. As they clattered to the floor, she reached over to the blaster of the guard to her left and fired the weapon, still in its holster, along his right leg.

And as he bellowed in surprise and pain, she yanked the blaster from its holster and swung it hard against the throat of the man to her right. She continued her turn as he collapsed to the floor, bringing the weapon to bear on the major only now beginning to react behind her. "Don't," she warned.

The major froze, his hand on his still holstered blaster, his face tight. "You can't escape," he warned, his voice under rigid control.

"Maybe I don't want to," Mara said. The guard whose leg she'd shot started to stagger toward her, and she shifted her aim away from the major just long enough to slam the side of her blaster across the guard's throat, sending him sprawling to the floor the way she had the other one. "Maybe I like living here," she added, bringing the weapon back to the major. "How about you?"

The major snarled something under his breath. But he was smart enough to know when further resistance would be a waste of his life. Still glaring, he lifted his hands and put them on his head.

"Thank you," Mara said. Dropping her aim, she blasted through the hobble chain linking her ankles. "Blaster and comlink on the floor."

Gingerly, the major drew his blaster with two fingers and lowered it to the floor beside him, following it up with his comlink. "Now your passkey," Mara continued.

"It won't do you any good," the major growled as he dropped the passkey beside the other items. "Governor Ferrouz doesn't rely on locks and droid sentinels. You'll never get to him—never. And you *certainly* won't get out of the palace alive."

"I appreciate the warning," Mara said. "Two steps back and lie down on your stomach, face to the wall."

Glowering, he obeyed. Mara picked up the passkey and retraced her steps to the door they'd entered through. Slipping the passkey into the slot, she keyed the release.

The door slid open. "LaRone?" she called softly, her eyes still on the major.

There was a breath of air, and the two stormtroopers slipped through the doorway into the corridor. "You all right?" LaRone asked. "We heard a shot."

"I'm fine," Mara assured him. "Give me the sonic—this blaster doesn't have a stun setting."

LaRone handed it over, and Mara headed back to the major. A minute later all three gray-suited men were asleep.

"Well, this looks nicely ominous," Marcross commented as Mara returned to them. "One exit, no doors, no monitors."

"Typical interrogation center entrance," Mara said, gesturing for him to turn around. "Consider yourself lucky you haven't seen one before."

"What happens now?" LaRone asked. "I hope you're not thinking of trying that turbolift."

"Hardly," Mara said, unfastening the endcap of Marcross's oversized thermal detonator casing and pulling out the lightsaber she'd concealed inside the empty shell. "Interrogation turbolifts typically only have two stops, and we're already at the less unpleasant of them. Is there anywhere out there you can hang around for a while without being challenged?"

"There's a guard station just north of the main gate," LaRone said. "Or we could just pretend we're one of the patrol teams. I doubt anyone will challenge us."

"At least not right away," Marcross added. "Eventually, someone's bound to notice that their stormtrooper count is off."

"If and when that happens, tell them Major Pakrie said he wanted you on courtyard patrol," Mara said, squinting at the name on her borrowed passkey. "No one will be able to prove you wrong for the next couple of hours."

"Assuming no one else wanders in here and finds him," Marcross said.

"Don't worry," Mara said, resealing Marcross's detonator casing. "I'll signal you if and when I need you."

"Any idea what that signal will be?" LaRone asked.

"Not yet," Mara said. "You'll know it when it happens."

"Along with half the city?"

"I'll try to keep it a little less visible than that," Mara said with a touch of dry humor. "Go on, get going."

A minute later they were outside, and the door was once again sealed. Mara took a quick look around, then ignited her lightsaber.

As she'd already noted, her plans hadn't included the palace's unofficial interrogation section. But they *had* shown what had been here before Ferrouz or his predecessors had retrofitted the area. This part of the palace had originally been a hospitality wing, with guest suites, private contemplation and entertainment rooms, and even a separate kitchen with human and droid chefs on call to attend to off-hour appetites. This particular corridor had once led from the kitchen and servant droid stations to a three-car turbolift cluster, continuing on into the rest of the palace.

Mara also knew that even with a completely sealed interrogation section like this one, most governors instinctively tried to keep prying eyes and ears at a distance. This implied that the kitchen and droid stations on either side of her were probably closed down and abandoned, which furthermore suggested that a quick exit from the corridor was only a couple of lightsaber cuts away.

The problem, as Marcross had pointed out, was that there was no guarantee someone wouldn't come looking for Major Pakrie and his men, either from the courtyard or from the underground interrogation room itself. A hole in the wall would be something not even the dimmest security recruit would miss.

But fewer people bothered to look up, especially when their eyes and hands were busy with something else—something such as lining up a passkey with a door's security slot.

The hallway was a bit above average height, but the ceiling was still easily reachable without Mara having to jump. Standing directly in front of the door, she swung her lightsaber blade in a conical pattern, cutting a beveled circle through the slab of duracrete above her. Closing down the weapon, she stretched out with the Force and lifted the plug she'd just cut, moving it away from the opening and setting it down off to the side. She leapt upward, catching the edge of the hole, and pulled herself cautiously through.

She was in the relaxation room of a nicely appointed guest suite. From the drawn shades and the faintly musty smell, it was clear the room had been unoccupied for some time.

That probably also meant that the room's computer wasn't active. But there would be other rooms nearby where she could tap into the palace system.

She dropped back to the corridor below and, using the Force, lifted the unconscious security men one by one up through the opening. The last of the three was a bit wobbly—for some reason, lifting bodies always seemed to take more out of her than moving the equivalent amount of inert matter. But she made it without dropping him. Then, jumping back up to join them, she lowered the duracrete plug back into place.

It was far from perfect. But the beveling would keep the slab firmly in place, and her cut was neat enough that even if someone spotted it, they might wonder if it was something that had always been there that they simply had never noticed before. By the time uncertainty and hesitation ran its course, the job should be finished.

And someone in the palace would have received Imperial justice.

In the dim light seeping around the closed curtains she discarded her hat and stripped off the blue-and-silver dress, readjusting the long, dark green tunic and leggings she had on underneath. It was a neutral but professional outfit, a style currently in vogue all across the Empire, and one she'd seen a handful of the palace's female employees wearing as they left for home the previous evening. She tore out the collapsed courier's shoulder pouch that had been concealed in the blue dress's inner lining, folded it back into its proper shape, and secured her lightsaber inside.

And with that, she was ready to roam the palace hallways.

The door had been double-locked, probably when it was first closed down, which normally prevented it from being opened from either side. But Major Pakrie's passkey had been coded even for off-limits areas and popped the lock without trouble.

A moment later Mara was moving silently down the hallway toward the murmurings of life and activity. Time to find herself a computer.

It was a quarter after ten, and Luke had just settled himself by one of the shops across the street from the governor's palace when he saw Axlon emerge from the crowd and head toward the small pedestrian door at the side of the main gate.

An unpleasant tingle ran through him. Axlon had his fancy pass from Governor Ferrouz, and so far neither the roaming stormtroopers nor the handful of men in bright blue-and-red uniforms had seemed inclined to do more than watch the older man's approach. But that didn't mean that the crowd milling around the area wasn't going to have its curiosity aroused if they saw a plainly dressed stranger just walk into the most secure place on Poln Major.

More important, how would the Imperial agent react if she, too, was wandering around here in the crowd?

Luke frowned, a second tingle shivering across his skin. For that matter, why was there a crowd outside the palace at all?

Maybe it was just the two landspeeders that had apparently crashed into each other in front of the gate. Luke hadn't been here when that happened, but it must have been fairly recent, given that gray-uniformed men were still working on the vehicles under the watchful gaze of a dozen stormtroopers.

But the crowd didn't seem like the usual collection of gawking onlookers that gathered at any disaster or near disaster. There was a restlessness to this crowd, a sense of anticipation that Luke could feel even without drawing on the Force. And as he stood there trying to look casual, it seemed to him that more and more people were sending lingering looks in his direction.

Something was about to happen. Maybe it was something the locals didn't want strangers to witness.

Luke grimaced. Common sense said to get out of there, to slip away and find someplace a little less conspicuous from which to watch. But Axlon was giving the orders, and Axlon had told him to be here.

To wait for an Imperial agent to show her face.

Luke swallowed hard. It made no sense. If the agent had even a modicum of lightsaber training, she would be able to cut Luke into pieces without breaking a sweat.

Unless Axlon knew something Luke didn't. Maybe the agent carried a lightsaber purely as a bluff, and had no more ability to actually fight with it than Luke did. Alternatively, maybe Axlon was right about the very existence of Luke's lightsaber slowing her down and buying Axlon the time he needed for whatever it was he and Governor Ferrouz needed time for.

Unfortunately, despite what Han seemed to think, Luke wasn't always let in on all the subtleties of the orders he was given.

But he *had* been given an order. And so he would wait here, until he received orders to do otherwise.

Ten twenty. Axlon reached the door and offered his pass to the guard. The guard plugged it into a datapad, then handed it back and said something on a comlink. The door opened, and Axlon went through.

There was still no sign of the mysterious Imperial agent who was supposedly here to stop him.

So where in blazes *was* she?

With a final jerk that jarred Han out of his fitful sleep, the speeder bus came to a halt.

He blinked as the repulsorlifts gave a final throaty growl and lowered the vehicle to the ground. They'd arrived just outside a large mined-out cavern, bigger even than the ones Dankcamp Village was built into.

Squatting in neat lines as far across the cavern as Han could see were ships. Decent-sized ones, too. They were about thirty-eight meters long, a bit bigger than the *Falcon*, with smooth curves and long, deep grooves running fore-to-aft along each of the sloping wings.

He nudged Leia. "Wake up, sweetheart," he murmured. "We're here."

"I'm not asleep," she murmured back, with a slightly slurred voice that told him that she *had*, in fact, been asleep until his nudge. "Where's *here*?"

"I don't know," Han said grimly. "But whoever these guys are, they came loaded for Togorian. Those things out there are warships."

Leia sat up a bit straighter. "How do you know?" she asked, peering out the window. "I've never seen anything like them before."

"Add it up," he told her. "Those grooves along the wings? That's the passive, low-tech version of enhanced slipstream stabilizers. Those weapons struts at the wing interfaces are ribbed like original equipment, not add-ons. That tall fin poking up from the top probably holds a set of vertically racked laser cannons, and that bulb all the way at the top is a dedicated targeting sensor. You can't see much of the sublights from this angle, but you can see enough of the nozzle flare to know they're big and have wide separation."

He pointed toward the nearest ship's bow. "And the only reason for a crosshatch wraparound cockpit canopy is to give a pilot maximum protection while still giving him a two-seventy viewing angle. No, they're warships, all right."

At the front of the bus, Ranquiv got to his feet. "All persons out," he called, his yellow insect's eyes glittering strangely in the bus's dim overhead light. "Your work now begins."

There was a general shuffle as the passengers stood up and began filing down the aisle to the door. "I don't know what's going on," Leia said quietly to Han. "But I *can* tell you we're nowhere near a thousand kilometers away from Dankcamp Village. I'm guessing we're no more than fifty or a hundred from Anyat-en."

Han stared out at the ships, the back of his neck tingling unpleasantly. "How do you know?"

"I was tracking the turns for the first couple of hours," she said. "We were doing a lot of weaving in and out, but we didn't seem to be getting much real distance." She nodded out the window. "I think they just don't want us knowing where we are."

"Yeah, well, if I had all these things stashed away down here, I wouldn't want anyone knowing that, either," Han agreed grimly.

"So what do we do?" Leia asked. "Try to get out of here and hope we can find our way back?"

Han leaned closer to her, trying to get a better look out the window. There were at least a dozen more of the black-haired, yellow-eyed aliens gathering in a loose circle near the front of their speeder bus, plus probably twenty other humans moving around among the warships.

Naturally, the whole bunch of them were armed.

"Han—" Leia began crossly, trying to lean away from him.

"We're going to have to stay for a while," Han said, pulling away from her and standing up. "Let's try to figure out what's going on, and look for an opening."

"An opening to do what?"

Han grimaced. "Don't worry," he assured her. "I'll figure something out."

CHAPTER TWELVE

With a sigh, Mara closed down the last of the files and shut down her borrowed computer. She'd hoped, she really had, that Ferrouz would prove innocent of the charges the Emperor had leveled against him. She'd wanted to believe that such a rising political figure had simply been duped, that the resources of the palace had been manipulated by someone else for their own advantage.

But the records were clear. Ferrouz had sent the first contact messages to the Rebel Alliance. He'd handled all the subsequent long-range negotiations as to sites and resources, discussing with Mon Mothma and General Carlist Rieekan all the quid pro quos of a full-stage political and economic agreement.

And to top it all off, the governor had personally gone to a local cantina only four days earlier to meet with the man the Alliance had sent in to finalize the plans.

She grimaced. First Choard, now Ferrouz. Was this a sign of things to come, a warning that the Emperor's New Order was starting to crack at the seams? Or was it simply a coincidence that two ambitious governors had decided to make individual bids for power at roughly the same time?

Mara didn't know. But one thing that was certain: treason could not be permitted to fester. It had to be dealt with, quickly and cleanly.

A governor's office and inner sanctum were always guarded, usually by a handpicked cadre of the governor's most competent and trusted people. But there were always ways to get through those final defenses. Some offices had drop ceilings, with enough space between the decorative and the real that a properly equipped agent could slip in that way. Nearly every governor also had a secret door and emergency exit, which could often be accessed for purposes of infiltration.

And sometimes, you could simply walk in the front door.

The computer had flagged the arrival of one Master Vestin Axlon at the gate just as Mara finished reading the last of the comm transcripts. Axlon's pass, she'd noted, was a suspiciously vague one, offering universal access and carrying the governor's personal authorization. Possibly he was Ferrouz's Rebel contact. Certainly he was someone no one would question once he was inside the building.

He would do nicely.

Axlon and the two palace security men escorting him had reached the turbolift leading to Ferrouz's fourth-floor office complex when Mara arrived. "I'll take it from here," she said briskly as she came up to them.

"Excuse me?" the senior guard, a lieutenant, asked.

"I said I'll take it from here," Mara repeated. "I'm to escort Master Axlon the rest of the way to Governor Ferrouz. Major Pakrie's orders."

The lieutenant made a little sniffing sound. Apparently, Pakrie's name didn't carry much weight among his troops. "We'll need to see your authorization."

"It was verbal," Mara said, pulling out her comlink. In front of them the turbolift door slid open, and she strode toward it. "The governor's waiting—we'll sort it out on the way." As she passed Axlon, she caught his arm and pulled him away from the guards and into the car with her.

It was instantly clear that neither guard was expecting anything so casually audacious, and for half a second both of them simply stood there gaping. Then they abruptly broke their paralysis and hurriedly clambered in with Mara and Axlon. "Hold on there," the lieutenant said sternly as he grabbed Axlon's other arm, clearly prepared to use force if necessary to get the man away from her.

For the second time in as many seconds a flash of bewilderment crossed his face as Mara simply let go of Axlon without struggle or argument. She keyed her comlink, lifting her hand for silence. "Give me a minute," she said. "The major will straighten this out."

The lieutenant squared his shoulders. "I have to insist—" He trailed off as Mara flashed him a hard-eyed look.

Major Pakrie, not surprisingly, hadn't answered the call by the time the turbolift car stopped. "Where *is* he?" Mara ground out to the universe at large as she jammed the comlink back into her belt and increased the level of simmering fury she was working hard to radiate. The key to keeping people from asking questions, she'd long ago learned, was to make any such questioning look more dangerous than it was likely to be worth. As long as she then kept her actions below the suspicion-trigger level, the same people who'd already decided not to ask would usually decide not to get in her way, either. "Fine," she growled as the car door opened, revealing another door ten meters away flanked by two guards and a clerk at an appointment desk. "We'll deliver him together."

"Yes, ma'am," the lieutenant said, relief in his voice at having found a compromise that would permit him to carry out his orders without simultaneously annoying an unknown but clearly connected person. Beckoning to Axlon, he and his partner stepped out of the car and headed toward the guarded door. Axlon strode out after them, with Mara taking her place behind him.

But then her whole stance, expression, and demeanor suddenly changed. Instead of the arrogant Imperial official she'd played for the first set of guards, she was now the lowly personal assistant, trailing after her employer with the quiet efficiency and quieter resignation of someone who knows she will never be anything more than a servant and helper to others.

And as she stretched out to the Force, she could see that the guards flanking Ferrouz's door had completely bought her act. Axlon, whom they would have been alerted to expect, had apparently brought an assistant whom no one had thought worth mentioning to them.

"Master Axlon to see Governor Ferrouz," the lieutenant said briskly as they approached.

"Yes," the receptionist said, her voice carefully neutral as she reached beneath her desk and triggered the door release. From the tension in her tone, Mara guessed that she either knew or strongly suspected who the visitor was, and didn't much care for the company her employer was keeping. "He's expecting you."

The lieutenant nodded and gestured to his partner. They stopped, stepping to either side out of the way as Axlon walked between them and the door guards and through the open door. Mara, still half a step back, went right in after him.

The lieutenant's expression, Mara reflected, would have been interesting to see. But she didn't give him the chance to show it to her. Glancing to the side as she cleared the door, she stretched out to the Force and hit the inside control, sliding the door shut again behind her. Another telekinetic twitch, and the door was locked.

The room she and Axlon had come into turned out to be a small waiting room equipped with couches, low tables, and a large transparisteel cylinder in the center inhabited by brilliantly colored butterflies. Five meters past the column, the door to Ferrouz's office itself was already open. "Come in, Master Axlon," a voice called.

Axlon continued forward. Mara stayed at his heels, still wearing her assistant's persona.

A moment later, she got her first look at the man she'd been sent here to kill.

Holos and vids, in Mara's experience, seldom captured the full essence of a person. Such was again the case here. On the surface, Governor Ferrouz certainly looked like his holos, with his lined but still-boyish face and thick brown hair that always seemed slightly mussed. But now, in person, Mara could see an overlay of tension to his face, a deep sadness the holos hadn't shown. His eyes were on Axlon as he and Mara came through his door, shifting almost unwillingly to Mara. "Good to see you again," he continued, rising slowly to his feet. "Who's your associate?"

Axlon turned, his jaw dropping as he saw that Mara had come in with him. "What are you—this is a private meeting."

"Go back into the waiting room, Master Axlon," Mara ordered. "I have business with the governor."

Axlon shot a hooded look at Ferrouz, then turned back to Mara, clamping his mouth firmly shut again. "What's this about?"

"The waiting room," Mara said, nodding her head back to the open door. "I won't tell you again."

"Go ahead, Master Axlon," Ferrouz said, his voice under rigid control. "Close the door behind you."

Axlon's throat worked. "As you wish, Your Excellency," he said. With a final look at Mara, he turned and retreated to the waiting room.

Mara didn't give him the chance to obey Ferrouz's order about closing the door. Stretching out to the Force, she did that herself.

She turned back to Ferrouz, half expecting to find a blaster in his hand. But he was just standing quietly, his hands empty. "Are you who I think you are?" he asked quietly.

"I'm the Emperor's justice," Mara said, striding across the soft carpet toward him. As she did so, she opened the pouch at her side and withdrew her lightsaber. "Is there some reason you're expecting justice to come calling?"

"I hardly think you need to ask that question," Ferrouz said. The tension was gone from his voice, a melancholy resignation in its place.

"No, I don't," Mara said. She pressed the lightsaber's activation stud, and with a *snap-hiss* the magenta blade appeared. "You're accused of treason, Governor Bidor Ferrouz. Of conspiring to hand over land and equipment belonging to the Galactic Empire to the Rebel Alliance. Do you deny these charges?"

"No," Ferrouz said. "Am I permitted to plead extenuating circumstances?"

"Not for treason," Mara said flatly. "The Emperor recognizes no excuses. Neither do I."

Ferrouz let out a quiet sigh. "No, I suppose not."

Mara stepped up to the front of the desk, putting herself within range of Ferrouz. "Judgment has been passed, Governor Bidor Ferrouz," she said formally, lifting her humming lightsaber high. "Have you any final words to say in your defense?"

"I have no defense," Ferrouz said. "But I do have a request."

Mara frowned. Pleas, excuses, and curses were all familiar parts of a condemned criminal's final moments. Requests weren't. "What sort of request?"

Ferrouz took a deep breath. "That once you've dispensed justice," he said, "you'll find my wife and daughter, and free them."

Mara felt her eyes narrow. There had been several notes in the records, she remembered now, where Ferrouz had asked his security staff to track his wife's comlink usage. At the time, it hadn't seemed important to her mission. "Explain."

"Three weeks ago my wife and daughter disappeared after returning from a shopping trip," Ferrouz said, his voice shaking with emotion. "The kidnappers sent me a holo of them in binders, along with a list of instructions." He swallowed hard. "This deal with the Rebellion was one of them."

"Are you saying the Rebels *kidnapped* your family?"

"Actually, I don't think it was them," Ferrouz said. His eyes flicked to the humming lightsaber, then back to Mara's face. "I think they're being manipulated the same way I am."

"By whom?"

"I don't know," Ferrouz said. "The note was sent by someone calling himself Warlord Nuso Esva. But who he is—or whether he exists at all—I haven't been able to discover."

For a long moment, Mara gazed hard at him, stretching out to the Force to try to read the emotions behind those tortured eyes. Treason was still treason . . . but if Ferrouz was really being coerced, it was worth holding off on his death sentence until she looked into it. "Do you still have the note?" she asked.

"Yes," Ferrouz said, reaching to his desktop and picking up a data card. He hesitated, then placed it in Mara's outstretched hand. "Please be careful with it," he said. "It's . . . it may be the last picture I ever have of them."

"I'll be careful," Mara promised as she slipped the data card inside her tunic. "Is there a time limit on his demands?"

"Just a general schedule," Ferrouz said. "Nuso Esva seems more concerned in getting everything done right than in getting it done quickly."

"Really," Mara said thoughtfully. "Interesting."

"Why interesting?" Ferrouz asked. "Does that mean something?"

"It might," Mara said. In fact, it meant or at least implied something rather important. But she was hardly going to share that thought with an admitted traitor. "All right, here's what we're going to do. I'm going to leave the palace and start looking into this. You're going to stay here and continue to play Nuso Esva's game."

She reached across the desk and picked up his datapad. "You'll also let me know *immediately* if he or any representative contacts you," she continued, balancing it in the crook of her arm and punching in her comlink number. "Needless to say, you won't mention this to anyone."

"I understand," Ferrouz said, a bit hesitantly. "What about the guards and my receptionist outside? They saw you come in."

"There are also the three guards I had to take out," Mara told him. "One of them is a Major Pakrie, who by the way has no business holding that rank if he doesn't know proper prisoner escort procedure."

"He's somewhat new to the job," Ferrouz murmured.

"It shows," Mara said. "You can tell Pakrie and all the rest of them that I'm an investigator checking on reports of Rebel activity in your sector, and that I decided to check out palace security while I was here. If they don't buy it, let me know and I'll throw together a preliminary report you can show them."

"They'll buy it," Ferrouz said firmly. "May I ask where the major and his men are?"

"Sleeping off a sonic in the guest suite above the interrogation room entrance," Mara said. "You can send someone to collect them after I leave."

"I'll do that." Ferrouz hesitated. "Agent, I'm . . . thank you."

"Don't thank me yet, Governor," Mara warned. "Understand that if your story doesn't check out, I *will* be back."

"Of course," Ferrouz said. "Understand in turn that all that matters to me is my family's safety. If you can bring them back, I'll accept whatever punishment you feel is necessary."

"Yes, you will," Mara said. "I'll check in with you if and when I find anything."

Ferrouz nodded, pulling another data card from a rack and handing it to her. "Here's my comlink information and my personal encryption."

Both of which Mara already had, of course. But it seemed impolite not to take the card anyway. "Right," she said, sliding it into her tunic with the other one. "I'll be in touch."

Closing down her lightsaber, she turned and headed back toward the door, her senses fully alert. She hadn't felt any duplicity in the man, but it was still marginally possible that this whole thing was a straight-up, face-less lie. If it was, Ferrouz's best move right now would be to try to shoot her in the back before she made it out of his office.

But she sensed no stealthy movement behind her, and no blaster shot sizzled across the room. Keying open the door, she stepped into the wait-ing room.

The lack of an attack didn't prove Ferrouz wasn't lying, of course. But it was a strong mark in his favor.

Axlon was still in the waiting room, pacing restlessly across the far side. He looked up as Mara entered, a flicker of something crossing his face. "What are you—I mean—"

"You can go in now," Mara said calmly, tucking her lightsaber back into her shoulder pouch. Circling the cylinder and its flapping butterflies, she headed for the outer door.

"But—" Axlon's eyes shifted briefly to the office door. "Aren't you—didn't you—"

"Relax, he's fine," Mara said. "We just had a little chat, that's all."

She was two meters from the door when its entire edge abruptly ex-ploded into a shower of sparks. Before she could do more than jerk to a halt, the door blew inward.

And as Mara stepped hastily back, blinking against the smoke and dust, two men with blasters strode through the jagged opening.

With her lightsaber tucked away in her shoulder pouch, the only thing that saved Mara in that first crucial second was the fact that the two men seemed as surprised to see her as she was to see them. They froze, their eyes going wide, their bulk blocking the doorway and the handful of other men she could see pressing in behind them.

But that moment wouldn't last, and Mara knew she would never have time to open the pouch and draw her weapon before they recovered and started shooting. She took a long step backward toward the cylinder enclo-sure, snatching up her pouch and squeezing, crushing the thin material inward around the lightsaber. Her searching fingers found the activation stud.

And suddenly the room lit up with a magenta glow as the blade lanced out, burning through the side of the pouch.

The sight of the blade seemed to snap the men out of their paralysis.

One of them shouted something, and abruptly the smoky air lit up with a blaze of blasterfire.

But Mara was no longer in the direct line of fire. She was already in motion, sidestepping the cylinder as she tried to deflect the incoming shots, even though the pouch strap across her shoulder severely restricted her lightsaber's movements. A few of the shots hit the cylinder, the direct fire blasting holes in the transparisteel, the more angled ones ricocheting off. Mara made it around to the far side, and with the cylinder temporarily blocking the bulk of the attack she finally managed to free herself from the strap. Still manipulating the lightsaber through the pouch, she made two quick slashes through the cylinder, one at knee height, the other angled upward from her shoulders, then slammed her shoulder as hard as she could against the side.

With a splintering crash, the section she'd cut free toppled over into the path of the men shooting at her. They jerked back, slamming in confusion into the ones trying to push their way in behind them, their shots abruptly going wild as a hundred frightened butterflies swarmed past them and escaped through the hole where the door used to be.

"Here!" a voice shouted from behind Mara. "In here! Come on!"

She glanced over her shoulder. Axlon was standing just inside the office door, beckoning frantically to her. Keeping her lightsaber blade between her and the intruders, Mara hastily backed up toward him.

The butterflies had completed their mad dash and the blasterfire was starting to come back to focus as she reached the doorway and backed through it. Axlon was ready, hitting the control to send the door sliding shut in front of her.

"What's going on?" Ferrouz demanded tautly as Mara reached out with the Force and double-keyed the lock.

"Someone wants my job," Mara told him, closing down her lightsaber and finally pulling it clear of the pouch.

"What?" Ferrouz asked, sounding confused.

"There's a mob out there that seems intent on killing you," Mara clarified. "Nuso Esva may have decided to go for the more direct approach."

"Wait a minute," Axlon protested. "Nuso Esva's trying to *kill* him? But why?"

"We'll worry about that later," Mara said, grabbing his arm and pulling him across the room toward Ferrouz's desk. The governor, meanwhile, had pulled out a blaster from somewhere, a small DDC Model 16 hold-out type that nestled in his hand.

At least he hadn't tried to shoot her earlier simply because he hadn't had a weapon available. Another point in his favor. "Let's focus on getting out of here before they blow this door, too," she told them.

The words were barely out of her mouth when there was a violent sizzling sound from behind her.

And as she spun around, shoving Axlon toward the desk, the office door exploded.

Luke was still looking around in vain for some sign of Axlon's Imperial agent when a sudden shout rose from somewhere in the crowd still milling around the area. "The governor is dead!" a voice called. "The governor is dead! Long live the Rebellion!"

Luke caught his breath. The governor was *dead*? But the Imperial agent hadn't even shown her face.

Or maybe she had. Maybe she'd slipped into the palace without him even noticing.

Luke winced. Of course she had. He had no experience at this sort of thing. No experience, and such little ability in the Force.

But excuses were of no comfort. The hard, cold fact was that he'd been given a job, and he'd failed.

Axlon would be furious. So would Han and Leia. So would Rieekan and Mon Mothma and all the rest. Ferrouz's death meant the collapse of the negotiations, and no hope of a Rebel base in Candoras sector—

"Here he is!" a voice shouted suddenly from behind Luke, practically in his ear. "Here's the man who freed us from Imperial tyranny!"

Luke spun around, his heart pounding suddenly in his chest. There was a burly, squint-eyed man with greasy hair and an unkempt mustache standing behind him, waving his hand over the crowd for attention. Was *that* the Imperial agent? But Axlon had said it was a woman.

And then, before Luke could react, the man stepped forward, jabbed a hand at Luke's belt, and stepped back with Luke's lightsaber gripped in his hand. Luke stared, chagrined, wondering how he'd been caught so unaware.

"Here he is!" the man shouted again, lifting the lightsaber high into the air. "Here's the man who saved us!"

And to Luke's horror he ignited the lightsaber, waving the blue-white beam up above the crowd. "Long live the Rebellion!" he shouted. "Long live the Rebel Luke Skywalker!"

Quiller's report was so unexpected that for the first couple of seconds LaRone was convinced he'd heard wrong. "Say again?" he demanded. "A *riot?*"

"Affirmative." Quiller's voice came tautly from LaRone's helmet speaker. "Some insane flash riot, kicking off without any lead-in that I saw. And you'll never guess who's in the middle of it: Luke Skywalker."

LaRone felt his mouth drop open. "*Skywalker?*"

"In the flesh, and waving his lightsaber around like he's trying to swat birds," Quiller said grimly. "You know, I didn't really buy Jade's story about Ferrouz and the Rebellion. But it's starting to look like she was right."

"Don't go jumping on any speeder carts just yet," Grave put in. "Skywalker's not the one waving that lightsaber. Someone grabbed it off his belt. In fact, it looks like all Skywalker's trying to do is get it back."

"Confirmed," Quiller said. "I've got a better look now. And—uh-oh; there he goes. A couple of the others in the crowd are trying to get him up on their shoulders."

LaRone looked at Marcross, wishing he could see the other's expression through his faceplate. This was rapidly passing from the bizarre to the utterly insane. "What's Skywalker doing?"

"Trying to get away from them," Quiller said. "And get this: the guy with the lightsaber is bellowing that Skywalker assassinated Governor Ferrouz."

LaRone felt his eyes narrow. "Okay, this is officially getting out of hand," he said. "Quiller, how far are you from Skywalker?"

"About a hundred meters," Quiller said. "And there's a fair amount of crowd standing between him and me."

"Wait a second—they're on the move," Grave said. "The whole crowd's heading across the street, moving toward the gate. Traffic's at a stop . . . that one clump of men is still holding back, still trying to get Skywalker up on their shoulders."

"LaRone, we've got a general order coming through," Marcross cut in.

LaRone keyed over to his helmet's palace comlink setting. "—at once to the gate and wall," a grim voice was saying. "Repeat: all roving patrols proceed at once to the gate and wall. Possible riot in progress; threat assessment at critical."

"Everyone's being ordered to the gate," LaRone relayed to the others. "This could get bloody."

"They're not going to fire on an unarmed crowd, are they?" Brightwater asked.

"I don't know," LaRone said. "But if they can't get the outside guards in fast enough, they may figure they have to."

"We've got warning shots," Quiller snapped. "Looks like they're coming from the wall defenses."

"Confirm that," Grave said. "Two of the lasers are laying down a pattern; the rest are tracking the forward edge of the crowd."

"Not good," Marcross muttered tensely. "Very not good."

"Which may be exactly what whoever started this thing is going for," LaRone said grimly. "A bloody confrontation, with multiple deaths and injuries."

"That doesn't sound like the usual Rebel tactics," Marcross said doubtfully.

"I'm not convinced it is the Rebels." LaRone glared across the grounds at the stormtroopers and gray-suited security men hurrying across the grass toward the wall. Skywalker in the middle of a riot, Jade inside the palace and out of contact, no idea who or what was driving any of this madness. "We need information," he said. "Right now, we're shooting blind."

"What do you want us to do?" Quiller asked.

LaRone pursed his lips. "Grave, what's your angle on Skywalker?"

"Reasonably clear," Grave said. "There are a few business flags and a couple of tapcaf table umbrellas in the way, but nothing serious."

"Quiller?"

"That man's still got Skywalker's lightsaber," Quiller reported. "There are another eight men still grouped around the two of them. From their positioning, I'm guessing they're there to keep Skywalker from leaving."

LaRone felt his throat tighten. Suddenly, like a flash of lightning from a roiling black storm cloud, he realized what was going on. Part of it, anyway. "Brightwater?"

"Within view of Quiller."

"Okay," LaRone said. "First job is to get Skywalker out of there. Quiller, you and Grave clear a path. Brightwater, you go in and grab him."

"Him and the lightsaber?" Brightwater asked.

"I doubt he'll leave without it," Grave said.

"Yes, absolutely get the lightsaber," LaRone said. "Destroy it if you have to, but don't let the mob keep it. Don't let them keep any pieces, either, if you have to blast the thing."

"Got it," Grave said. "What about you two?"

"We're heading inside to find Jade," LaRone said. "If I'm reading this right, she may be in serious trouble in there."

"Be careful," Brightwater said.

"Believe it," LaRone assured him. "Come on, Marcross. Let's see if the Emperor's Hand needs a little help."

"You want it?" the mustached man asked mockingly, waving the lightsaber in front of Luke. "Well, come on, Master Jedi Skywalker. You want it? Come and get it."

Luke clenched his teeth, watching the blade weaving back and forth in front of him, fully and painfully aware that the whole thing was hopeless. With better control of the Force, he might be able to get a telekinetic grip on the handle and wrench it aside. Or he might be able to pick up one of the chairs from the tapcaf's outdoor tables and hurl it at the man. Or he could even pick up the man himself and physically move him aside.

But he couldn't do any of those things. He wasn't the "Master Jedi" the other had derisively called him. He wasn't any kind of Jedi.

And even if by some miracle he was able to get the lightsaber back, what then? There were eight other hard-looking men gathered around him, all of them big, all of them probably armed, all of them clearly intent on keeping him here until the palace guard or a stormtrooper patrol got here. Even with the lightsaber, there was no way he would be able to cut all of them down before one of them got him.

Behind the ring of thugs, a shout rang out, and the crowd suddenly surged away from them. Luke glanced over his shoulder and saw them streaming into the street, halting the landspeeder traffic that had already slowed to a crawl.

"They're heading to the palace," the mustached man confirmed. "They're going to storm it."

Luke winced. "They'll be killed."

"Or they'll get in and take it over," the mustached man said offhandedly. "Makes no difference to me. Not so long as the Rebellion gets the credit."

"You're not part of the Alliance," Luke bit out.

"Yeah?" The man grinned evilly. "Good luck proving it."

With an effort, Luke pushed back the shifting sands of despair threatening to roll over him. The Force was with him, and there *was* a way out of this. All he had to do was find it. The mustached man swung the lightsaber again, casually, mockingly.

And as Luke watched him wielding the clearly unfamiliar weapon, he had an idea.

He couldn't yet call on the Force for the strength to physically attack the man. But his full-throttle flight down the Death Star trench had showed that he *could* call on the Force for guidance.

Maybe that would be enough.

"I don't have to prove it," Luke said, reaching down and unfastening his belt buckle. "All I have to do is bring you in. *You* can prove it."

The mustached man frowned as he watched Luke pulling his belt free. "What do you think you're doing?" he demanded.

"Like I just said," Luke said, sliding the belt through his hands. As he did so, he slipped the comlink free, palming it in his right hand. "Fighting with a lightsaber isn't as easy as it looks," he continued, finishing the belt slide with the tip in his left hand and the buckle hanging free. "Let's see how fast a learner you are."

The other looked down at the belt as Luke began swinging it loosely in his hand. "You're joking," he said flatly.

"I've got a friend who says that hokey religions and ancient weapons are no match for a good blaster at your side," Luke said, glancing to his right and left. The rest of the men in the circle, at least those he could see, were watching the unfolding drama with the same fascinated disbelief as the mustached man was. With luck, that would slow their reaction time when Luke made his move. "That goes for stun whips, too."

The other snorted. "You have a stun whip in your *belt?*"

"You'd be surprised at what I've got," Luke said, swinging the belt a little wider and adjusting his grip on the comlink. This would take both timing and accuracy. Hopefully, the Force would supply both. Stretching out as best he could, he snapped his wrist, sending the belt swinging in a wide arc toward the other man's right knee as if trying to get the buckle past the glowing blade between them.

But the belt wasn't long enough, and the man was far quicker than Luke's swing. As the buckle arced toward him, he twisted his wrists, swinging the lightsaber down and to his right and slashing it across the belt.

And with the mustached man's hands now turned over and fully exposed, Luke threw his comlink as hard as he could into the man's right thumb, the one pressing down on the activator stud. The man bellowed in pain, reflexively yanking his injured hand away from the lightsaber.

And with the usual sizzling hiss, the blade vanished.

The man recognized his mistake instantly, of course. But it was already too late to fix it. Even as he tried to get his hand back to the lightsaber's activation stud Luke was on him, grabbing the hilt of the lightsaber with his left hand and slamming the knuckles of his right fist into the back of the man's left hand.

With another bellow the other let go, lunged forward, and gave Luke a shove that sent him staggering two meters backward. Then, shaking his injured right hand once, he reached into his jacket and pulled out a blaster.

He wasn't alone, either. All around the circle, there was a sudden flurry of motion as the onlookers also went for their weapons.

Clenching his teeth, Luke ignited the lightsaber, stretching out to the Force again and trying not to think about the impossibility of getting all nine of them before they took him down. The mustached man leveled his blaster.

And jerked backward as a blaster bolt from above sizzled into the ground in front of him, blowing small splinters of permacrete from the walkway.

Startled, Luke looked up. Standing on one of the nearby rooftops was an Imperial stormtrooper with a long sniper rifle pressed against his shoulder. The trooper fired again, this shot blowing more permacrete from the ground somewhere behind Luke and eliciting a yelp from one of the men in the back.

"Behind you!" the mustached man shouted, and dodged to the side as a fresh volley of blasterfire erupted from that direction.

Luke spun around, dropping into a crouch. Another stormtrooper was on the ground barely thirty meters away, charging toward them in that loping run that Luke had seen both Imperials and Rebels use when they wanted to cover ground and shoot accurately at the same time.

One of the thugs on that side of the ring opened fire, his first shot glancing off the stormtrooper's shoulder. He didn't get a second shot; he fell, cursing, as a pair of blaster bolts burned through his leg. Another of the thugs yelped as a bolt from the sniper on the rooftop cut through his right forearm, sending his blaster flying into the street. Behind the stormtrooper, a scout trooper on a speeder bike swung into view around the line of landspeeders that had been stopped by the rampaging mob and headed toward them.

With that, the mustached man had finally had enough. "Get out of here!" he shouted, already heading for one of the side streets leading away from the palace. "Rendezvous point three. *Move* it!"

With a speeder bike and its underslung blaster cannon bearing down on them, the other thugs didn't have to be told twice. They took off, a few of them heading for the same side street down which the mustached man had disappeared, the others running into the tapcaf or nearby shops. Two of them paused long enough to shove their blasters back into concealment and grab the man with the wounded leg. Lugging him between them, they headed for the closest doorway and disappeared inside.

And now, instead of facing nine thugs, Luke was facing three armed stormtroopers. All in all, the thought occurred to him, it wasn't much of an improvement.

So why did he feel an unnatural calmness flowing into him from the Force?

The running stormtrooper had jogged to a halt, his eyes and blaster turned away from Luke and toward the swirling mob and the sounds of blaster- and laserfire that Luke suddenly realized were coming from that direction. Focused on the Force and his own danger, he'd completely lost track of what was happening on the far side of the street. He winced as someone screamed with pain or rage—

And jerked back as the speeder bike braked to a halt beside him. "Get on," the trooper's filtered voice ordered. "LaRone says you need to get out of here."

For a second the name didn't register. Then Luke got it, and he felt his eyes widen. LaRone, Marcross, Grave, Quiller, and—"*Brightwater?*" he asked.

"You were expecting Lord Vader?" Brightwater growled. "Come *on.*"

Luke still had no idea what was going on. But with a rampaging mob and Imperial firepower in one direction and nine armed and irate thugs in the other, this was no time to get picky. Closing down his lightsaber, he retrieved his comlink from where it had bounced off the mustached man's hand and swung his leg over the bike's saddle behind Brightwater. He'd barely gotten settled when the trooper hit the speeder's throttle and took off.

"Where are we going?" Luke called, gripping the trooper's utility belt as they shot past both the mob scene and the street and shops where the thugs had fled. "Brightwater?"

"Don't know," the other called back. "LaRone just said to get you out of there and find out what you know about this lunatic attack on the palace."

"I don't know anything," Luke told him. "It's nothing we're doing, that's for sure."

"Who's *we,* and what *are* you doing?"

Luke hesitated. When he and Han had last dealt with LaRone's group, the former stormtroopers had renounced their Imperial connections and were working on their own for the people of the galaxy, delivering justice and aid wherever they saw a need. But now here they were, apparently fully integrated into Governor Ferrouz's security forces. Did that mean they were back on the Empire's side? Or were they simply on Ferrouz's side?

And did he know anymore what Ferrouz's side really was?

"Skywalker?" Brightwater prompted. "Come on, we've got our necks stretched from here to Imperial Center on this one."

"We were invited here by Governor Ferrouz to support him against an alien warlord named Nuso Esva," Luke said. He still didn't fully understand what was going on, but the Force had given him a sense of calm as Brightwater came up. He would take his cue from that and assume LaRone and his group could be trusted.

"You sure that was the name?" Brightwater asked, his voice suddenly odd. "Nuso Esva?"

"Pretty sure, yes," Luke said. "There was also some talk about Candoras sector seceding from the Empire, but I'm not so sure about that. Ferrouz might have just thrown that in to persuade us to bring a good-sized force here."

"Anything else?"

Again, Luke hesitated. He trusted LaRone and the others, trusted them implicitly. But he had other loyalties, too, and he couldn't betray them. "Nothing else I can tell you," he said. "But our plans definitely don't involve a riot at the palace. Or anywhere else."

For a moment Brightwater was silent. Then, abruptly, he made a hard left into another of the side streets, this one lined mostly with apartment buildings. "I have to get back," he said, bringing the vehicle to a halt. "You have someplace you can go?"

"I don't know," Luke said, trying to think as he climbed off the speeder. "My ship's back at the spaceport. But our chief negotiator is still in the palace. If that riot breaks through, he may need my help getting out."

"So you're staying here?"

"For now, anyway," Luke said. "I need to talk with our people. I have no idea what's going on anymore."

"Join the club," Brightwater said darkly. "Good luck."

"Thanks," Luke said. "And thanks for the rescue."

"No problem," Brightwater said. "Wait a second." Reaching to his waist, he unfastened his utility belt. "There's emergency rations and a few other items in there that you might find useful," he said, handing the belt to Luke. "If you're going to ground, you may need some extra gear."

"Thanks," Luke said.

"Good luck, and watch yourself," Brightwater said. "Whatever's going on, it's probably going to get worse before it gets better." Swinging the speeder around in a tight circle, he roared down the street and headed back toward the palace.

Luke took a deep breath and glanced around. There were no vehicles and only a few pedestrians in sight, and none of them was paying him any attention, despite the fact he'd just been dropped off by a scout trooper. Apparently the citizens of Whitestone City had learned to keep their curiosity to themselves.

That was fine with Luke. Cracken needed to be brought into this right away, and Luke had no time to look for a private place from which to call him. Looping Brightwater's utility belt over his shoulder, he pulled out his comlink.

Only to discover that it was broken.

He stared at the device, a hard knot forming in his stomach. Even granted that he'd thrown the comlink at the mustached man's hand as hard as he could, he hadn't thought he'd thrown it hard enough to break it. But clearly, he had.

Which meant he was alone here. Even more alone than he'd realized.

He took a deep breath.

He wasn't alone. The Force was with him.

He looked around, getting his bearings, and set off toward a group of small shops clustered at the street corner beyond the apartment complexes. The first thing he needed to do was get some new outerwear, in case the mustached man and his gang were still on the hunt for him. Then he would find a quiet place to empty the pouches of Brightwater's belt and find out what he had to work with.

And once he'd done all that, hopefully he would be able to come up with a plan for getting Axlon out of the palace.

CHAPTER THIRTEEN

T HE FIRST WAVE OF ATTACKERS THROUGH THE REMAINS OF FERROUZ'S office door were careless or untrained or both. They charged through the ragged gap firing blindly, most of the shots going wide but a few of them coming straight at Mara as she stood in front of the governor's desk.

Unfortunately for the attackers, those straight shots were the ones most easily deflected directly back at them. Three of them died, and two or three more were wounded, before the rest got the message.

Unfortunately for Mara, calmer heads had taken over since that first mad rush. The remaining attackers were crouched at the edges of the opening, or behind the bodies of the fallen, shooting in coordinated volleys that were becoming increasingly difficult for her to deflect.

Worse, sooner or later it would probably dawn on them that if they stopped firing, charged in, and fanned out to both sides, they could present her with a crossfire that even she couldn't survive.

The only thing preventing them from doing that right now, in fact, was that Ferrouz was crouching by the side of the desk with his blaster, firing carefully measured shots through the doorway. Charging in now would merely give the governor better targets, and even though he couldn't stop a concerted rush, it didn't seem like any of the attackers was all that eager to sacrifice himself for whatever cause it was they were fighting for.

Still, the standoff couldn't last much longer. A fully charged DDC-16 only carried about twenty shots, and although Mara's attention had been too focused on her own defense to keep count, she knew he had to be run-ning low. Unless he had a spare power pack in his desk, she was soon going to be on her own.

Completely on her own, in fact. The battle had dragged on for at least five minutes now, more than long enough for Ferrouz's security forces to have been alerted and come running to the rescue. The fact that no one had done so implied that they'd been killed, locked out, or otherwise co-erced into inaction.

Which meant Mara was going to have to either get Ferrouz out of here fast or else drastically switch tactics.

There would be an emergency exit somewhere in the office, she knew. Nearly all governors and Moffs had one, for precisely this sort of situation. But with Ferrouz pinned down by his desk, there was no way he was going to make it over to wherever his bolt-hole was and get it open.

She was just going to have to do this the hard way.

Moving toward the attackers would be dangerous, since closing the gap would shorten the time she had to react to their shots. But it was the only way to push them back. Once they were out of the doorway, she might buy herself some breathing space and Ferrouz some mobility. She took a step forward.

And then, even as the enemy gunfire increased, a new sound flicked into her straining consciousness: the deeper, heavier sound of a stormtrooper's BlasTech E-11. The barrage coming at her faltered, then stopped completely, and for a handful of seconds the two different sounds competed with each other. Then both sets of weapons trailed off and stopped.

As Mara lifted her lightsaber back into defense position, two stormtroop-ers appeared, easing their way over the bodies and through the blasted doorway. "Are you all right?" one of them called.

Taking a deep breath, Mara closed down her lightsaber. Even through the vocoder's mechanical filtering she had no trouble recognizing that voice. "Good timing, LaRone," she said. "Yes, we're fine."

"No, we're not," Axlon called tautly from behind the desk. "I need help back here."

They found Ferrouz lying stretched out on the floor, his head cradled in Axlon's lap, a blackened line sliced across a mass of swelling skin on the left side of his scalp. "I think he must have caught a ricochet," Axlon said grimly as Mara knelt down beside them. "I tried to tell you, but I don't think you heard."

"No, I didn't," Mara said, checking his vital signs and leaning closer to the wound. It looked mostly superficial, possibly scorching the cranial bone but not penetrating through to the brain. For the second time today, it seemed, Governor Ferrouz had cheated death. "Medpac?"

LaRone already had his out and open. "Doesn't look too bad," he said.

"No, but his heartbeat's a little thready," Mara said, pulling out the spray hypo and loading an anti-shock booster vial into it. She injected the dose, then put the hypo back and selected a pair of burn patches. "Any ID on our attackers?"

"No," Marcross said. "But I'm guessing they're with the rioters out front."

Mara frowned up at him. "We have a *riot* going on?"

"Reasonably big, very loud, and getting nastier by the minute," Marcross told her. "The whole palace security contingent has been ordered to the wall to stop the people who are trying to climb over."

"Which could also be accomplished by opening fire and slaughtering a few of them," LaRone added. "Fortunately, the general in charge seems to be trying to avoid that."

"That would be General Ularno," Mara said as she laid the patches across Ferrouz's burns. "Very stolid, very by-the-book. Not very imaginative."

"I can believe that," Marcross said. "He keeps calling for Governor Ferrouz to check in. Probably hoping for some fresh ideas."

"You're not actually going to take him out there, are you?" Axlon asked anxiously.

"You mean out where someone else can take a shot at him?" Mara countered, closing the medpac and handing it back to LaRone. "Don't worry. We're going to find someplace to go to ground until we get this mess straightened out."

"You mean the riot?" Marcross asked.

"I mean the fact that someone set me up," Mara said bluntly. "They set up Ferrouz to commit treason, then they set me up to kill him." She gestured toward the bodies lying in the doorway. "*And* they wanted to catch me in the act."

"There may be another possibility," LaRone said. "There's a person—"

"Can this wait?" Mara interrupted.

"Yes, of course," LaRone said, sounding a little embarrassed. "Sorry."

"I assume we're not going out the front?" Marcross said, nodding toward the office door.

"That depends," Mara said. "How many dead guards did you see outside the office suite on your way in, and did you see any of our attackers cross the courtyard while you were waiting out there for me?"

The two stormtroopers exchanged looks. "There were two dead guards and a woman I assumed was a receptionist," LaRone said.

"We didn't see anyone in the courtyard who wasn't security or a stormtrooper," Marcross added.

"What does any of that have to do with anything?" Axlon asked.

"A lack of dead guards would have meant that a sizable fraction of Ferrouz's security force was in on it," Mara told him. "The guards would have simply stepped aside instead of letting themselves get killed defending him."

"And since the attackers didn't come in through the front gate in the last half hour, they either had a private way in, or they came in earlier and were hiding somewhere inside," LaRone said. "The security corps in general may still be loyal, but *someone* in the palace is helping them."

"So we go for Ferrouz's bolt-hole," Mara said, looking around the room. "Let's spread out and find it."

"Try back that way," Axlon said, pointing toward one of the rear corners. "I think he was getting ready to move in that direction when he was hit."

Mara studied the corner. The walls back there included a lot of hand-carved scrollwork that would be more than adequate to conceal release buttons. "LaRone, watch the door," she said, heading across the room. "Marcross, pick up the governor and come with me."

"That's all right," Axlon said. "I can carry him."

"I apparently didn't make myself clear," Mara said, pausing and looking back at him. "*We're* leaving. *You're* staying here."

"Governor Ferrouz is my friend," Axlon said firmly. "More than that, he's my ally. I won't desert him in his time of need."

"So you're a Rebel."

Axlon flinched, but nodded. "Yes, I am," he said, with no regret or embarrassment in his voice. "But like it or not, sometimes enemies have to work together against a bigger enemy." He gestured at Ferrouz. "Whoever's trying to kill the governor is that bigger enemy."

"Just one small problem," Mara said. "I don't trust you."

"I don't trust you, either," Axlon countered. "So let's get practical. There may be more trouble out there, trouble you'll need to shoot your way through. You really want to find out the hard way whether stormtroopers can lug an unconscious man and shoot at the same time?"

Mara grimaced. They didn't have time for this.

Besides which, the man had a point. "You should have been in politics," she said, resuming her trip across the room. "Don't drop him. Marcross, you're with him."

Most governors, Mara knew, had their private exits locked mechanically, with no circuitry that could be located by someone with an energy scanner. Mechanical locks worked only in certain specified ways, and under normal conditions she could have found the release within a couple of minutes.

But today she didn't have the luxury of time or finesse. Igniting her lightsaber, she slashed through the wall at waist height until a puff of cool, stale air told her she'd hit the hidden door and the tunnel behind it. Quickly she carved out the rest of the opening and then thrust the lightsaber inside. By the faint glow of the blade, she could see that there was a short passageway leading away from the office wall and ending in a narrow stairway. "Axlon, can you handle stairs?"

"No problem," Axlon said. He had Ferrouz up over his shoulder now, holding him in a standard rescue carry. "You want me to take lead?"

"I'll take lead," Mara said, stepping into the doorway. "Marcross next, then you. LaRone, you're on rear guard. Give Grave and the others a call and tell them to get back to the truck, unsuit and dump their gear inside, and wait for my call."

She turned back to the corridor and took a deep breath. Sometimes, she knew, governors set traps in their emergency exits to discourage pursuit. "Let's go."

Caldorf VII interceptor missiles were big and bulky, and even with a couple of ASP-7 lifter droids to assist, Han quickly found out why Ranquiv was willing to pay two hundred for each one of the things that his workers could successfully jostle into place.

Leia wasn't any help, of course. She tried to be, and Han was pretty sure she *thought* she was being helpful. But mostly she just got in the way, or handed him the wrong tool, or offered advice that he didn't want.

But he couldn't tell her that. She would just get into a snit, and a public argument would draw attention that they couldn't afford.

So he suffered and sweated and swore, and let her help, and occasionally accepted her orders even when he already knew what he was doing.

He had attached the nesting rack to the ship and had the first four bolts of the missile casing in place when he spotted one of the humans, a man with spiky brown hair, having an animated conversation with one of the yellow-eyed aliens off to the side of the cavern near the tunnel where the speeder bus was parked. As he watched, two more of the aliens drifted into the group, and a casual look around showed another three in other parts of the cavern also moving in that direction.

Something was going on. Han should probably find out what.

He turned away from the discussion. "Hydrospanner," he told Leia, gesturing toward the tool kit they'd been given. "Biggest one you've got."

She peered into the box and pulled out a five-centimeter version. "This big enough?" she asked, holding it up.

"Perfect," Han said, taking it and putting one of the bolts wrong-end first into the tool's hydraulic receiving collar. Glancing around surreptitiously to make sure no one was watching, he triggered the tool, squeezing the collar down onto the bolt. There was a soft grinding of metal on metal, and when he unlocked the collar he found that the bolt's threads had been mashed just a little on one side.

"What are you *doing*?" Leia asked as he pulled the bolt out and put in a second one.

"Making an excuse to go eavesdropping," Han told her, squeezing the hydrospanner down on that one, too. "What do you think? Two enough? Or should I make it three?"

She didn't answer, but just stared at him as if he'd lost his mind.

"Yeah, let's make it three," Han decided, and mashed the threads on a third bolt. "You can put this away," he told her, handing her the hydrospanner. Collecting his three damaged bolts, he turned again and headed across the cavern toward the conversation.

The other aliens had joined the party now, but Spikes seemed to be doing most of the talking. "— *have* any more men inside," he was snarling as Han got into hearing range. "The frilty little bittern took them down. Every last frilting one of them."

"Then send in more," Ranquiv said, his voice dark. "You said you would bring enough."

"Numbers aren't the problem," Spikes retorted. "The problem is, no one else can get into the palace until our man inside comes out of wherever he's hiding."

"Did she kill him as well?" one of the other aliens asked.

"I *don't know*," Spikes ground out. "Stelikag was on the outside, organizing the riot. He doesn't know what happened in there any more than I do."

"You must find him," one of the other aliens insisted.

"You think?" Spikes said sarcastically. "Don't worry, we've still got—" He broke off as he spotted Han. "What do you want?" he demanded.

"How about workable equipment?" Han growled, holding up the bolts. "You see these? Threads are crushed. *Three* of them with threads crushed. How do you expect me to do my job if you don't give me decent stuff?"

"There are more bolts there," Ranquiv said, pointing to a set of tool and supply cabinets along the side wall. "Get what you need. Do not bother us further."

"Yeah, I can see how busy your schedule is," Han said sourly. Turning, he headed for the cabinets.

And as he walked he kept an eye on Leia, standing beside his half-finished install. It was hard to tell at this distance, but it looked like her eyes were on the group of aliens.

Which probably meant Spikes and the aliens were watching him.

He made it to the cabinet without anyone shooting him in the back, found replacement bolts, and headed back to the ship.

"What was that all about?" Leia asked as he picked up one of the hydrospanners and got back to work.

"They looked like they were talking about something interesting," Han said. "I wanted to find out what it was."

"Did they tell you?" Leia asked drily.

"Not exactly," Han said, grunting as he snugged one of the bolts in place. "But I got enough to know there's trouble on Poln Major. Trouble involving the palace."

Out of the corner of his eye he saw Leia stiffen. "Han," she said quietly, her eyes on something past his shoulder.

"We need to get hold of Luke—" he continued.

"Who's Luke?" Spikes's voice asked from behind him.

With an effort, Han managed not to jump. He'd expected a follow-up, but not quite this quick. "Buddy who flies with us sometimes," he said casually, setting the next bolt in place and giving the hydrospanner a couple of cranks. "I was telling her that if you've got more of these things to do, we should bring him in on it," he added, turning around as Spikes walked up to him, a data card in his hand.

"We already have plenty of help," the other growled, eyeing Han suspiciously. "If it hadn't been a rush job we could have done all the work ourselves."

"Yeah, I can see you knocking yourselves out over there," Han said. "I just thought if you needed more help—"

"We don't," Spikes said shortly, peering up at Han's work. "Adequate," he said. "Nothing special, but it should hold. You're still missing those last three bolts."

"Yeah, I'm working on it," Han said, setting one of the bolts into the hydrospanner. "Anything else?"

"Not from you." Spikes pointed at Leia and jerked his head toward the ramp running from the ground up to the side of the ship. "But I need her inside."

Han glanced at Leia. "What for?" he asked warily as he put down the hydrospanner, freshly aware of the blaster at Spikes's hip.

"I want to get her started on the calibration," Spikes said. "No—you stay put. I just need her."

"Call me curious," Han said, stepping to Leia's side.

"How about I call you *dead*?" Spikes retorted.

Han stayed where he was. Spikes glared at him for another moment, then muttered a curse. "Fine," he growled, gesturing at the ramp again. "Go."

"Where?" Han asked as he walked past the other and headed for the ramp.

"Cockpit," Spikes said. "Come on, move it."

Han nodded. Rounding the ramp, he headed up, his back itching as Spikes started up the ramp behind him. Still, Leia was now behind Spikes, and hopefully she would be fast enough to do something if he went for his blaster.

Fortunately for all of them, he didn't.

The cockpit systems were in standby mode, half the instruments and displays dark, the rest glowing softly. The controls were also lit, with identification labels in blue and red script that was as alien as the ship itself. "Okay," Han said as he dropped into the pilot's seat. "Now what?"

In answer, Spikes stepped up to the board and slid his data card into a slot on the lower part.

And with a multiple flicker, all the control labels simultaneously switched from alien characters to standard Basic.

Han looked at Spikes.

"Don't look so surprised." Spikes said, a mocking smile on his face. "There are a lot of different alien types who fly these ships. This is the smart way to make sure they know what button to push." He pointed to the upper part of the board. "That's the calibration setup. She can start on that—and you can get your butt out of that seat and finish with the hardware." Without waiting for a reply, he turned and pushed past Leia as she stood in the cockpit doorway. A moment later, the ship vibrated with his footsteps as he headed back down the ramp.

Han climbed out of the seat and gestured to Leia. "You're on, sweetheart," he said. "I'll go run the rest of those bolts in and be right back."

"Take your time," Leia said, grimacing a little as he brushed closely past her. "I don't really need you here."

"*I* need me here," Han told her. "I'll be right back."

He got the rest of the bolts secured in two minutes, and was back in the cockpit in three. "That was fast," Leia commented, not looking up from her work as he took up position behind her, leaning one hand on the back of her seat. "I've barely started."

"Take your time and do it right," he told her. "It's not like we need the money they're paying."

"Hey!" Spikes's distant voice called.

Han leaned forward and peered out the crosshatch canopy. Spikes was standing at the foot of the ramp, pointing imperiously toward the ground beside him. "What does he want?" Leia asked.

"Me, probably," Han said. Waving back genially, he returned his attention to the board. "Ignore him—maybe he'll go away."

No such luck. A moment later, the ship once again began to vibrate with the tramp of feet on the entrance ramp. They didn't sound like happy footsteps, either. "You need me," Han said softly in Leia's ear.

She frowned up at him; and then Spikes was at the cockpit door, glaring at them. "You deaf, Shrike?" he bit out. "She can handle this herself. You need to get started mounting another missile."

"I need him here," Leia said in that firm, no-argument voice that Han had heard her use on him so many times over the past few months. "You'll have to wait until I'm done."

Spikes snorted. "What does he do? Hold your hand?"

"No, he does all the double-mark, ginlay, and parity checks," Leia told him. "If you had any real professionals out there, you'd already know that's the accepted procedure."

Spikes snorted again. "You think anyone here gives a womp rat about accepted procedure?"

"I assume they give a womp rat about getting the job done right," Leia said calmly. "Single-eyetrack calibrations have a twelve percent error rate, which means that in one job out of eight you'll have to go back to dirt and do the whole thing over." She waved a hand. "But hey, you said you'd pay for calibrated missiles. You never said you needed the calibrations to be any good."

Spikes took a deep breath. "Fine," he growled. "Do it your way. You've got one hour." He leveled a finger at her. "And I'll be checking every line of your work later. Personally."

Turning, he walked away, and again the ship vibrated as he stomped down the ramp. "Thanks," Han said quietly.

"You're welcome." Leia looked up at him. "If you *were* planning to hold my hand, forget it."

"What I'm planning is to memorize these controls," Han told her, nodding toward the board. "I somehow don't think Spikes is going to let you keep that translator card once the missile's been calibrated."

"Why do you need to memorize the controls?" Leia asked, looking puzzled. "The only way out that's big enough for these things is that conveyance tunnel at the far end."

"Yeah, I saw it," Han said. "I also saw that they've got enough firepower clustered there to level a city block. No one's getting in or out that way, not until Ranquiv says so." He considered. "Unless someone tries for a suicide run."

Leia's eyes were suddenly very steady on his face. "You're not serious."

"You never know," he said casually. He gestured to the board. "You'd better get busy before *he* decides to come hold your hand. And get it right."

"Don't worry," she said stiffly, turning back to the board.

"I won't," he said, just to get in the last word.

He would worry, of course. Whatever was going on here was well worth worrying about. But right now his main job was to figure out how to fly one of these things. Just in case he wound up needing to.

He really *wasn't* planning a suicide run. But you never knew.

Watching over her shoulder, the faint scent of Leia's hair wafting up at him, he got to work.

Ferrouz's secret exit, to Mara's relief, turned out not to be booby-trapped. Also to her relief, the switchback stairway only went down three floors before becoming an equally narrow but more easily navigable slight downward slope.

Some governor bolt-holes dead-ended in a safe room, which would be heavily fortified and usually stocked for a long siege. But most such escape routes also continued on past the safe room to a hidden exit some-where well beyond the palace grounds, where a vehicle of some sort waited to provide a fugitive with quick transport elsewhere.

Such was indeed the case here. Mara led them past the entrance to the safe room—which, interestingly, was nearly as well camouflaged as the se-cret door back in the office had been—and continued on down the long, dark corridor.

The permacrete around them had changed subtly, indicating to her that they'd left the palace grounds and entered some forgotten part of the city's infrastructure, when Axlon finally spoke up. "How far *is* this safe room, anyway?" he asked, his breathing labored.

"We're not going to the safe room," Mara told him, pausing and plac-ing her hand on the side of the tunnel. It was cool to the touch, cooler than it should have been, and she could feel a faint vibration. A relatively thin wall, she concluded, with open air on the other side.

"Then where *are* we going?"

"Here," Mara said, motioning the others to a halt. Taking a step away from them, she drew her lightsaber. "Into the sewer."

"Whoa, whoa," Axlon protested. "What kind of sewer are we talking about here? Sewage, or storm drainage?"

"We're about to find out," Mara said. Igniting her lightsaber, she deli-cately cut a small opening in the tunnel wall at eye level. Closing down the weapon, she stepped forward and gave the gap a cautious sniff.

There was a faint smell of mustiness, plus a combination of rotting vegetation and dirt, but no stench. "Storm drainage," she reported. Ignit-ing the lightsaber again, she sliced a person-sized opening and stepped through.

It was indeed a storm drainage conduit, rounded on the bottom but tall enough for her to stand more or less upright. The vibration she'd felt had been from the air streaming down the conduit, along with the flow com-ing in from a grating set into the top of a short vertical cylinder a dozen meters away. Carried on the breeze were the muted sounds of the city around them. "Wait here," she murmured. "Keep quiet."

She crossed to the grating and for a moment stood beneath it, gazing up and listening. From the lack of passersby and the distance of the traffic sounds, she tentatively concluded that the grating opened into an alley. There was a short ladder set into the vertical cylinder; climbing it, she stretched out to the Force and eased the grating up and away from the opening. She shifted her grip to the edges of the hole and pulled herself cautiously up to eye level.

The grating did indeed open onto an alley, a narrow service passageway tucked in between two rows of buildings, very similar to the one where she'd taken out the two palace stormtroopers earlier that morning. The shop doors opening up onto the alley had small signs identifying the various businesses. The signs, unfortunately, were too small for Mara to read from her distance and vantage point.

But five doors down from the grating was the top of a hydraulic lift platform tucked closely in to one of the buildings. That implied a tapcaf or cantina, with the lift there to lower full kegs from supply trucks down to the cellar and bring the empties back up to be discarded.

For the moment, a tapcaf storage cellar was probably their best bet. Taking a final look around the alley, she dropped back into the conduit and returned to the rest of the group.

"There's a tapcaf five doors down on the south side of the alley," she told them. "LaRone, you and Marcross will go around to the front—get rid of everyone and close the place down. When everyone's out—"

"Close it *down*?" Axlon asked, his eyes widening. "How are they supposed to do *that*?"

"Understood," LaRone said, ignoring the interruption. "What then?"

"Lock up, go down to the cellar, and raise the supply lift," Mara told him. "We'll get the governor in that way."

"We're going to hide in a *tapcaf cellar*?" Axlon asked.

"And if Master Axlon's very lucky," Mara added, looking Axlon in the eye, "he may still be alive by then."

Axlon clamped his mouth shut.

"Understood," LaRone said again. "If you'd rather keep Marcross here on guard, I can do the job alone."

Mara shook her head. "I can handle things here, and people react faster to two stormtroopers than they do to one. Have the others finished suiting down?"

"Yes, and they're waiting in the truck," LaRone said.

"Get the tapcaf's name and get them over here," Mara instructed. "Better have them stay on foot for the moment, with minimal equipment. Have them do a quiet sweep of the neighborhood and then join us."

"Via the supply lift?"

"Yes," Mara said. "And have them bring the green bag at the back of the truck—it has my combat suit in it." She gestured to the grating. "You going to need any help getting up there?"

"No, we can handle it," LaRone said. "We'll see you soon."

The two stormtroopers walked over to the open grating and, one by one, pulled themselves up and out into the alley. "Now we wait?" Axlon asked.

"Now we wait," Mara confirmed. "But we wait over there, where we can watch."

They went over to the grating, and Mara helped the Rebel ease Ferrouz off his shoulder and onto the conduit floor. The governor's heartbeat seemed steadier now, but his breathing was still slow. Mara eased her fingers across the edges of the burn patches, wishing she'd had more medical training.

Without warning there was a catch in Ferrouz's breathing and he opened his eyes. "Wha—" he croaked.

Axlon was on his knees beside Ferrouz in an instant. "Governor!" he said, sounding relieved. "Are you all right?"

"I don't know," Ferrouz said, his eyelids fluttering a little as he looked at Axlon and then Mara. "What happened?"

"Your friend Nuso Esva apparently didn't trust me to kill you all by myself," Mara told him grimly. "He had some hired guns standing by to help."

"Yes," Ferrouz murmured, his forehead creasing with concentration. "I remember now. They attacked us. In my office, right?"

"Right," Mara said. "And you blocked one of their shots with your head. Generally not a good idea."

Abruptly, Ferrouz's eyes widened. "Where are we?" he said, his gaze shifting past Mara to the open grating above them. "I have to get back—he said I wasn't supposed to leave the palace."

"Who said?" Axlon asked.

"Nuso Esva," Ferrouz said, fumbling his hands against the cold perma-crete and struggling weakly to get up. "He said he'd kill them if I left. I have to go back."

"Easy," Mara soothed, gently but firmly holding him down. "No one's killing anyone. Not today."

"But he said he would," Ferrouz pleaded.

"Who's getting killed?" Axlon asked. "What's going on?"

"A self-styled alien warlord named Nuso Esva has kidnapped the gover-nor's family and given him a list of demands." Mara raised her eyebrows. "One of which was to make this deal with you and the Rebel Alliance."

Axlon drew back. "What?" he asked carefully.

"You heard right," Mara said, stretching out with the Force. Axlon's face was under rigid control, but she had no trouble sensing the turmoil of anger and frustration swirling behind it. "You haven't found a corrupt gov-ernor you could manipulate, Master Axlon. You found a loyal governor under extreme coercion."

Axlon took a deep breath. "I see," he said. "What now?"

"Don't worry, I'm not going to turn you over to Lord Vader," Mara as-sured him. "Even if I knew where to find him. More important, I can still use you. So here's the offer: Until we get Governor Ferrouz's family back, we have a truce. Once that happens, I'll give you and your fellow Rebels two hours to get out of the Poln system. Deal?"

Axlon huffed out a breath. "I doubt I'll get a better offer anywhere else today. Yes, deal."

Mara looked down at Ferrouz. "You okay with that, Governor?"

"I am," Ferrouz said grimly. "Provided they weren't involved with the kidnapping. If they were, I want them all dead."

"By the time I have your family back, I'll know who was involved," Mara promised. "Tell me about the other ways into the palace compound besides the main gate."

Ferrouz frowned. "There aren't any."

"Sure there are," Mara said. "Your secret exit, for one. We used it to get out, which means someone else could have used it to get in."

"No one came in that way."

"Then they came in some other way," Mara said. "Or else someone in high authority passed them through the gate and then tucked them away somewhere for at least several hours and possibly a day or two."

Ferrouz exhaled softly. "It's a big palace," he said. "I don't even know how you'd ever find out that there'd been someone hiding there."

"There are ways," Mara said. "It usually comes down to an analysis of the palace food, power, computer, and water usage. But hiding people's always risky. I'm inclined to think our attackers were slipped in earlier today, around the same time I came in."

"But there aren't any other entrances," Ferrouz protested.

"Maybe something you wouldn't normally think of as an entrance," Mara suggested. "A garbage shaft or sewage outflow whose safeguards and defenses can be removed. Or some passage or doorway that was retrofitted after the palace was built, like that interrogation room and access corridor."

"Like maybe the way they get rid of the bodies after their interrogations," Axlon muttered.

Ferrouz looked sharply at him. "You're right," he said. "There's a disposal chute leading from the interrogation room. And it was specifically designed to be large enough for a human body to pass through."

"Where does it go?" Mara asked.

"Supposedly, a secure facility where any waste can be processed and put into the city's regular sewage system," Ferrouz said. "But I've never seen it, so I really don't know."

Mara nodded. There were still other possibilities to be explored, but her gut was telling her that they'd indeed identified the attackers' entrance. "New subject: who has access to the interrogation area?"

"Only the top staff and security people," Ferrouz said. "Myself, General Ularno, Security Chief Colonel Bonze, and about five of his top people."

Mara felt her eyes narrow. "Including Major Pakrie?"

"Yes," Ferrouz said, frowning at her sudden change in tone. "You're not seriously suggesting . . ."

"Why not?" Mara said. "You said earlier that he was new to his position. Explain."

"He was promoted to major about a month and a half ago," Ferrouz said, his eyes unfocused and thoughtful. "After his predecessor was killed in an airspeeder accident."

"This was about three weeks before your family was kidnapped?"

Abruptly, Ferrouz's face went rigid. "Are you saying *he* was the one who arranged that?"

"More likely he was one of a group," Mara said. "I'll know better after I run his profile. If you can give me all the palace security passwords and access codes, it'll save me the trouble of slicing them myself."

Ferrouz shook his head, his mind clearly still on Pakrie. "No use. You can't access the computer system from out here."

"That's why I'll be going back in as soon as I have you settled," Mara said. "If Pakrie is involved, he'll have left a trail somewhere. Maybe I can use it to backtrack to the kidnappers and figure out where they're holding your family."

"Won't they be looking for you in there?" Axlon said.

"Probably not," Mara said. "Even if they are, they won't find me."

"But you'll be finding Pakrie?" Ferrouz said darkly.

Mara shrugged. "If he's smart, he's already on the run. If I do run across him, we may have a short chat."

In the distance, she heard the faint creaking of machinery. "Sounds like LaRone's got our door open," she said, standing up. "Let me check, and then we'll get you up there."

Marcross was waiting at the supply lift when she and Axlon and a still-shaky Ferrouz arrived. "Welcome back, Governor," the stormtrooper greeted them.

"Thank you," Ferrouz said.

"Any trouble?" Mara asked as they gathered together on the lift.

"No," Marcross said, touching the control and starting the platform back down. "LaRone told the owner his place was suspected of harboring Rebel operatives and that we were shutting him down while we investigated. He couldn't have been more helpful in kicking everyone out and giving us the passkey."

Axlon muttered something. "Good," Mara said, ignoring him. "That won't buy us more than a couple of days, but it might be enough."

The supply cellar was about what Mara had expected: a single large room with rough permacrete walls and floor, its walls lined with kegs and racks of bottles.

Though not as many as Mara had anticipated. Either the owner had been preparing to reorder, or else business wasn't going so well.

"We spotted a couple of long couches upstairs," Marcross said as Mara gave herself a quick tour of the room. "The stairway's a little narrow, but I think we can probably get one of them down here for the governor."

"I'm all right," Ferrouz said.

"Yes, good idea," Mara said to Marcross. "Take Axlon and go get one of them. LaRone still upstairs?"

"Yes, checking for supplies," Marcross said, beckoning to Axlon. "No point eating ration bars if there's something better available. Come on, Axlon."

The two men crossed to the stairway and disappeared upstairs. "You trust them?" Ferrouz asked quietly.

"I trust mine," Mara said. "You trust yours?"

Ferrouz grimaced. "He's a Rebel. Can any of them truly be trusted?"

"Point," Mara conceded. "Still, simple self-preservation ought to keep him in line long enough for us to end this."

"Yes." Ferrouz hesitated. "Is there really a chance, Agent—You know, I don't even know what to call you."

"Call me Jade," Mara said. "And yes, there's a chance. A good chance, I think. Whatever Nuso Esva hopes to accomplish, killing his hostages won't get it for him. If we're fast enough, I should be able to get to them while he's still trying to figure out how to play this new situation we've suddenly presented him with."

"I hope you're right," Ferrouz said, his face sagging a little.

"I am," Mara said, stepping to his side and taking his arm. Conscious or not, he was still in pretty bad shape. "I'm also very good at my job. As soon as we've got you settled and resting, I'll get to work on it."

Three minutes later, with much huffing and under-the-breath cursing, Marcross and Axlon had the couch down the stairs and set up beside a row of racked bottles. Five minutes after that, Grave, Brightwater, and Quiller arrived, reporting that the neighborhood seemed quiet and that their speeder truck was stashed near a mechanic's shop where it would be unobtrusive but within reasonably quick reach.

Five minutes after that, dressed now in her skintight black combat suit and boots, with her lightsaber and hold-out blaster at the ready, Mara was once again in the underground passageway, heading back upslope toward the palace.

And as she walked, it occurred to her that she would be going right by Ferrouz's emergency safe room. If Pakrie or some of Nuso Esva's other allies had missed Ferrouz by now, they might assume he'd gone to ground. If so, they might even now be gathered around the armored door, trying to break their way in.

She rather hoped that they were.

CHAPTER FOURTEEN

T HE HELM OFFICER PEERED AT HIS MONITOR, THEN LOOKED UP AT Pellaeon. "Course reading confirmed, Commander," he said. "We have a positive tracking on the vector given us by Lord Odo."

"Thank you, Lieutenant," Pellaeon said, nodding. "Carry on."

"Yes, sir."

The officer turned back to his console, and Pellaeon continued his solitary walk along the command walkway. Ahead of him, the forward viewport was filled with the flowing hyperspace sky.

Normally, Pellaeon found the view rather soothing. Appealing, even, in an artistic sense. But not today. Today, that sky was ominous and threatening, with unknown dangers behind it.

They weren't running some well-known route, where every sizable astronomical body had been carefully identified and mapped. They were in the Unknown Regions now. There could be anything lurking in their path—gas giant planets, brown dwarf stars, even full-fury supernovae. No one on the *Chimaera* would even know the danger was there until it was too late.

And even if they made it through, what then? Lord Odo had been suspiciously evasive on the topic of what they might face when they arrived at his destination and dropped out of hyperspace.

"Commander?" the comm officer called. "Lieutenant Commander

Geronti requests your immediate attention in the main engine control room."

Pellaeon turned, focusing on the engineering monitor station. "What's the trouble?" he asked.

"Nothing indicated here, sir," the engineering officer reported, running quickly through the paging sequence on his displays. "All systems appear to be functioning normally."

"Sir?" the comm officer called again. "The lieutenant commander *urgently* requests your presence. He says you'll need to see this for yourself."

Pellaeon swallowed a curse. Geronti better have a *really* good reason for this. "Lieutenant Tomslin, you have the bridge," he called to the second duty officer as he headed for the turbolift.

Two minutes later, the car came to a halt. The door opened to the sound of tinny, mechanical music, and Pellaeon stepped out into the vast control room that served as the nerve center for the *Chimaera*'s huge sublight ion drive engines.

And came to a sudden, startled halt.

Gliding across the control room floor were a dozen MSE-9 droids, their squat little boxy shapes weaving back and forth like some sort of strange mechanical ballet. They were also, he realized now, the source of the strange music cutting across the hums and muted rhythmic throbbings of the massive engine machinery a couple of bulkheads away.

The mastermind behind the bizarre display wasn't hard to identify. Sorro was standing off to one side, waving his arms in slow, dreamy movements, as if conducting a genuine orchestra or chorus.

Like any good ballet, the performance also had an audience. All thirty crew on duty in the vast room were sitting or standing frozen at their posts, gazing in fascination at the droids crisscrossing one another's paths.

Again, Pellaeon bit back a curse. Crewers on duty were supposed to be on *duty*, sitting at their stations, watching their monitors, and not being distracted by every eye-catching thing that happened by. The fact that the sublight engines were on standby while the *Chimaera* traveled through hyperspace was totally irrelevant. He took a deep breath, preparing a command-class bellow that would be loud enough to be heard three decks away—

"I'm not sure when he arrived," Geronti said from beside him.

Pellaeon turned, temporarily canceling the bellow as he realized with embarrassed chagrin that he hadn't even noticed Geronti's arrival. The MSEs' dance was strangely hypnotic. "You're not *sure?*" he growled. "How in the Empire could you miss *that?*"

"I'm not talking about Sorro," Geronti said, pointing across the room. "I'm talking about *him.*"

Frowning, Pellaeon looked in that direction. Walking slowly but purposefully in the relative shadow of a bank of control junction boxes was Lord Odo. "What's *he* doing here?" he asked.

"As far as I can tell, giving himself a walking tour of my control room," Geronti said nervously. "I tried to ask him what he wanted, but he just walked away. I know Captain Drusan ordered us to give him access to any area he wanted, but this is just—" He broke off. "I didn't want to wake the captain, so I called you."

"Yes," Pellaeon said, watching Odo. The other paused, apparently studying the readouts on the junction boxes, then moved on toward the mixture-feed control station, whose three crewers were staring in complete oblivion at the droid ballet. "Well. Let's go talk to him."

They were halfway to the mix station when the crewers there suddenly seemed to notice the approach of senior officers. They spun back to their stations with guilty speed, followed by a collective twitch of their shoulders as they apparently only then noticed Odo's presence, as well. One of them glanced back at Pellaeon, made as if to speak, seemed to decide that the officers would deal with the situation, and turned back to his post without a word.

Odo had finished his inspection of the mix station and was moving on when Pellaeon and Geronti caught up with him. "Lord Odo?" Pellaeon said. "May I ask what you're doing here?"

"Captain Drusan has given me full access," Odo said, not breaking stride in the least. "I assumed you were aware of that."

"I am," Pellaeon said. Taking a few quick steps, he passed Odo and then turned sharply, putting himself directly in the other's way. "That's not what I asked."

Odo stopped just short of running into him. "I've given you all the answer you need, Commander," he said. "You will remove yourself from my path."

"No," Pellaeon said firmly. "You may have free run of this ship, but the *Chimaera* is still a warship of the Imperial fleet. You and your pilot are currently turning it into a Mon Cal opera, and I want to know why."

The blank eyepieces in Odo's mask seemed to bore into Pellaeon's face. Pellaeon forced himself to stare back, and after a moment Odo's shoulders twitched in a shrug. "Very well," he said. "Have you ever heard of the Troukree?"

Pellaeon searched his memory. The name wasn't familiar, but there were so many alien species. "I don't think so," he said. "Should I have?"

"Not yet," Odo said. "But if Warlord Nuso Esva has his way, you soon will."

"Warlord who?" Geronti asked.

Pellaeon gestured him to be silent. "Why is that?" he asked Odo.

"Because the Troukree are Nuso Esva's stealth weapon of choice," Odo said. "Expert saboteurs, dangerous warriors, cunning and deceitful beyond measure."

"Sounds like they'll be worth keeping an eye on when they surface," Pellaeon said. "What does this have to do with you and Sorro?"

Odo inclined his head. "I believe the Troukree may have infiltrated the *Chimaera*."

A shiver ran up Pellaeon's back. "That's impossible."

"Is it?" Odo countered. "Even in the Empire there exist creatures like the Clawdites with limited mimicry of face and form. Who's to say what secrets of stealth or disguise the Troukree may have developed or been given?"

Pellaeon pursed his lips. On the surface, it was a ludicrous claim. Even the most expert of Clawdite shape-shifters would have severe difficulty getting through the security procedures of a modern warship.

But Odo was right. There were many strange peoples in the known galaxy. What even stranger creatures might exist in the unexplored darkness outside the Empire's boundaries? "And this performance?" he asked, gesturing behind him toward Sorro and his musical droids. "This is supposed to draw these Troukree out?"

"The performance is to distract and bemuse them." Odo brought his left hand out from a concealing fold of his cloak. "*This* is to identify them."

Pellaeon focused on the object in his hand. It was a metal sphere, about ten centimeters across, with a pair of sensor antennas, a large circular visual scanner, a small air analysis grille, and a triad of repulsorlift ridges. "Looks like a vintage seeker," he said.

"It is indeed," Odo confirmed. "An Arakyd Mark Two, to be precise. An old one, as you say, and not in the best of shape. The repulsor drive no longer works, but the sensors are still functional. I'm traveling about the critical parts of the ship searching for traces of Troukree biomarkers."

"And if you find them?"

A sound that an imaginative man might have deciphered as a chuckle came from behind Odo's mask. "Never fear, Commander," he said. "I'm not a being of personal action and violence. If I detect the presence of the Troukree, be assured that I will immediately communicate that information to Captain Drusan and the commanders of the trooper and stormtrooper forces aboard the *Chimaera*." He lowered his hand back to his side, concealing the seeker again beneath his cloak. "If your curiosity is satisfied, may I now be permitted to continue?"

"Yes, of course," Pellaeon said, stepping aside.

"Thank you." Odo continued on his way, heading now toward the fusion-feed controller station.

"Did any of that actually make sense to you, sir?" Geronti murmured.

"Enough of it, yes," Pellaeon said grimly. "More than enough, in fact."

"I see," Geronti said. "I presume I'm to keep everything I've heard strictly confidential?"

"Extremely so," Pellaeon confirmed, watching as Odo paused by the fusion controller. "Do me a favor and keep an eye on him. He can go where he wants, but keep an eye on him. I'd appreciate it if you'd also pass that word—*quietly*—to the rest of the duty officers."

"I will, sir," Geronti said.

"And take down the register numbers of those MSEs," Pellaeon added, pointing toward Sorro's collection. "When Sorro's finished with them, I want each and every one of them examined, down to their wiring and microgears. *And* make sure they're reprogrammed back to whatever they were supposed to be doing when Sorro hijacked them."

Geronti nodded. "Yes, sir."

"I'm heading back to the bridge," Pellaeon said. "Let me know if you find anything out of place in the droids, or if anything else odd happens down here."

"I will, Commander," Geronti said. "Sorry to have disturbed you."

Pellaeon looked across at Odo's back. "That's all right," he said. "I'm not sorry. Not at all."

The first group of shops Luke had seen at the end of the apartment complex didn't include any clothing stores. But half a block away he found a small secondhand shop that had two full racks of cast-off clothing. A few minutes and twenty credits later, he emerged wearing a blue tunic and yellow sash, a set of gray military-style trousers from some army and war he'd never heard of, and a hooded poncho that not only concealed his hair and shadowed his face but also conveniently hid the stormtrooper utility belt now looped around his shoulder.

The sounds of the mob at the palace had faded away during the time he'd been inside the shop. Just the same, he knew better than to go back in that direction anytime soon. Sticking to the quieter residential side streets, he headed farther out into the central part of the city, looking for a place where he might have a little privacy.

He found it four blocks away: a small park with benches and trees with interlocking branch canopies. There was a low wall around the park and, more useful for Luke's purposes, several stands of aromatic, meter-high plants with bright pink-and-orange flowers, multicolored leaves, and furry stems. Sitting down on the soft grass a meter away from one of the stands, turning his back to the rest of the park and the city beyond it, Luke slipped the stormtrooper belt off his shoulder and began opening the pockets.

Brightwater had said there might be items in there that Luke would find useful. He'd been right. Along with three days' worth of emergency rations, there were two ion flares, a syntherope dispenser and grappling hook, a medpac, two small key-locked grenades of unknown type, a compact electromonocular, a glow rod, and a spare comlink. There were also two spare blaster power packs, somewhat less useful given that Luke didn't have a blaster to go with them, and an old coin that looked a little like the druggats they sometimes still used back on Tatooine.

Setting aside the rest of the equipment, he picked up the comlink. Finally, he could check in with Cracken.

Only, to his chagrin, he discovered that he couldn't. The comlink wasn't a standard, general-use model, but was binary-linked to a single comlink system—presumably the system Brightwater and LaRone were working on.

Luke rolled the comlink across his hand, wondering what he was supposed to do now. A city this size would have a few public comm stations scattered around, mostly for the use of citizens whose own comlinks had been lost or damaged. But Rieekan had warned repeatedly against using anything that wasn't running an Alliance encryption. Especially public comms that were probably under regular governmental surveillance.

Of course, he also doubted that Rieekan would approve of Luke calling *anyone* on a stormtrooper's comlink. But right now, he was out of ideas. Bracing himself, he keyed the comlink.

LaRone answered almost instantly. "LaRone," he said in a clipped, professional tone.

"It's Skywalker," Luke identified himself.

There was just the briefest pause, as if LaRone had been expecting someone else and was having to reset his brain to this new reality. "Skywalker," he said, a little flatly. "You all right?"

"Yes, thanks to Brightwater and the others," Luke said. "I wanted to call and thank you for that."

"You're welcome," LaRone said. "I hope you're on your way out of the city."

"Not yet," Luke said. "I was hoping—"

"Well, then, *get* out of the city," LaRone interrupted him. "They're trying to frame you for Governor Ferrouz's murder."

Luke felt the breath catch in his throat. He'd hoped all that stuff the mustached man was shouting had been nothing but mob rhetoric. "He *is* dead, then?" he asked.

"Actually, no, he's not," LaRone said, his voice suddenly sounding odd.

"Hold on a second—someone else wants to talk to you." There was a moment of silence as the comlink apparently changed hands, a murmur of distant conversation too faint to hear—

"Skywalker?"

Luke felt his jaw drop. "Master *Axlon*? What are you doing there?"

"Staying alive, thanks to your friends here," Axlon said grimly. "I don't know how or why you met up with Imperial stormtroopers, and I don't think I want to. But never mind that. Where are you?"

"Somewhere in the city," Luke said, looking around for a street sign. There was nothing visible from where he was sitting. "Where are *you*?"

"In a tapcaf," Axlon said. "It's the—what's the name here? It's the Whistling Wind, about three blocks south and west of the palace gate. You need to get here as quickly as you can."

"Wait a minute." LaRone's voice cut back in, and Luke had a quick impression of him snatching the comlink from Axlon's hand. "Cancel that, Skywalker. You aren't to come anywhere *near* this place."

"What are you talking about?" Axlon demanded, his voice faint. "We need as much help as we can get."

"We don't want—"

LaRone's voice broke off, and Luke heard a faint scuffle as if he and Axlon were fighting for the comlink.

"Luke, listen to me," Axlon said. "No, Governor Ferrouz isn't dead. But he's injured, and we could be under assault at any time by the people who tried to kill him. I appreciate the fact that LaRone's trying to protect you, but the fact of the matter is that we need you here. More than that, I'm your superior and I'm *ordering* you here. Do you understand?"

"Yes," Luke said, grimacing. "I'll be there as soon as I can. Have you heard anything about Han and Leia?"

"Not since you called me about them last night," Axlon said. "But if you'd like, I'll give Chewbacca a call as soon as we're done. Hopefully, I'll have some news by the time you get here."

"Good enough," Luke said. "See you soon."

He keyed off the comlink and clipped it onto his new sash. He was under Axlon's authority, and if Axlon wanted him at the Whistling Wind, he had no choice but to obey.

But he'd also seen LaRone and the others in action. If they didn't want Luke there, there had to be a very good reason for it.

So he would go to the Whistling Wind as he'd been ordered. But he would go there very carefully and very watchfully, using every bit of observational skill and subterfuge that he had.

Which wasn't all that much. But he had the Force. Maybe that would be enough.

He looped the utility belt over his shoulder again beneath the poncho and stood up. Adjusting the hood to hide his face, he got his bearings and headed out.

Axlon clicked off the comlink and held it out toward LaRone. "Thanks," he said. "I appreciate it."

"I wish I could say the same," LaRone said, holding hard on to his temper. "What possessed you to tell Skywalker to come *here*?"

"We need him," Axlon said in a tone of strained patience. "We need all the fighters we can get." He waved a hand. "Or are you depending on *this* to keep us safe?"

He had a point, LaRone had to admit as he looked at the redoubt they'd hastily put together. Ferrouz, stretched out on his couch, had drifted back to unconsciousness, and LaRone and Marcross had laid the pieces of their armor across him to protect him as best they could.

Two meters in front of the couch they'd set up a row of meter-tall metal kegs, with the two-meter gap allowing them enough space to crouch, shoot, and reposition themselves if necessary. Stacked together on the stairs were thirty bottles of the highest-proof liquor they could find, ready to be blasted and their contents ignited to create a fire barrier between them and any attackers from that direction. Marcross had questioned the wisdom of that, but LaRone had pointed out that enough of the cellar was permacrete and other nonflammable material to ensure that any fires they started shouldn't get out of control. More bottles had been gathered behind their keg barrier to serve as makeshift grenades, along with all the actual grenades the team had carried in their utility belts. More bottles, should they need them, were close at hand in the floor-to-ceiling rack ris-

ing behind Ferrouz's couch. Finally, Marcross and Brightwater had cre-
ated a pair of trip wires with their syntherope, one each in front of the stairs
and across the room by the lift.

It was a decent enough redoubt, given the materials they'd had to work
with. And it would certainly slow down any assault.

But it wouldn't stop it. Not if the attackers were determined.

"You're right, we could use some more fighters," he told Axlon as he set
his BlasTech E-11 on one of the kegs of their barrier and started laying his
spare power packs beside it. "But Skywalker's not the one we need. More
to the point, we don't *want* him here."

"How do you figure that?" Axlon countered. "He's a Jedi, isn't he? The
Jedi were supposed to be good fighters."

"He's not a Jedi yet," Marcross said, his elbow crooked with his own
E-11 pointed at the ceiling as he walked over from the stairs to join the
conversation. "At least, not as of three months ago."

"Things change," Axlon said, circling the end of the barrier and going
over to peer at Ferrouz's closed eyes. "The point is that, until Jade comes
back, Skywalker's our best bet."

"Our best bet for what?" Grave asked, straightening up from behind
the barrier where he'd been rearranging their stack of alcohol bombs.

"Weren't you listening?" Axlon growled, turning to face him. "For defense, of course."

"Are you sure that's why you want him here?" Grave asked.

"It's not because of his sparkling personality," Axlon said acidly. "You
been wearing your helmet too tightly or something?"

"It's the higher altitude that snipers have to work at," Quiller said, slapping a fresh power pack into his blaster as he came up beside Grave.

"Maybe that's it," Grave said. "Because there's something here I'm still
not getting. Maybe you can explain it to me."

Axlon sighed. "I'll do my best. What's the problem?"

"It was something that happened just before the riot started," Grave
said. "Someone in the crowd shouted that Governor Ferrouz was dead,
then grabbed Skywalker and his lightsaber and announced that Skywalker
was the one who'd done it." He cocked his head. "What I don't understand
is why anyone would think the governor had been killed with a lightsaber."

The cellar was suddenly very quiet. "Obviously, he heard somehow that Jade was in town," Axlon said. "Probably from Major Pakrie, whom we know is working with them."

"Only Pakrie was stunned and out of commission at the time," Marcross pointed out thoughtfully. "LaRone and I watched Jade do it."

"I didn't say he heard about Jade *today*," Axlon said. "You've been in town at least a couple of days, right?"

"True," Grave said. "Let me rephrase the question, then. How did he know to claim *right then* that the governor had been—"

Without a word, Axlon pulled a small blaster from his tunic and shot him.

It was so unexpected that for a heartbeat LaRone found himself frozen. A long, fatal heartbeat. Axlon shifted aim, blazed a shot into Quiller's leg that sent him tumbling to the floor beside Grave, then swiveled ninety degrees and fired a third shot over the barrier, this one hitting and shattering the power pack on Marcross's E-11 and sending shards of plastic and metal scattering.

And as LaRone belatedly grabbed for his blaster, he found Axlon's weapon pointed directly at his face. "Easy, stormtrooper," the Rebel said softly. "You don't have to die. None of you has to. Put down the blaster, and you can all live."

LaRone didn't move, his hand on the grip of his E-11, his mind dropping belatedly into tactical mode. Axlon's blaster was already centered, while LaRone's was still a good half second from pick up, aim, and fire. Trying to beat out the Rebel would almost certainly mean his death, but he might get off a dying shot that would save the others.

Axlon might have been reading his mind. "Don't try it," he warned. "I don't want to kill you—I don't want to kill any of you—but I will if I have to."

LaRone took a deep breath. "Grave?" he called, keeping his eyes on Axlon.

"He took one in the right abdomen," Brightwater reported grimly, and out of the corner of his eye LaRone saw the other kneeling over the wounded man. "Low down, possible kidney graze. Doesn't look immediately life threatening, but he's going to need a bacta tank."

"The sooner this is over, the sooner you can get him to one," Axlon said.

"Quiller?" LaRone asked.

"Right thigh," Quiller said, the words coming from between clenched teeth. "I'll be okay. Pulls his shots to the left, I see."

"That assumes he was going for my blaster and not my head," Marcross said. He still had his now useless E-11 pointed at Axlon, a couple of trickles of blood running down his cheek from the burst power pack.

"Of course I was going for your gun," Axlon said, starting to sound a little angry. "I could have killed all three of them, LaRone. But I didn't. Consider it a gesture of good faith."

"So I'm the only one you want to kill?" Ferrouz asked weakly from behind him.

LaRone tensed in sudden anticipation. If Axlon turned even partway around toward the governor . . .

But the Rebel wasn't foolish enough to make such an obvious mistake. "Awake again, are we, Your Excellency?" he asked, his eyes and blaster still rock-steady on LaRone's face. "How's your head?"

"You mean where you shot me?"

Axlon shrugged fractionally. "My apologies. Of course, you *were* already unconscious, since I had to slam your head against the side of the desk in order to get your blaster away from you. No, please, don't try anything. I helped stack that armor, remember? You can't move more than three centimeters without bringing one of the pieces clattering down."

"What do you want, Axlon?" Brightwater asked.

"I want you to lower your weapons and relax," the Rebel said. "Just until Skywalker arrives. Once he's here and we've completed a little business, you'll all be free to go, and to take your wounded with you."

"That business being the murder of Governor Ferrouz?" LaRone bit out.

Axlon's lips compressed briefly. "For whatever it's worth, it wasn't supposed to go this way," he said. "I was told that the Emperor would almost certainly send the young lady known as the Emperor's Hand to investigate Ferrouz's treason. *She* was supposed to kill him. Skywalker was simply supposed to take the blame."

"I'm sure he'd have been thrilled," Marcross said.

"He killed nearly a million men aboard the Death Star," Axlon said tartly. "I seriously doubt one more death will be a burden to his reputation."

"You might be surprised," LaRone said. "There's a huge difference between combat death and murder."

"This from the people who destroyed Alderaan?" Axlon snarled. "You think those were combat deaths, *stormtrooper?*"

Out of the corner of his eye, LaRone saw Brightwater start to ease back to his feet from beside the two wounded men. "And you can hold it right there, Brightwater," Axlon ordered, the brief flash of anger back under control. "I *can* still kill all of you if I have to, you know."

"No, actually, you can't," LaRone said. "You need us alive and looking more or less normal when Skywalker arrives."

Axlon's eyebrow twitched. "Very good," he said. "You're smarter than I would ever have given a stormtrooper credit for. Yes, that's what I want. But we don't always get what we want, do we? If I have to, I can explain to that naïve fool why all of you are dead. Certainly long enough to get hold of his lightsaber." He shrugged. "No matter how it goes down, it'll certainly be safer than waiting for Jade to come back and trying to get hold of *hers.*"

"Why do you care about Skywalker's lightsaber?" Ferrouz asked, his voice still weak. "You have a blaster. Why not just shoot me?"

"Because *everyone* has blasters," Axlon retorted. "Aren't you listening? I need to guarantee that the Rebellion gets the credit for Ferrouz's death. The only way to do that is to use a lightsaber and then blame it on a known lightsaber-carrying Rebel."

"Yes, we've got that part," Brightwater said. "But why do you care that the Rebels get the blame?"

"You really want to know?" Axlon countered. "I'll make you a deal. Lower your weapons to the floor and you, Brightwater, get over there on the other side of the barrier with LaRone and Marcross, and I'll tell you all about it."

"What about Grave?" Brightwater asked, still crouched beside the two wounded stormtroopers. "He needs a pair of burn patches. My medpac's right there by that keg—let me treat him, and then I'll do whatever you say."

Axlon's eyes flicked briefly to them, unfortunately not long enough for LaRone to make any move of his own. "I think right now Quiller's as functional as I want to have on this side of the barrier," he said. "Hand him the medpac, and he can do whatever patching is required. *After* you and the others are together where I can keep an eye on you."

Brightwater sighed. "Fine," he said. Reaching past Grave, he retrieved the medpac and handed it to Quiller. Murmuring encouragingly in the other's ear, he put his hands on top of his head and got to his feet. Giving the wounded men one final, lingering look, he turned and walked around the end of the keg barrier.

And as he came around to their side, he flashed LaRone a look.

LaRone felt his heart pick up its pace. Brightwater hadn't just given up. Not that easily, certainly not with that look in his eye. He was up to something.

Only what? He was walking with a slight limp, LaRone noticed, dragging his right foot across the floor as he walked. Had he caught part of one of Axlon's shots?

"You two, same as him," Axlon ordered, twitching his blaster at LaRone and Marcross. "And take a long step back while you're at it. I don't want any heroes trying to throw themselves over the kegs at me."

Silently Marcross laid his E-11 on the keg in front of him and took the requisite step backward. He put his hands on his head, sending a sideways look at LaRone as he did so, a look that said that he, too, had picked up on Brightwater's subtle attitude. Reluctantly, LaRone released his grip on his own E-11, placed his hands on his head, and stepped back. Brightwater, still dragging that foot, came up to Marcross's side. Axlon, his eyes and blaster still on the three of them, moved up to the barrier and picked up LaRone's E-11, then backed up all the way to the rack of bottles and propped the blaster rifle by the foot of Ferrouz's couch where it would be within easy reach. "Fine," Brightwater growled. "How about that story now?"

"In a moment," Axlon said. He glanced briefly to his left at the governor, to his right at Quiller and Grave, then finally returned his gaze to LaRone and the others. "I first need to make a call," he continued, pulling out his comlink. "I have to make sure Skywalker gets the proper reception."

His lip twisted. "And *only* the proper reception."

CHAPTER FIFTEEN

T HE TRAITORS, TO MARA'S MINOR REGRET, HADN'T GATHERED IN THE corridor outside the governor's emergency safe room.

More surprising was that no one had gathered in Ferrouz's office, not even the security men who should have been there trying to figure out what had happened to the governor.

The man sitting at Ferrouz's desk with his back to Mara was the likely reason for that. "Hello," he said, not turning around. "Is he dead?"

"Should he be?" Mara countered, focusing on the man's white hair and gray-green army uniform. She couldn't see the rank bars from her vantage point, but she was pretty sure who this was.

"I don't know," the man said. "If you're who I think you are, you only appear when treason is involved. Yet there's no body. What should I assume from that?"

"You can assume that my investigation is still ongoing," Mara said. "Where is everybody?"

"You mean the security investigators?" the man asked. "I sent them away, of course. As soon as they ascertained the governor had been taken and that a lightsaber was involved."

"Why?"

He shrugged slightly. "I assumed you wouldn't want anyone . . . stumbling into you."

"Very thoughtful," Mara said. "You know, it's considered polite to face a person when you're speaking to them."

"I wasn't sure you'd want that," he said. "I've heard that to look on you is to look on death."

"Not always," Mara said. "Turn around, please."

For a moment the man didn't move. Then, with obvious reluctance, he swiveled his chair around.

One glance at his face and rank bars was all the confirmation Mara needed. "Certainly not in this case, General Ularno," she said. "What do you know of Governor Ferrouz's recent activities?"

"A little," Ularno said, his eyes still avoiding Mara's face. "Not much. Should I have known more?"

"You know what you know," Mara said. "I'm looking for information, General. There's no right or wrong answer."

He smiled sadly. "Of course there are right and wrong answers. This is the Empire."

Mara felt her stomach tighten. So this was the legacy of the ISB and men like Vader and Grand Moff Tarkin. Not the rule of law or justice, but of fear. "I'm an interrogator, General, and a dispenser of Imperial judgment," she said. "But first and foremost I'm an investigator. All I want from you is the truth."

Carefully, Ularno lifted his eyes to her face, and for a moment he looked at her in silence. Then he gave a short sigh, the kind that came from a man who has nothing left to lose. "Governor Ferrouz has been having quiet communications with various persons," he said. "Persons very likely unfriendly to the Empire."

"Rebels?"

"Some were Rebels," Ularno said. "I wasn't sure what to make of that, but decided to give him the benefit of the doubt. I hoped it was some officially sanctioned operation, that he was trying to lure the Rebels into a trap."

"I see," Mara said, keeping her voice neutral as she stretched out to the Force. Ularno was seriously worried about his own skin, but she could sense no hint that he knew about the kidnapping of Ferrouz's family. "You said some of his contacts were Rebels. What about the others?"

"He's also spent a great deal of time recently bringing in various alien groups that have drifted to Poln Major and Whitestone City over the past few years. Those talks were always in private, and he was always vague afterward whenever I asked him what they'd talked about."

Mara nodded. That one, too, made sense. Once Nuso Esva had made his move, Ferrouz would naturally try to find out as much as he could about the warlord. Travelers and refugees coming in from the Unknown Regions would be an obvious source of such information. "What's your opinion of Major Pakrie?"

That one got a snort. "In a word, ambitious," Ularno said. "He'll do anything necessary to advance his own career and fortune."

"Up to and including murder?"

Ularno grimaced. "You're referring to the circumstances under which he achieved his most recent promotion. Yes, some of us wondered about that. But no one ever found proof that it was anything but an accident."

Mara felt a sudden flicker of hope. If they'd suspected Pakrie of murder . . . "Did these interested parties include Security Chief Bonze?"

"Very much so," Ularno said. "Colonel Bonze is very conscientious about the quality of the men under his command."

"Excellent," Mara said, smiling grimly. "That means he'll have run a complete profile on Pakrie, including full tracks on his activities, his travel, and his communications."

"Probably," Ularno admitted. "You'd have to ask him about that."

"Or we could skip a step and tap into the security files," Mara said, waving Ularno back as she walked toward him. "A little room, please."

Ularno's eyes widened briefly. Apparently, the thought of doing anything so outrageously out of protocol was a shocking and disturbing one. "But I don't know the colonel's passwords," he protested, hastily getting up out of the chair.

"That's all right," Mara said. "Governor Ferrouz was kind enough to give me all the codes." She stopped beside the chair and looked Ularno in the eye. "You interested in finding some truth, General? Or would you rather go back to your duties and pretend you never saw me?"

Ularno drew himself up, as if from a permanent slump he hadn't even realized had become a part of his bearing. "Thank you, Agent," he said softly. "I'd very much like to stay."

"Call me Jade," Mara invited, seating herself and turning on the computer. "Let's see what we can find."

If sheer volume of collected data was any indication, Colonel Bonze had been seriously suspicious of his newly minted Major Pakrie. He'd run Pakrie's entire life under the scanner, from his finances and friends to his eating and drinking habits, his casual associates, and his taste in desserts.

Moreover, the security chief hadn't limited his investigation to the period immediately before and after Pakrie's promotion. Instead, he'd continued it all the way up to the present day, with the last entry time-stamped that very morning.

Pakrie apparently spent a lot of off-duty time visiting cantinas, gambling halls, and recreation dens. But all such activities were legal, and as far as Mara could tell none of them took place in a location where a halfway competent kidnapper would feel safe stashing his victims. Not surprisingly, there was also no mention in any of the files of anyone named Nuso Esva.

But there were several references to Pakrie's recent association with someone named Dors Stelikag. Bonze's file on the man was sketchy, but it included holos of him and several of his gang. It also suggested that one of Stelikag's goals in life was to quit the low-rent thug business and carve out a second career acting as intermediary or recruiter among the Poln system's various criminal and semi-criminal types. Making a mental note to look further into that when she had a chance, Mara went back to the log of Pakrie's recent activities for a more detailed look. "Any idea where Pakrie is now?" she asked Ularno.

"As of half an hour ago, he hadn't checked in," the general told her. "I know because that was when Colonel Bonze ordered a search for him."

"Do you know if they've checked the area above the interrogation room access hallway?"

"I believe the interrogation suite was the first place they looked," Ularno said. "That was where he was supposed to be going when the . . . when you came in."

Mara frowned as a line on the log caught her attention. "Do Pakrie's duties involve the governor's residence floor?"

"What do you mean?" Ularno asked, leaning closer.

"Pakrie seems to have spent a lot of time in that area," Mara said, pointing to the display. "Particularly during business hours, when Ferrouz is in the business part of the palace."

"That's not what you think," Ularno said, sounding faintly embarrassed. "The governor's wife and daughter aren't there at the moment. They went to their country estate about three weeks ago for some quiet relaxation."

Mara nodded as she keyed for a different page. It was an obvious but reasonable enough cover story, one that Ferrouz could come up with quickly and which most people would accept at face value.

Except that there was no record in the vehicle log of airspeeder travel between the palace and the estate during that time period, official or otherwise. What *was* there was a record of Pakrie again being on the residence floor the day Ferrouz's family disappeared. Not just once, but twice.

And one of the characteristics of virtually all governors' residences was that they also had access to the governors' emergency exits and safe rooms.

"May I ask a question?" Ularno asked tentatively.

"Go ahead," Mara said, running a cross-check on the palace's vehicle inventory. All three airspeeders registered to Ferrouz and his family were still marked as being in the palace garage. But there was one general-use airspeeder that hadn't been checked out and for which no location was given. Had it been Ferrouz's official escape vehicle, parked perhaps at the far end of the tunnel she and LaRone had taken Ferrouz down? That might explain why the palace records showed no extra vehicle activity, and perhaps how Nuso Esva's kidnappers had gotten their hostages out without being seen.

"*Is* Governor Ferrouz involved with the Rebel Alliance?"

"There are indications in that direction," Mara said absently as she keyed for the specs on the missing airspeeder. She would need to know exactly what she was looking for when she tapped into the planetary vehicular monitor system.

"Were the Rebels responsible for the attempt on his life today?" Ularno persisted.

"It's possible," Mara said, frowning up at him. "Why does it matter who's trying to kill him?"

"I suppose it doesn't, really," Ularno said. "It's just that I need to know how to handle that new directive from Imperial Center. As Governor Ferrouz's second in command—"

"What new directive?"

"Directive Four Seventeen, the one that came through about two months ago," Ularno said, frowning in turn. "I assumed you were familiar with it."

"Remind me," Mara said.

"It states that if a governor is assassinated by Rebels or suspected Rebels, his successor is to immediately broadcast an alert to all Imperial forces," Ularno said. "The forces are then supposed to converge on the location of the assassination."

"No, I hadn't heard about that," Mara growled. It sounded like something Vader had come up with, which would explain all by itself why she'd somehow been left out of the comm ring. Vader and Mara had never gotten along very well, and he was utterly focused on making sure he had the first crack at reacting to any Rebel operations.

Which was nothing but unfounded paranoia on his part, of course. The Emperor had tasked the Sith Lord with the job of dealing with the Rebellion, and Mara had no interest whatsoever in poaching on that territory. She had more than enough work to keep her busy as it was.

"Our copy's on file," Ularno said, as if afraid Mara wouldn't believe him. "I assume the idea is to prevent the Rebels from taking advantage of the chaos following—"

"Yes, I understand the intent," Mara cut him off as that part of the puzzle fell into place. So that was why Nuso Esva had forced Ferrouz to play nice with the Rebel Alliance. He'd hoped the Emperor would get wind of it, which he had, and send Mara to execute the suspected traitor, which she hadn't.

But how had Nuso Esva planned to tie Ferrouz's execution to the Rebels? And how did bringing a group of Imperial warships to Poln Major gain him anything?

"I only ask because the directive doesn't cover this situation," Ularno continued. "I need to know what action to take."

Mara sighed to herself. For a brief moment, the general had been stretching beyond his usual boundaries. Thinking ever so slightly past the accepted norm. But the strain had apparently been too much. He was pulling back from such unfamiliar territory, retreating to the safety of official guidelines and requirements. From now on, it would be up to Mara to make the decisions.

On the other hand, pushing it all back on Mara might show that Ularno was smarter than he looked. Because the next decision facing them—her—was a potentially lethal one.

It all boiled down to what Nuso Esva would do if things didn't go exactly according to his plan. Would he kill the hostages if Ularno announced to the galaxy that Ferrouz was still alive? Or would he kill just one as a way to put extra pressure on Ferrouz to get himself murdered like he was supposed to?

Alternatively, if Ularno pretended that Ferrouz was dead, would Nuso Esva decide that the hostages had served their purpose and release them? Or, again, would he simply kill them both?

And who exactly was Nuso Esva expecting to draw to Poln Major with an announcement of Ferrouz's death, anyway? Mara had done only a cursory check on her way into the system, but as far as she knew only Ferrouz's own small Candoras sector forces were close enough to Poln Major for the kind of quick response the directive obviously envisioned.

She had to let Ularno make *some* kind of announcement. Nuso Esva would be expecting news, and Mara couldn't afford to let him become suspicious.

She would have to gamble. Not with her own life, but with those of an innocent woman and girl.

"Go ahead and make the broadcast," she told Ularno. "But instead of saying Governor Ferrouz has been assassinated, just say that there was an attempt on his life and that Rebel involvement is suspected."

"I can do that," Ularno said slowly. "It's not *exactly* what the directive indicates."

"It's close enough," Mara assured him, shutting off the computer and standing up. "Get on that right away. And don't tell anyone else that I was here."

"Not even Colonel Bonze?" Ularno asked. "Protocol states—"

"Not *anyone*," Mara repeated firmly. "Understood?"

Ularno swallowed. "Understood."

"Good," Mara said. "I'll contact you via comlink if I have any further instructions."

"Understood," Ularno said again. "Good luck."

Mara was halfway down the first flight of stairs in the escape passage and had already pulled out her comlink when it occurred to her that it would probably not be a good idea to call LaRone right now. If the kidnappers had used the escape tunnel once, they might do so again, especially now that Mara was threatening the surface world with her particular brand of chaos. She still might run into them here, and it would not be good if they heard her before she heard them.

There would be plenty of work for the stormtroopers soon enough. Until then, she might as well let them rest.

Putting away the comlink, she drew her lightsaber and, holding it loose and ready in her hand, continued down the stairs.

"No, *you* listen, Stelikag," Axlon bit out, glaring into his comlink as if the other could actually see him. "You *will* clear your crew out of the palace neighborhood, and you will *not* try to find, capture, obstruct, or even look cross-winked at Skywalker. Do you understand?"

The person on the other end of the transmission said something LaRone couldn't hear. But he could see Axlon's face darken still further, and his finger press a little harder on his blaster's trigger. "Maybe we should offer to talk to him," he murmured to Marcross. "They tell me stormtroopers can be very persuasive."

"Stelikag doesn't sound like the persuadable sort," Marcross murmured back. "North low, when you have a moment."

LaRone felt his forehead crease in a frown. *North* was currently to his left, *low* meant down at the floor. Had Marcross spotted something down there they needed to deal with? Some vermin roaming silently around the cellar?

"Because he trusts me," Axlon said in a voice as strained as his trigger finger. "And because once I get him and his lightsaber, we won't need to deal with Jade anymore. You of all people should be happy about that."

He paused, listening again, his mouth working with his frustration. Casually, LaRone eased his head a few degrees to his left and lowered his gaze to the floor . . .

To Brightwater's feet, and the fancy knife the alien Vaantaar had given him, which now balanced across the top of Brightwater's right foot.

Just as casually, LaRone looked back up at Axlon. So that was why Brightwater had been walking with that dragging limp earlier. While he was crouched over Grave and Quiller, he'd managed to loosen the knife from its spot at the small of his back. When he stood up, the weapon had slid down his trouser leg to the floor, held upright between the material and Brightwater's leg.

Now, as he'd stood here with LaRone and Marcross, he'd worked it free and maneuvered it with his left foot up onto his right.

Which was also why he'd been so quick to surrender. Axlon facing down three functional stormtroopers was a panicky slaughter begging to happen. Axlon in what he thought was a position of strength might be lulled into making a mistake.

LaRone grimaced. It would, however, have to be one oversized bantha of a mistake. Axlon was four meters away, on the other side of a meter-high barrier, and LaRone had never heard anything about Brightwater being especially proficient at knife throwing. Nor was anyone else in their group, for that matter. Axlon was going to need a serious moment of inattention for this to work.

Maybe Brightwater had already thought of a way to get that moment. Or maybe he was counting on one of the others to buy it for him.

"No, just let them go," Axlon said. "We don't need your mob anymore—enough people have already seen Skywalker and his lightsaber. Just pay them off and let them go."

If Brightwater was waiting for an opening, LaRone was the only one who could give it to him. If he dodged to his right, moving as if he was going to go around the far end of the barrier, he might draw Axlon's eyes and fire in that direction.

"I don't know," Axlon said. "Go back to Poln Minor, I guess, and help Ranquiv mount those Caldorfs. We'll need them when—" He broke off, rolling his eyes. "Then help him guard the ones who *do* know how," he growled. "It sounds like he's got the scum of the system in there. Maybe someone'll need shooting—you'd like that. Just get out of there before Skywalker spots you. I'll call you after we're finished, and you can talk to Ranquiv about—"

He stopped, his eyes narrowing. "Really," he said. "Did Ranquiv give you a description?"

"Uh-oh," Marcross said quietly. "Ferrouz."

LaRone looked at the couch. Somehow, the governor had managed to work a hand free without rattling any pieces of the stormtrooper armor piled across him. Moving his arm almost imperceptibly, he had reached up and over the top of the couch back and was slowly working one of the liquor bottles free of the rack behind him.

Not yet, LaRone pleaded silently across the gap, giving his head an urgent, microscopic shake. *Not while he's still on the comlink. Stelikag and his gang will hear, and they're already in the neighborhood.*

But Ferrouz wasn't looking at him. His full attention was on Axlon as he slid the bottle silently along the rough wood. Another minute and he would have it free.

"Try to catch his eye," Marcross murmured. He cleared his throat. "Hey, Axlon?" he called loudly. "You promised us a story. Quit jabbering and talk to us."

Axlon shifted his aim slightly, pointing his blaster at Marcross. "Just one of my prisoners," he said into the comlink. "No, Solo shouldn't be a problem—he's a smart-mouth, but he usually knows what he's doing. You should still tell Ranquiv about him, though, make sure he doesn't break anything. And warn him not to tell Solo about the deal—I want to spring that one on Cracken myself. I'll finish things up here, then check in with Hapjax and clear him to clean up the rest of it. An hour, maybe less, and it'll be done."

Without waiting for a reply, he keyed off the comlink. "Well, that's that," he said, putting the comlink away. "Don't look so intense, LaRone. It'll all be over soon."

"I'm sure it will," LaRone said. "But maybe not the way you're hoping. Skywalker won't be nearly as easy to get the drop on as we were."

"Or as easy to kill," Marcross added.

"I already said I wasn't going to kill you," Axlon said. His voice was low, controlled, and so sincere that LaRone almost believed him. The man must have been a politician before he joined the Rebellion. "I'm not going to kill Skywalker, either. I just need to borrow his lightsaber for a minute."

"You think he'll just stand there and watch you kill Governor Ferrouz?" Marcross persisted.

Axlon shrugged. "By the time he realizes what's happening, it'll be too late for him to stop me. He'll accept it with whatever grace he chooses, and then it'll be off to the spaceport where Chewbacca and the *Millennium Falcon* should be ready to whisk him off the planet."

"Wait a minute," LaRone said, frowning. "Chewbacca is *here*? I thought you said Solo was up on Poln Minor."

"Solo is," Axlon said. "Apparently he's slipped into one of Nuso Esva's work crews."

"Yet another loose end for you to tie up," Marcross commented. "Looks to me like the whole thing's starting to unravel."

"Hardly," Axlon assured him. "Even if it was, Nuso Esva could put it back together. He's a military genius." He smiled tightly. "Who will soon be on *our* side."

"He's told you that, has he?" Marcross asked.

"That's the deal, yes," Axlon said. "Once General Ularno sends out his panic-stricken plea for help and Nuso Esva and Alderaan have both been fully and properly avenged, Nuso Esva will bring the full strength of his fleet onto the side of the Rebel Alliance." He shrugged. "At that point you can tell your story to anyone you want and it won't change a thing. So there's no reason to kill you, as I've already said."

"And you trust this Nuso Esva, do you?" Marcross asked. "A being who deals in manipulation and casual murder?"

" 'The enemy of my oppressor is my brother,' " Axlon said, quoting the old saying. "Nuso Esva has a score to settle with the Empire, just as we do. And the fact that his enemy is also the one who ordered Alderaan's destruction will simply make our vengeance that much sweeter."

LaRone frowned. "What are you talking about? I've seen the reports. Alderaan was Tarkin's idea, and he's already dead."

"So little you know," Axlon said contemptuously. "But Nuso Esva knows the truth. He told me who it was who was pulling Tarkin's strings."

"No one pulled Tarkin's strings," Marcross said. "I know people who knew the man personally. No one ever told him what to do except the Emperor. He barely even accepted suggestions from Vader."

"You've been lied to," Axlon said bluntly. "You've all been lied to. But I know the truth."

"You're sure about that?" LaRone put in, raising his voice a bit. Ferrouz almost had the bottle free now, and there might be some scraping as the end came off the rack. "You sure Nuso Esva wasn't just dangling Alderaan's memory in front of you so that you would get Skywalker here for him?"

Axlon snorted. "You really have no idea. Up on Poln Minor, at this very moment, Colonel Cracken and his team are loading tons and tons of Imperial weapons, equipment, and supplies aboard our transports, all of it ordered there by Nuso Esva. If he was just using us, why not keep it all for himself?"

"Spoken by a man who's never had to actually spend his own money," Marcross said scornfully. "Any one of those Caldorfs is worth half of whatever junk he's got you busy loading aboard your transports. Give the kiddies a few toys to keep them happy while he makes off with the *real* treasure."

"You might have a point," Axlon said. "Except that he's already agreed to give us all the ships—*and* missiles—that survive the upcoming battle."

LaRone felt his skin tingle. An upcoming *battle*?

"All of that negotiated personally by me, in fact," Axlon went on. Behind him, Ferrouz pulled the bottle free of the rack. "I can hardly wait to see Cracken's face when I present him our new—"

And as the governor began to shift his grip on the bottle's neck, one of the stacked stormtrooper chest plates fell clattering to the floor.

Axlon spun around, his blaster tracking toward the noise. "Well, well," he said tightly. "Nicely done, Governor." He stepped around the end of the couch toward Ferrouz and the bottle gripped in his hand. "I'll take that, if you please."

And as Axlon reached out his free hand, Brightwater flipped the knife up off his foot and into the air.

But not toward Axlon, or even toward Brightwater's own hand. Instead, the weapon made an almost lazy curve over the keg barrier toward the spot where Quiller and Grave were lying wounded. The knife topped its arc and started down again—

With a grunt of pain, Quiller lurched upright into LaRone's view. He caught the knife in midair and threw himself forward toward Axlon's back, wrenching the weapon from its sheath as he loped, his face contorting with pain with each impact of his injured leg against the floor.

Axlon heard him coming. But it was already too late. Even as he turned back around Quiller was on him, ducking beneath his blaster hand and stabbing upward into the center of Axlon's tunic.

And as Quiller's leg finally collapsed and dropped him to the floor, Axlon also collapsed, falling heavily across Quiller's back, the blaster dropping from his slackened hand.

LaRone and Marcross were there almost before the weapon finished bouncing, each grabbing one of Axlon's arms and hauling him up and off their friend. "You all right?" LaRone asked.

"Ask me again when the room stops spinning," Quiller said, his face twisted in pain. "Okay, I took out the bad guy. Can I get another pain shot now?"

"I'm on it," Brightwater said. He had circled the opposite direction around the barrier and was crouching beside Grave and the medpac, loading the proper vial into the spray hypo. "Nice work, Quiller."

"Nice work both of you," LaRone said. "Marcross, can you handle him the rest of the way? I'm thinking we can dump him in that gap beside the stairs."

"No problem," Marcross said as LaRone handed him Axlon's other arm. "What are you going to do?"

"Call Skywalker and wave him off," LaRone said grimly as he pulled out his comlink. "Axlon's friends may still be in the area, and we do *not* want him leading them here."

LaRone's call wasn't unexpected.

LaRone's news definitely was.

"I can't believe it," Luke said, his stomach churning, his mind trying to wrap itself around the very thought of Axlon's betrayal. "He was involved with kidnapping and *murder?*"

"Up to his eyebrows," LaRone said, his voice grim. "For whatever it's worth, I think he was mostly duped into it by this Nuso Esva character—the guy found Axlon's Alderaan button and leaned on it." He hesitated. "Also for whatever it's worth, I'm sorry."

Luke took a deep breath, trying to stretch out to the Force for calm. For once, it didn't work very well. "So what do we do? What do I do?"

"Depends on what you *want* to do," LaRone said. "You can go back to your Rebel friends, tell them what happened, and be done with the whole thing."

"Or?"

"Or you can stick around awhile and try to help us find Governor Ferrouz's wife and daughter."

Luke grimaced. The deal with Ferrouz had been a complete and utter fraud, Nuso Esva was apparently preparing some kind of battle, and Cracken was so entangled with the supply operation on Poln Minor that he might be days extricating himself and his team.

And on top of that, Han and Leia were still missing. This quiet little mission was rapidly falling apart. "Tell me again what Axlon said about Han."

"Just that he was helping mount missiles for Nuso Esva's people," LaRone said. "Does that sound like something Solo would know how to do?"

"I'm still amazed at all the stuff Han knows," Luke said. "No idea where this was happening?"

"Just somewhere on Poln Minor, which I gather you already knew," LaRone said. "But Axlon also said Nuso Esva was going to be giving the ships to the Alliance, so it's possible your leaders already know about this."

"If they do, they haven't mentioned it to me," Luke said. "I don't think I believe it."

"Oh, I'm *sure* I don't believe it," LaRone growled. "So far everything I've seen of Nuso Esva pegs him as a fraud and a swindler. Or worse. What does your side know about him?"

"Not much," Luke said. "Axlon was the one who brought his name up to the leadership, and given what we now know about Axlon I don't trust anything he said. You have any idea where to start looking for the governor's family?"

"Not a clue," LaRone admitted. "At this point our best bet is to try to find Major Pakrie and see if we can beat it out of him. But I doubt he's just sitting around waiting for us to swoop down on him."

"How about if we found someone else who's involved?" Luke suggested. "Like the one Axlon was talking to earlier. Stelikag, you said his name was?"

"That might do," LaRone agreed. "Problem is, he's probably gone to ground, too."

Luke smiled tightly, raising Brightwater's electromonocular to his eye and focusing the ranging cross-mark on the distant tapcaf window and the man with the scraggly mustache seated behind it. "Not necessarily," he told LaRone. "He's sitting in a tapcaf exactly one hundred thirty-eight meters from me."

"You're kidding," LaRone said, sounding as surprised as Luke had ever heard him. "That's great. Tell me where—one of us will come take over."

Luke hesitated, a nagging sensation tugging at him as he gazed at Stelikag. It certainly made sense for LaRone and the other stormtroopers to take over at this point. They were trained at this sort of thing, and Luke wasn't. More to the point, Governor Ferrouz was an Imperial. That meant this was their business, not his.

But he was feeling a subtle but definite tugging of the Force in the other direction. Logical or not, smart or not, his business or not, this was where he was supposed to be. This was what he was supposed to be doing. "How about instead you concentrate on finding Major Pakrie?" he suggested. "I'll keep an eye on Stelikag. That'll give us two chances for a lead instead of just one."

"You sure?" LaRone asked. "This isn't really your area of expertise. It's also not your fight."

"There are innocent people in danger," Luke reminded him. "There's also some sort of unknown threat heading this way. You may be right about the expertise part, but this is definitely my fight."

"Well, I'm not in any position to turn down free help," LaRone said. "Fine—you watch Stelikag. If he makes any comlink calls or leaves the tapcaf, let us know."

"I will," Luke promised. "Listen, I need to let my commander know what's happened. Is there any way to unlock this comlink?"

"Not that one, no," LaRone said. "But don't worry—I'll call someone in your group and give them an update."

Luke felt his eyes widen. "*You'll* call them?"

"Don't worry, I won't spook them," LaRone assured him. "Axlon's comlink should have the contact information I need. You just keep an eye on Stelikag. And *don't* let him spot you."

"No problem," Luke said. "Good luck."

He clicked off, a flicker of uneasiness running through him. He hadn't thought about Axlon's comlink, or his datapad, or any of the other things he might be carrying that might compromise some aspect of Alliance security.

He took a deep breath, forcing himself to relax. It would be all right. LaRone and his friends might be serving the Empire right now, but they would never again be true Imperials.

Across at the tapcaf, the server brought Stelikag and his friends a large plate of something steaming. Pulling out one of Brightwater's ration bars, Luke settled down to watch.

"*We're* going to contact the Rebels?" Marcross asked, looking stunned as LaRone put away his comlink. "Are you *insane*?"

"I don't see that we have a choice," LaRone said, heading over toward where they'd dumped Axlon's body. "Skywalker's right—they need to know about Nuso Esva's manipulation, and we're the only ones who can tell them. Brightwater, how's Grave doing?"

"Not good," Brightwater said grimly. "We're never going to be able to move him. Even if we got a doctor in here first to stabilize him, a landspeeder ride might kill him before we could even get him to a bacta tank."

"Understood," LaRone said, running through Axlon's clothing and relieving him of his comlink and data pad. "I think I may have an alternative."

"We also have another problem," Marcross said. "We're down to three of us, and this place is not exactly the most defensible position I've ever seen."

"Three and a half," Quiller put in. "I may not be mobile, but I can still shoot."

"My recommendation is that we pull the governor out," Marcross continued. "Get him settled somewhere safe, then worry about getting Grave some help."

"No," Ferrouz said.

They all turned to look at him. "No?" Marcross asked.

"We don't leave here," the governor said firmly. "Splitting a force this small is a bad idea, especially when one of you is badly injured." He waved a hand around the room. "Besides, until we know the full extent of the treason inside my palace, there's nowhere we could go that would be safer than right here."

"What about your safe room?" Quiller suggested. "It's just a little way back along the tunnel."

Ferrouz shook his head. "They somehow got my wife and daughter out of a heavily guarded Imperial facility. I don't trust anyplace connected with that facility, not even my safe room. No. Whatever stand we make, we make it here."

"We appreciate your confidence," Marcross said. "But the fact of the matter is that successfully holding any location boils down to numbers. We simply don't have them."

"No, we don't," LaRone agreed, an odd thought suddenly occurring to him. "Brightwater, you up to taking a little drive?"

"Sure," Brightwater said, frowning as he got to his feet. "Where am I going?"

"Back to the spaceport," LaRone told him. "If we can't get Grave to a bacta tank, maybe we can get a bacta tank to him."

"You mean ours, out of the Suwantek?" Marcross asked. "Come on — even a subminiature is way too heavy for Brightwater to handle on his own."

"I know," LaRone said. "And as long as he's going to be out there anyway, maybe we can get some of those extra numbers we need."

"You're going to call in the *Rebels*?" Ferrouz asked, his tone and face unreadable.

"Yes," LaRone said. "And, actually, no."

CHAPTER SIXTEEN

THIS TIME MARA WENT ALL THE WAY DOWN THE ESCAPE TUNNEL, PAST the hidden safe room, past the spot where she'd taken Ferrouz out into the city's storm drain, and past two more places where the permacrete structure around her again changed for the worse. Eventually, she reached the end.

Which was exactly that: the end. There was nothing there but a crumbling wall that blocked further progress. There was no hangar, no sign of an airspeeder, no sign that an airspeeder had ever been there, no access to the outer world.

She took a couple of minutes to check the walls and ceiling anyway, just to be sure. Then she pulled out her comlink and called LaRone.

"You all right?" he asked when she'd identified herself.

"Yes, but no farther along than we were when I left," she told him. "How's the governor?"

"He's doing better," LaRone said grimly. "Right now, he's the exception."

In a few terse sentences, he laid out the story of Axlon's betrayal, his attack on Grave and Quiller, and his death. "I hate it when I leave a party early," Mara growled when he'd finished. "What do you need me to do?"

There was a faint voice from somewhere on the other end. "Governor Ferrouz says what you can do is find his family," LaRone relayed. "I agree. We can handle things here for the moment."

"You said Grave was badly injured."

"We've got a bacta tank coming," LaRone said. "I have someone pulling the one out of the Suwantek and bringing it over in our other landspeeder."

Mara frowned. "Some*one*?"

"It's covered," LaRone said firmly, in the tone of someone who didn't want to talk about it. "What do you think about Axlon's comment that it would be over in an hour or less? Does that mean the hostages are somewhere nearby?"

"Not necessarily," Mara said, mentally sifting through the possibilities. If the kidnappers hadn't gotten out through the escape tunnel . . . "It could be that he was just going to call them and tell them to close up shop."

"Wouldn't that be risky?" LaRone asked. "Even our Suwantek has gear that can track a comlink call if you know which one's being used. I imagine a more complete ISB or Intelligence setup could also decrypt the conversation in more or less real time."

"Not always," Mara said, frowning with a sudden thought. Maybe the kidnappers had gotten into the tunnel but never left it. "But you're right, it would be dangerous for them. Put Ferrouz on, will you?"

There was a brief pause, then: "You have something?" Ferrouz asked.

"Maybe," Mara said. "What do you know about your emergency safe room?"

"It was built by one of my predecessors—Moff Frisan, I think it was. I've only been inside twice. It's much larger than I expected: six rooms, laid out along the same lines as the palace residence suite, only with a food prep area and considerably more storage."

"How do you get in?" Mara asked. "Biometrics, or is there a keypad code?"

"Keypad code, plus a voiceprint verbal code," Ferrouz said. "A precise code, with specific intonations and inflections on the words."

Mara keyed her comlink to record mode. "Give it to me."

It was short, only half a dozen words. "Keypad code?" she asked, shutting down the recording.

The numerical sequence was also short, only nine digits long. Whoever had set up the system had clearly chosen to sacrifice extra security for speed of access. "Who besides you has the code and an on-file voiceprint?"

"Just my wife, daughter, General Ularno, and Colonel Bonze," Ferrouz said, his voice gone dark. "You think they're in *there*?"

"It makes a certain amount of sense," Mara said. "They didn't leave by airspeeder, the exit tunnel dead-ends, and getting out through the gate would have required a lot of bribery or coercion."

"But how would they have gotten into the room?"

"That's the beauty of having two hostages," Mara said. "You can threaten one to make the other do what you want. I'm guessing a blaster to your wife's head would have quickly gotten the code out of your daughter."

Ferrouz swore, quietly and feelingly. "I want these people, Agent Jade."

"I fully intend to get them, Governor Ferrouz," Mara told him. "You just rest and recover. I'll let you know when I find something."

"All right. Just a moment—LaRone wants to speak with you again."

There was another pause, a longer one this time, with the sort of background noise that gave Mara the sense that LaRone was moving somewhere else with the comlink. "There was one more thing," his voice came on quietly. "I don't know if the governor caught the significance, and I don't want to worry him any more than he already is. But Axlon also said something about Nuso Esva's people mounting Caldorfs. Is there any other use of that term you know of other than ship-based interceptor missiles?"

Mara felt her stomach tighten. Nuso Esva had a supply of *Caldorfs*? "No, they're interceptors, all right," she said grimly. "Did he say where they were, or what they were doing with them?"

"Just that they were mounting them," LaRone said. "But there are other indications that say it's happening on Poln Minor."

"Big help," Mara growled.

"I know," LaRone said. "I may be able to get it pinned down a little more."

"Do that," Mara said. "Meanwhile, keep a close eye on the governor."

"We will," LaRone promised. "One other thing. We have someone with eyes on one of Axlon's associates, a man he called Stelig. He's going to let us know if Stelig makes any moves, so if you plan to stir things up a heads-up would be appreciated."

"If I have any advance notice myself, I'll be sure to let you know," Mara assured him. "Is this watcher someone you trust?"

"Yes," LaRone said. "We've dealt with Skywalker before."

Mara frowned at her comlink, a months-old memory flashing to mind: Lord Vader in the Emperor's library, doing a private search that Mara had subsequently been able to reconstruct.

A search for the name Luke Skywalker.

Firmly, she shook away the sudden odd sense of foreboding. *Skywalker* was a common enough name, especially in the Mid and Outer Rim areas of the Corellian Run. The odds were slim that this particular Skywalker was the one Vader was hunting.

Still, it was an interesting coincidence. "Tell him to stay sharp," Mara said. "From here on, things are likely to move fast. There's no guarantee of advance warning."

"I'll make sure he knows that," LaRone promised. "Good luck."

"And stay sharp yourselves," Mara added. "I'll let you know when I find something."

Keying off the comlink, she started back up the tunnel. No, LaRone and Skywalker weren't likely to get any advance warning.

With a little luck, neither would the kidnappers.

Han was halfway through his third missile mounting when Leia suddenly stiffened. "Ranquiv's heading this way," she murmured. "He's got two armed men with him."

"Hand me the big hydrospanner," Han murmured back, focusing on the missile's shiny surface. There were three figures coming up behind him, all right, though the reflections in the curved metal were too distorted for him to see any details. "On a scale of one to ten, how unhappy do they look?"

"Very," Leia said grimly as she handed him the hydrospanner. "There are two more men and two more of Ranquiv's yellow-eyed friends coming in about ten meters behind them."

"Yeah, I see them," Han said. Still, he'd known from the beginning that they were running on borrowed time. "Get ready to move."

"Where?"

Han did a quick assessment. Their current ship was obviously the closest, but getting to the ramp would mean heading toward the trouble currently marching in their direction. The next one over, the one behind Leia, would at least let them run away from Ranquiv's thugs. "Up that ramp," he said, nodding over her shoulder.

"Okay," Leia said. "Let me know when."

Han grimaced. "Trust me. You'll know."

He lifted the hydrospanner, making a show of adjusting it as he watched the approaching figures. The two men's arms shifted subtly as they reached for their blasters.

Spinning around, Han hurled his hydrospanner toward the group and grabbed for his own blaster.

Reflexively, the two men ducked as Ranquiv snapped both forearms up between his face and the spinning hydrospanner. The men recovered their balance and reached again for their weapons.

And twitched their hands away as Han put a shot squarely into each of their holsters, blowing the blasters apart and sending bursts of Tibanna gas out into the air.

"Go!" Han snapped, waving behind him. The two backups were on the move now, breaking into a run as they pulled out their weapons. For an instant Han considered sending a couple more shots in their direction to try to slow them down, decided it wasn't worth it, and turned and took off for the ship ramp he'd pointed out to Leia.

Fortunately, she hadn't waited for his order to run. As he ducked under the missile he'd been working on he saw that she was already halfway up the ramp. He leaned into his run, and by the time the blaster bolts started flying around him he'd made it to the top of the ramp and through the hatch, throwing out his free hand in front of him as he slammed into the bulkhead on the far side of the narrow entryway.

He was spinning around to close the hatch when Leia, who'd been standing to the side out of his way, slammed it shut for him. "Now what?" she demanded, spinning the door's old-fashioned locking wheel.

"We get out of here," he told her, pushing off the wall and through the cockpit door. He dropped into the pilot's seat and grabbed the straps, glowering at the controls and their softly lit alien-script labels. He'd hoped to have at least one more chance to study the translation before he tried this.

But he didn't, and he would just have to make do. "Strap in," he ordered as Leia tumbled into the seat beside him. The starter sequencer . . . there. He keyed the switch, and a soft rumble began to build from somewhere behind them.

"You're sure you know what you're doing?" Leia asked, leaning forward to peer out the side of the crosshatch canopy.

"I always know what I'm doing," Han assured her. A row of glowing markers shifted abruptly from red to blue. Standby? Probably, since that hadn't been long enough for repulsorlifts to warm up all the way. The drive activation was over *here*—he probably wouldn't need it, but it wouldn't hurt to have it ready. He keyed it on, glancing over at the red-lit weapons section of the board and wondering if he should bother trying to activate the laser cannons, as well.

Abruptly, the whole ship shook as something slammed violently against the outer hatch. "You forgot to raise the ramp!" Leia snapped.

"No, I didn't," Han said. The blue repulsorlift markers winked, then changed again, this time into a deep purple.

"What are you talking about?" Leia demanded, jabbing a finger. "I can see the end of it from here."

"I mean I didn't forget," Han said as whoever was out there again slammed himself against the hatch. "Hang on." Getting a grip on the steering yoke, he gave the throttle palm wheel a quick spin.

The ship leapt like a scalded mynock, heading straight for the ceiling, and Han heard a faint scrabbling sound as whoever had been on the ramp slid unceremoniously off of it again. Hastily, he spun the wheel half a turn back, and his stomach lurched as the ship ended its upward bounce and started back down again. Leia gurgled something as Han tried it again, turning the wheel a quarter turn this time.

The ship wobbled a bit and then stabilized, hovering a few meters off the ground. "See? Nothing to it," Han said, taking a moment to look out the canopy. From their new vantage point above the rest of the missile ships he could see across the cavern to the big conveyance tunnel at the far end. The two sets of quad lasers Ranquiv had installed over there were starting to swivel around on their mounts, shifting from the task of guarding the cavern's approach to the more immediate job of swatting down this unexpected hijack attempt. Between the quads, half a dozen other men were wrestling with one of the concussion launchers, also turning it to face into the cavern, while another group of aliens was hurrying to the entrance with heavy blaster rifles in their hands. Clearly, no one was getting out that way.

Just as well that wasn't the direction Han was planning to go.

Leia had seen the assembled firepower, too. "Han?" she warned, pointing.

"Don't look," Han advised, returning his attention to the control board. The banking controls . . . there? No; *there*. Shifting one hand from the yoke to the sliders, he gave them a turn. The ship leaned to portside, then began drifting sluggishly in that direction as the angled position unbalanced the repulsorlifts. Han gave the slider another push, glanced out the side of the canopy and twitched the control yoke. Blasterfire was hitting the ship now, the bolts thudding into the hull and splashing off the canopy as the ship's sideways skid picked up speed.

Across the cavern, he could see that the quad lasers were almost ready. He gave the slider one final nudge, remembering just in time that he also wanted the landing gear retracted. He found the right switch on the second try, then grabbed the throttle wheel and braced himself.

With a violent crash, the ship slammed into the side of the cavern right above the tunnel where he and Leia and the others had arrived. Spinning the throttle wheel all the way back, he dropped the ship to the ground.

And with the landing gear retracted and its hull on the ground, the ship was now completely blocking off the tunnel.

"Out," Han ordered Leia, pulling out his blaster and thrusting it into her hands. "Get to the speeder bus—see if you can start it. If you can't—"

"Open the access panel so that you can hotwire it," Leia called back over her shoulder as she disappeared through the cockpit door.

"Open the access panel so I can hotwire it," Han finished under his breath. He keyed off all the systems, then unstrapped and headed out after her.

With all the firepower at the other end of the cavern, he'd expected Ranquiv to have at least posted a guard or two at this equally obvious escape point. But there was no sound of blasterfire as he picked his way down the now slightly battered ramp, and he saw no bodies as he sprinted to the bus. Even insect-eyed aliens who could pull Caldorf missiles out of thin air, he reflected, sometimes made mistakes.

He found Leia inside the bus, the access panel already open. "It's frozen," she told him as she stepped back out of his way.

"Yeah, no problem," he grunted, kneeling down and giving the wiring a quick look. Something this old and decrepit ought to be a snap. "Thirty seconds," he promised. "Time me."

"Just hurry," Leia bit out. "They could be here any minute."

"Relax," Han said, poking at the wires. "They're not moving that ship anytime soon."

"Maybe they already have people out here," she countered, looking over her shoulder at the darkened tunnel stretching out behind them. "Where are we going?"

"Away," Han said. There was the starter line. A little tweaking . . .

"That's not an answer," Leia said. "We need to get back to Cracken and the others. Or at least close enough to one of the inhabited areas that our comlinks will work."

There was a click, and a low rumble suddenly filled the bus as the repulsorlifts came to life. "There you go," Han said, straightening up and turning to the driver's seat.

Leia was faster, slipping past him and dropping into the seat. "You're better with this," she said, handing him back his blaster. "I'll drive."

"How are you at driving backward?" he countered. "Because there's no room in here to turn arou—"

He grabbed for the seat back as she keyed in the repulsorlifts, sending the bus lurching up off the ground. A second later, as he was still trying to regain his balance, she shifted into reverse and they took off, backing full speed down the tunnel. "Get to the back," she ordered. "Let me know when we hit the next cross-tunnel so I can turn this thing around."

"So you've figured out where we're going?" Han asked as the bus once again settled into its periodic lurching side dips.

In the faint light from the control console readouts, he saw her lips tighten. "Like you said, the first thing we need to do is get away," she said reluctantly. "I don't suppose you were keeping track of the turns on our trip here."

"I thought that was your job," Han said. The bus made another of its dips, this one accompanied by a faint crunch of rock. "You're the one who said we were only about a hundred kilometers from the Anyat-en caverns, right?"

"I was only watching the first part of the trip," Leia said. "I fell asleep at the end."

"You should have woken me up."

"I didn't realize I'd dozed off until I woke up," Leia countered. "You didn't happen to see how the driver was navigating, did you? I don't see any map readouts anywhere on the control board."

"He had a datapad propped up on the console," Han told her. "Ranquiv took it with him when we all left."

"I was afraid of that," Leia said. "I guess we'll just have to poke around until we find something we recognize."

"That's what I was thinking," Han agreed. The bits of light coming from around the missile ship he'd crashed were fading into the distance, and he turned around to look out at the even darker tunnel behind them. "You might want to switch on some lights," he added. "It could be handy to see where we're going."

"If you can figure out a way to turn on the rear glow panels without turning on the front ones, go ahead," Leia said. "Otherwise, get the glow rod out of the emergency kit under the seat there and go shine it out the back. I don't want to have the headlights showing Ranquiv where we are. What *is* that noise?"

Han frowned, playing back the last couple of seconds through his memory. It had just been one of the bus's dips, along with another of the skittering-stone accompaniments he'd heard earlier. "The regulator squid's got a feedback problem," he told her. "It pops the repulsorlifts on one side—"

"I know *that*," she growled. "I'm asking—oh."

Abruptly she kicked in the brakes, forcing Han to again grab for a handhold as she brought the bus's speed down to a crawl. "What are you *doing*?" he demanded. There was another dip, and another soft crunch, and Han lurched again as she brought the vehicle to a complete halt.

He winced away as she turned on the headlights, blowing away the night vision he'd built up over the past couple of minutes. "Look," she said.

"At what?" he growled.

"At that," she said impatiently. "Right there, in front of us on the left side. That little circle. You see it?"

Reluctantly, Han opened his eyes to slits, giving them a moment to adjust to the glare. There was a faint circle there, all right, a slightly clearer spot in the layer of gravel covering the tunnel floor.

And suddenly he got it. "It's the backfeed sputter," he said, opening his eyes all the way as he studied the circle. "The stones get an extra kick when the repulsorlifts shunt back in."

"Leaving us a trail to follow," Leia said, cautious hope in her voice.

"Going to be tricky, though," Han said doubtfully. "A sputter every couple of seconds at a hundred kilometers an hour only gives us one marker every fifty meters or so. And *that* assumes there's gravel at all those spots for the sputter to make a circle in."

"It still beats wandering aimlessly around Poln Minor," Leia said. She shut off the lights, and in the sudden darkness Han heard her climb out of the driver's seat. "Think you can drive backward?"

"At least as good as you can drive forward," Han told her. "You planning to take a nap?"

"I'm planning to open the rear hatchway and watch for our trail of grapes with this," she said, and as Han's eyes again readjusted to the dim radiance from the console he saw her pull the glow rod from the bus's emergency pack. "At least until we find a place to turn around."

"Okay," Han said, sitting down behind the wheel. "You *do* remember how that story ends, don't you? The birds ate all the grapes the kid had dropped and he ended up dying lost in the woods."

"Is *that* the way they told it on Corellia?" she called back as she headed down the aisle. "On Alderaan, it turned out that the sun had fermented the grapes, and the birds who ate them got drunk, so the boy just followed the line of sleeping birds back home."

Han rolled his eyes. Leave it to the Alderaanians to slap a cheery end on a nice little grisly children's morality tale.

Of course, he'd always thought the kid in the story was an idiot anyway. "You ready back there? Okay. Here we go."

The hyperspace sky cleared, the starlines flashed back into stars, and the *Chimaera* arrived at a blue-green world spinning lazily through space.

Right at the edge of a massive battle.

"Full alert!" Drusan was bellowing as Pellaeon stepped hurriedly from the turbolift into the aft bridge. "Deflector shields activate; turbolasers to full power. Senior Commander Grondarle?"

"I read forty-two ships in the engagement sphere," the first officer called from the tactics station in the portside crew pit. "We have an Imperial heavy attack line: one Star Destroyer—the *Admonitor*—two *Strike*-class medium cruisers, and four *Carrack*-class light cruisers. Opposing are eight ships of Dreadnought size and twenty-seven escort vessels of system patrol craft size, all of unknown configuration and weaponry."

"Line array?"

"Unknowns are using a modified drinking-cup with center-focus fire," Grondarle reported. "The Imperials . . . I'm not sure, Captain. It looks almost like a standard engagement line, except that the *Admonitor* isn't hanging back out of enemy range like it should. And the Carracks are doing a sort of sweep pattern around and in front of it."

"Take us into combat range," Drusan ordered, frowning out the viewport as Pellaeon came up beside him. "That Carrack maneuver makes no sense," he added, lowering his voice. "The *Admonitor* has far more armor and shielding than any light cruiser. Putting the Carracks in front like that is practically begging for them to be blown out of the sky."

"It does look that way," Pellaeon agreed, gazing out the viewport at the distant battle.

"Obviously someone incompetent running the show," Drusan said darkly. "I suppose we'd better go and fix it for him."

"Sir, the *Admonitor* is hailing," the comm officer called.

"Put them through," Drusan said. "*Admonitor*, this is Captain Calo Drusan of the *Chimaera*."

"Welcome to Teptixii, Captain Drusan," a voice came from the bridge speakers. "Captain Voss Parck, currently commanding Task Force *Admonitor*. I don't know what you're doing this far out, but your timing couldn't have been better. I have the enemy ships nearly pinned, but my closest reinforcements are still nearly twenty minutes away. I need your help to finish this."

"We're on our way," Drusan said. "In the meantime, you're putting your Carracks at severe risk. I suggest you pull them back."

"He's not risking his Carracks, Captain," Lord Odo said from behind them. Pellaeon turned to see the masked figure striding along the walkway, his cape rippling behind him.

"Excuse me, Lord Odo, but he *is* risking them," Drusan said stiffly.

"Forgive me; I misspoke," Odo said, coming to a halt beside Drusan. "He *is* risking his Carracks, but he's doing so in order to gain victory. Observe how each time the Carracks block fire from the enemy cruisers the *Admonitor* is freed to lower its shields long enough to send a volley at one of the enemy's other ships."

The words were barely out of his mouth when there was a multiple flicker of turbolaser fire from the distant Star Destroyer and one of the enemy patrol ships flared and then exploded in a blue-white fireball.

"That's all well and good," Drusan grunted. "But having the Carracks block the larger ships means Parck's only available targets are the patrol craft. That leaves the larger ones intact, and he's risking his own screening ships to do it."

"He has little choice," Odo said. "The larger ships, the Firekilns, are more powerful than you realize. Laser to laser, five of them are an even match for his Star Destroyer, and Nuso Esva currently has eight of them in place."

"That's *Nuso Esva* out there?" Drusan asked, leaning forward as if that would give him a better view of the battle.

"Those are his ships, at any rate," Odo said. "Captain Parck would know better whether or not the warlord himself is on the scene. The point is that while the Firekilns are heavily armed, their shields are inferior to those of the Imperials. They rely on the screening ships to block the *Admonitor*'s attacks."

Pellaeon looked over at the tac display. "Except that the screening ships aren't just running defense, but are also armed," he said. "If they can take down the cruisers while the *Admonitor* is picking at them, he'll be left all alone."

"Not while we're here he won't," Drusan said grimly. "Let's see if Nuso Esva has the stomach for a fight when he *hasn't* got the odds on his side.

Helm, increase to flank and take us across the edge of the enemy formation."

"Not to the edge," Odo said. "Angle thirty degrees to portside and set our vector to cut behind the formation."

"That'll take too long," Drusan objected. "We're still a good eight minutes from firing range."

"It'll also put us inside the planet's gravity-well anchor point," Pellaeon warned. "If we get in trouble, we won't be able to make a quick escape."

"Never mind our escape," Drusan growled. "The point is that any delay on our part will give Nuso Esva the time he needs to take out Parck's cruisers."

"Fortunately, I don't think Nuso Esva is interested in destroying cruisers today," Odo said. "The Firekilns could have done that long ago. I suspect he's hoping to disable or destroy the *Admonitor* and capture the smaller ships intact as additions to his fleet. If, on the other hand, we come around behind him as I suggested . . ." He paused expectantly, like a teacher waiting for his students to come up with the correct answer.

Pellaeon got there first. Or at least, he spoke up first. "We'll force him to split his screening ships into two distinct and non-overlapping groups," he said. "Which I'm guessing he can't afford to do."

"Can't, and won't," Odo agreed. "He'll instead break off and make his escape as soon as he recognizes our intention." His mask turned toward Drusan. "There's no need for the *Chimaera* to reach actual firing range in order to drive them off, Captain. Nuso Esva will do the driving for us."

"Yes, I understand," Drusan said sourly. "Helm: thirty degrees to portside."

Odo's prediction proved to be correct. Less than a minute after the *Chimaera* altered its course, the Firekilns broke their formation, wheeling about in all directions, the smaller escort ships scrambling to draw in close to the larger cruisers. As the *Admonitor* intensified its fire the alien ships flickered with the pseudomotion of a hyperspace jump and vanished.

"And that," Odo said, "is that. Senior Captain Parck, are you still there?"

"I am," Parck said. "Thanks to you. One correction: I'm merely

Captain Parck. My superior, Senior Captain Thrawn, is currently away from the ship."

Pellaeon felt his back stiffen. This was *Thrawn's* attack force? Thrawn, the alien whose ineptitude at court politics seemed to have him permanently on the edge of being thrown out of both the fleet and the Imperial court?

And yet he had not only a Star Destroyer but an entire attack force? Who at Command would have risked giving him *that*?

"I'm sorry to hear that," Odo said. "His presence is urgently needed at Poln Major in Candoras sector."

"For what reason?" Parck asked.

"A response to possible insurrection," Odo said. "You've received no transmissions concerning the threat?"

"I've had no recent transmissions of any sort from the Empire," Parck said.

Odo muttered something behind his mask. "As I feared," he said. "Even this close to Imperial territory you're still out of HoloNet range."

"We're not *that* far out," Parck corrected. "Full transmissions can reach us considerably farther into the Unknown Regions than this. Rest assured that if there had been any messages we would have received them."

"Yet clearly, you have not," Odo said. "I must therefore deliver General Ularno's request myself. Your presence is urgently requested at Poln Major. Yours, Senior Captain Thrawn's, and the rest of your task force."

"And you are?"

"A representative of the Emperor himself," Drusan put in. "I can personally confirm his credentials. I can also confirm his claim of Rebel activity in the Poln system."

"I sympathize with the Poln system," Parck said. "But I'm afraid I must refuse your request. We have orders of our own, and vital work to do."

"This situation is more vital than anything you may be doing," Odo insisted. "A few hours' delay will surely not impact your mission."

"If necessary, I can invoke Directive One-Oh-Three," Drusan threatened. "In the absence of orders to the contrary, all fleet officers—"

"I'm familiar with the directive," Parck cut in stiffly. "It doesn't apply to us."

"You're part of the Imperial fleet, aren't you?"

"Technically, we're detached from the fleet command structure," Parck told him. "And as I said, Senior Captain Thrawn has his own set of orders that he needs to comply with."

Drusan took a deep breath. "Captain Parck—"

"One moment, Captain," Parck said, his tone suddenly changed. "We're receiving a transmission. Possibly the very one you've been expecting."

Drusan turned to the portside crew pit. "Comm officer?"

"Yes, sir, we're picking up the same transmission," the other confirmed. "There's been an attempted assassination on Poln Major, with a possible Rebel insurrection also involved."

"An *assassination?*" Pellaeon asked, feeling his eyes widen. There hadn't been any hint of any such trouble when they'd passed through the system a few hours earlier. "Who was the target?"

"Governor Ferrouz," the officer said. "The message is unclear as to whether or not the attempt succeeded."

"It was the Rebellion," Odo said darkly. "Of course it succeeded."

"General Ularno would seem to agree with you," Parck came back on the speaker, his voice grim. "Even in the absence of physical proof, he's invoked Directive Four-Seventeen, requesting the support of all nearby Imperial forces."

"And your response?" Odo asked.

"*This* directive is, unfortunately, quite clear," Parck said reluctantly. "Very well, Captain Drusan. We'll make ready immediately to head to the Poln system."

"And the rest of your force?" Odo asked. "You stated you had reinforcements in the area."

"A few," Parck said. "At their current positions, assuming we leave within the next half hour, we should all arrive at Poln Major at roughly the same time."

"Excellent," Drusan said. "Whatever resources the Rebels have brought in, a full Imperial task force ought to be more than enough to take them down."

"We'll do what we can," Parck promised. "If you can give us a few minutes to assess our damage and begin some running repairs, we can head back together. Otherwise, you can leave now and we'll follow."

Drusan looked at Odo, and Pellaeon spotted the latter's microscopic nod. "We'll wait," the captain told Parck. "It would be best if we all arrive together. Besides, Nuso Esva's ships might come back while we were gone."

"There's that," Parck conceded. "Thank you."

"One other thing," Odo said. "Will Senior Captain Thrawn be arriving at Poln Major with the rest of your force?"

"I'm not sure precisely where he is at the moment," Parck said. "However, the summons I've sent should reach him."

"And?"

"I can't speak for the senior captain," Parck said. "But under the circumstances, I presume he'll find a way to join us. Now if you'll excuse me, I need to see to my ships."

"Of course," Drusan said. "Let us know when you're ready to go."

Car'das looked up from the board, wincing at the clammy feel of the dried sweat that had gathered beneath his collar. "That was close," he commented.

"Not really," Thrawn said, his glowing red eyes narrowed in concentration as he gazed at the *Admonitor* and the other ships floating in the center of the display. "Nuso Esva wants us at Poln Major, remember?"

"No, I *don't* remember," Car'das said, eyeing the other suspiciously. "You've never told me exactly what he's up to."

"He wants to eliminate me as a threat, of course," Thrawn said calmly. "Just as I wish to do to him."

"Yes, but how exactly is he planning to do that?" Car'das persisted.

Thrawn shrugged. "There are two ways to destroy a person, Jorj. Kill him, or ruin his reputation."

"I suppose that makes sense," Car'das said, feeling a twinge of guilt and sadness. How long had it been, he wondered, since he'd had any kind of reputation himself that was worth guarding? "Any idea which approach Nuso Esva's planning?"

Thrawn smiled faintly. "If I know Nuso Esva," he said, "very likely both."

CHAPTER SEVENTEEN

THE SAFE ROOM ENTRANCE, MARA HAD NOTED ON HER FIRST TRIP through the escape tunnel, had been well disguised. The keypad and mike were hidden even better, and it took her nearly five minutes to locate them.

But once she did, Ferrouz's voiceprint and key code did the trick. The thick door, another hinged type, popped open. Easing it open a crack, she looked in.

The doorway led into a guard foyer with a pair of reinforced hardpoint firing positions flanking the foyer's only other door. The hardpoints were simple half cylinders, a meter in diameter and two meters tall, with their curved sides pointed toward the main door. Each had two slits—one at eye level for observation and one waist-high, for firing—and was big enough to provide cover for two guards at a time. A single person, crouched out of sight beneath the firing slit, would be in perfect position to launch an ambush on someone heading for the door into the safe room proper.

But Mara's Force-enhanced hearing could detect no surreptitious breathing. The guard foyer was empty.

Pulling the door wider, she stepped inside. She went to the hardpoints first, double-checking that they were unoccupied. Then, pushing the exit door closed behind her, she crossed between the hardpoints and keyed the other door.

It slid silently open. Lightsaber in hand, she stepped inside.

Ferrouz had already said the suite was large. What he hadn't mentioned was the fact that whoever had designed the retreat had apparently felt that, just because a governor was running for his life, there was no reason he had to put up with less-than-ideal accommodations, as well. The suite was beautifully appointed, with expensive furniture, marble and brass and cut-gem décor, thick carpets, and an extensive entertainment center. The food prep area was built along the lines of a master chef's kitchen, well stocked with cookware, dining settings, and food supplies. The whole apartment was spotlessly clean and meticulously cared for.

Like the guard foyer, it was also empty.

Mara went through the place twice, just to make sure there was no one hiding in a closet or beneath the hand-carved desk in the even more elaborate study. Her hopes lifted for a moment when she found a closet full of housekeeping droids, but a quick check of the settings showed that all of them had been shut down and on their chargers for the past six days. No help or information for her there.

It was on her third, more careful pass through the suite that she found a small dusting of glowglitter on one of the bedroom pillows. Glowglitter-painted ear helixes were one of the current fads among upper-class Imperial Center girls, and Mara had long ago learned that such fads propagated across the Empire with HoloNet speeds. Ferrouz's daughter had been here, all right. Probably his wife had, too.

So where were they now?

She continued on with her examination of the rooms, finding more sprinkles of glowglitter in one of the entertainment room couches and, oddly enough, in the massive but currently empty soaking tub. Aside from the glitter, though, she could find no trace of either of the hostages.

She ended her search in the office, sitting at the desk, glaring at the computer.

Ferrouz was safe, but only for the moment, with a guard that had started out marginal and was now down to little more than half its strength. Ferrouz's family was presumably also alive, but their safety was even more tenuous than the governor's, and she had no clue as to their whereabouts. The Poln system was overrun with Rebels, and there was an alien warlord and would-be conqueror lurking somewhere in the shadows calmly pulling strings within both the Rebel Alliance and the Empire.

For the first time in years, Mara was at a complete loss as to what to do.

Settling herself into the comfortable chair, she closed her eyes. What she would *not* do, she told herself firmly, was contact the Emperor and ask for help. She was the Emperor's Hand. She was supposed to be able to handle this sort of thing on her own.

But maybe there was another way to get the assistance she needed. Taking a deep breath, willing calmness into her thoughts, she stretched out to the Force.

For a moment nothing happened. Then her mind cleared, and she felt the Force flowing through her, twisting and rippling like a mountain brook, drawing her up and out and into itself.

She seemed to be floating outside the palace, rising above the ground, soaring through and then over the clouds. She saw Poln Major beneath her, and Poln Minor floating against the starry blackness in the distance. Multiple lines of ship traffic cut across her view, some of the vessels traveling between the two worlds, the rest incoming or outgoing from the system. The big Golan I defense platform orbited silently past her, and she could see the much smaller shape of the Dreadnought *Sarissa* holding similar guard over Poln Minor. Both of them guarding the Emperor's worlds with their turbolasers and missiles and—

Their missiles.

Mara shook her head, snapping back to herself and the safe room around her. She took a moment to blink away the rest of the vision, then leaned forward and keyed the computer. LaRone had said Nuso Esva's agents had gotten hold of some Caldorf missiles . . . and as she thought about it, she seemed to remember that Caldorfs were precisely the sort of missile being deployed on Dreadnoughts these days.

It was a crazy thought. An insanely outrageous thought. But Nuso Esva had made the necessary contacts, and he'd already demonstrated the icy nerve necessary to kidnap an Imperial governor's family.

Two minutes later she leaned back from the computer again, a prickly sensation creeping up her back. He'd done it. He'd really and truly done it. Grimacing, she pulled out her comlink and keyed for General Ularno.

"This is Jade," she identified herself when he answered. "Are you alone?"

"Yes," he said. "You have news?"

"Yes, of the bad to worse variety," she told him. "Are you aware that all fifty of the *Sarissa's* Caldorf VII interceptor missiles were removed four days ago?"

"Yes, of course," Ularno said. "The notice came through last week—some possible malfunction in the guidance systems, I'm told. They're at the Spillwater Fleet base being recalibrated."

"Not anymore they're not," Mara said. "Nuso Esva is currently loading them aboard his own ships somewhere on Poln Minor."

There was a brief silence. "I see," Ularno said, his voice almost calm. "He seems to have his fingers in a great number of soup bowls, hasn't he?"

"Having a top security officer like Pakrie in his pocket will go a long way toward doing that for him," Mara said. "Speaking of Pakrie, has there been any sign of him?"

"Not yet, no," Ularno said. "But Major Pakrie couldn't have done this for Nuso Esva or anyone else. The memo and order came from outside the Poln system."

"My point is that all such information would be on the military system, using military codes and encryptions," Mara said. "Yet Nuso Esva knew about the missiles and where they were going. Ergo, Pakrie must have had access to the messages."

"He shouldn't have," Ularno said. "Military and administrative encrypts are supposed to be strictly separate."

"But he obviously does," Mara said, punching out a quick message on the computer. "So if we can't find him, let's see if we can get him to find us. I'm sending you a note in military encrypt, signed by Governor Ferrouz, saying that he's managed to get to the safe room. I want you to pull it up and read it, then make a big show of calling off the search parties you have out looking for him. With luck, Pakrie will get wind of the change in orders, slice into your messages, and find the note."

"Yes, I see," Ularno said slowly. "I trust you realize that if he comes, he won't come alone."

"He can bring as many friends as he likes," Mara assured him. "I'll be ready for them."

"Understood," Ularno said. "I'll get on this right away. Good luck."

Mara keyed off her comlink, then took a final walk through the suite.

Turning off all the glowplates, she returned to the guard foyer. The glowplates there couldn't be completely shut off, so she merely lowered them to their minimum, dusk-level settings. Folding the right-hand hardpoint's seat out of the way, she sat down cross-legged on the floor behind the curved metal, out of sight of either the main door or the one leading into the suite. She checked her hold-out blaster, then returned it to its sleeve holster and pulled out her lightsaber. Setting it on her lap, she settled against the cold hull metal to wait.

The agreed-upon signal came from across the room: three dull thuds on the top of the supply lift. Proper signal or not, though, LaRone made sure he and Marcross were crouched behind more of the metal kegs, their E-11s aimed at the lower open door, before he signaled Quiller to send up the lift. There was a brief clanking and banging, and then the three-thud signal came again. LaRone nodded to Quiller, and again hunched ready over his blaster rifle.

And as the lift started down, and he got his first look at the newcomer's big clawed feet and hairy legs, he raised his blaster, breathing a quiet sigh of relief. In a day filled with errors and near-fatal mistakes, *one* thing at least had gone right.

For the moment, at least, that welcome trend continued. Chewbacca lugged the Suwantek's bacta tank into the cellar, growling away LaRone's and Marcross's offers of help. He set up the device against the wall near the lift door where it would be out of the way and wired it to pair of standard-current lines that together gave the tank the necessary power. Then, still refusing any assistance from the others, he affixed the breath mask to Grave's face, carefully lifted the injured stormtrooper, and laid him out in the tank. He peered for a moment at the readouts, then lowered the hinged lid down and filled the tank the rest of the way up.

Apart from the big Wookiee's muttered growlings, the whole thing was carried out in complete silence.

"Thank you," LaRone said when it was done. "We owe you."

Chewbacca rumbled something, gave Ferrouz a single, unreadable look, then gathered up Axlon's bloody body and returned to the lift.

A minute later, he was gone.

LaRone took a deep breath. "Marcross?"

"Looks good," Marcross confirmed as he crouched by the tank's readouts. "He's stabilized, and his blood count is rising nicely. Assuming he's given enough time in there, he should be fine."

"That *is* the question, isn't it?" LaRone agreed. "Time, and how much of it we have." He turned to Ferrouz. "Your first Wookiee, Governor?"

"Certainly the first one I've seen up close," Ferrouz said, sounding a little shaken. "I'll be honest—for a minute I thought he was going to rip me apart right here."

"Chewbacca wouldn't do that," LaRone assured him. "But you have to understand he's had some pretty unpleasant treatment under the Empire's rule, including torture and a stint or two as a slave. Some of his people have suffered even more. He doesn't like Imperials."

"I didn't know that," Ferrouz said in a low voice. "I know Kashyyyk is on the Empire's unfriendly-system list, but I always assumed there was a good reason for that."

"Like you probably assumed Alderaan was full of Rebel sympathizers?" Quiller asked, an edge of challenge in his voice.

"I don't know what happened there," Ferrouz said evenly. "All I know is that I swore an oath to uphold the Empire and its laws. I intend to carry out that oath." His throat worked. "Until my death."

"Hopefully, that'll be a long time coming," LaRone said, giving Quiller a warning look. This was no time to get into politics.

"Maybe," Ferrouz said heavily. "Jade *did* come to Poln Major to execute me."

"You may find she's more reasonable than you think," Marcross assured him. "She knows you were coerced into dealing with the Rebels."

"Which doesn't alter the fact that it *was* treason," Ferrouz pointed out. "As far as the letter of the law is concerned—"

"Hold it," LaRone said as his comlink gave a double-ping signal. "They're here. Marcross?"

Marcross nodded and keyed the supply lift. It rose to the street level, and once again there was the sound of feet and the thud of equipment from above them. LaRone's comlink pinged again, and he gestured again to Marcross.

This time, it wasn't a Wookiee and a bacta tank that came into view as the platform returned to the cellar. This time it was Brightwater, heavy satchels full of stormtrooper equipment from their speeder truck—

And five of the knife-making, green-scaled, badly dressed Troukree.

"Welcome," LaRone said, his eyes flicking across the aliens and picking out Vaantaar. "We're very grateful for your willingness to come."

"No thanks needed," Vaantaar said, his dark green scales and fur patches looking even darker in the cellar's artificial light. "I regret that I could not bring more of my people. But our defenseless must not be left alone."

"Understood," LaRone said. "Rest assured that whatever Brightwater pledged in return for your aid, you will receive it."

"Brightwater pledged a great deal of money," Vaantaar said, looking at Brightwater as he and the other Troukree began lugging the bags into the cellar. "We accepted nothing, save your promise that we would be fighting against Nuso Esva's forces." His white-rimmed eyes looked over at Ferrouz. "This is not one we have met."

"Not yet, no," LaRone confirmed. "Governor, this is Vaantaar and his fellow Troukree, master knife crafters and enemies of Warlord Nuso Esva. Vaantaar, this is Governor Bidor Ferrouz, Imperial administrator of Poln Major and Candoras sector."

"We are honored to serve with those who also stand against Nuso Esva," Vaantaar said, bowing toward Ferrouz. "We are doubly honored to serve he who has graciously permitted us refuge on this world, we and our defenseless."

"Glad we're all friends here," Quiller said, wincing as he sat down on the floor beside Grave's bacta tank, his wounded leg stretched out awkwardly to the side. "Tell me, Vaantaar, can any of you shoot a blaster?"

Vaantaar exchanged glances with one of the other Troukree. "Our skill is with our knives," he said, tapping the pair sheathed at his waist. "In a space so confined, that is all we shall need."

"Maybe," Quiller said. "But a little additional training wouldn't hurt."

"Agreed," LaRone seconded. "Marcross?"

"That's okay—I can do it," Quiller volunteered, popping the back of his E-11 and readjusting it to practice mode. "I'm not much use with anything else at the moment. Get your people over here, Vaantaar." He gave

LaRone a humorless smile. "Let's see how fast we can turn you into Imperial stormtroopers."

Leia had been hanging out the side of the speeder bus for what seemed like hours, and her eyes were aching with the task of staring continuously at the gravelly tunnel rolling by beneath them, when her comlink suddenly signaled.

"Han, stop," she ordered, pulling herself back into the bus and setting down her glow rod.

Typically, infuriatingly, he ignored her, if anything picking up his speed a little. Sending a useless glare at the side of his head, Leia pulled out her comlink and thumbed it on. "Yes; Leia."

"Finally," Cracken's voice growled. "Where have you *been?*"

"I don't even know where we are now, let alone where we've been," Leia admitted. "At least we're close enough to civilization to get a comlink relay. Han, can we at least stop long enough to figure out where we are?"

"Not a good idea." Han grunted, pointing back over his shoulder. "We've got company."

Leia turned to look. In the distance behind them were a set of distant headlights. Several sets, actually. "How long have they been there?" she asked.

"Maybe three minutes," Han told her. "They came out of a couple of the cross-tunnels at that last big intersection."

"You think they're after us?"

"You seen any other traffic around here?" he countered.

Leia grimaced. "Not since we left."

"Leia?" Cracken called.

"We've picked up some tails," Leia told him grimly. "At least three landspeeders, maybe more behind them."

"And you're in what?"

"A speeder bus," Leia said. "An old one, too. Once they figure out it's us, we're not going to be able to outrun them."

"They have to spot us first," Han said. "This far ahead of them, with no lights showing, they might not realize we're here."

"You get all that?" Leia asked into her comlink.

"Enough of it," Cracken said. "You said you just passed an intersection. Any idea which one it was?"

"I wasn't looking in that direction," Leia said. "Han? Did you get a number on that intersection?"

"The biggest of the tunnels was labeled AF-two-two-seven-five," Han said. "I didn't catch the others."

"We just passed AF-two-two-seven-five," Leia told Cracken. "But I don't know which one we're in right—"

"There's another tunnel coming up," Han interrupted, pointing ahead.

Leia peered out the windscreen, tensing. The tunnel markers at each of the intersections were small, and if they shot past it with their headlights still off they probably wouldn't be able to read it.

But if they turned the lights on now, the landspeeders behind them would instantly spot them.

It was a gamble. But she and Han had no choice but to take it. Reaching to the console, she flipped on the lights.

"No!" Han barked, lunging toward the switch.

Leia batted his hand aside, her squinting eyes on the blaze of light in front of them. The tunnel marker flashed past—"RK-oh-one-four-oh," she called into the comlink, reaching for the light control.

And winced as Han's hand closed around hers. "Don't bother," he said, pushing her hand aside. "If they didn't already know we were here, they do now. Might as well have the light."

"Sorry," she said, pulling her hand free of his grip.

"Don't tell me sorry," he said. "Tell me Cracken's got a roadblock on the way ready to slide in behind us."

"I think I can do better than that," Cracken said. "Can you hold out another five or six minutes?"

Leia looked behind them. The lights back there didn't seem to be getting any closer. "We can try," she said. "Tell us what to do."

"There's a conveyance tunnel cutting across yours about six kilometers ahead," he said. "Turn left into it and run the best speed you can manage."

"I think we're already doing that," Leia said, frowning. Why *weren't* the lights back there getting closer? Surely they'd figured out this was their renegade bus by now.

"I gather that means Solo's driving," Cracken said. "Keep the link open, and hang on."

The minutes ticked slowly by. Leia alternated her attention between the tunnel ahead and the lights behind. As far as she could tell, their pursuers still weren't gaining on the bus.

Which could only mean one thing. "They must have friends up ahead," she told Han. "They're herding us, trying to run us into an ambush."

"You just figure that out?" Han asked.

Leia felt her face warming. "Forgive me for not thinking like a smuggler," she growled. "You have an actual plan? Or you just like the satisfaction of knowing in advance what's about to hit you?"

"Of course I've got a plan," Han said. "Their comlinks couldn't have hooked up with the system any faster than ours did. That means they've just started putting the ambush in place. All we have to do is get there and get past it before they do."

"Brilliant," Leia said. "And what if they've got full-power comms instead of comlinks, and have been in contact with the ambush squad the whole time?"

A muscle in Han's cheek twitched. "In that case, the plan is to shoot our way through and hope that Cracken's got a really good countermove in the works."

Leia grimaced. "I thought so," she said. "Look—there. There's the conveyance tunnel."

"I see it," Han said. "Hang on. This could get a little rough."

"Right." Leia slipped into the seat behind him and got a two-handed grip on one of the support bars.

The bus roared up to the conveyance tunnel and careened around in a tight circle, nearly slamming into the far wall before Han got it back under control. In the distance, Leia could see a few faint glow panels in the tunnel ceiling, too far away to illuminate anything nearby. For a moment the bus fishtailed wildly, and then Han got it straightened out. He did something to the console, and Leia could hear the repulsorlifts straining as he tried to get more power out of them. She looked ahead at the distant ceiling lights, wondering if they marked another tunnel intersection —

She caught her breath, her eyes and brain abruptly registering the fact that the glow panels weren't as far away as she'd thought, and were in fact moving toward them. She opened her mouth to shout a warning to Han.

And right at the top edge of the bus's headlight glow, three airspeeders appeared and shot past over their heads.

Leia spun around, catching another view as they reappeared behind the bus, heading toward the corridor she and Han had just left. Only with that longer view she realized now that the vehicles weren't just air-speeders.

They were X-wing fighters.

Taking a deep breath, she raised the comlink to her lips. "You could have told us what you were planning," she said as calmly as she could.

"They there already?" Cracken asked. "Great. That's Antilles for you — flies as crazy as Solo does."

"Good thing, too," Leia said. "What now?"

"Just keep going," Cracken told her. "He'll have left one of the X-wings ahead to guide you back."

"I see him," Han called over his shoulder. "About half a kilometer ahead."

"You should be only about twenty minutes away," Cracken went on. "Get here as fast as you can."

"We will," Leia said. "In the meantime, get all the crew chiefs together. We've got some bad news."

"They're already assembled," Cracken said grimly. "Because whatever your bad news is, I guarantee mine is worse."

It had been a long, hard day, and Mara was dozing lightly behind the guard foyer hardpoint when the soft click of the lock release snapped her fully awake. By the time the door swung open she had shifted from a sitting position into a crouch, lightsaber in hand.

She'd expected Pakrie to be the cautious, thorough type and send a small army of thugs or mercenaries, like the group who'd attacked

Ferrouz's office earlier. But she could hear only a single set of footsteps coming through the door on the other side of the hardpoint. Midway through the foyer the steps paused, as if their owner was listening, then resumed their path toward the door leading into the suite.

Could Pakrie really have come alone? Or was her visitor someone else? General Ularno, maybe, whose rigidly simplistic mind had decided he should drop in and check on her? The footsteps passed Mara's hiding place, and she leaned a few centimeters out for a look.

Fortunately for Ularno, it wasn't him. It was indeed Pakrie, a blaster in his hand and a grimly determined look on his face.

Yet he was still alone. *Why* was he still alone?

It was, Mara decided, a question worth asking. Shifting her lightsaber from her right hand to her left, she reached out with the Force and tapped the outside edge of Pakrie's right boot, as if something alive had brushed against him.

Pakrie reacted instantly, leaping to his left as he spun around to see what was down there. Silently, Mara rose to her feet, took a long step up behind him, and tapped him gently on the right shoulder.

Pakrie twitched violently and again spun around. But a second sudden movement right on top of the first was too much for his coordination. Even as he flailed for balance, Mara caught his hand, deftly wrenched the blaster from his grip, and turned it around to point at him. At the same time she jabbed the hilt end of her lightsaber into his stomach, then turned the weapon sideways and pressed it against his stomach, shoving him backward.

An instant later she had him pinned to the foyer wall by the safe room door, lightsaber hilt still pressed against his stomach, his own blaster jammed up under his chin. "Now," she said conversationally. "You've got ten seconds to tell me why I shouldn't execute you for treason."

For another two seconds he just stared at her from wide, panicky eyes. Then, suddenly his mental gears seemed to catch, and Mara sensed his fear change into an almost righteous indignation. "*Me?*" he countered. "I'm not the traitor—Ferrouz is. He's made a deal with the Rebels—"

"Yes, I know," Mara interrupted. "How does any of that give you the authority to kidnap his wife and daughter?"

"They weren't kidnapped, they're in protective custody," Pakrie said stiffly. "It was for their own good."

"*Their* good?" Mara asked. "Or yours?"

Pakrie's throat worked. "I don't know what you're talking about."

"Let me tell you what I think," Mara said, stretching out toward him with the Force, sifting through every nuance of thought and emotion. "*I* think someone came and dangled the chance to be a hero in front of you. They told you Ferrouz was a traitor, and that with your help they could prove it, and your career would take off like a Star Destroyer out of dry dock. Any of this sounding familiar?"

Pakrie didn't answer. But he didn't have to. The rigidity of his face and the unpleasant swirling of his emotions were all the evidence Mara needed. "Of course, they didn't mention that you were going to have to commit high crimes to do it," she went on. "And by the time you realized that you were already in too deep to get out."

"Ferrouz is still a traitor," Pakrie insisted, an edge of desperation in his voice. "I'm a security officer. I can do whatever is necessary to find and expose treason."

"So can I," Mara said, suddenly thoroughly disgusted with the man. "Only *I* don't have to answer to anyone afterward. You do. Tell me where Ferrouz's wife and daughter are." Out of the corner of her eye she saw the door to the suite inexplicably slide open.

And from inside the suite came a thunderous burst of blasterfire.

Mara reacted instantly, shoving hard off Pakrie's stomach with her left hand as she hurled herself to the floor, firing a couple of random shots back at her unknown attackers to try to throw off their aim. She could see a group of figures moving back there, silhouetted against the light streaming through the door from inside, and caught a glimpse of rainbow-tinted skin, flowing black hair, and glittering yellow eyes.

And then her back hit the floor, and as she fired off a couple more shots she turned her momentum into a flat somersault that carried her to temporary safety behind the far side of the hardpoint where she'd been hiding a few minutes earlier. The incoming fire shifted in response, some of the bolts cutting through the air behind her back, the rest splattering off the metal or else finding its way through the observation and firing slits.

Through the screaming of the barrage she could hear her attackers moving single-file through the door and spreading out to both sides of the foyer in an attempt to flank her.

Reaching up, she wedged the muzzle of Pakrie's blaster into the firing slit, flipping it to full automatic as she did so. She squeezed the trigger, sending a spitting firestorm back at her attackers, and jammed her comlink into the trigger guard to keep the fire coming. Then, using the Force to sweep the weapon back and forth, she slipped around the far side of the hardpoint.

Coming from a lighted suite into the relative darkness of the guard foyer, with their attention focused on the gyrating blaster spitting its arc of death toward them, they probably never saw the black-suited figure come around toward the end of their flanking line. The first hint that their ambush had failed was most likely the sudden blaze of light at the side of the room as Mara ignited her lightsaber.

The battle was short and sharp, the attackers hampered by the fact that the very flanking line they'd been setting up left them in position to interfere with one another's fire. Quickly, systematically, Mara walked down their line, alternating between cutting down the attackers within reach and blocking the blasterfire from those were weren't. Somewhere along the way the blaster she'd set to automatic fire ran out of power and went quiet, still hanging by its muzzle from the firing slit.

Eight bodies later, it was over.

For a moment Mara stood in the center of the carnage, her lightsaber humming in her ears, confirming to herself that they were all dead. Then, stepping to the wall beside the open door, she closed down the weapon and used the Force to enhance her hearing. If the attackers had left a second wave in reserve, now was the time for them to show themselves.

But there was no second wave. There was nothing. The suite was empty.

It was only then, as Mara returned her hearing to normal, that she realized Pakrie was gone.

Sprinting to the outer door, she pulled it open and stepped out into the tunnel. But he was nowhere in sight. Nor was there any sound of footsteps, even with enhanced hearing.

Cursing under her breath, she returned to the guard foyer, closing the heavy door behind her. Even preoccupied with her defense, she should have seen Pakrie making his break. Only she hadn't, and now it was too late.

Or maybe not. Crossing to the hardpoint, she retrieved her comlink from the drained blaster's trigger guard and keyed for LaRone. "Status?" she asked.

"All quiet," he reported. "Grave is being treated, the governor is recovering, and Quiller and Brightwater are running our new recruits through some quick training. Yours?"

"Not as good," Mara said. "Pakrie got into the safe room, along with a bunch of aliens who fit the description of Nuso Esva you gave me. Best guess is that these are his personal shock troops, sent to make sure the job was done right this time."

"I assume they didn't do any better than the last bunch?"

"Not really," Mara said. "The bad news is that Pakrie got away. Are you still in contact with Skywalker?"

"I can be," LaRone confirmed. "What do you need?"

"I'm guessing that Pakrie will be calling Stelikag, if he hasn't already, with the bad news," Mara said. "I'm not sure which way they'll jump, but with Pakrie warning them I'm on the scene, I assume they'll either intensify the hunt for you or else run off to bolster the guard on the hostages. Hopefully, it'll be the latter. Either way, I need Skywalker to stay on top of Stelikag."

"Got it," LaRone said. "I'll call him right away."

"And watch yourselves," Mara added. "Stelikag could just as easily decide to jump in your direction."

"We'll be ready."

Mara clicked off the comlink and returned it to her belt, her eyes on the alien corpses littering the foyer floor.

They hadn't been in the suite an hour earlier. They hadn't come in the front door with Pakrie. Ergo, there was another entrance somewhere in the suite, one she hadn't spotted on her last trip through the facility.

It was time to correct that omission.

Shifting her lightsaber to her left hand, she drew her hold-out blaster and headed back inside.

CHAPTER EIGHTEEN

"THEY LEFT THE TAPCAF ABOUT HALF AN HOUR AGO," LUKE TOLD LaRone, holding the comlink surreptitiously at the edge of his hood as he moved casually along the busy walkway. "They picked up a couple of small portable scanners from their landspeeder, split up into two groups, and are walking the side streets near the palace. I think they've finally realized that Axlon's call is overdue and are hunting for you."

"They'll be hunting a lot harder in a minute," LaRone said. "We think they're about to get a call—"

"Hold it," Luke interrupted, peering through his electromonocular. "Stelikag's got the call, all right. And he does *not* look happy."

"You need to stay with them," LaRone said. "They may lead you to the hostages."

Luke grimaced. Great . . . except that Stelikag had a landspeeder, while Luke was on foot. If the kidnappers decided to drive to their destination, there was no way he could keep up with them.

Sure enough, Stelikag made an abrupt U-turn and headed rapidly back down the walkway in the direction of their landspeeder. "They're on the move," Luke reported. "You have any vehicles parked southwest of the palace gate that I can borrow?"

"No, nothing," LaRone said. There was a faint, indistinct voice from somewhere at the other end. "Marcross says to knock a citizen down and steal one if you have to. Just don't let Stelikag get away." He clicked off.

Luke returned the comlink to his sash. It was all very well, he thought darkly, for Marcross to talk about stealing a landspeeder. They were former stormtroopers who'd probably commandeered vehicles all the time. But that wasn't something Luke was either comfortable or experienced with.

But there were lives at stake. If he didn't have to hurt anyone along the way, maybe he would be able to steal something.

Unfortunately, that would take time, and Stelikag was already on his way back to the gang's landspeeder. Luke was closer, but he wasn't close enough to find a vehicle of his own before Stelikag got to his.

Unless Luke could find a way to sabotage it.

He wasn't sure how he was going to do that, not without the damage being obvious. But it was worth a try. Ducking into one of the narrow alleyways that paralleled the street, he broke into a run.

Stelikag had parked their vehicle in a similar alley behind the tapcaf where they'd been waiting for the confirmation call that Axlon never made. Luke glanced around the bales of compacted garbage and rows of bins as he jogged up to it, confirmed that he was unobserved, and popped open the hood.

The landspeeder was larger and more ornate than the battered SoroSuub X-34 he'd owned back on Tatooine, but the engine layout was basically the same. He leaned over the opening, getting a grip on the lightsaber tucked into his sash, searching for a likely wire to cut.

He froze as something hard pressed suddenly into his back. "Well, well, look who we have here."

Carefully, Luke turned his head a few degrees, his hand still gripping his lightsaber. It was one of Stelikag's men, the man Quiller had shot twice in the leg during the stormtroopers' rescue outside the palace gate. His injuries must have gotten him assigned to watch over the gang's vehicle. Clearly, Luke's quick check of the area had missed him.

And unless he did something fast, this whole thing was going to fall apart. "It's not too late to change sides," he told the thug. "You can't win— the governor's well hidden and you don't have the numbers to find him. But you can still make a deal to get out of this."

"Nice try," the man said. "Thing is, Skywalker, you've already been seen in public, so we really don't need you anymore. And Stelikag will pay the bounty he put on you whether you're alive or dead." The blaster pressing against Luke's back shifted slightly as the man repositioned it directly in line with Luke's heart. "So long, kid."

There was nothing Luke could do. No time for thought, no time for any other action. Bracing himself, wincing with anticipation and regret, he ignited his lightsaber.

The blade *snap-hiss*ed through his sash, the back of his tunic, and the gunman standing behind him. The pressure of the blaster muzzle against his back vanished, and without a sound the man crumpled to the ground.

Luke closed down the lightsaber and turned around, his heart thudding in his throat as he stared at the body lying at his feet. It had been fully justified, he told himself firmly. The man was a kidnapper, a traitor, and a would-be murderer. And he'd clearly stated his intention to kill Luke where he stood.

Still, killing this way felt different than it did from the isolation of his X-wing cockpit. Enormously, painfully different. It tore a fresh line across his heart every time he did it, and he suspected that it always would.

And it would all be for nothing if he couldn't hide the body and sabotage the landspeeder before Stelikag and the rest of the gang arrived.

Or maybe there was another way.

Luke's X-34 hadn't had any real storage space. Stelikag's did, an impressively large lidded compartment in the rear, complete with a dozen large blaster rifles laid out on top of a blanket. A minute later, having dumped the blasters in the nearest garbage bin, Luke heaved the dead thug up over the edge and dropped him into the storage compartment in their place.

And then, realizing all too well the horrible risk he was taking, he climbed in behind the body. Closing the lid over him, he covered himself with the blanket and laid himself as flat as he could, working a few folds into the material so that it would look like it was simply bunched up.

Just in time. Even as he made his last adjustments to the blanket he heard voices approaching. He stretched out to the Force, trying to hear better.

"—the blazes is Kofter?" he heard Stelikag snarl as the men hurried up to the vehicle. "Bams, get him on the comlink. Everyone else get in—"

The voice suddenly cut off as, beside Luke, the comlink on the dead thug's belt began to signal.

The sound went on for a solid five seconds, accompanied by an utter silence from the men gathered outside. Luke braced himself, gripping his lightsaber tightly.

And then, with a sudden violent creaking from the hinges, the storage compartment lid was flung open.

For another moment the comlink was again the only sound Luke could hear. He held his breath . . .

The comlink went silent. "Well," Stelikag said into the rigid stillness, a bitterness in his voice that sent a chill up Luke's back. "At least now we know where Skywalker and those stormtroopers went. Seems they've got our spare blasters."

"How did they get the drop on Kofter?" someone demanded. "No, wait a second—I want to see what they did—"

With a swoosh, the lid slammed shut. "You want to do an autopsy right out here?" Stelikag snarled, his voice muffled now by the closed lid. "Where anyone can look out of those windows up there and see that we're lugging around a corpse? And never mind the blasters—there are more where those came from. Mikks, get in. Everyone else, get back out on the street. I want Ferrouz, and I want him *now*."

"What about Kofter?" someone asked.

"We'll take him back and deal with him when we've finished the job," Stelikag said. "You just find Ferrouz."

"And Skywalker?"

"Oh, yes," Stelikag said, almost too quietly for Luke to hear. "You find him, too." The landspeeder leapt forward, the acceleration shoving Luke back against the body beside him.

He took a careful breath. So far, the gamble was working. Stelikag's reaction to a dead body in his landspeeder had been to get it out of sight instead of pausing to investigate more closely. Until they reached their destination, and probably even for a while past that, Luke should be able to avoid detection.

Now, if only LaRone was right about them heading to the place where Ferrouz's family was being held.

Sliding his lightsaber back into his sash, Luke stretched out to the Force for calm and settled in to wait.

Han had never liked Axlon. The man had been condescending and irritating, and more than once on the way to the Poln system Han had toyed with the idea of giving him a walk out the *Falcon*'s air lock.

But never in his wildest dreams had he suspected *this*.

"You're sure?" he asked Chewie across the makeshift conference table Cracken had set up in his transport.

The Wookiee warbled a grim confirmation. "I'm sure Chewbacca is telling the truth as he was told it," Cracken said. "The question for you, Solo, is whether you believe this LaRone character."

"Absolutely," Han said without hesitation. "Chewie and I worked with LaRone and his pals before. So did Luke. Besides, he's got no reason to lie."

"Why?" Cracken pressed. "Because Governor Axlon was a Rebel and LaRone is a stormtrooper?"

"*Former* stormtrooper," Han corrected. "And yes, because Axlon was a Rebel. There's a bounty on all our heads. You know that. An Imperial— *any* Imperial—can shoot any of us down in the street. He wouldn't need to concoct a story."

Cracken pursed his lips. "What about Luke?" he asked. "You think he was telling the truth on that, too?"

Han looked over at Leia. But she was just sitting quietly at her end of the table, staring at her datapad like she had been ever since the meeting started. As if she wasn't even listening to the discussion.

"If LaRone says he's all right, then he is," he said, looking back at Cracken. "And no, I don't know why he hasn't contacted us. You can ask him when he gets back."

"Assuming travel between here and Poln Major isn't about to be violently disrupted," Cracken said grimly. "Which brings us to *your* cheerful bit of news. First of all, do you have any idea whose warships they are?"

Han shook his head. "They weren't any design I've ever seen. But given that Nuso Esva's the only alien in the equation, and given that everything Axlon told us about him being on our side was probably a lie, I'm guessing they're his."

"You think he's working for the Empire?" one of the chief techs asked.

"Not unless the Empire's started assassinating its own governors," a major whose name Han hadn't caught growled. "The big question is what an independent contractor could possibly need with that much firepower. Especially *here.*"

"I see three possibilities," Cracken said. "Straight-up piracy against Poln Major's shipping, an attack on one of the Imperial facilities in the system, or an attack on us."

"I vote for the latter," the major rumbled. "No point in luring us here otherwise."

"Agreed," Cracken said. "Which leads to the next question: how fast can we pack up and run?"

"Well, that's going to be a problem, isn't it?" the major said grimly. "Even if we abandon everything that's not already on the transports, it'll take a couple of hours just to collect everyone and get them aboard the ships."

"*And* then to get them out of here," one of the transport captains put in, "we either have to get the transports back to Yellowstrike Spaceport or else maneuver them through the conveyance tunnel maze and find a different way out."

"Something Nuso Esva will already have thought of," one of the other captains pointed out. "Odds are that private hangar of his is within easy striking distance of the spaceport."

"We'll never get those transports out through the spaceport," the major warned. "Not with enemies sitting that close. The blasted things take off like overstuffed waddle birds."

"Which means we need to find that nest and neutralize it," Cracken said, turning to Wedge. "Antilles?"

Wedge shook his head. "Sorry, Colonel. We tried every tunnel in the whole area where we intercepted Solo and Princess Leia. There was no sign of the landspeeders that were chasing them, or anything else we could track."

Han grimaced. He knew now that the landspeeders hadn't been trying to catch their speeder bus, but had been simply following behind them in order to wipe out the telltale repulsorlift marks he and Leia had been using to find their way back.

With all the twists and turns they'd made along the way, it was for sure

they weren't going to get back to the cavern without those marks. Not anytime soon. "There has to be some way to find them," he insisted.

"There is," Leia said, looking up in triumph from her datapad. "And I
have."

Han glanced around the table. Practically everyone there was staring at
Leia with one degree or another of astonishment or disbelief.

All of them except Cracken. But then, he'd probably known her the
longest. "Explain," he said.

"When Han and Chewie first landed at Quartzedge Port, three of Nuso
Esva's men were there on guard," she said. "It wasn't anything to do with
us, because once Han told them he was heading for the Anyat-en caverns
they basically lost interest in him."

"Because they were there to keep an eye on something else," Han said
as he saw where she was going. "They were moving the missiles from the
port to their cavern."

"That's my guess," Leia confirmed. "Because we also know it was only
a couple of days later that they started hiring outside people to mount and
calibrate them. That must be when they realized the job was going to take
too long for them to handle on their own." She tapped her datapad.
"There's only one other long-distance tunnel coming out of Quartzedge,
and it only connects with a certain number of others that are wide enough
for heavy-lift speeder trucks. Add in the conveyance tunnel we know is at
the other end of the target cavern, add in the tunnel area where Wedge
picked us up, throw in the fact that the cavern is close to the surface, and
we get—"

"Wait a second," Han interrupted, frowning. "How do you know we
were close to the surface?"

"Because the whole ceiling was wired with shaped charges," Leia said,
frowning. "That's probably how they plan to get the ships out—they'll
want to bring them out all together, and with the conveyance tunnel
they'd have to go one at a time. Didn't you notice?"

" 'Course I did," Han lied. All that time studying the ships, the tunnels,
the aliens, and the hired thugs, and he'd never once thought to look up.
That was just plain embarrassing. "I meant how do you know blowing the
ceiling won't just take them into another cavern or a different conveyance
tunnel?"

"Because the conveyance tunnels aren't that close together, and just moving to a different cavern makes no sense," she said patiently. "Anyway, put that all together and assume they're within a couple hundred kilometers of here, and you get only one possibility." She gave the datapad a push, sending it sliding across the table to Cracken.

"So we do," he said, picking it up and peering at the screen. "Excellent work, Princess. Okay. How do we want to take them out?"

"It won't be with X-wings," Han said. "The tunnel we were using is too small, and the conveyance tunnel's too well defended."

"How about our new T-47s?" Wedge suggested. "Ten of them have been checked clear, and they'll get through anything a speeder bus will."

"They aren't nearly as well armed as the X-wings," Cracken warned.

"Firepower won't matter if we can't get to them," Wedge pointed out. "Besides, they think they're hidden. We'll have surprise on our side."

"Possibly." Cracken looked around the table. "Any other suggestions?"

There was a moment of silence. "Then we have a plan," the colonel concluded. "Let's get busy and—"

"One other thing," Han said, lifting a finger. "What were you planning to do about the Dreadnought and the Golan out there?"

"I thought your Duros friend said neither of them was a threat," Leia reminded him.

"Maybe not to smugglers in little freighters," Han said. "But big fat Rebel transports are a different matter. Especially since the safe-conduct ID code Axlon got from Ferrouz may have expired."

The major hissed something under his breath. "He's right, Colonel," he said grimly. "Even if the code's still functional, we may very well find it was only good for getting our ships *into* the Poln system, not out of it."

Cracken gestured to Han. "You have a suggestion?"

"Yeah," Han said, nodding. "Chewie and I take the *Falcon* over to the Golan, get aboard, and start shooting at the Dreadnought. In all the confusion, you and the transports lift and get clear."

There was a moment of stunned silence. "You're not serious," Leia said.

"Why not?" Han said. "Even a full-complement Golan One carries only four hundred men—"

"*Only* four hundred?"

"—and this one's running at maybe thirty percent," Han continued. "I figure eighty or ninety, tops, and most of them will be techs and turbolaser gunners. There probably won't be more than ten with any actual ground combat experience."

"How would you get aboard?" Cracken asked. Of all of them, Han noticed, he was the only one who seemed to be taking the idea seriously.

"We use the pass Ferrouz gave Axlon," Han said. "It came back with the body, didn't it?"

"It should be there, yes," Cracken said. "But it's probably only good for getting into the palace."

"That's okay," Han said. "I can make it good for the Golan, too."

"How?" the major asked.

"By being the best loud, overbearing Imperial undercover officer the Poln system has ever seen," Han told him. "Trust me, I've seen some of them. I know how to play it."

"And once you're aboard, you take over and shoot everyone who gets in your way?" the major persisted. "Just the two of you?"

"Pretty much," Han said. "Unless you've got a few soldiers you think could use some exercise."

"Get back to the armaments locker and draw whatever you need," Cracken ordered. "We'll make it a small team, I think—Toksi and Atticus should do. They'll meet you at the *Falcon*."

"Wait a minute," Leia said, sounding stunned. "You're actually going to let him *do* this?"

"It's that or risk losing everything," Cracken said. "You know how we have to play these things."

Leia looked across at Han, her face tight, and he thought he saw her slump a little. "Understood," she murmured.

Cracken looked back at Han and cocked an eyebrow. "You still here?"

"Nope," Han said, standing up and beckoning to Chewie. "Come on. Let's go see if they've got anything we can use."

And as he strode down the narrow corridor toward the transport's stern, he permitted himself a small smile.

Oh, yeah. She was crazy about him, all right.

————

Luke had been settling himself down for a long, uncomfortable ride when, suddenly, it was over.

He frowned in the darkness, wondering if they could really have arrived already. But the landspeeder had stopped and the repulsorlifts shut down, and he felt the double rocking dip as Stelikag and Mikks got out. For a few seconds he heard their footsteps, then they faded away.

This was apparently it.

Leaning over the body beside him, Luke fumbled for the lid release. He found it, pulled it, and the lid popped open a few centimeters. Leaning over a little more, he peered out.

He was in a long tunnel, dimly lit by what seemed to be randomly placed overhead glow panels. Here and there along the walls he could see clusters of crates, drums, cabinets, and workbenches. In the far distance, the tunnel's end was a faint glow of what appeared to be diffuse daylight. Half a dozen other landspeeders were parked against the walls, along with two airspeeders. Now that the storage compartment lid was open, he could again hear the two men's footsteps, and once again listened as they faded away into silence.

For another moment he waited, listening hard. But there was nothing. Drawing his lightsaber, he eased himself over Kofter, raised the lid just far enough to squeeze through, and rolled over the lip onto the permacrete floor. He glanced around the tunnel, confirming that he was alone, then eased himself to the rear corner of the landspeeder and looked carefully around its side.

There was more of the tunnel stretching out in front of the vehicle, but it was blocked by a heavy metal-and-permacrete barrier that had gaps only wide enough for pedestrians to get through. Twenty meters past the barrier, the tunnel abruptly opened up into a big cavern whose walls glowed with soft reddish light.

Checking one last time behind him, he pulled out his comlink and thumbed it on.

"I'm here," he said softly when LaRone answered. "Looks like a tunnel leading into a cavern or cave with white walls. At least, I think they're white—the place is being lit by red glow panels, so it's a little hard to tell."

"Any idea where exactly this tunnel is?"

"No, but the landspeeder ride was less than fifteen minutes," Luke told him. "We must be still in the city. Maybe even somewhere near the palace."

"Okay," LaRone said. "Hold on."

The comlink went dead. Luke started to close the storage compartment lid, then on impulse reached in and retrieved the blanket he'd been hiding beneath. He closed the lid, folded the blanket and tucked it under his arm, then straightened up and ran as quietly as he could over to the barrier and crouched down beside it. From his new vantage point he could see that there were buildings inside the cavern, low, rough-looking structures, clearly decades old. He couldn't see anyone, but he could hear voices, one of them Stelikag's, conversing angrily from somewhere inside the cavern.

The comlink clicked back on. "You need to stay there," LaRone said. "Find a safe place to hide, and watch and listen."

"What about the governor's family?" Luke asked. "If they're in there, I may be able to get them out."

"You're more likely to get yourself killed," LaRone said bluntly. "Don't worry, help is on the way."

"One of you?" Luke asked.

"Never mind who," LaRone said evasively. "You just stay out of sight and let us know if anything changes."

Luke grimaced. "Right," he said. "Just tell whoever it is to hurry. Stelikag's out for blood."

"Understood," LaRone said. "Watch yourself."

For another moment Luke peered through the barrier. Han would go for it, he knew. Leia probably would, too.

But he, Luke Skywalker, Jedi-in-training and son of the best star pilot in the galaxy, had been ordered to sit this one out.

A meter past the barrier were a pair of deep, human-sized niches carved into the tunnel wall, one on each side. Guard or maintenance posts, probably, now no longer in use. Watching the cavern closely, Luke eased through the barrier and slipped into the right-hand niche.

He would wait. But he wouldn't wait forever.

Mara was in the middle of searching the governor's safe room office when she suddenly remembered the glowglitter in the soaking tub.

There was no reason for anything that powdery to have remained intact through the tub's draining and filtering process. Unless, of course, the girl and her glitter had been in there without any water.

It took her two minutes to find the hidden door built into the rear section of the tub, designed to be partially covered and totally inaccessible when the tub was full. Turning out the bathroom's glow panels to make sure the sudden appearance of light didn't alert any watchers who might be on the other side, she popped the catch and swung the door out and up on its hinges.

Apparently the Moff who'd designed this whole place had been a big fan of tunnels. Beyond the door was yet another narrow passageway, this one leading down yet another flight of steps. In the distance, she could see a hint of a reddish glow. Returning her lightsaber to her belt, Mara drew her hold-out blaster and headed down.

She'd gone three steps when her comlink signaled.

Grimacing, she hurried back up the steps and closed the hidden door. If she couldn't afford Stelikag's men seeing stray lights, she certainly couldn't afford them hearing unfamiliar voices. Pulling out the comlink, she clicked it on. "Report."

"Skywalker's found the nest," LaRone said. "He says it's a white-walled cavern with red glow panel lighting at the end of a long vehicle tunnel. From the description he gave of the tunnel and the structures inside the cavern, it didn't sound like the place has been used for a while."

Mara smiled tightly as it finally clicked. "Not for the past hundred years or so," she agreed. "It would seem that the secret emergency exit from the governor's secret emergency safe room leads into one of the old underground mines beneath the big crystal mounds. Probably the mound the palace itself was built into."

"All the way down there?" LaRone said disbelievingly. "Sounds a little like overkill."

"Not for the truly paranoid," Mara said. "The more barriers and secret doors you put between yourself and your enemies, the longer it takes for those enemies to track you down. The more tunnels that connect those secret doors, the more the enemy has to come at you one at a time, which gives you better odds on defense. And by putting the end point in a big, spacious cavern with a built-in vehicle exit, you've got the option of getting out of town or even off the planet while your security team fills the tunnels with your enemies' bodies."

"Still sounds like overkill to me," LaRone said. "What do you want Skywalker to do?"

"Find cover and stay put," Mara said. "He can watch and listen, but nothing else. I'll go in and see what needs to be done."

"Acknowledged," LaRone said. "Good luck."

The stairway was shorter than Mara had expected, only fifteen steps. The tunnel beyond was also short, running about twenty meters before opening up into the red-lit cavern Skywalker had described for LaRone. It was just as well, she thought as she eased her way down the passageway, that she'd been extra careful with the lights and voices. She reached the end of the tunnel and lowered herself into a crouch.

If the tunnel had been shorter than Mara expected, the cavern was surprising in the opposite direction. It was *huge*, a good 150 meters across, 60 or 70 wide, and 20 to 25 deep. She had come out near the center of the cavern's narrower end, about three meters below the ceiling. Three-quarters of the way from her end of the cavern, a vehicle-sized tunnel headed off to the left, probably the tunnel where Skywalker was hiding. Right beside Mara, also to her left, a wide metal catwalk led from the tunnel mouth to a metal-mesh switchback stairway leading down to the cavern floor. Lowering herself to her belly, Mara crawled forward onto the catwalk for a better view.

It didn't look promising. There were fifteen structures of various sorts down there, ranging from small supply and toolsheds all the way up to long but flat half-broken bunkhouse-style buildings. Any but the very smallest of the structures was large enough to hold Ferrouz's family, particularly if the kidnappers weren't concerned about the hostages' comfort. There were various other bits and remnants of the old mining operation, including a few rusted or broken ore cars, occasional tools, and a lifter truck canting heavily to one side on a broken tread. A small group of barrels, also rusted, were stacked against the wall near the vehicle tunnel, their prominent FLAMMABLE warning emblems visible even at Mara's distance. Probably fuel, now well aged, for the broken lifter truck. Walking a random-walk guard pattern through the cavern were at least thirty armed guards, some of them human, others more of the yellow-eyed aliens she'd dealt with upstairs in the guard foyer.

And as she watched, it seemed to her that several of them were casting casual but lingering looks upward toward her tunnel.

Which led to an interesting and ominous question. By now Pakrie had surely alerted his allies that Mara had disposed of their latest attack squad. They had to assume that sooner or later she would find the door in the tub and come down to join them.

So why were they still casually roaming the floor down there instead of lining up here with their blasters pointed down the tunnel?

Over the years, the catwalk Mara was lying on had pulled a couple of centimeters away from the long bolts that anchored it to the cavern wall. Easing herself backward, she lined up her eyes with the gap and gave the switchback stairway a good, hard look.

There was no line of blaster-wielding aliens up here because Pakrie had also told them about her skill at defending against such attacks. But no lightsaber artistry would protect her from a stairway mined with high explosives. Through the mesh she could see that sections of each flight of stairs had been mined with grenades, with the entire top two flights also rigged with motion triggers. The minute Mara stepped from the catwalk onto those stairs the booby trap would go off.

And if the twenty-meter fall didn't kill her, the cloud of metal shrapnel from the disintegrating stairway would.

She raised her eyes again. There were ways to bypass even well-rigged explosives traps, but such techniques tended to be noisy. Noise would bring the guards running, and taking on thirty armed guards wasn't something even the Emperor's Hand went into lightly. Especially since there could easily be more guards out of sight inside the buildings.

But there might be a more subtle approach. Immediately to her right was a crane rail that stretched the entire length of the cavern, starting from an old decaying overseer's control cabin at the right end of the catwalk and ending in another such cabin at the far end. The crane itself was missing, but the rail looked solid enough, and most of the two-meter-long, V-shaped struts connecting it to the ceiling were still intact. The cabin at the far end had another switchback stairway, similar to the one at Mara's end, leading down to the main floor. The crane rail was about half a meter wide, easily crawlable, and with nearly two meters between it and the ceiling there was plenty of room for her to move along it without getting hung up on anything. If she could get up there, she could probably crawl across the cavern and get down the stairway that no one was paying any attention to.

The catch was getting up there in the first place. There was a three-meter section of catwalk with no cover that she would first have to get across, and with all the discreet attention the kidnappers were aiming in her direction she knew she would never make it without being spotted. What she needed was some kind of distraction.

Or maybe what she needed was a surprise attack from the vehicle tunnel over there.

Taking one last look around the cavern, she crawled backward into her tunnel and headed back up the stairs to the safe room.

"Here's the good news," she said when LaRone answered. "I've found Skywalker's cavern, and I think Ferrouz's family is here. If not, they're wasting an awful lot of guards and blasters on a crystal mine that was probably worked out decades ago."

"And the bad news?"

"There are too many for me to take on alone," she said. "You think you can organize a diversionary attack?"

"Just a moment."

The comlink went dead. Mara pulled out her syntherope dispenser, checking the gauge. There was fifty meters' worth of the quick-drying liquid left, more than enough for her to rappel down from either the catwalk or the crane rail if that became necessary. But if LaRone could get his force here and launch a sufficiently loud attack—

Abruptly, the comlink came on again, the speaker bursting with a flurry of distant but heated-sounding voices. "LaRone?" Mara snapped.

"We've got trouble," LaRone came on, his voice tight. "Governor Ferrouz has just called Pakrie and told him where we are."

"*What?*" Mara demanded.

"He says he wanted to draw some of them away from his family for you," LaRone growled, sounding even angrier and more frustrated than Mara felt. "He pretended he didn't know Pakrie was a traitor, and made it sound like he was calling him like he would any other security officer if he was in trouble."

Mara ground her teeth. Of all the *stupid* stunts—

She took a deep breath, stretching to the Force for calm. What was done was done.

Besides, there was something to be said for a man who would deliberately put himself into deadly danger to help those he loved. "I don't suppose there's any way you can get out of there," she said.

"We'd have to leave Grave behind," LaRone said. "We can't disengage him from the bacta tank that quickly. Quiller's not exactly mobile, either." There was another faint voice in the background. "Quiller is offering to stay here and guard Grave while we find a safe place to hide the governor."

Mara grimaced. No way would LaRone and the others actually consider walking away and leaving two of their own behind to die. They and Ferrouz really did deserve each other. "It's probably already too late," she said. "Stelikag wouldn't have pulled all his people off search duty. At this point all you can do is call General Ularno—"

She jerked back as a burst of static erupted from the comlink. Reflexively, she shifted frequencies, hit the squelch, then tried the reset. But nothing worked.

Not only had Stelikag's men reached the tapcaf, but they'd set up a comlink jammer nearby.

She smiled tightly. Fine. If LaRone couldn't call Ularno for backup, Mara would do it.

She paused with her finger poised over the call button, the smile fading. Unfortunately, she couldn't do that. Not yet. Pakrie was surely still monitoring palace security activities and communications. The minute Ularno ordered a security force to the tapcaf Stelikag would immediately pull his men back, including however many he'd been planning to send from the cavern detail.

Even worse, if Stelikag decided they'd lost all chance of getting to Ferrouz, there would be no reason for him to keep the hostages alive.

With a grimace, Mara put the comlink away. Stupidly reckless though it had been, Ferrouz had given her the best shot she would have to rescue his family.

It was up to her to make sure she didn't waste that chance. Or to waste the lives it was going to cost.

CHAPTER NINETEEN

ONCE AGAIN, THE STARLINES FLASHED AND BECAME STARS. ONCE again, the *Chimaera* had arrived safely at its destination.

For Pellaeon it was cause for a quiet sigh of relief. Just because they'd passed safely through this same tiny but potentially lethal segment of the Unknown Regions once before didn't mean the return trip would be equally uneventful.

And as he gazed out the bridge viewport at the Poln system's twin planets, he felt an unexpected flicker of respect and even admiration for Senior Captain Thrawn and the men in his task force. They took this same gamble every single time they jumped to lightspeed in those uncharted wastes.

Thrawn might not have the raw political skill that a fleet officer needed to keep himself moving smoothly up the ladder of success. But he did have courage.

"Signal from the *Admonitor*," the comm officer called. "Captain Parck reports that his task force has arrived safely."

"The entire force?" Drusan asked.

"Yes, sir."

"Confirmed," the sensor officer spoke up. "We have the *Admonitor* and the six cruisers from the Teptixii engagement to portside, along with five light cruisers and three heavy cruisers of unknown configuration."

Drusan grunted. "Aliens," he said under his breath. "None of our business, I suppose." He raised his voice again. "Signal the *Admonitor* that all ships are to move into close planetary deployment. Sensor officer, any other warships in range?"

"No warships, sir," the other said. "But the shadow has reappeared and—"

"Belay that!" Drusan snapped, spinning around to glare at the man.

Pellaeon turned, too, in time to see the sensor officer wince back from the captain's sudden anger. "Yes, sir," he said in a subdued tone.

"Shadow?" Pellaeon asked, looking at Drusan.

The captain grimaced. "You weren't supposed to know," he said reluctantly. "No one was. We've had a ship shadowing us ever since our last pass through the Poln system."

Pellaeon felt his mouth drop open. Ships didn't follow Imperial Star Destroyers just for the fun of it. "What kind of ship? Who's aboard?"

"It's a simple, low-threat freighter," Drusan assured him. "A modified Mon Cal *DeepWater* class. Decent armor, decent shields, nothing special. Certainly nothing to be concerned about."

"But what's he doing there?" Pellaeon asked. "And he's a Mon *Cal?*"

"It's a Mon Cal *ship,*" Drusan corrected tartly. "I didn't say there were any Mon Cals aboard." He grimaced again. "Actually . . . Lord Odo thinks it's one of Warlord Nuso Esva's people. Possibly even Nuso Esva himself."

Pellaeon shot a look out the viewport. "*Here?*"

"So Odo thinks," Drusan said, frowning as he looked around the bridge. "I assumed we would be finding out for certain . . . comm officer, signal Lord Odo. He was supposed to have joined us by now."

"Yes, sir." The officer bent to his board. A few seconds ticked by—"Sir, Lord Odo's not responding, not to his comlink or the comm in his quarters."

"Find him," Drusan ordered darkly. "Security teams to all likely places aboard ship." His glaring eyes flicked to Pellaeon. "You—Commander— go and help them."

"Me?" Pellaeon asked disbelievingly. Hunting down wayward crewers or passengers was hardly the sort of duty a senior bridge officer was supposed to be handed.

"You've spent as much time with him as any of us," Drusan growled.

"And you've spent *more* than the rest of us with that little weasel pilot of his. Find Odo, or find Sorro and have *him* find Odo. Just *get* him here."

Pellaeon suppressed a grimace. "Yes, sir."

Turning, he headed down the command walkway at a fast walk, annoyance simmering inside him. He would find Odo, all right. And the arrogant masked figure had better have a good excuse for leaving Drusan hanging this way.

A *really* good excuse.

The stealthy footsteps had been moving about the tapcaf above the stormtroopers' sanctuary for several minutes before the attack actually began. When it finally did, it was with an equally stealthy opening of the cellar door.

LaRone got just a glimpse of the blaster, the unshaven face, and the startled look before the shot from his E-11 blew the man back.

And as pandemonium erupted from the other three men who'd been silently gathered by the door, LaRone and Marcross stepped through the opening, their armor gleaming in the sunlight coming through the tapcaf windows, and opened fire.

The battle was short. But not quite as short as LaRone had expected it to be. The four men standing stupidly by the cellar door turned out to be only the sacrificial decoys, probably drifters or thugs that Stelikag's men had hired off the street on their way over. Even as the last one fell, his blaster firing uselessly into the ceiling, the men crouched behind the tapcaf's tables and half concealed in its booths opened fire.

But they weren't shooting at helpless citizens or fellow smugglers now. They were targeting Imperial stormtroopers, and Imperial stormtroopers were light-years better at this sort of thing than they were. With Marcross firing coolly at his side, LaRone systematically cleared out the attackers on his side of the zone, ignoring the shards of plastic and metal scraping across his armor from the near-misses, ignoring even the sudden twinges of pain as a better-aimed shot or two or three made it through his armor and burned into the skin beneath.

Ninety seconds later, it was over. Two of the attackers had managed to get out more or less unscathed. The rest lay dead.

"Let's hope the next one is that easy," Marcross commented as they headed across toward the bodies, their E-11s sweeping back and forth just in case Stelikag had been clever enough to add a third layer to their attack.

"It won't be," LaRone told him as they reached the first pair of bodies. He began turning a slow guard circle, running his helmet's vision enhancements for any signs of trouble as Marcross holstered his own E-11 and checked the blasters of their late opponents. "The minute the survivors get out from under their own comlink jamming they'll be screaming for help. If Stelikag's capable of learning, the next batch will be way more professional."

"Good," Marcross said with a grunt as he stood up with a pair of scavenged weapons. "Maybe it'll clear out the hostage cavern enough for Jade to get in there."

"Maybe," LaRone agreed, grimacing behind his faceplate. Of course, a situation like this was very much a zero-line game. The fewer opponents Jade ended up with, the more LaRone and Marcross and the others would be facing.

But then, that was the job they'd taken on when they joined the ranks of the Imperial stormtroopers. To fight, and to eventually die, so that others might live. "Make it fast," he urged Marcross. "We need to get back and get those bottles back up on the stairs." He bent over and picked up another of the attackers' blasters. "And if we get enough weapons for all of the Troukree, we might want to rethink our fire-line arrangement a bit."

"In what little time we have to make any alterations," Marcross warned.

LaRone grimaced. "Yes," he conceded. "There is that."

Han had the *Falcon* on course for the Golan when Chewie rumbled a sudden warning. Han frowned, peering out the canopy.

He felt his jaw tighten. The distant sky was filling up with ships.

Not just any ships, either. Imperial warships. The readout tagged a pair of *Strike*-class medium cruisers, four *Carrack*-class light cruisers, a few more ships of unknown alien design—

—and two Imperial Star Destroyers.

Chewie growled again.

"Yeah, I see them," Han growled back, staring out at the newly arrived task force. So it had been a trap all along. Just like he'd thought, and just like he'd told Rieekan.

"What is it?" Toksi asked from the passenger seat behind him.

"Trouble," Han said, frowning out at the distant ships. On the other hand, if this was a trap, it was a pretty incompetent one. The whole Imperial force had come out of hyperspace together, all of them grouped in a screen formation on the same side of Poln Minor instead of in a proper encirclement pattern. Even the Dreadnought that was supposed to watch over Poln Minor was currently on the far side of the planet near the rest of the Imperials. If Cracken had been ready to go, the transports could have just lifted off Poln Minor and burned space in the opposite direction, with nothing but an undermanned Golan between them and a clean escape.

Of course, Cracken *wasn't* ready to go. Maybe that was the point. Maybe the Imperials knew they had plenty of time to reconfigure and still catch the Rebels on the ground.

"What *kind* of trouble?" Atticus asked from the other passenger seat.

"The Imperial kind," Han told him. "Two Star Destroyers plus escorts, thirty degrees to starboard. Quiet and let me think."

"What's there to think about?" Atticus demanded. "We need to get back and help Cracken—"

Chewie snarled over his shoulder. This time, Atticus got the message and shut up.

Han drummed his fingers on the control board, alternating his attention between the distant Imperials and the much closer Golan. One of the Star Destroyers had left the group now, its pointed bow turning toward the *Falcon* and Poln Major. But the rest of the ships were still just sitting over Poln Minor, moving slowly inward but showing no signs of breaking formation. At the very least the Strikes and Carracks should be running for the planet's far side by now to cut off any escape in that direction.

Was it possible that the Imperials didn't know the Alliance was here? Because they sure weren't acting like it. In fact, it was almost like the newly arrived ships and the governor's palace weren't even talking to each other.

Maybe they weren't. Chewie had said that LaRone had Governor Ferrouz in protective custody. Maybe in all the chaos on Poln Major no one down there was talking to anyone at all.

And if the palace wasn't talking to the Imperial ships, maybe it wasn't talking to the Golan, either.

Abruptly, he came to a decision. "We're going in," he told the others. "Same plan."

"We're *what*?" Atticus demanded. "Solo—"

"We've still got the pass, and so far no one's challenging us," Han cut him off. "And we still need to buy the others some time."

"What about that Star Destroyer?" Toksi asked, pointing over Han's shoulder at the incoming ship. "It's heading straight for us."

"Sure is," Han agreed. "You rather be out here or inside a big metal battle station when it gets here?" He craned his neck to look over his shoulder. "Or I could just let you off here," he offered.

Atticus glared at him. "Just do it," he growled.

Han turned back to the massive station now almost filling the canopy and keyed the comm. "Golan Defense Platform, this is Major Axlon aboard the civilian freighter *Gateling*," he said. "Acknowledge."

"*Gateling*, Golan acknowledging," a young-sounding voice responded. "Please confirm identification."

"Major Axlon," Han repeated. "Don't bother looking me up on your complement listing—I'm not there. Clear your number one port for immediate docking—I'm coming aboard."

"Ah . . . one moment."

The comm went silent, and Chewie warbled a question.

"Just keep going," Han told him. "Make it look like we'll ram the port if they don't open it."

There was a click—"Major, this is Commandant Barcelle," a cautious new voice came on. "May I ask your business aboard?"

"Not on an open comm," Han said. "Open port one and meet me there."

"Yes," Barcelle said uncertainly. "Ah—"

"And do *not* call anyone to confirm my presence," Han said coldly. "This is a *highly* sensitive operation, and I will *not* have it compromised by loose talk or careless name-dropping. No one—*no* one—except Governor

Ferrouz knows I'm even in the Poln system. Now stop stuttering and *get that port cleared.*"

"Yes, sir," Barcelle said, his voice abruptly gone both briskly efficient and quietly terrified. "Sending docking data to you now."

With a flick of his wrist, Han cut off the comm. "Okay, we're in," he told the others.

"So who exactly does he think we are?" Toksi asked suspiciously.

"Imperial agents, or maybe ISB," Han said. "Either way, no one he wants to mess with."

Atticus grunted. "Let's hope he's still in terrified awe of us when he sees that all we've got for ID is a pass from the governor."

"We'll make that jump when we get there," Han said, throwing another quick look at the approaching Star Destroyer. No problem—the *Falcon* should be at the station long before the ship reached firing distance. "Let's just concentrate on getting there in one piece."

Leia had always known that T-47 airspeeders weren't exactly overgenerous in the accommodations department. But as she snuggled into the gunner's seat at the rear of Wedge's vehicle, she realized she'd had no idea of how cramped the things really were.

"You all right?" Wedge called back to her.

"I'm fine," Leia assured him, struggling to get her straps fastened. "It's just cozy, that's all."

"Yeah, they are," he agreed. "This isn't really necessary, you know," he went on. "We *have* the location. You don't have to come with us."

"I'm the only one who's actually been there," she reminded him. "That may turn out to be useful."

Besides which, she'd never liked the idea of sending men and women into danger without having someone in authority share it with them. Her father Bail had never flinched from standing on the front lines with his men, and she wasn't going to, either.

"Well, we're glad to have the company," Wedge said diplomatically. "Here we go."

With a lurch, the airspeeder lifted from the cavern floor and headed for the tunnel that she and Cracken had calculated would give them their best approach to the missile ships. Behind her, Leia could see the rest of their ten-ship raiding party lift and flow into following positions.

She grimaced. She'd never liked riding backward, but it had been so long since she'd had to do it that she'd completely forgotten the queasy feeling it always stirred in the pit of her stomach. Next time she ended up in a T-47, she promised herself, she would make sure *she* was the one facing forward and doing the actual flying.

She looked out the side of her canopy at the rocky wall shooting past the airspeeder's wingtips. On second thought, maybe not.

With a grimace, she settled back into her seat, gazing at the long line of dark airspeeders trailing behind her and sternly ordering her stomach to calm down.

It was going to be a very long trip.

Pellaeon's first thought was that Odo might have returned for some reason to his old quarters near the bay where the *Salaban's Hope* was docked. His second thought was that he might have gone back to one of the engine control rooms, either the main or one of the secondaries, for a repeat of the MSE droid ballets that had so disconcerted Lieutenant Commander Geronti and his techs. His third thought was that he or Sorro had gotten someone to unlock the docking bay and gone aboard the *Salaban's Hope* itself.

But the first two options came up dry, and the docking bay was locked. Wherever they'd disappeared to, they'd done an extremely good job of it.

Pellaeon was back in the turbolift, wondering what he was going to tell Captain Drusan, when the emergency alarms suddenly began blaring.

He had his comlink out in an instant, keying to the emergency channel. "Pellaeon," he snapped. "Report."

"Massive explosions in all engine-control centers," the damage-control officer snapped back. "Possible thermal detonators; massive damage; massive casualties. Contact has been lost with the bridge; no indication of explosions there. All command level doors have been sealed; all turbolift cars are frozen and locked down."

Pellaeon frowned, his eyes flicking to his car's indicator. *His* car wasn't frozen. "I'm about five seconds from the bridge," he told the other. "Stay on this link—I'll report again once I've assessed the situation." He jammed the comlink, still on, into his belt as the car came to a halt. The door slid open.

And a cloud of thick white smoke burst in through the open door.

Pellaeon lunged toward the control panel, trained fire-response reflexes sending one palm slamming into the emergency-close button as he grabbed for his nose and mouth with the other. The slight whiff he'd gotten before he got his nose covered had identified the smoke as vertigon gas—nonfatal, but a couple of lungfuls would wreck his sense of balance and send him gasping to the deck. His only chance to avoid that fate was to get the door closed and hope the car's ventilation system could clear out the gas before he needed to breathe again.

Only the door wasn't closing. Pellaeon hit the emergency button again, harder this time. Still nothing. His lungs were starting to ache now, the tendrils of gas pressing at the fingers pinching his nostrils and covering his mouth. He hit the emergency button one last time.

And then, abruptly, he remembered the emergency firefighter pack fastened to the wall to the right of the turbolift. A firepac that included a full-face breath mask and an emergency oxygen supply.

Squinting against the swirling smoke, he sidled out of the car, keeping a hand on the wall lest he get disoriented in the white nothingness and lose his bearings. The firepac, he remembered, was about two meters from the edge of the turbolift . . .

Sooner somehow than he'd expected, there it was: a bright orange rectangle faintly visible even through the smoke. Pellaeon punched the release, popping open the cover, and ran his hand across the contents until he hit the familiar form of the breath mask. He snatched it out and slapped it over his face, pressing it tightly against forehead, nose, and mouth as he twisted the oxygen valve. The cold delicious air flowed across his skin and into his nostrils, filling his lungs and banishing the last hints of the gas that had suddenly and inexplicably invaded the *Chimaera*'s bridge.

He was securing the mask's straps when he caught a flicker of light from his right and heard the sharp *crack* of a blaster shot.

He spun around, his heart pounding suddenly in his chest. Another shot cracked, its light again showing faintly through the smoke.

And in that single heartbeat, everything changed. This wasn't some accident, or group of accidents. The *Chimaera* had been sabotaged.

The *Chimaera* was under attack.

Two more shots cut through the smoke and stillness as Pellaeon stumbled backward. What had happened to the pair of troopers who'd been on guard when Pellaeon had left the bridge earlier? Were they the ones firing? If so, what were they firing at?

Or had the troopers merely been the first ones to die?

He had to get off the bridge and find some troopers or stormtroopers who could deal with this. The turbolifts were frozen, except for the one he'd arrived in, and given what he now knew of the situation, he wasn't about to trust that one to still be working. But there were other ways out of the aft bridge—

Abruptly his foot caught on something on the deck. He flailed his arms, trying to recover his balance. But he was moving too fast, and his foot was still caught. Throwing out his hands to catch his fall, hoping he could land without attracting the attention of whoever was firing in there, he fell heavily to the deck.

Squarely on top of Captain Drusan.

Pellaeon caught his breath. "Captain?" he breathed. The other's eyes were closed, his face screwed up with pain, the center of his chest blackened with a close-range blaster burn. "Captain!"

Drusan's eyes flicked open. "Pellaeon?" he murmured.

"Yes, sir," Pellaeon said, glancing once toward the main bridge and then scrambling back to his knees. The aft bridge's emergency medpac should have something he could use to treat the captain's injuries.

He started to get to his feet, but wobbled off balance again as Drusan caught his sleeve. "No," the captain murmured.

"Sir, you're injured," Pellaeon said, trying to pry away the other's hand. But Drusan was gripping him tightly, with far more strength than a man in his condition ought to have. "I have to get the medpac."

Drusan shook his head weakly. "He lied to me," he murmured. "He said that together we would bring a stunning defeat down on the Rebel Alliance. A victory they would never recover from."

"Yes, sir, we will," Pellaeon assured him, pulling vainly at the clutching fingers. "But I have to get to the medpac—"

"That's why I endorsed his credentials," Drusan said. "Don't you see? He was going to bring us victory."

Pellaeon stared at the other, a sudden taste of bile in his mouth. "You endorsed—You *knew* he was a fraud?"

"Victory over the Rebellion," Drusan said, his hand finally loosening. "And then . . . it would be Admiral . . . Drusan . . . Admiral . . ."

His hand slipped from Pellaeon's sleeve, his arm fell to the floor, and he was gone.

"Commander?" The faint voice came from Pellaeon's belt.

Pellaeon grabbed for the comlink and clicked it off, cursing under his breath as he once again looked toward the main bridge. Comlink voices didn't usually carry, but this was no time to take chances. Fortunately, the firepac breath mask had its own built-in comlink, with its speaker right up against Pellaeon's ear where no one except him would be able to hear. Turning it on, he again keyed to the ship's emergency channel. "The bridge is under attack," he murmured urgently. "Repeat: the bridge is under attack. They're using vertigon gas, and I think they're shooting the crewers—"

"Identify yourself," an unfamiliar voice ordered.

Pellaeon frowned. "This is Commander Pellaeon," he said. "Third bridge—"

"Commander, this is Senior Captain Thrawn," the voice said. "What's your personal status?"

Pellaeon felt his eyes widen. Thrawn was *here*?

Of course he was. Parck had said that Thrawn would likely join them at the Poln system. "I have a breath mask from the bridge firepac," he said. "Sir, Captain Drusan's been killed, and I think Lord Odo is the one who murdered him."

"His name isn't Odo, Commander," Thrawn said grimly. "The man in the mask is Warlord Nuso Esva."

For a moment the name didn't register. Then, in a sudden flush of recognition: "*Nuso Esva?*"

"Yes," Thrawn confirmed. "Are you armed?"

Pellaeon took a deep, calming breath. "No, sir," he said. "But if I can find the guards who were on duty I may be able to find a blaster."

"There's no time," Thrawn said. "You need to keep Nuso Esva from leaving the ship. How did you get to the bridge?"

"Turbolift," Pellaeon said mechanically, his mind still trying to wrap itself around this new revelation.

"Which was obviously functional even though I'm told the rest of the system has been shut down," Thrawn said. "It follows that he's planning to use that particular turbolift to make his escape. Are you still with me, Commander?"

Pellaeon took another deep breath of the cold oxygen. "Yes, sir, I'm here."

"Very good," Thrawn said. "Here's what you're going to do . . ."

The Golan's commandant was waiting as Han rode the *Falcon*'s lift to the upper hatch and into the docking entry bay. So were half a dozen of his fellow officers, plus every single one of the ten trooper types Han had estimated would have ground combat experience. Unlike the officers, those particular ten were wearing belted blasters.

Han didn't even glance at them as he strode toward the assembly. The commandant stirred and opened his mouth—

"Commandant Barcelle," Han said briskly. Imperial agents and ISB, he knew, always got in the first word. "I need a quick rundown of your current operational status."

"Major Axlon, you can't just come in here—" one of the other officers began.

"Operational status!" Han snapped, not bothering to look at him as he thrust Axlon's pass into his hands. "If I have to ask again—"

"No, sir," Barcelle said hastily. "We're at thirty percent capacity, with nine turbolaser batteries and one proton torpedo launcher still functional. Our tractor beam projectors are all down, but—"

"Commandant!" a frantic voice barked from the bay speaker. "Sir, you have to get up here right away. We've got trouble. We've got big trouble."

Barcelle's eyes flicked to the speaker, then back to Han. "On my way," he called. "Major—"

"We're wasting time," Han bit out. He had no idea what the trouble was, but it probably had something to do with him and the *Falcon*, and he absolutely didn't want the commandant finding out about it before he did. "Let's go."

The bridge ventilation system had begun to make some headway against the billowing vertigon gas as Nuso Esva's shadowy figure swept through the archway that separated the main bridge from the aft bridge. He turned toward the turbolift, his cloak rippling through the air.

From his crouched concealment by the consoles at the other side of the aft bridge, Pellaeon moved toward him quickly and silently, the air-filled hypo he'd taken from the aft bridge medpac gripped in his hand. As he reached Nuso Esva, he raised the hypo over his head and plunged it past the edge of the black metal mask and into the side of the other's neck.

Nuso Esva twitched violently, his hand flailing as he tried to slap Pellaeon's hand away. But it was too late. He half turned, twitched again, and collapsed to the deck.

Pellaeon took a deep breath, gazing down at the crumpled figure. Thrawn had assured him that an air embolism would kill his target quickly. He hadn't said whether it would be painful.

With Captain Drusan dead, plus all those mangled bodies scattered around the *Chimaera*'s engine room, Pellaeon rather hoped it would be very painful.

"He's down," he announced, dropping to one knee beside the figure. He checked the other's hands first, knowing it would be a hollow victory indeed if Nuso Esva got a final shot at him.

But both hands were empty. He must have dropped the blaster somewhere along the way. Turning the other over, Pellaeon got his fingers under the edges of the mask and pulled it off. "Hello, Nus—"

He broke off, his eyes widening. It wasn't an unknown enemy alien behind the mask. It was a human.

It was Sorro.

"*Sorro?*" he breathed.

The other's eyes fluttered. "My family," he murmured. "Have I now redeemed them?"

Pellaeon stared into the gray face, feeling his heart sink. With those four words, it had suddenly become clear. The hold Nuso Esva had had on the melancholy pilot, a hold that had even extended to the lengths of sabotage and murder. The whole obscure Arkanian legend of a tragic figure named Salaban.

And the reason the man had taken the name *sorrow*.

"Yes, you've redeemed them," Pellaeon said quietly. "They'll be released now."

A small, bitter-edged smile touched Sorro's lips. "Thank you."

The smile was still there as his breathing came to an end.

"Commander?" Thrawn's voice came.

Swallowing hard, Pellaeon got back to his feet. "It wasn't Nuso Esva," he said bitterly, turning to the archway leading into the main bridge. The smoke was definitely clearing, and he could see the hazy figures of collapsed crewers scattered across the deck and crumpled in the crew pits. Some were starting to move a little. Others had the immobility of death. "It was Sorro, dressed in Nuso Esva's mask and clothing."

"You didn't really think I would be so easy to catch, did you?" a new voice cut into the circuit. "Is Sorro dead yet, Commander Pellaeon?"

Pellaeon felt his breath catch in his throat. The voice was subtly different without the mask. But it was definitely the voice of Lord Odo.

The voice of Nuso Esva.

"Yes," Pellaeon said through stiff lips.

"Pity," Nuso Esva said. "He rather liked you, you know. I think he might have told you all about me, had he cared less for his family. Well, Captain Thrawn. Our paths cross one final time."

"Perhaps," Thrawn said. "Commander Pellaeon, a quick assessment of the bridge control settings, if you would."

"No need, Commander," Nuso Esva said as Pellaeon picked his way carefully through the scattered bodies. "I can tell you exactly what your settings will show. The *Chimaera* is currently under low power, its course locked and, for the moment at least, completely unchangeable."

"Commander?" Thrawn prompted.

"Yes, sir, I'm almost there," Pellaeon said as he headed down the steps toward the helm station.

"Your Star Destroyers are remarkable instruments of war," Nuso Esva continued, his tone almost that of a training course lecturer. "But they have serious weaknesses. The ventilation system, for one. Not only is it totally inadequate for the rapid clearing of a gas attack, as Commander Pellaeon has already discovered, but it also provides a perfect pathway for Arakyd Mark Two seekers."

Pellaeon frowned. "You were *holding* that seeker," he said. "It wasn't in the ventilation system."

"*That* one wasn't, no," Nuso Esva said scornfully. "That was the one the other seekers were set to search for."

Pellaeon clenched his teeth. Seekers in the vents, following Odo as he carefully walked the target seeker along the proper pathway to the engine-control consoles. With the big MSE droid show purely there to distract the crewers' attention.

And as Pellaeon stood over the remains of the bridge's blaster-wrecked helm console, he saw why.

"The helm station has been destroyed, sir," he reported, his pulse pounding suddenly. "The *Chimaera* is locked on a collision vector with the Golan defense platform orbiting Poln Major. ETA—" He swallowed. "ETA, fourteen minutes."

"Sir!" another voice cut in. "Commander Pellaeon? Aft sensors are reporting that a new group of ships has entered the region. Configurations match those of the alien warships of Captain Parck's engagement at Teptixii."

"I mean to destroy you, Captain Thrawn," Nuso Esva said, his voice soft and cold. "But first, your soldiers and subordinates are going to watch as you make your final, fatal choice."

"What choice is that?" Thrawn asked.

"In fourteen minutes, unless something is done, the *Chimaera* and the Golan will destroy each other in a fiery collision," Nuso Esva said. "The other ships of your task force are helpless to interfere. I have all of them trapped here by Poln Minor, and should any of them attempt to leave their current positions my Firekilns have been ordered to intercept and destroy. The only way to prevent the collision is for either the *Chimaera* or the Golan to open fire and destroy the other."

Pellaeon looked up at the bridge viewport. Through the last remaining tendrils of smoke he could see the blinking lights of the Golan defense platform in the distance.

And the *Chimaera* was indeed heading straight toward it.

"You, Captain Thrawn, will make that decision," Nuso Esva said quietly. "You will decide which of your Empire's precious war machines you will order destroyed.

"You will decide which of your Emperor's warriors will die."

CHAPTER TWENTY

L UKE'S FIRST WARNING WAS A SUDDEN BARKING OF ORDERS FROM THE cavern, the clink of weapons being yanked off racks, and the sound of scrambling feet.

His first, horrified thought was that they were on to him. But a second later he realized that couldn't be the case. If Stelikag knew or suspected someone was out here, he wouldn't be making nearly this much noise about it. He would instead order a quiet, stealthy search, hoping to catch the intruder napping.

So all the noise and flurry out there wasn't on account of him. But then who *was* it on account of?

His stomach tightened. It was LaRone, of course. LaRone, the other stormtroopers, and Governor Ferrouz.

And whatever they'd done, they'd managed to make Stelikag extremely angry.

That didn't sound good. Not for them, and not for Luke. He was still huddled in the firing niche beside the vehicle barrier, where he would be in the direct view of anyone who happened to look to his left as he hurried past.

For a second Luke wondered if he had time to get back out into the main tunnel, where there was more cover. But it was way too late for that.

But he still had the blanket he'd taken from Stelikag's landspeeder. If the kidnappers were in as much of a hurry as they'd been back in the city, the same trick might work again.

At this point he had little choice but to try it. Scrunching himself down into as small a package as he could all the way at the back of the niche, he flipped the blanket up and over his head, draping it into a casual covering over his torso, legs, and feet.

Three seconds later, the hurrying footsteps became a thundering stampede as the men charged past.

Luke held his breath, reaching out to the Force. Back on Tatooine, Ben Kenobi had been able to deflect stormtrooper interest away from himself, Luke, and the two droids Leia had sent. Unfortunately, Luke had no idea how to do that particular trick. All he could do was stay motionless, try to look innocent, and hope that would be good enough.

Apparently, it was. The running footsteps rose to a crescendo, then faded echoing into the near distance. The steps stopped, were replaced by the hum of half a dozen repulsorlifts and the opening and closing of doors, and then the repulsorlifts too faded into silence.

Cautiously, Luke eased the blanket away from his head and focused his senses. There were still the sounds of footsteps coming from the cavern, plus the murmur of low voices.

How many of the kidnappers were left he couldn't tell. But the number was certainly much smaller than it had been a few minutes ago.

Small enough, maybe, that he could now risk going in there to try to find Ferrouz's family?

He chewed at his lip. Not yet, he decided reluctantly. LaRone had said there was someone else on the way. For now, he would sit back and let whoever it was take the lead.

Moving back up to the edge of the niche, he gazed into the cavern, fingered his lightsaber restlessly, and settled down to wait.

Lying on her stomach on the catwalk, Mara permitted herself a small smile. The comlink call had come in, Stelikag had gone berserk, and twenty men and aliens had grabbed blasters and grenades and taken off down the vehicle tunnel. There they'd loaded themselves into what had sounded like at least half a dozen landspeeders and burned out of there as if Lord Vader himself were after them.

Whatever LaRone had done to the team back in town, it must have been highly impressive. She just hoped he hadn't pushed Stelikag into handing him and the others more than they could chew.

Resolutely, she pushed the thought away. They were Imperial stormtroopers, and they would handle their part of the operation.

It was time for Mara to get busy and handle hers.

The remaining guards, she noted, were still glancing up occasionally in her direction. But the looks seemed now to be more casual than they had been before, more from rote obedience to orders rather than from a sense that they would actually see anything. At this point, in fact, it was quite possible that they were assuming Mara wasn't coming in at all, but had gone back into the city and joined forces with LaRone.

The more she thought about it, the more likely that seemed. It would certainly help explain Stelikag's decision to send more than half of his force away.

Unless Stelikag had decided that there was no need for them because there would soon be no one left for anyone to guard.

Mara squeezed her hand around her hold-out blaster, then consciously relaxed her grip. Allowing tension to get hold of her would do nothing but block her access to the Force. Willing calmness to flow into her instead, she gazed down at the men wandering around below. They all knew where the governor's family was being kept. If she could read their eyes and body language accurately enough, maybe she could figure it out, too.

Stelikag was standing near the vehicle tunnel, next to one of the shed-sized buildings, talking with two other men. His face looked calm enough, but Mara could tell from the way he was drumming his thumb against the side of his hand that he was still on the bleeding edge of fury.

She focused on his eyes. They seemed to be gazing mostly on his discussion companions. Even when he glanced away it wasn't toward any of the cavern's structures but to the vehicle tunnel. The other two men had their backs to Mara, but their head movements didn't seem to indicate any particular interest in any of the buildings, either.

And then, just as she was wondering if they were simply talking about weather or politics, Stelikag gestured behind him. Behind him, and above him.

The direction of the stairs at the far end of the cavern, and the decrepit overseer control cabin up at the ceiling.

Mara grimaced. Of course Stelikag hadn't simply stashed Ferrouz's wife and daughter in some random building, a place that would require binders or else a circle of guards to keep his prizes from making a run for it at an opportune moment. He'd put them twenty meters above the ground, with a single stairway exit that would have them in plain sight of the entire guard force for a solid minute if they tried to leave.

And would put any prospective rescuer in the same indefensible position.

Unless that prospective rescuer got clever.

Mara had already considered using the crane rail stretching the length of the cavern as a way to get across to the other stairway. Now the idea sounded even better.

The trick was still going to be how to get across the three-meter gap and up onto the rail without being seen. Even with the enemy's numbers decreased, there were enough random glances coming in her direction to make that risky.

For a moment her thoughts flicked to Skywalker, presumably still lurking out there somewhere in the vehicle tunnel. But she quickly dismissed them. Whoever he was, he was clearly an amateur, and this was a job for professionals.

Maybe with a little extra help from the kidnappers themselves.

It took her a minute of slow crawling to make her way down the catwalk to the beginning of the stairway. Being careful not to set off the motion triggers, she worked a length of syntherope from her dispenser and slipped the end through part of the metal mesh of the upper stair riser, then threaded it around one of the guardrail supports. With both ends of the syntherope in hand, she backed down the catwalk again and returned to the tunnel mouth. Leaving the cord there, she slipped into the tunnel and headed back to Ferrouz's safe room sanctuary.

Three minutes later she was back, one of the dead alien bodies from the guard foyer draped over her shoulder. At the tunnel mouth she laid it out flat and tied one end of her syntherope loop around its chest beneath its arms. She eased it out onto the catwalk, maneuvering it around so that it was pointed toward the stairs.

Picking up the free end of the syntherope, she began to pull.

Slowly, awkwardly, the body moved down the catwalk. Mara continued to pull, keeping the body moving, the bulk of her attention on the kidnappers wandering the floor below. Unlike the stairs, the catwalk itself was made of solid metal, but it was just possible the top of the body would be visible from below.

But so far no one seemed to have noticed it. The body was nearly to the stairs now, and Mara eased herself a little farther into the cover of the tunnel mouth. When the rigged stairs went off, she didn't want to be anywhere within range of the explosion.

The body reached the end of the catwalk and teetered for a moment on the edge. Mara gave the syntherope a final jerk, and the body went flopping forward onto the stairs.

And with the multiple thunderclap of a midsummer electrical storm, the stairway explosives went off.

Mara pressed herself against the tunnel wall, wincing as the sonic shock wave hammered across her head, wincing a little more as pieces of the stairs and the shredded end of the catwalk ricocheted off the tunnel wall and bounced more or less harmlessly off her back and legs. The hail of metal stopped, and she eased back to the tunnel mouth.

Below her, the whole cavern was on the move, the kidnappers running toward the demolished stairs, their blasters aimed and ready. A couple of them looked up at the tunnel mouth, but those glances were even more perfunctory than before. Those who'd looked quickly enough had surely seen a body falling toward the floor, and there was logically no one that could have been except the Imperial agent they'd been expecting.

And with all eyes focused on the pile of shattered debris, and the dust and smoke of the multiple explosions billowing upward and obscuring everything in its path, Mara stepped onto the catwalk and slipped over to the control cabin. A two-handed grip on the edge, a pull and leg-swing upward onto the roof, a roll and another grab on the nearest of the crane rail's support struts —

And as the dust began to clear, she slid up onto her belly on the rail.

It wouldn't be long, she knew, before the searchers down there picked their way through the debris and discovered to their consternation that the body was one of their own. When that happened, the search for her would be on.

By then, if she was lucky, it would already be too late.

Hunching up her shoulders to get her elbows beneath her, she started to crawl.

"Eleven minutes to impact, sir," the kid at the Golan's sensor board said, his voice tight, his eyes wide. "Commandant? What do we do?"

It was, Han thought as he gazed out the viewport at the distant shape bearing down on them, a really good question.

And so far, Commandant Barcelle didn't seem to have the slightest idea how to answer it.

Han looked around the command room. Eighty-three men, Barcelle had said, were aboard. Eighty-three men, and no escape pods. They were supposed to have them, but like everything else aboard the station the safety equipment had been allowed to slowly fall apart. There were no pods, no ships, no escape. Nothing but Han and the *Falcon*, and there was no way the *Falcon* could take on eighty-three passengers.

"Can we move this thing?" he asked Barcelle. "At all?"

"All we can do is rotate," Barcelle said, his face and voice as tight as that of the sensor operator. "We're an *orbiting* station. Once we're in place we're not supposed to have to go anywhere."

Han grimaced. That was, unfortunately, the answer he'd been expecting.

But the Golan *did* have its weapons, or at least some of them. If they opened up on the Star Destroyer . . .

Then the Star Destroyer would open up on them. And given the disparity in firepower, the Golan would definitely be the loser in the exchange.

Not that it would make any difference either way. The Star Destroyer's weapons were probably already powering up with exactly that plan in mind. The Golan's comm system was in as bad a shape as the rest of the station, and with all the static Han hadn't caught the name of the Imperial in charge. But enough of Nuso Esva's challenge had gotten through to make it clear that this was some kind of personal issue.

And no Imperial commander could afford to lose a Star Destroyer *and* a Golan I in the same day. Especially not in the same incident.

"We could rotate to put our long axis toward them," one of the other officers offered hesitantly. "We'd be a smaller target that way."

"You mean they might miss us?" someone else asked.

"Not likely," Barcelle said grimly. "But it would at least be doing *something*. Kater, fire up the flywheel. Let's see what we can—"

"No," Han cut in suddenly. "You said you still had a torpedo launcher. Where is it?"

"Sector One-One cluster," Barcelle said, frowning at Han. "This end of the station. Are you suggesting we *shoot* at them?"

"I'm suggesting we shoot torpedoes at right angles to the *Chimaera*'s vector," Han said. "Full-power rail launch, minimal propellant, aimed so they don't hit anything. If we can give the platform enough sideways momentum, maybe we can get out of the way."

"That's impossible," someone insisted. "The relative mass—"

"You want to sit here and just watch them run us down?" Barcelle snarled. "Pastron, fire up the launchers. Nills, what's the rack status?"

"We just have the standard two torpedoes in place," one of the men reported tensely. "That's all we're supposed to have racked in peacetime."

"This look like peacetime to you?" Han snapped, gesturing toward the distant alien ships and the not nearly distant enough Star Destroyer. "Get more of them to the racks. *Now*."

"Yes, sir," Nills said hastily, punching at his controls. "But that'll take time. Number three crane's the only one that's functional—"

"Oh, for—" Swallowing the curse, Han yanked out his comlink. "Chewie, get up here," he ordered. "Bring the other two with you. Commandant, get someone down to my ship to show them where the racks and storage cradles are."

"Opfo, make it happen," Barcelle ordered. "You do realize, Major, that these are considerably bigger than your average starfighter-sized torpedoes."

"Trust me—Chewie's considerably bigger than your average handler," Han said. "I'll put my Wookiee up against your crane any day of the month."

"You have a *Wookiee*?" someone asked incredulously.

"What we *have* is ten minutes until that Star Destroyer gets here," Han bit out. "Everyone who's not on some other job, get over to the racks and give them a hand."

"You heard the man," Barcelle confirmed. "*Move* it."

"There!" Car'das said, pointing at the display. "There he goes."

"Who?" Thrawn asked.

"Nuso Esva," Car'das said. "Or at least, a freighter that shouldn't be out there. Backtrack says it came from the *Chimaera*. It has to be him." He looked over at Thrawn. "I may still be able to hit him from here."

Thrawn shook his head. "Focus on the task at hand, Jorj," he said. "Nuso Esva will keep for later."

Car'das grimaced. The task at hand: trying to keep the *Chimaera* and the Golan from destroying each other in a fiery collision that would send repercussions rippling all the way back to Imperial Center. Nuso Esva had called it, all right: Thrawn's entire reputation and career were on the line here. "You really think this is going to work?"

"The theory is perfectly sound," Thrawn reminded him. "The only question is whether or not the *Lost Reef* will be able to handle the strain."

"Don't worry about that," Car'das assured him, tapping the edge of his ship's control panel in emphasis. "The Mon Cals build their ships to last, and I put in a lot of extra modifications after you gave her to me. She'll hold together." He jabbed a finger at the display. "*My* question is whether Commander Pellaeon and the *Chimaera* will be able to pull off their end."

"We'll soon find out," Thrawn said. "Position?"

Resolutely, Car'das turned away from the oh-so-tempting target that was the fleeing Nuso Esva. Thrawn was right, of course—they needed their full attention and the *Lost Reef*'s full power on the *Chimaera* operation. But he still ached to take the shot. "Ten seconds."

"Captain Thrawn?" Nuso Esva's mocking voice came from the *Lost Reef*'s cockpit speaker. "Your time is running out."

"Not at all," Thrawn said calmly. "You ask me to choose between the death of the *Chimaera* or the death of the Golan. I've made my choice."

He looked at Car'das, and it seemed to Car'das that a small smile touched the other's lips. "I choose neither."

"There it is," Wedge called over his shoulder. "Here we go . . ." There was a hint of reflected light bouncing off the walls flying past the T-47's wings.

And suddenly they were there, and Leia was thrown against her straps as Wedge ran the airspeeder into a sharp up-and-right turn. For a second she was looking down at the missile ships, and then Wedge straightened them out again. Behind them, Leia saw the other Rebel airspeeders file into the cavern and break off into their own attack runs. Turning her attention to her weapons monitors, she got a grip on the firing controls—

And with a sudden jolt the T-47 twitched sideways, tipped up on the starboard wing, and headed down.

Leia had just enough time to get out a startled gasp before Wedge leveled them off again. "We've got trouble," he called back to her.

"What sort—?" She broke off as the T-47 gave another jolt, this time spinning a quarter turn before Wedge got it back under control.

It was only then that Leia saw that, as the Rebel airspeeders buzzed around the cavern firing at the missile ships, the missile ships' fin-mounted laser cannons were firing back.

The ships weren't just sitting around waiting for the Rebel transports to break the Poln Minor surface. They were prepped, energized, and ready to fly.

Fifty warships. And she'd brought Wedge and ten lightly armed airspeeders in to face them.

"Stay high!" Wedge called. "Their lasers are forward-firing. Stay above them and you'll be out of range."

Leia grimaced. Or at least they would until the missile ship pilots got into the air.

But there was nothing they could do about that. Nothing, except make sure that as many of those ships as possible were no longer fit to fly. Gripping her controls, peering into her targeting displays as Wedge swooped over the alien warships, she opened fire.

The second attack began much as the first had, LaRone noted, with quiet footsteps moving across the tapcaf floor above their heads.

But this time, there was no stealthy opening of the cellar door in an attempt to sneak up on the defenders. Instead, the door was flung violently open and a pair of grenades was hurled down onto the stairs. There was a crash as the impact shattered two of the stacked bottles and scattered several of the others.

A second later there was a second, more violent crash as Marcross fired up the stairwell from his post to the left of the stairway's base. A body hurled down the stairs, scattering another dozen bottles as it slid to a halt. Marcross kept firing, and LaRone heard a scream and another muffled thump from the floor above.

With a deafening explosion that rattled LaRone's ears all the way across the cellar and through his helmet's audio protection, the grenades detonated.

For probably three seconds the air was a swirling mosaic of flying bottle fragments. The hail ended, and LaRone looked cautiously up over the kegs of their redoubt.

He'd half expected to find that entire third of the cellar blazing with the ignited alcohol. But to his surprise, there were only a few small isolated fires, most of them little more than smoldering pools. Even as he focused on the two that were actually showing flames one of Vaantaar's people leapt up from his own defensive position to the right and ran across to hastily stomp them out.

But fires notwithstanding, the grenades had definitely made a mess of that end of the cellar. "Marcross?" he called.

"I'm okay," Marcross called back, and LaRone saw him emerge cautiously from behind the kegs of his firing point. He seemed mostly intact, unlike the kegs themselves, which were currently spraying their contents over the blast debris and the permacrete anchoring stubs that was all that remained of the stairway. "The body helped smother the blast."

"The bottles probably helped, too," Brightwater said from LaRone's left. "It looked like the idea was to bounce the grenades off the stairs and give them more distance. Only the bottles absorbed the momentum and kept them at that end."

LaRone nodded. Not exactly the way he'd envisioned the bottle defense working, but in battle any positive result counted as a win.

"What will they try next?" Vaantaar asked from LaRone's right, fingering his borrowed blaster restlessly.

The answer came in a sudden firestorm of blaster bolts down through the cellar door that hammered the permacrete floor where the stairs had once stood.

Powerful blaster bolts, too, very hot, with the kind of cycle rate that even a T-21 couldn't sustain. It had to be an E-Web heavy repeating blaster, or something similar.

LaRone frowned, his combat instincts tingling a warning. It was a highly concerted, highly profligate attack, yet none of the shots were coming anywhere near either Marcross or the Troukree. In fact, the fire pattern wasn't doing anything except tearing an arc of shattered permacrete and setting off a few more small fires in the pools of spilled alcohol.

And then, suddenly, he got it. An *arc* pattern.

The E-Web wasn't just firing to make noise and create gravel. It was creating a fire shield. "Incoming!" he shouted, lifting his E-11 over the barrier and aiming for the center of the E-Web's fire arc.

Just as a figure dropped through the door from the tapcaf above, landing neatly behind the sheet of fire.

Or rather, two figures. The one in front was human, its head sagging against its chest, while the one close behind him was one of Nuso Esva's yellow-eyed aliens.

They had barely hit the floor when LaRone opened fire.

To his surprise, the shots seemed to have no effect. The human twitched a couple of times as the blaster bolts struck him, but he didn't fall. Behind him, the alien stretched a hand over the man's shoulder, and LaRone twitched reflexively as a pair of blaster bolts sizzled past his helmet.

Marcross had already opened up with fire of his own, his shots having no more effect than LaRone's. The alien swiveled to his right, both he and the human moving in unison, training his blasterfire now toward Marcross as he screamed a warbling, high-pitched wail.

And then, the wailing abruptly cut off, and with a violent jerk both figures crumpled together to the ground. As they fell, LaRone caught a
glimpse of a Troukree knife hilt protruding from the alien's back.

But the withering arc of blasterfire was still raining down from above.
"Vaantaar?" LaRone called.

"He was a scout," the Troukree called back. "He carried the dead
human as a shield while he called out our numbers and positions."

LaRone scowled. That had been his conclusion, too. "Any idea how far
he got with his description?"

"They now know that our main position is here," Vaantaar said. "Marcross and the others by the stairway were not yet located when he died."

"Means they'll probably be sending down a replacement to get the
rest," Brightwater said. "Grenades?"

"Grenades," LaRone agreed. "Stay here—I've got it." Shoving his E-11
into its holster, he grabbed a grenade and leapt up onto the keg barrier,
landing on his back as he flipped his legs into the air. The momentum carried him across and forward, and he rolled over the barrier to land on his
feet on the far side. Regaining his balance, he sprinted across the cellar
toward the arc of blasterfire still raining down the stairwell. The tricky part
would be making it through the sheet of fire without collecting enough
blaster bolts to get himself killed, while simultaneously making sure the
grenade itself didn't take a hit and explode right there in his hand. His best
bet would be to cross the fire at a dead-on run, try to pop the grenade accurately through the door, then keep going the short distance to the back
wall.

And hope the E-Web gunner couldn't shift his aim fast enough to nail
him before the grenade went off.

He was five steps from the blasterfire when, out of the corner of his eye,
he saw two of the Troukree leave their firing positions and break into a run
toward the stairway. One of them pulled ahead.

Abruptly, LaRone realized that both aliens were on an intersect course
with his own vector. "Get back!" he shouted.

But it was too late. The Troukree in front came to a sudden halt right
at the edge of the E-Web's fire arc. He spun around as the second alien
continued running toward him.

As LaRone reached the fire arc, the second Troukree leapt up into the waiting hands of the first and was hurled up into the air in a gymnast's shoulder throw.

His body crossed the line of blasterfire directly above LaRone's head just as LaRone charged through.

The Troukree might have screamed as the bolts tore into his body. Or maybe it was a scream of anger from the alien operating the E-Web. LaRone didn't know. All he cared about in that split second was putting his grenade directly under the center of the E-Web's tripod. He threw the explosive, then put his hands out to catch himself as his momentum carried him toward the cellar's back wall.

And as his palms hit the permacrete the grenade exploded. LaRone bounced back off the wall, staggering as the grenade's shock wave hit him, and spun around, drawing his E-11.

The blaster wasn't necessary. As the explosion faded, and his helmet's audio protection eased back, silence again descended on the cellar.

Taking a deep breath, LaRone looked across the floor. The dead Troukree was lying where he'd fallen, his body half torn apart with multiple blaster wounds, his companion crouched over him. To LaRone's right Marcross rose from behind his barrier, looking first at the two Troukree and then at LaRone.

Faces weren't visible through stormtrooper helmets, but LaRone had been with the others long enough that their body language was as clear to him as open expressions would have been to anyone else.

It was very clear that Marcross was feeling the same awe and humility about the Troukree's sacrifice that LaRone was.

Exhaling a sigh, LaRone started back across the room. The crouching Troukree looked up as he approached, and a dozen different words of sympathy or compassion flashed though LaRone's mind. But every one of them felt somehow shallow, blasé, or inadequate.

In the end, he could think of only one thing to say. Focusing on the Troukree lying dead in front of him, he lifted his hand in salute. "Well done, soldier," he said quietly.

The trip back to the redoubt seemed longer than it ever had before.

"Incredible," Quiller murmured as LaRone rounded the barrier and came up beside him. "I've seen stormtroopers sacrifice themselves that way for each other. But never an alien. At least, not for someone they barely even knew."

LaRone nodded. "You were the one who said we were going to make stormtroopers out of them."

"I did, didn't I?" Quiller agreed soberly. "Sometimes I don't know my own strength." He gestured. "If the scout gave them our setup here, we should probably think about moving."

"Yes, we should," LaRone agreed, looking around the cellar.

The problem was that there wasn't anywhere else to go. All the biggest kegs had already been lined up to create the redoubt and the firing nests for Marcross and the Troukree, and it would take a dangerous amount of time to reposition them. More serious was the fact that anywhere else they tried to go would move them closer to either the demolished stairway or the supply lift.

Which, so far, the attackers had ignored. Could they possibly be unaware of its existence? Or were they planning something special from that direction?

He frowned as a new sound filtered through his helmet and his thoughts. A dull thudding sound, like someone tapping on a wall.

Or on the side of a bacta tank.

He turned toward the tank parked beside the supply lift door. Sure enough, Grave's eyes were open above the breath mask, the back of his hand tapping against the transparisteel. Slipping off his helmet, LaRone circled the redoubt barrier and crossed over to him. He keyed the system to draw the fluid back into the supply tank, and when the level was low enough he popped the lid and swung it open. "Welcome back," he greeted Grave as he carefully took the breath mask off the other's face. "How are you feeling?"

"I'm fine," Grave said, his voice weak. "I was going to say that you're making one jink of a lot of noise out here. You have any idea how hard it is to sleep through all that?"

"Sorry," LaRone apologized as Brightwater came up beside him. "I wish I could promise it won't happen again."

"You ready to stop loafing and join the party?" Brightwater asked.

Experimentally, Grave shifted his shoulders, the movement sending little ripples through the half-full tank. "Sorry," he said, wincing. "Not quite."

He looked back at LaRone. "But maybe there's something I can do from the sidelines. Fill me in, and let's see if we can come up with something clever."

CHAPTER TWENTY-ONE

LUKE WAS STILL WATCHING THE KIDNAPPERS FROM THE EDGE OF HIS guard niche when the cavern abruptly thundered with a violent explosion.

Reflexively, he ducked back, his ears ringing with the sound, a wash of musty-smelling air flowing past him. The air flow faded away, and he eased back to the edge of the niche and looked out—

—to find that the entire cavern was on the move.

His first impulse was to duck back again in case one of the kidnappers looked his way. But it was clear that none of them had the slightest interest in anything that might be going on in the vehicle tunnel. Everyone he could see was racing toward the right-hand part of the cavern. From the flow of dust and smoke and the fading reflection of light on the far wall, Luke guessed that that was the direction the explosion had come from.

Only from the tone of the shouting voices he could hear now that the echoes had faded away, the kidnappers didn't seem all that distressed by the blast. In fact, he could hear at least one whistle that sounded decidedly triumphant.

Had they been expecting the explosion? Had they planned it?

Had it been a trap for the help LaRone had said was on the way?

Luke grimaced. Of course—that had to be it. They'd set a booby-trap, and whoever it was had walked straight into it.

It was up to Luke now.

A last man ran past the tunnel, and now there was nothing but buildings and drifting smoke in Luke's sight. He gave it another five-count, just to be sure, then slipped out of the niche and moved up to the edge of the cavern.

The place was considerably bigger than he'd realized. It was 150 meters long at least, and 20 meters or more from floor to ceiling. At the end of the cavern to his right were the results of the explosion: a frozen dune of crumpled and shattered metal on the floor, with a darkened and scored wall behind it. Most of the kidnappers were still headed in that direction, with a few of them already there and starting to pick their way cautiously through the rubble.

But not all of them. As Luke turned to look in the other direction, he saw that there were still three men at the other end of the cavern. They were huddled together, apparently in deep conversation, near the foot of a staircase leading up to a small structure set against the wall near the ceiling.

Hurriedly, Luke backed again into the tunnel until he was out of their sight. Moving across to the left side of the tunnel, he returned to the cavern and again peered around the corner.

The men had finished their conversation. One of them was walking back in Luke's general direction, while the other two remained by the stairs.

Luke frowned, an unpleasant sensation tugging at him. The two men weren't just standing there, and they weren't simply talking together. One of them was speaking on a comlink, his free hand fiddling restlessly with a knife belted at his side. The other was standing close to him, obviously listening in, his body tense, his eyes turned upward.

Suddenly, with the kind of utter certainty that Luke was slowly learning to associate with the Force, he realized the truth. The small room at the top of the stairs was where Ferrouz's wife and daughter were being held.

The first man put away the comlink and drew his knife. He turned it over in his hands a few times, saying something to the other man. Then, waving it one last time as if for emphasis, he slid it back into its sheath.

And both men started up the stairs.

Luke swallowed hard, half a dozen possibilities flooding in on him. Maybe the attack team Stelikag had sent had succeeded in killing Governor Ferrouz. Maybe they hadn't, and had decided he was out of their reach. Or maybe someone had decided that they no longer needed either Ferrouz or the hostages.

But one thing was certain, as certain as the flash of insight that had told Luke where the hostages were. The two men were heading up to confront Ferrouz's wife and daughter, and kill them.

There was no time to think. No time to plan. The two men were on the stairs, and there was only Luke to stop them, and there was just a single opponent standing in Luke's way.

It was now or never. Ripping off his bulky hooded poncho and throwing it into the tunnel behind him, Luke rounded the corner into the cavern and charged at full speed toward the strolling kidnapper.

The man spotted him instantly, a startled and slightly puzzled frown crossing his face. "Who are you?" he demanded as his hand dropped to his blaster.

Luke's answer was to put on an extra burst of speed. There were only ten meters separating them now. If he could cover the distance before the other got his blaster out . . .

But the man was faster than he'd hoped. Before Luke made it three more steps he had the weapon clear and leveled at Luke's chest. Luke saw his finger tightening on the trigger.

Suddenly there seemed to be two images shimmering in front of Luke's eyes. One was of the man and his blaster, the weapon pointed at Luke's chest. The other was of the same man and same blaster, only this one had a hazy bolt shooting from the weapon in a dream-like slow motion. Reflexively, Luke brought his hands up from his sides, watching the bolt drifting toward him as he swung his lightsaber into position—

As the blue-white blade snap-hissed into existence, the two images abruptly came together, and the slow-motion blaster bolt abruptly burst toward Luke at normal speed—

—and ricocheted from the blade straight back into the man's shoulder.

The other bellowed with surprise and pain, his blaster flailing to the side as he jerked with the unexpected impact. He recovered his balance and tried to bring the blaster back on target.

Luke slammed into him, his shoulder connecting solidly with the man's chest and knocking him a full meter backward to land with a thud on the ground.

The man swore viciously, again trying to bring his blaster to bear. Stepping hastily to the side, Luke swung his lightsaber again, slashing the blaster in half. The man rolled up onto his side, then collapsed again as Luke kicked him hard in the stomach. This time, he stayed down.

For a second Luke just stared at him, his breath coming in quick heaves, the reality of what he'd just done flooding in on him. *Good against remotes is one thing.* Han's mocking comment on their first trip together came drifting back. *Good against the living? That's something else.*

Luke had done it. He'd gone against the living. And he'd survived.

He looked up at the stairs. The two men who'd been climbing had stopped one flight up from the floor and were staring down in open-mouthed astonishment.

But that wouldn't last long. Squaring his shoulders, Luke took a step toward them.

And ducked as a pair of blaster bolts shot past his head.

He'd forgotten all about the mob of kidnappers at the other end of the cavern.

Another bolt shot past, closer this time. Luke glanced down at the blaster he'd just cut in half, wishing too late that he hadn't done that, and took off toward the stairs. There was a shed over that way, plus an abandoned and extremely rusty ore car. Either of them should give him cover while he tried to figure out his next move.

Unfortunately, he already knew what that move was. He had to chase the two men up those stairs, and he had to do it fast enough to stop them. Even if it meant doing so in full view and full blaster range of the rest of the gang. Even if it meant taking a few blaster bolts along the way.

Even if it meant dying in the attempt.

Mara had made it perhaps a quarter of the way along the beam when she heard a shout from the cavern below.

She froze, her eyes flicking toward the sound. Ahead, between the stairs and the vehicle tunnel, one of the kidnappers had drawn his blaster and was lining it up on a badly dressed and clearly insane figure that had appeared from nowhere and was running straight at him.

She winced. Skywalker—that had to be LaRone's contact Skywalker. He'd broken cover, like he'd been ordered not to, had charged in here alone, like any intelligent life-form should have known better than, and was about to pay the ultimate price for his foolishness.

And there was nothing Mara could do to prevent it. Her hold-out blaster didn't have nearly enough range to take out the kidnapper, and even if it had she couldn't have risked using it. The minute she fired, the rest of the kidnappers down there would be on to her, and Ferrouz's family would be doomed.

Maybe they were doomed anyway. Now that her attention had been drawn forward, she could see that there were two men climbing the stairs, their expressions and body language that of men preparing for murder.

Cursing under her breath, she focused on the track in front of her. She would never make it in time. Not at her present speed. Probably not even if she stood up and ran.

Ferrouz's wife and daughter were going to die. And like Skywalker's own impending death, there was nothing Mara could do about it. The man on the cavern floor ahead aimed his blaster and fired.

And with the *snap-hiss* of a lightsaber, a blue-white blaze lanced out from Skywalker's hands and deflected the shot straight back at the gunman.

Mara felt her mouth drop open. Skywalker had a lightsaber? And actually knew how to use it?

Then, without slowing down, Skywalker rammed his shoulder into the kidnapper's chest and knocked him down. Before the man could recover the lightsaber flashed again, cutting his blaster in half. The gunman tried to get back up, and Skywalker kicked him, putting him down for good.

Mara felt her lips twist. Hardly the tactic of a lightsaber artist. That first deflection must have been a lucky shot.

On the stairway, the two would-be killers had stopped and were gawking at the scene below. The kid turned toward them.

And nearly died right there as a pair of blaster shots lanced past him from the rest of Stelikag's group at Mara's end of the room.

Mara came to a sudden decision. She couldn't get to the men on the stairway, not in time. But Skywalker might be able to. *If* he had a blaster.

Clenching her teeth, she hunched up onto her knees on the crane rail. Skywalker was a long way away, and even with a Force assist she was going to need all the upper-body strength she had. The figure below had resumed his run toward the stairs, and the two men there had broken their own mesmerized paralysis and were starting upward again.

Drawing her hold-out blaster, Mara cocked her arm over her shoulder and threw it as hard as she could toward Skywalker.

It clattered to the ground three meters in front of him, and for a second she thought he was going to just run straight past it. Then, abruptly, he stopped, and with the blaster bolts from behind starting to fill the air around him he stooped and picked up the weapon.

And then, like a complete idiot, he paused and looked around him.

Don't look, Mara pleaded silently as she dropped flat onto the rail again. *They're watching you. Don't look for me.*

But of course he did.

And he spotted her.

Mara winced, pressing herself tightly against the rail. Maybe Stelikag wouldn't notice. Maybe he hadn't tracked the direction the blaster had come from.

But Stelikag noticed. Of course he noticed.

"There!" she heard a shout from below her. "Up there."

And suddenly the bulk of the blasterfire that had been directed toward Skywalker sizzled through the air around Mara.

She clenched her teeth. *Now* she was well and truly trapped.

But at least Skywalker seemed to have figured out why she'd sent him a weapon. He was on the move again, running toward the stairway, the hold-out blaster spitting its small but deadly fire at the men on the stairs.

The kid wasn't a bad shot, either. One of the men jerked like a twitched puppet and dropped to his knees, clutching his leg. The other man took two more steps up to the next landing and dropped into the partial shelter of the guardrail. He yanked out his own blaster and trained it at his attacker.

Suddenly Skywalker was dead center in the middle of a crossfire.

Mara winced. Fortunately, the kid knew what to do in that situation. He continued running until he reached an abandoned ore car lying on its side near the base of the stairs. Dropping into a crouch in the partial shelter, he resumed his attack on the stairway.

Only the attack couldn't succeed . . . and as Mara looked below her again she realized with a sinking heart just how little time they had. About half of Stelikag's remaining force had come to a halt level with her position and were standing or crouching in sharpshooter stances, keeping her pinned down with a steady rain of blasterfire. The rest of the crowd was heading toward Skywalker, moving slowly and warily but keeping up their attack on him as well.

When they reached him, he would die. And then Mara, still lying here, would watch helplessly as Stelikag or one of his men climbed leisurely to the control cabin and killed Ferrouz's family.

She looked up again, focusing on the rail stretching out in front of her. It hung two meters from the ceiling, as she'd already noted, with enough room for her to walk or run.

The problem was the fire coming from below, and the V-shaped struts that held the rail to the ceiling. If she didn't block her attackers' shots she wouldn't last long. But if her lightsaber sliced through enough of the struts neither would the rail.

Which left her only one option. A desperate, borderline-insane option.

But she was the Emperor's Hand, and there were Imperial lives hanging by a thread.

Taking a deep breath, she ignited her lightsaber.

"There!" Pellaeon said, jabbing a finger at the monitor. "That freighter there."

"I see it, sir," the young tractor operator said, his fingers dancing across the controls. "Tractor activated . . . firing."

Pellaeon held his breath, watching as the *Lost Reef* cut swiftly across the *Chimaera's* bow from starboard to portside. Crewer Mithel was hardly the ship's most senior tractor beam operator, and in fact Pellaeon suspected the boy was fresh out of training at this particular post.

But with the command deck's doors still locked Mithel was the only one available. Pellaeon could only hope he was good enough to pull this off.

Above the monitor, a green light winked on. "Got him," Mithel said.

"Confirmed," Thrawn's voice came over the speaker. "Now draw me in—slowly, slowly."

"Yes, sir," Mithel said, adjusting his controls. "Drawing you in now."

Pellaeon craned his neck, looking out of the crew pit at the bridge viewport. The Golan was still looming directly ahead, and he could almost see it growing larger. An optical illusion, of course, born from the tension of the moment. That, plus the knowledge that there were only nine minutes left until impact. He watched the Golan another minute, then looked back down at the monitor.

He caught his breath. "It's getting away!" he snapped, pointing at the *Lost Reef*'s image. "You've lost the lock."

"No, sir, I haven't," Mithel said. "I have to let him get farther out, then draw him back in. Otherwise this won't work."

"But—"

"He's correct, Commander," Thrawn put in calmly. "Draw in, then reel out to allow a buildup of momentum, then draw in again."

Pellaeon swallowed. "Yes, sir," he muttered reluctantly. On the display, he saw the freighter come to a hesitant halt as Mithel again added power to the tractor beam and once again began drawing him in.

"It's simple physics, Commander," Thrawn said. "Strictly speaking, a tractor beam doesn't pull in its target, but instead pulls the target and generator toward their common center of mass. Since the *Chimaera* vastly outmasses nearly everything you've ever drawn in, it's never before been an issue for you."

"Yes, sir," Pellaeon said again.

"The question now, of course, is whether the *Lost Reef* and I can provide you enough of a nudge to pull you off Nuso Esva's predetermined path," Thrawn continued. "What do you think, Nuso Esva?"

"Very clever, Thrawn," Nuso Esva said through the speaker. The mocking tone had vanished from his voice, replaced by a cold bitterness that sent an icy dagger digging into Pellaeon's stomach. "Very clever indeed."

"More than just clever," Thrawn said. "Your entire battle computation depended on me having only the *Admonitor* and her escort ships. Now I

have the *Chimaera* and the Golan defense platform, as well. You may wish
to withdraw your Firekilns while you still have the chance."

Nuso Esva gave a sort of whistling snort. "Don't insult me, Thrawn. Do
you truly believe I hadn't prepared for this possibility?"

"Yes, I do," Thrawn said calmly. "The moment is now, Nuso Esva."

"Agreed," the alien said. "The moment is indeed now."

It was obvious right from the beginning that the Golan crew didn't much
know how to deal with Chewie. Even as they worked frantically to load
the torpedo racks, Han caught some of them throwing surreptitious
looks at him, or twitching aside to get out of his way. Maybe they'd heard
stories about Wookiee rages. Maybe they were just in awe of his massive
strength as he lugged torpedoes all by himself from the storage cradles to
the launch racks.

Or maybe Han was just imagining it. Maybe all they were thinking
about was that if this didn't work, they had seven minutes left to live.

"We're ready, Major," one of the crewers called. "Racks loaded and set
for rapid fire."

"Got it," Han said, crossing to the fire-control station where Nills was
standing stiffly with his hands poised over the launch controls. "Commandant, give me an update on the fire trajectory," he called toward the comm
as he keyed the display for a forward view. "Confirm no vessels in the target zone."

"Trajectory confirmed," Barcelle said tightly. "Clear to launch. Nills—"

"Hold it," Han said, frowning at the display. The incoming Star
Destroyer looked different somehow.

"There's no time," Barcelle ground out. "Nills, launch when—"

"I said *hold it*," Han interrupted, putting a hand between Nills and the
board. Suddenly he realized what was different about the looming warship. "The Star Destroyer's veering off."

"That's impossible," Barcelle insisted. "The readout on the damage . . ."
He trailed off. "You're right," he said, sounding relieved and puzzled at the
same time. "Still running under low power, but his vector's now . . . I don't
understand. How is he *doing* that?"

"Don't know," Han said, taking a deep breath and letting it out in a huff. That had been way too close. Even for him. "Don't care. Secure the torpedoes. Doesn't look like we're going to need—"

"Incoming!" Nills said, pointing a rigid finger at one of his displays. "Commandant, we've got . . . we've got *eight* more alien ships coming in from hyperspace—sector three. Correction: eight large ships plus thirty smaller escorts. The big ones show the same configuration as the group already squared off against the *Admonitor*."

Han hissed between his teeth as he studied the display. Apparently, he'd relaxed too soon. "Commandant, we have anything on those ships?" he asked.

"No, nothing," Barcelle said. "But from the way the *Admonitor* is repositioning escorts, they're not taking them lightly."

Han crossed over to the tactical holo. There were now sixteen of the unknown ships heading across the Poln system toward the *Admonitor* and its escorts. "Is the *Chimaera* going to be able to get over there in time to join the party?"

"Assuming it continues its current rate of turn, it should at least have a fire angle," Barcelle said. "And the *Sarissa's* also now moving up to support the *Admonitor*."

"Right," Han confirmed. He'd already spotted the Dreadnought leaving its orbit and heading for the *Admonitor's* group. "Looks like whoever's in charge is pulling in every turbolaser he's got."

Barcelle hissed out a frustrated sigh. "Except ours," he said. "Looks like we're the only ones who are out of the fight."

Han grimaced. "Yeah, we are," he agreed. We, the Golan; more important, we, the Rebel Alliance. He just hoped Cracken would be ready to move before the big battle started.

He stiffened, his mind making a hard right-angle turn. The missile ships hidden on Poln Minor weren't there to intercept the Rebel transports, as he and Cracken had assumed. They were the card Nuso Esva had hidden up his sleeve.

He keyed the tactical to add an overlay of Poln Minor's geological features. If Leia had been right, the cavern should be just about *there* . . .

He nodded grimly. If Leia was right, the missile ships were, in perfect position to blow the cavern roof, fly out, and regroup themselves for an attack around the curve of the planet. With all the Imperial ships currently on the other side of the planet, the missile ships could hit their rear before anyone could do anything about it.

Anyone, that was, except the Golan.

Or, given this bunch, anyone except Han.

For a long moment he gazed at the holo, watching the incoming alien warships rearranging their lines, wondering what to do. He and Leia had helped *arm* those missile ships, blast it. If they got out and tore into the *Admonitor*'s rear, they would do some serious damage before they were stopped.

On the other hand the Alliance was *trying* to topple the Empire. Doing anything to help the Imperials seemed a little crazy, even if it was to help stop an alien who'd already demonstrated he was ready and willing to use the Alliance for his own purposes.

Surreptitiously, Han looked around the fire-control room. Leadership, Rieekan had lectured him, was all about responsibility and consequences. Whatever Han did right now would have consequences, some which he might never know about, others of which might come along three minutes from now and smack him in the back of the head.

But there was no way around it. He'd helped arm Nuso Esva's missile ships. He had to make sure that Nuso Esva didn't get to use them. Against *anybody*.

On the other hand, if he could do that *and* help the Alliance at the same time . . .

He caught Chewie's eye and gestured him over. "Get back to the *Falcon* and call Cracken," he said quietly when the Wookiee joined him. "Tell him to pull Leia and the assault squad off their attack and get them out of there."

Chewie rumbled a question.

"Yes, *now*," Han confirmed tartly. "I don't care if they're winning or losing—probably losing. Just get them out."

The Wookiee acknowledged and started to turn away. Han caught his arm. "And then get her ready to fly," he added. "I'll grab Toksi and Atticus on my way down."

Chewie nodded and headed away. "Commandant?" Han called toward the comm. "We've got a new target. Pull up a map of Poln Minor, and I'll give you the coordinates."

Wedge threw the T-47 into yet another sharp turn, and once more Leia fought against her bouncing head and motion-blurred vision to fire a double laser blast at the missile ship in her sights. She saw the bolts slam into the ship's armor, fired off another shot as Wedge dived straight toward the vessel—

And then at the heart-stopping literal last second he pulled up, shoving Leia hard into her seat. "Good shooting," he called.

Leia clenched her teeth as he arced them across the cavern and swung back for another attack. Maybe she was shooting well. Maybe he was just being polite.

But all the good shooting in the galaxy, whether by her or by the rest of the Rebel gunners, didn't seem to be doing much good. The missile ships were more heavily armored than she'd realized, and were ray-shielded on top of it, and while probably half of them now sported burns and warped hull plates, not a single one had been destroyed or even disabled.

And their time was running out. All fifty of the ships were rumbling with the sound of pre-flight warm-up, and the last few humans who'd been operating the quad lasers when the T-47s first blew into the cavern had abandoned their weapons and disappeared somewhere down the conveyance tunnel. The missile ships were about to leave, ready to fly over and position themselves for an attack on the Rebel transports when they emerged from underground.

Or if they didn't feel like waiting, they could probably use a few of the Caldorf missiles to blow their way through the surface and destroy the transports right where they currently sat.

Caldorf missiles she and Han had helped load.

The comm crackled in her ear, cutting through the curt orders and reports from the other T-47s. "Command to Rogue Team," Cracken's voice came tartly. "New orders: break off—repeat, break off—and return."

Leia frowned. Break off? *Now?*

Wedge obviously didn't believe it, either. "Rogue One to command: confirm order," he called.

"Break off and return," Cracken repeated.

"Command, strongly recommend against that," Wedge warned. "Once they break cover, they'll disperse. We won't get another chance like this."

"You don't like it, you can take it up later with Solo," Cracken said. "Chewbacca says he's got something special planned, and it doesn't involve any of you still being there."

Leia felt her eyes widen. This was *Han's* idea? "What's the plan?" she asked.

"Chewbacca didn't say," Cracken said. "I'm not really sure he knows. Now kick afterburners, or I'll kick them for you."

"Acknowledged," Wedge said. "All Rogues—"

"Wait a minute," Leia said, her eyes focused on the bulbs at the top of the weapons fins. "Whatever Han's up to, it will probably work better if these ships can't shoot straight."

"We've already tried," Wedge said. "The sensor bulbs are as ray-shielded as the rest of the hull."

"Then let's try something new," Leia said. "I'll need a wingmate."

"Rogue Three, form up on my portside," Wedge ordered.

"Copy," another voice said, and as Leia looked out her canopy one of the other T-47s dropped into parallel formation a few meters away. "What's the plan?"

"Just hold position," Leia said. Swiveling her harpoon gun all the way to the side, she aimed for Rogue Three's starboard braking flap and fired.

There were twin yelps from both the pilot and gunner as the magnetic harpoon slammed into the airspeeder's side. "What the—?"

"Now we swing low and sweep," Leia said. "See if the cable can take off one of the sensor—"

She gasped as the T-47 dipped suddenly and then jerked hard. It jerked again as Wedge got it back under control and pulled up—and as he sent them flying toward the far end of the cavern Leia saw the mangled metal at the top of the fin they'd just passed. The metal, and the missing sensor bulb.

Rogue Three gave a war whoop. "It works!" he crowed.

"Time's up," Wedge said. "All Rogues, break off and head home. At your earliest convenience."

There were a cluster of acknowledgments . . . and as Leia watched, the

T-47s linked up in pairs, one of each pair shooting a magnetic harpoon at the other. They circled at the far wall of the cavern and swung smoothly around.

And as they flew one last time over the rows of missile ships, the stretched cables snicked off at least another dozen of the sensor bulbs.

"Release!" Wedge snapped.

Leia nodded and punched the cable release. Just in time, as Wedge did a quick sideways jink and inserted them once again at full speed into the dark, claustrophobic confines of the tunnel. Behind her, Leia saw the rest of the airspeeders also disentangle their cables from one another, form up, and slide in a neat single file behind them.

The last of the ten T-47s had just made it inside when there was a sudden burst of reflected light from the distant cavern behind them.

The aliens had blown the ceiling. The missile ships were about to fly.

Leia rubbed her shoulders where her straps had dug into them. "There you go, flyboy," she murmured. "Whatever you're planning, I hope that helps."

"What was that?" Wedge called.

Leia shook her head. "Nothing."

"Commander?" the sensor officer called, his voice still slurring a bit with the aftereffects of the vertigon gas. "I'm reading an explosion on Poln Minor."

"Where?" Pellaeon called back, looking up from the tractor station toward the bridge viewport.

"Seventh Octant, right at the edge of our view," the officer reported. "I've got a visual feed from the Golan, too, but it's not much better."

Pellaeon looked back at the tractor display. The *Chimaera*'s vector was well clear of the Golan now. The ship's engine control was still crippled, but at least they were out of imminent danger. "Can you handle the rest of this?" he asked Mithel.

"Yes, sir," the tractor operator said. "Unless Lord Odo—" He glanced up at Pellaeon. "—I mean unless Nuso Esva has left us more surprises, we should be all right."

"Carry on," Pellaeon said, a tight smile tugging at his lips as he turned away and headed for the crew pit stairs. Mithel was barely out of his training, yet he had the casual boldness to offer his assessment of the *Chimaera*'s condition to a ranking command officer.

Pellaeon's smile faded. On the other hand, why shouldn't he? The *Chimaera*'s senior officers certainly hadn't done a very good job of taking care of the ship, Pellaeon himself included.

"Senior Captain Thrawn?" he called as he climbed back up to the command walkway. "Did you hear that?"

"I did, Commander," Thrawn's voice came back. "Maintain your present operation."

Pellaeon grimaced. Like they had any real choice with their drive locked down the way it was. "Shall I launch TIE fighters to investigate the explosion?" he asked.

"Negative," Thrawn's voice came back. "I'll need all of your fighters available once Nuso Esva brings in the rest of his ships"

"Understood," Pellaeon said, his stomach tightening as he looked out over the distant battle array. "Sir, Nuso Esva told us earlier that five Firekilns were the equivalent of a Star Destroyer. Was that an accurate assessment?"

"Quite accurate, Commander," Thrawn confirmed calmly.

And there were already sixteen of the big alien ships out there facing off against the *Admonitor* and the still-crippled *Chimaera*.

Thrawn wasn't going to need the *Chimaera*'s TIE fighters. Thrawn was going to need a miracle.

"Commander, I have ships at the explosion region," the sensor officer spoke up suddenly. "Looks like they're rising out from underground. Midsized fighters, alien design, with underslung—" He broke off. "Commander, those underslung missiles are *Caldorf* VII *interceptors*."

"Turbolasers!" Pellaeon snapped, turning sharply to the viewport. A group of ships armed with interceptor missiles in the rear of Thrawn's battle array would be devastating. "Target those ships."

"Sir, weapons-control systems are nonfunctional," another voice called. "I've signaled the crews to set for manual."

"Tell them to hurry," Pellaeon snarled. Once the alien ships gained some altitude and speed, there would be no way the *Chimaera*'s crews could hit them on manual control. *"Move* it, Lieutenant," he said. "We're the only thing standing between them and the *Admonitor."*

"Fire!" Han called.

With a crackling stutter from the Golan's electromagnetic rail launchers, the racks of heavy proton torpedoes began emptying themselves out into space. Six—eight—ten—twenty—Han gazed out the viewport at the stream of torpedoes heading for the missile ships' lair, feeling a strange mixture of awe, approval, and uneasiness. It was good to have this level of firepower on their side.

Problem was, it usually *wasn't* on their side. Usually, this was the kind of weaponry the Rebel Alliance was facing.

"All torpedoes away," Nills reported tensely. "More ships rising from concealment; still clustered. Leading edge impact . . . *now."*

With a distant flash of light, the first torpedo detonated. And then the second, and the third, and the fourth.

Suddenly the whole edge of Poln Minor lit up like the inside of a small star.

"What the—" Barcelle gasped as a visible ripple of firestorm shock wave blew outward through the planet's thin atmosphere. "Major, what *was* that?"

"That was a whole bunch of Caldorf VII interceptors getting hot enough to self-ignite," Han told him with grim satisfaction.

"Ah." Barcelle watched the fading fireball in silence for a few seconds. "And, uh, we're sure those were *enemy* ships, right?"

"Trust me," Han said. He looked over at the tactical holo. "Or trust him," he added pointing. "Eight more Firekilns have just jumped into the system. I guess Nuso Esva was counting on those missile ships."

"So what happens now?" Nills asked anxiously.

Barcelle squared his shoulders. "We get on the turbolasers," he ordered. "We may be out of the main battle over here, but we still have a world to defend. Let's get to it."

CHAPTER TWENTY-TWO

As LaRone had expected, the final assault on the cellar came from the supply lift.

Though technically, it came from the crater where the supply lift had been before the massive set of shaped charges from above ripped through the top, tore across the shaft walls, and blew the inner door halfway across the cellar.

Through the smoke and flying debris eight men and aliens dropped from the alley above into the charred hole, their blasters blazing.

"Get down!" LaRone shouted, ducking his own head a bit as he and the others opened up with their E-11s. Fortunately, he'd anticipated their insertion point well enough to have thrown together a new redoubt in the cellar's far rear corner.

Only he and the others hadn't had time to move the big kegs that had formed their original defensive barrier. Their new position was mostly made up of smaller kegs, piled on top of one another where necessary, with the old redoubt still in its original position barely five meters away from them.

Brightwater had wondered if the attackers would spot the old barrier and simply settle into its protection for their attack. As LaRone's blasterfire staggered one of the aliens in the middle, the group did exactly that.

"Now what?" Marcross shouted over the staccato screams of the blasterfire. "LaRone, we're trapped!"

"Keep firing," LaRone shouted back, keeping an eye on the other end of the room. If whoever was running this attack was smart, he ought to be opening up a second battle vector just about now.

Right on schedule, there it was: three more figures dropping from the stairway door to the cellar floor, their own blasters silent. Keeping low, they headed stealthily toward the loud exchange of blasterfire at the other end of the room, clearly hoping to catch the defenders in a crossfire.

Just as stealthily, two Troukree rose up from concealment under broken pieces of walls and stairs as the three attackers passed them.

"Keep firing!" LaRone shouted again. The blasterfire itself ought to drown out any sounds the Troukree or their victims might make, but a little extra noise couldn't hurt.

He needn't have worried. The Troukree reached their targets, and with a flicker of light from their knives all three attackers collapsed silently to the floor.

LaRone returned his attention to the eight attackers crouched behind the keg. Or rather, to the five attackers who were still firing, apparently unaware through the ongoing firestorm that three of their original number were down. Beside him Marcross gave another shout, some kind of alien-sounding battle cry, clearly calculated to keep the noise level up. The number of attackers at the barricade went to four, then three, then two.

Abruptly, the last two survivors seemed to wake up to what was happening. They both spun around, dropping down with their backs to the kegs, their weapons tracking around to their rear . . .

Toward Grave, lying in his now open-topped bacta tank, the blaster he'd concealed as the attackers ran past with barely a glance braced against the edge of the opening. His weapon spat one last shot, with his usual deadly accuracy, and one of the two aliens collapsed to the floor, his own final bolt shattering another piece of wall.

The last attacker was still lining up his blaster when Quiller fired from his own stack of concealing debris across the room and ended the battle.

Cautiously, LaRone rose to his feet. "Governor?" he asked, turning to look at the figure curled awkwardly behind the extra pair of kegs behind him.

"Don't worry about me," Ferrouz said. He'd argued against the stormtroopers giving him any extra protection, but LaRone could tell from his face that he was just as glad he'd had it. "What about you and the others?"

"I'm fine," LaRone assured him, wincing as he turned back around. With the adrenaline of the battle fading, the pain of a dozen blaster burns was starting to throb in his arms, chest, and left cheek. "Report?" he called.

One by one, the others checked in. It was the usual: blaster burns, damaged equipment, drained power packs. But they'd all made it through alive, as had the four remaining Troukree. If anything, in fact, the green-scaled aliens had gotten through it with fewer injures even than the stormtroopers.

A fact that Vaantaar had clearly noticed, and was apparently not happy with. "You take too much of the battle upon yourselves," he chided LaRone as he awkwardly swapped out the power pack on his blaster for a new one.

"I don't see how you can say that," LaRone said. "Especially since the only death so far has been one of yours."

"We serve and die willingly," Vaantaar said. "But we wish fuller service against the enemies of our people. The next battle will be ours."

"Actually, there may not be another battle," Marcross pointed out. "They have to be running low on people by now."

"Not to mention that even with shaped charges, blowing the supply lift was a little on the noisy side," Brightwater added. "Hopefully, there are some patrollers on the way by now."

"If not, maybe we can call them," LaRone suggested, checking his helmet's comlink as he left the redoubt and headed over to Grave. But the crackle of static in his ear showed that the jamming was still in place. "Or not," he added. "Good shooting, Grave."

"Thanks," Grave said, breathing heavily, his gun hand hanging limply over the edge of the tank opening. "Not my best work, I'm afraid."

"It was more than good enough," LaRone assured him. "How are you feeling? Will you be ready for—what are we up to?—Round Four?"

"There will be no further rounds," a voice called from the top of the open lift shaft beside them.

LaRone spun around toward the shaft, snapping his E-11 up into firing position. Out of the corner of his eye he spotted Marcross circle quickly to the other side of the shaft. He settled into covering position and nodded.

Carefully, LaRone eased forward and peered up the shaft. Nothing was visible except the tops of the surrounding buildings and a darkening evening sky. "Hello?" he called.

"You have been worthy opponents," the voice said, and now that LaRone was listening closely he could hear the faint alien intonation in the words. "But it comes now to the end."

"Fine with me," LaRone said. "Come on down, and we'll have it out."

"It comes now to the end," the voice repeated. "Our master has achieved his goal of luring his enemy to this system. We no longer require that the governor die in any specified way."

LaRone gripped his blaster a little tighter. That didn't sound good. "Commanders are always changing their minds that way," he commiserated. "So we'll be going our separate ways, I assume?"

"We shall go our way," the voice said. "But you have caused deaths among my people. Deaths among we who are the Chosen. Those deaths will not go unavenged."

LaRone grimaced. He'd been afraid that was the direction the conversation was heading. "No problem," he said. "As I said, come on down and we'll see what we can do about giving you your revenge."

"The revenge is already prepared," the voice said. "Die in agony, enemies of the Chosen."

There was the faint sound of footsteps moving away. LaRone keyed up his helmet's audio enhancers, listening hard as the steps faded down the alley. Heading away to the east, he decided.

He stepped back to the bacta tank, gesturing the others to join him. Marcross nodded and moved around the blackened shaft, his eyes and blaster still pointed cautiously upward. Brightwater was already on his way from the redoubt, where he'd been standing guard over Ferrouz, and across the room Quiller was hobbling toward them on his injured leg, two of the Troukree supporting him as he walked.

"Thoughts?" LaRone asked as Marcross and Brightwater reached him.

"I'm guessing more explosives," Marcross said.

"Certainly the simplest approach," Brightwater seconded. "Probably going to lay them where the tapcaf joins the stores on either side. Hitting those supporting walls properly should bring both buildings falling inward on top of us."

"They'll probably be planting them on the alley side," Quiller added as he limped up beside Marcross. "Street side's a little too public."

"Especially after that last blast," LaRone said, nodding. "And if they're in the alley, that means there's a chance we can still stop them. I think their spokesman went east, but we should probably send two of us in each direction."

"Agreed," Marcross said. "Well, gentlemen. It's been an honor to serve—"

"What's this *two* stuff?" Grave put in, grabbing the edge of the bacta tank and hauling himself gingerly up into a sitting position. "What am I, chopped entrails?"

"We'll need to do some jumping to get up there," Marcross reminded him. "I don't think you're up to that just now."

"Neither is Quiller," Grave retorted, pointing to Quiller as he hung somewhat precariously onto Brightwater's shoulder. "If he goes—"

"Hold it," LaRone said, staring at Quiller. He'd come over with the help of two of the Troukree.

Why was he hanging on Brightwater's shoulder now?

He took a quick step back from the group, looking around the cellar.

Just as two of the Troukree took off from opposite directions, running toward the lift shaft. "Wait!" LaRone snapped, trying to get around Marcross.

He stopped short as Vaantaar put a restraining hand on his arm. "No," the Troukree said softly. "I already said it. This battle is ours."

There was nothing LaRone could say. Nothing he could do. The first Troukree reached the center of the shaft and was thrown up through the opening by the third Troukree, who was waiting for him there. Even as the first alien disappeared from LaRone's sight, the second reached the shaft and was similarly hurled upward, arcing toward the other side of the alley. There was a warbling call, followed by a multiple burst of blasterfire.

And then, nothing.

LaRone looked at Vaantaar. "It is over," Vaantaar said, letting go of LaRone's arm, his expression oddly serene. "Come. We may now leave this place."

LaRone nodded. There were some alien cultures, he vaguely remembered, that used the phrase as a term for death.

But it didn't really matter. There was still a wounded Imperial governor in here, and a threat to his life out there, and LaRone and the other stormtroopers had no choice but to head out and try to stop it. "Marcross?" he said.

"On it," Marcross called back, already rolling one of the smaller kegs into the shaft. "You and me?"

"You and me," LaRone said, popping a fresh power pack into his E-11.

And it occurred to him that he'd been right, way back when this whole thing started.

One way or another, the Hand of Judgment was most definitely going to go out with a bang.

The two men on the stairs fired again, one of their shots blasting some of the rust from Luke's ore car, the other shot missing completely. Leaning out from his cover, Luke fired a shot back at them—and quickly ducked back in as another burst of fire burned past from behind him. The kidnappers from the other end of the cavern, coming up fast.

With a curious sense of detachment, Luke realized he was about to die.

He was pinned down. So was whoever that was up there on the crane rail. Luke's only weapons were a small borrowed blaster, which had to be nearly out of power by now, and a lightsaber that he barely knew how to use.

Maybe the blaster had been the other intruder's only weapon. Certainly he hadn't heard any return fire from up there.

And against the two of them were at least twelve men, counting the two on the stairs. With death sentences facing all of them for the kidnapping of Ferrouz's family, they had nothing to lose by adding another murder to their list of crimes.

Another two murders, actually. With a lot of their fire trained upward, it was a toss-up as to which of them would die first.

And then, through the scream of blasterfire, Luke heard the *snap-hiss* of a lightsaber. Frowning, he leaned out.

He was facing an extraordinary sight. The person on the rail—a woman, he could see now, her hair glittering strangely in the red lighting—was on the move, running along the rail toward the stairs and the small room where Ferrouz's family was being held. She was swinging a lightsaber as she ran, the blade deflecting the sudden extra fury of blaster bolts now coming from Stelikag and the other kidnappers below her.

But the blade wasn't simply cutting across the incoming fire the way Luke blocked such attacks in his practice sessions. It was flickering rapidly on and off in an irregular pattern, flashing like a magenta strobe light. She kept running, gradually twisting her torso around as she moved past her attackers, keeping the lightsaber blade between her and their fire as it began to come more from behind than from beside her.

Axlon had said there was an Imperial agent on Poln Major who carried a lightsaber. But after all the rest of the traitor's lies, Luke had assumed he'd been lying about that, too. Apparently not.

But what was she *doing*? The lightsaber was still flickering as she ran, and each time it went off it opened up the possibility that one of the blaster bolts would get through. Was there some kind of defect in the weapon?

Luke caught his breath as he suddenly understood. She was turning her lightsaber on and off as she ran to keep from slicing through the rail's support struts while she swept the blade across the incoming fire.

For a moment he just stood there staring, frozen in amazement by the level of sheer control and artistry the maneuver demonstrated. She deflected a shot, swung the lightsaber toward the next one, flicked the blade off and then on to bypass a strut, deflected the next bolt—

A shot from the stairs sizzled past Luke's shoulder, abruptly breaking the spell. "Right," he muttered to himself, spinning around and firing another two shots of his own at the men on the stairs—

—only to discover that while he'd been watching the lightsaber display above him both men had managed to make it up another section of the stairway.

And he realized to his horror that they were now out of his blaster's range.

He dropped back into the ore car's partial cover and turned to face the group still running toward him. If the ones on the stairway were out of range, those in the distance were even more so.

But even useless shots fired in their direction might distract them from the agent running along the rail above him. It was, he realized heavily, all that he could do.

Luke was out of the fight. From this point on, it was all up to her.

Dimly, through the Force-created combat tunnel vision, Mara saw she was nearly to the control cabin.

So were the two men climbing the stairs toward it.

With an effort, she pulled a little of her focus away from her defense. The men were climbing, but she saw now that both of them were moving slower than they should have been. She pulled a little more of her focus and saw that both were limping badly. Apparently in all the shooting he'd been doing, Skywalker had managed to wound both of them.

At least he was good for *something*.

The crane rail jerked and twisted beneath her feet as her lightsaber slashed through one of the support struts. Clearly, she'd diverted a bit too much of her attention. She brought her mind into focus again, blocking the attacks on her as she ran.

Suddenly she was there.

She braked to a halt, nearly slamming into the cavern wall before she was able to stop. Below her was the roof of the control cabin, and she slashed her lightsaber at it, slicing out a circle of old metal and plastic and sending it crashing to the cabin floor below. Deflecting the last two blaster bolts sizzling toward her, she dropped through into the cabin.

They were there, all right: Ferrouz's wife and daughter, looking tired and disheveled and scared, but with the hint of quiet defiance in both their expressions that Mara would expect from the family of an Imperial governor. They were sitting in rough wooden chairs at the back of the cabin, the woman's arms protectively around the girl.

"Don't move," Mara ordered, and headed across the small room toward the door.

She was halfway there when the door was thrown open and one of the men loomed in the doorway, panting from his climb up the stairs. Lifting his blaster, he opened fire—and died instantly as Mara deflected the bolt into the center of his chest. He jerked, his blaster going flying, his body slamming into the man behind him and sending them both tumbling backward off the landing and halfway down the first flight of stairs.

Swearing viciously, the second man shoved the body of his companion away and lifted his own blaster. He fired, his curses turning to a scream of rage and pain as Mara caught the bolt on her lightsaber and sent it back into his weapon, shattering both the blaster and the hand gripping it.

Another shot came at Mara from the floor. Crouching down on the landing, she looked over the guardrail.

Any reasonable kidnappers would have realized by now that it was over and would be heading down the vehicle tunnel in a frantic attempt to get away. But not this bunch. This bunch was still heading for the stairway, still firing their blasters, still apparently convinced that they could salvage something out of the mess.

Even if it was just to kill one of the people who'd wrecked their plan.

She looked down. Skywalker was still crouched beside the ore car, the blaster she'd sent him silent, his lightsaber gripped in his hand but not ignited. Waiting for them to come to him.

Mara grimaced. She had no idea who he was, or how it was LaRone knew him. But he'd been helpful, whether he'd really planned to be or not, and he'd played his own small part in saving the governor's family. She couldn't just stand here and let him die.

From this distance, with no weapon other than her lightsaber, there was no way she could kill the rest of the kidnappers. But maybe she could do something to dissuade any further action. Just past the vehicle tunnel, between Skywalker and the kidnappers, was the stack of barrels she'd noted earlier, the ones emblazoned with FLAMMABLE warnings. Standing up, she locked her lightsaber on and threw it toward the stack.

The weapon arced through the air, its blade spinning like a child's twist toy. Mara stretched out, using the Force to guide the weapon's path as best she could, sending the blade slicing through the bases of three of the barrels. They burst open, and a gush of thick, evil-looking liquid flowed out.

She had no idea whether the stuff was still flammable. If it was left over from the mine's heyday, probably not.

But she would bet heavily that none of the men down there knew whether it was flammable, either. Even thirsting for Skywalker's death, maybe they would decide they weren't thirsting for it enough to face the possibility of going up in flames.

With that, they finally got the message. Even as Mara stretched out to call the lightsaber back to her hand, they slowed and then stopped. Their blasters were suddenly silent, their eyes no longer on Mara but on the stream of bubbling liquid flowing across the cavern in front of them.

All of them except one. Stelikag didn't even slow down, his eyes still burning toward Skywalker as he splashed unheeding and apparently uncaring through the stream.

And with no blaster within her reach, there was only one thing Mara could do. "Shoot it!" she shouted at Skywalker as her lightsaber flew the last couple of meters into her hand. "Shoot the pool. *Now!*"

"Shoot the pool!" the voice shouted from above Luke, the words echoing in the cavern. *"Now!"*

He glanced at the power indicator on his blaster. There were perhaps two shots left. Not nearly enough to stop the entire group of kidnappers who'd been charging at him moments before. But maybe enough to ignite the pool of liquid.

But could he do that? Could he deliberately spark a fire that he knew would kill someone?

And as he looked at Stelikag, splashing across the liquid, Ben Kenobi's words seemed to echo in his mind. *For over a thousand generations the Jedi Knights were the guardians of peace and justice in the Old Republic.*

Justice . . .

Stelikag was a kidnapper. He'd tried to murder an Imperial agent with his booby-trapped stairway, and he was involved with the plan to murder Governor Ferrouz and his family. If he'd had the chance, he would certainly have carried out those murders.

And at this immediate moment, he was planning to kill Luke.

Luke wasn't a Jedi yet. He might never become one.

But the pursuit of justice was something even non-Jedi could choose. Raising his blaster, he fired.

With a thunderous roar, the liquid on the cavern floor below exploded.

The shock wave slammed into Mara, throwing her back through the door into the control cabin. The whole structure, maybe even the whole cavern, shook as she retreated across the room and grabbed the woman and girl, pulling them to the floor and wrapping her arms protectively around them. There was a *crack* from above, and she winced as part of the ceiling near where she'd cut her way in fell with a crash. There was a second, somewhat softer explosion from below.

And then the echoes of the blast faded into a distant crackling.

"Stay here," Mara ordered the others. Getting to her feet, picking up her lightsaber from the floor where she'd apparently dropped it, she made her way to the door and cautiously looked out.

The stuff had been flammable, all right. Nearly half the floor below was roiling in bright yellow flames and a black, evil-smelling smoke. At the far corner of the cavern, she caught a glimpse of the remaining kidnappers pressed together against the far wall, as far away from the flames as they could get.

There was no sign of Stelikag. Blinking against the smoke, she looked down toward the ore car where Skywalker had been crouching. But the roiling smoke was too thick now for her to see whether he was still there or not.

What she *could* see was that the slope of the cavern floor had directed most of the blazing liquid away from the vehicle tunnel. A few more minutes to let the fire burn down, and she and the former captives would be able to get out of here.

Returning her lightsaber to her belt, she pulled out her comlink. While they waited, she would give Governor Ferrouz the good news.

Taking a quick three-step run, LaRone jumped up onto the keg and from there up to the edge of the shaft. He dropped his E-11 out onto the duracrete and simultaneously grabbed the edge with both hands, pulling himself up. His swinging legs made it to the top, and with a final heave he got his torso up, as well. He grabbed his E-11 from where he'd dropped it, rolled away from the opening, and came to rest on his stomach with his blaster aimed down the alley.

As he heard Marcross repeat the procedure behind him, he discovered to his stunned disbelief that it was all over.

At the end of the tapcaf, right where Brightwater had said they would plant the explosives, three of the yellow-eyed aliens were lying stretched out in the alley beside a half-assembled shaped charge. On the ground beside the explosives was the familiar boxy shape and oversized antenna of a Sanchor III comlink jammer. Standing over them were the two Troukree who had been thrown up out of the shaft a minute ago, the ones LaRone had tried to stop, the ones he'd assumed had gone straight to their deaths.

Beside those two Troukree were three more, all of them hefting heavy blasters.

With an effort, LaRone found his voice. "Clear," he called.

"Likewise," Marcross called back, his voice sounding as stunned as LaRone felt. "LaRone—"

"Yeah, me neither," LaRone conceded. The Troukree were looking back at him, and he suddenly realized his E-11 was still pointed at the group. "Mind you, it's nice to occasionally have some of the heavy lifting done by somebody else," he added as he lowered his blaster and stood up.

There was the patter of running feet below him, and Vaantaar suddenly came flying out of the shaft, landing with casual ease on the duracrete beside LaRone. Without a word, he strode down the alley toward the group of Troukree.

Marcross stepped up to LaRone's side. "Any idea who they really are?"

"Not a one," LaRone said, turning and looking past Marcross's shoulder. There were three more Troukree at that end of the tapcaf, guarding two more yellow-eyed alien bodies. "But I would say that Vaantaar's got some serious explaining to do."

To his mild surprise, there was a ping from his helmet comlink. Apparently, while they were shutting down the attackers the Troukree had also shut down the jammer. "LaRone," he said.

"Jade," the Emperor's Hand's voice came. "The governor's family has been secured."

LaRone breathed a sigh of relief. "He'll be very happy to hear that," he told her. "We seem to be in the clear, too. Do you need any assistance?"

"I don't think so," she said. "We're just waiting for the fire to die down a little before we head out."

"All right," LaRone said, frowning. That didn't sound like a very secure situation to him. Still, Jade usually knew what she was doing. "Have you seen anything of Skywalker?"

"He the one with the lightsaber?"

"That's him."

"He was helpful," she said. "If you're in contact with him, tell him to clear out. He's closer to the fire than we are, and he's probably roasting by now."

"We'll call him," LaRone promised. "You want us to take Governor Ferrouz back to the palace?"

"You should probably call General Ularno first and arrange an escort," Jade said. "We still don't know who else Nuso Esva might have suborned. Make sure Ularno brings men he can trust."

"Acknowledged," LaRone said. "We'll see you there."

"Good." The comlink clicked off.

Down the alley, Vaantaar had finished his discussion with his fellows and was heading back. "Marcross?" LaRone called.

"Call Skywalker and get him out of there," Marcross said, nodding. "Got it."

He turned away, and LaRone heard him key his comlink. Pursing his lips, LaRone headed toward Vaantaar.

They met halfway. "I think you owe us an explanation," LaRone said evenly.

"And an apology," Vaantaar agreed, ducking his head in an abbreviated bow. "But the rules of engagement forbid us to fire upon an enemy without positive identification. With all other communications blocked, any counterattack had to wait until my warriors could physically appear and indicate the proper targets to our backup."

"Very responsible of you," LaRone said. "The fact remains that you didn't tell us who you really were. Why not?"

"All beings have secrets," Vaantaar said. "And in truth, we were no more dishonest with you than you were with us."

LaRone felt his throat tighten. "Meaning?"

"Meaning you are deserters," Vaantaar said bluntly. "As such, you carry the death penalty from the leaders of your Empire."

"Only if we're caught," LaRone said through clenched teeth. If he reset his E-11 for stun, and fired fast enough to drop Vaantaar and the others . . .

"You have already been caught," Vaantaar said. "I know. So do others." He cocked his head slightly. "So does our master."

"This master being . . ."

"The great one," Vaantaar said. "The leader of we who consider ourselves the *true* Chosen."

A shiver ran up LaRone's back. One of the yellow-eyed aliens lying dead over there had used that same term. "Does this great one have an actual name?"

"Of course," Vaantaar said. "Soon you will learn it, for he wishes greatly to meet you."

LaRone leaned his head slightly to look over Vaantaar's shoulder. The rest of the Troukree back there had spread out now, no longer in range of an easy burst shot, their weapons not quite pointed at him. "Sounds exciting," he said. "When?"

"Now."

"And if I refuse?"

Vaantaar cocked his head again. "I would prefer not to insist," he said. "Please gather the others. A vehicle is waiting to take us to the spaceport."

The *Chimaera* came through its last small turn into the battle line, and as it did so Pellaeon finally saw with his own eyes what the tactical had already shown him.

Nuso Esva's fleet filled nearly the entire bridge viewport: twenty-eight Firekilns, plus nearly a hundred of the smaller escort ships, arrayed against the *Admonitor*, the *Chimaera*, the *Sarissa*, and a handful of cruisers. Hopeless odds, by anyone's reckoning.

But at least the enemy missile ships that had been lurking on Poln

Minor were gone. He'd received that bit of good news from Commandant Barcelle only ten minutes earlier. All fifty had been destroyed, thanks to Barcelle and some timely assistance from a mysterious Major Axlon whose place in the fleet's overall chain of command Barcelle had seemed a bit hazy on.

But if Axlon's role was hazy, the effect of the missile ships' destruction on Nuso Esva had been anything but. The alien warlord hadn't said much, but it was only after Thrawn had reported the incident to him that the last four Firekilns and their escorts had finally jumped in from hyperspace.

Nuso Esva meant to destroy the Imperial ships. That much was abundantly clear.

What *wasn't* clear was why Thrawn continued to taunt him about it.

"Twenty-eight Firekilns against two Star Destroyers," the senior captain commented as the final group began to deploy to their spots in the battle line. "Are you so frightened of me, Nuso Esva?"

"I fear nothing," Nuso Esva ground out. "You may hide behind your Imperial underlings if you wish, aboard that freighter, and allow them to die before you. But you *will* die. And when you are dead, I will batter the worlds below you into rubble."

Pellaeon winced as Nuso Esva launched into a detailed description of what exactly that battering would consist of. He wasn't bluffing, either, Pellaeon knew. There were a handful of other ships in Governor Ferrouz's sector fleet, but they were old and weak and even if Thrawn somehow got them here they would make little impact. If the Firekilns were as powerful as Nuso Esva claimed, once they'd destroyed the Imperial force, they could slag Poln Major's surface at their leisure.

Unless they *weren't* that powerful.

Was that what Thrawn was banking on? That the *Admonitor* and *Chimaera* still had surprises Nuso Esva wasn't ready for?

Then, suddenly, he understood.

The TIE fighters. Both Star Destroyers had hangar bays full of the small, deadly, starfighters.

Pellaeon smiled tightly. No wonder Thrawn hadn't wanted him to launch the TIEs to check out the Poln Minor explosion. The TIE fighters had been the key in taking down many a Rebel ship. They could do the same to Nuso Esva's arrogant Firekilns.

"Sir?" the comm officer spoke up quietly. "Something's not right here."

Pellaeon stepped back and looked down into the crew pit. "Explain."

"The *Lost Reef*'s putting way more power into his current transmission than he needs to," the officer said, pointing to one of his displays. "What's even stranger is that he's also echoing Nuso Esva's part of the conversation in the transmission, not just transmitting his own side."

Pellaeon frowned. That made no sense. Why spend power sending Nuso Esva's arrogant boasts farther than they were already going? "How far does his signal reach?"

"That's the other thing, sir," the officer said, pointing to a different display. "I'm also getting the edge of a relay. A *powerful* relay. Someone out there is taking Captain Thrawn's signal, boosting it, and kicking it out into the Unknown Regions."

"Monitor it," Pellaeon ordered. "See if you can locate that booster." Turning back to the main viewport, he tuned back in on Nuso Esva's ravings.

Apparently just in time for the end. ". . . as will all who dare oppose me," Nuso Esva finished with a verbal flourish.

"You assume the people below us are your enemies," Thrawn pointed out. "*I* am, certainly, but they may not be. The people of this sector have no particular love for the Empire. If given the chance they may choose to become your allies, as have the Stomma and Quesoth."

"Allies?" Nuso Esva made a sound that sounded like he was spitting. "*You* have allies, Thrawn. All to me except the Chosen are mere tools. They can be useful tools, or they can be broken tools."

"Interesting," Thrawn said. "I imagine the Stomma and Quesoth leadership will be interested to learn what their true positions will be should they choose to join your realm."

"I imagine in turn that you would delight in telling them," Nuso Esva said. "Not that they would believe you."

"There's no need for them to believe *me*," Thrawn said calmly. "They can hear it from your own mouth. In fact, they're hearing it right now."

For a moment, Nuso Esva was silent, and Pellaeon permitted himself a small, grim smile. So that was where the boosted signal was going. Thrawn had taunted Nuso Esva into personally sowing distrust between him and some apparently hoped-for partner species.

"Your cleverness is wasted," Nuso Esva said coldly. "Once we've dealt with you, my fleet will travel to the Stomma homeworld and I *will* once again make them useful tools. Your time is ended, Thrawn. My ships are now in their places."

"They are indeed," Thrawn agreed. "And the time is indeed ended, Nuso Esva. Signal cherek, signal esk, signal krill."

Pellaeon looked over at the comm officer. *Cherek, esk, krill*—that wasn't any Imperial code he was familiar with. It certainly wasn't a TIE fighter launch order. What in the Empire was Thrawn up to?

"Commander!" the sensor officer snapped, his voice barely recognizable. "New signals coming in from hyperspace." He looked up from the crew pit, his eyes wide. "Sir, it's—" He broke off, pointing at the viewport. Frowning, Pellaeon turned to look.

There they were, flickering with pseudomotion as they decanted from hyperspace. Coming into the Poln system in perfect synchronization, into perfect attack positions behind the wall of Firekilns.

Star Destroyers. Six of them, their names already the stuff of legend across the Empire. *Devastator. Accuser. Stalker. Adjudicator. Tyrant. Avenger.*

And in the center of the formation the pride of the entire fleet. The massive bulk of the Super Star Destroyer *Executor*.

It was the Death Squadron.

It was Lord Darth Vader.

"Senior Captain Thrawn," the Dark Lord's voice boomed over the speaker. "Are these the enemies of the Empire you spoke of?"

"They are, Lord Vader," Thrawn confirmed.

"And you wish them destroyed?"

"I've offered the possibility of a treaty between us," Thrawn said. "That offer has been repeatedly refused."

"Then it would seem there is nothing more to be said," Vader concluded.

"Agreed, my lord," Thrawn said. "I am currently detached from my ship. I would consider it an honor if you would personally assume command of the *Admonitor* for the purposes of this battle."

Pellaeon cleared his throat. "The *Chimaera* also stands ready to receive your orders, my lord," he called.

"Then let us make an end of it," Vader said. "All ships: engage at will."

The distant battle was at the height of its fury when Leia finally got the word that the transports were ready to go. "Good," she said. "All captains: you're cleared to launch. We'll meet at the rendezvous point. Good luck."

She got a chorus of acknowledgments. "What about the others?" Cracken asked as their transport lurched off the ground and started to move down the wide conveyance tunnel.

"I'm on it," Leia said as she rekeyed the comm. "Han? Luke? We're almost clear. Wherever you are, get out of there."

"Getting out now," Luke said, the comm tag showing he was calling from his Z-95 Headhunter. "Listen, you'll never believe—"

"Save it for the debriefing, Skywalker," Cracken put in. "Solo? You there? Solo?"

"Yeah, I'm here," Han said. "We'll be along in a minute."

"What are you waiting for?" Leia asked, frowning.

"I thought we'd stick around the Golan and watch the battle a little longer," Han said. "You don't get a view like this very often."

Leia felt her eyes narrow. Was he *serious*?

Of course he was serious. He was Han. "Han—"

"I also thought we should stay here until you're *completely* clear, not just almost clear," he added. "Just because we ran the Golan dry of torpedoes doesn't mean someone won't notice you and ask Commandant Barcelle to figure out something else to do about it."

Leia glared at the speaker, feeling the familiar sensation of having had the ground cut out from under her. Why did he *do* that? "Fine," she said between clenched teeth. "Just make sure you *do* get out."

She slapped her hand across the comm control, shutting off the mike. "No doubt about it," Cracken murmured.

"No doubt about *what?*" Leia demanded.

"The man's got a future with the Rebellion," Cracken said, carefully keeping his eyes forward. "Not sure what kind. But he's definitely got a future."

The fire was still burning as Mara helped Ferrouz's wife and daughter down the stairs. She kept a close eye on the men still huddled against the far wall, but they'd finally had enough for one day. Possibly for one lifetime.

Some of them, she mused, might come out of this experience ready to make changes in their lives. The rest would die someday, probably violently.

But it would be by someone else's hand. Right now, Mara had more important things to do.

"Are we going home?" the little girl asked uncertainly, looking up from Mara's side.

"Yes," Mara assured her, looking at the ore car as they passed it. There was no sign of Skywalker, alive or dead. Hopefully, LaRone had gotten him out before he picked up any serious burns or other injuries.

Skywalker.

She frowned, wondering again if the kid could possibly be the same Skywalker that Lord Vader was searching for. On the face of it, the odds of such a coincidence were vanishingly small. But in this crazy universe, with the Force subtly guiding all life, one could never be sure.

Just the same, she decided, she probably shouldn't mention it to Vader. Just in case.

"And my daddy?" the girl asked. "Will he be okay?"

Mara felt her throat tighten. She'd been sent to Poln Major to investigate possible treason. And she'd determined beyond any doubt that Ferrouz had indeed committed that crime.

She was the Emperor's Hand. She was investigator, judge, and executioner.

Sometimes, she reflected, it was good to be a law unto herself.

"Yes," she told the girl. "He'll be just fine."

The ship Vaantaar led them to was tucked away in one of the darker, more out-of-the-way docking bays. It was a style LaRone hadn't seen before: thirty meters long, sloping wings with long grooves running along them, crosshatched cockpit canopy, large sublight nozzles, and a tall dorsal fin that seemed to be home to vertically racked laser cannons. "Nice ship," he commented.

"We are pleased by it," Vaantaar said. "Come—our master awaits."

LaRone looked behind him. Marcross and Brightwater were standing silently between a pair of Troukree, their faces giving nothing away. Behind them, two more Troukree carried Quiller, his injured leg stretched out awkwardly in front of him, while six more lugged Grave, still in his sloshing bacta tank. Even if the Troukree hadn't been armed, there would have been no way for them to make a break for it. At least, not together. "You never told us what your master wants with us," he said.

"You have left the Empire," Vaantaar said.

"It was the Empire that left us," Marcross corrected.

"Even better," Vaantaar said, half turning to look at him. "Our master offers you the chance to even the scales."

"How?" LaRone asked.

Vaantaar smiled, his white-rimmed eyes glistening. "Come and see."

CHAPTER TWENTY-THREE

Car'das had seen Darth Vader on occasion, back in the days when his smuggling organization was supplying Palpatine's freshly minted Empire with data. But he'd never seen the Dark Lord this close.

And he'd *definitely* never seen him this angry.

"That was the agreement, Senior Captain," Vader ground out, leveling a finger at Thrawn across Governor Ferrouz's still-battered office. "My assistance, on *your* schedule, in exchange for the Rebels. Yet they are gone." He swung the accusing finger a quarter of the way around the room to where Ferrouz sat quietly at his desk. "And *your* forces also did nothing to stop them."

"My forces were also engaged in the battle, my lord," Ferrouz reminded him. "We had no way of stopping them."

"I accept no excuses, Governor," Vader rumbled. He turned back to Thrawn. "From *anyone.*"

"I make no excuses, my lord," Thrawn assured him. "But if you'll recall, our agreement was that I would deliver the Rebel leadership. Surely you don't think they were gathered at Poln Minor."

"The leadership—" Vader broke off, looking again at Ferrouz. "There are others in the Rebel Alliance besides the leadership that I also seek," he said, his tone oddly reluctant.

"I see," Thrawn said, he forehead wrinkling. "My apologies, my lord. You said nothing of this to me beforehand."

"What does it matter?" Vader said, the momentary reluctance vanished back into his simmering anger. "They're gone."

"Information always matters," Thrawn told him. "Bad information leads to bad tactics. Incomplete information leads to flawed strategy. Both can lead to defeat." He raised his eyebrows slightly. "May I ask the name and identity of this person or persons of interest?"

"What you may do is fulfill your side of the agreement," Vader said ominously. "What you may do is deliver the Rebel command."

"Governor?" a voice asked tentatively from across the room. Car'das turned to see a young man standing in the ruined doorway, clearly wondering if he should enter the room, or perhaps whether he really wanted to. "I have the data you requested."

"Give it to Senior Captain Thrawn," Ferrouz told him.

"Yes, sir." Hurriedly, the assistant crossed the room, making a wide circle around Vader, and handed Thrawn a data card. Thrawn already had his datapad out, and as the assistant beat an equally hasty retreat he slid the card into place.

"What data is this?" Vader asked.

Thrawn didn't answer, his glowing eyes narrowed in concentration as he manipulated the datapad's controls. "It's the listing of the material Nuso Esva had me leave in the Anyat-en and Lisath-re mining complexes for the Rebel team to find," Ferrouz said.

Slowly, Vader turned to face him. "You gave them *supplies*?"

"I was so ordered, my lord," Ferrouz said. Oddly enough, or at least oddly enough to Car'das's mind, the governor seemed almost calm in the face of Vader's quiet rage. Maybe he was simply the calm, imperturbable type, like Thrawn.

More likely, it was the fact that his family was the most important thing in his life. Now that they were safe, even a Sith Lord's anger was almost inconsequential.

"Did you at least damage the equipment?" Vader countered. "Or otherwise render it useless?"

"He couldn't," Thrawn put in absently, his eyes still on the datapad. "Nuso Esva couldn't anticipate when the Emperor's Hand would arrive, nor when she would conclude her investigation and move against Governor Ferrouz. The Rebels had to be given a reason to stay long enough for that to happen."

For another few seconds Vader's empty faceplate remained fixed on Ferrouz. Then, with a muffled sound that might have been a curse, he turned away. His eyes lingered for a moment on the gaping hole across the office that had once been Ferrouz's hidden escape hatch. Then, with another huff, he turned back to Thrawn. "Well?"

Thrawn lowered the datapad. "Here's what they took, in order of loading. Cold-weather equipment and cold-weather modification kits. Critical replacement parts for a SURO-10 power generator, a KDY DSS-02 shield generator, and some Atgar P-tower laser cannon. They probably also have at least one Golan Arms DF.9 anti-infantry cannon, along with several combat-modified T-47 airspeeders and the equipment to modify more." He paused expectantly.

For a long moment Vader just stood there, facing Thrawn, his stance giving no clue as to what was going on inside that black armor. Car'das felt himself tensing . . .

"A cold world," Vader said, his voice almost shocking in its quiet calmness. Not angry, not simmering, but merely thoughtful. "Uninhabited, or nearly so. No useful resources."

Thrawn inclined his head. "I agree, my lord," he said.

"Wait a minute," Ferrouz said, sounding confused. "I understand the cold part. But how do you know it's uninhabited."

"The SURO and DSS-02 are designed to operate in the open," Vader said, his faceplate still turned to Thrawn. "On a cold world, with no cover available, they would quickly be spotted anywhere except on an uninhabited world. And any world with appreciable resources would hardly remain uninhabited."

"You know now where to look for them," Thrawn said. "And the knowledge that they'll be using Atgars, DF.9s, and T-47s will enable you to tailor your attack for quick victory."

"Yes." Vader held out his hand.

Pulling out the data card, Thrawn gave it to him. "My lord," he said, inclining his head again.

"Captain." Vader turned and nodded to Ferrouz. "Governor."

"Lord Vader," Ferrouz said, nodding back.

Vader looked briefly at Car'das, apparently decided he wasn't worth mentioning, and with a swirl of his cloak strode from the office.

Two minutes later, with Ferrouz's fervent thanks still ringing through his mind, Car'das followed Thrawn in the same direction. "I presume you'll be heading back to the *Admonitor*?" he asked as they reached the turbolifts.

"Yes," Thrawn said. "Nuso Esva's Eastern Fleet has been shattered, but he has two more of equal strength. I have to return immediately to seize our temporary advantage."

"Not to mention paying a visit to the Stomma and Quesoth," Car'das murmured. "I imagine they'll be more receptive to you now that they know the truth."

"If not, they'll have only themselves to blame for the consequences," Thrawn said. "What about you?"

Car'das grimaced. What about him? "I don't know," he confessed. "There's still one possibility, way out by the Kathol Rift, that I've been told might let me put my life back together. But I don't know."

"Whether it can be done?" Thrawn asked quietly. "Or whether you want to try?"

Car'das snorted. "I never could fool you, could I?"

"Not often."

The turbolift car came, and they stepped inside. "While you're considering whether or not your life still has purpose," Thrawn continued as the car started down, "there's one more job I would very much like you to do for me. Commander Pellaeon's report said that after Nuso Esva came aboard the *Chimaera* he made a short visit to a planet called Wroona."

"Plus a longer one to a place they still haven't identified," Car'das said, nodding. "Yes, I read the report."

"The unknown world is of no lasting importance," Thrawn said. "That would have been the place Nuso Esva chose to meet with his commanders and finalize his plans for the operation. But the other one, Wroona, is where I believe Nuso Esva's agents are holding Sorro's family hostage. Possibly his entire town, considering the legend the *Salaban's Hope* was named for. My hope is that Sorro's family may still be alive and can be freed."

Car'das felt his stomach tighten. "By me."

"There's no one else who can do the job," Thrawn said. "The *Lost Reef* has the weaponry, and I'm sure you have the necessary contacts to locate them." He eyed Car'das closely. "The question is whether you have the will."

The door opened, and they headed across the palace's main floor. Car'das watched the other employees as they walked past, noting the wondering looks and furtive glances.

But no one stopped them. They reached the door, passed between the pair of 501st Legion stormtroopers standing guard there, and headed outside.

Car'das thought one of the stormtroopers nodded to Thrawn as they passed. But it might have been his imagination.

They were halfway to the outer wall before Car'das made up his mind. "I suppose it wouldn't hurt to at least take a look," he said. "There's an arms dealer named Ba'Seet on Wroona—probably where Nuso Esva got the thermal detonators he used against the *Chimaera*. I could start there."

"Thank you," Thrawn said, inclining his head. "I'm certain Sorro would have appreciated it, too, had he lived."

"Yes." Car'das looked sideways at Thrawn. "By the way, I noticed you didn't mention to Vader that you were the one who ordered the Caldorf VII missiles taken off the *Sarissa* and sent to Poln Minor where Nuso Esva's people could grab them."

Thrawn shrugged. "Merely following Nuso Esva's own philosophy. He wanted the Rebels to be so heavily invested in their newfound material wealth that they couldn't quickly or easily extricate themselves. I wanted Nuso Esva to have the same incentive, to assure he would bring in his entire available force."

"Could have been awkward if those ships had gotten out intact," Car'das pointed out.

"I was counting on the Rebels to destroy them," Thrawn said. "I admit they did the job more inventively than expected, but the result was the same."

"Really," Car'das said, looking closely at him. "Sounds like you're feeling more charitable against the Rebellion these days."

"Not at all," Thrawn said, his tone going grim. "Their military abilities are undeniable, but their chances for long-term stability are nonexistent. Multiple species, with multiple viewpoints and racial philosophies, simply cannot hold power together for long. The dominant voice must certainly be wise enough to adopt ideas and methods from its allies and member peoples. But there must *be* a dominant voice, or there is only chaos. In this part of the galaxy, that voice is the Empire."

"And in your part of space?" Car'das asked.

Thrawn shrugged slightly. "A work in progress," he said. "But we will succeed." His throat tightened. "I've seen the future, Jorj. We will succeed, because we have no other choice."

Mara waited in the Suwantek for two days before she regretfully concluded that LaRone and the others weren't coming back.

What had happened to them was still a mystery. She'd made inquires and checked all the Imperial databases, both the official and the not-so-official ones. But there was no sign of them.

Had the 501st caught them after the battle, when Vader sent them down to handle security while Ferrouz and Ularno sorted out which of their people could be trusted? But Vader was a stickler for proper procedure, at least among his subordinates, and *someone* should have filed a report somewhere. Major Pakrie, then, or some of Nuso Esva's other agents? But Pakrie was in hiding, and from the tapcaf body count it seemed highly unlikely there were any of Nuso Esva's fellow aliens left to make trouble. Even if there were, and even if they'd managed to kill the stormtroopers, there was no reason for them to hide or dispose of the bodies.

Mara had no idea how it had happened. But the fact was that they were gone.

And so it was, at the end of the second day, that she found herself sitting in the Suwantek's pilot's seat, gazing moodily out at the spaceport beyond.

Missing them.

It was a new sensation, she thought, to miss someone. The only true constants she'd ever had in her life had been the Emperor and a handful of people like Vader. Vader she could take or leave, his moods permitting him to be an occasional ally but little more. The others of the court or fleet were the same.

As for the Emperor, he was available anytime she needed him, just the stretch of her mind away. She could hardly miss someone who was always there.

She didn't like missing LaRone and the others. It felt weak and vulnerable, and she didn't like it at all.

But she missed them just the same.

And what made it all the worse was the hard and bitter knowledge that whatever had happened to them had happened because of her. She was the one who'd ordered them here, and had then left them to stand alone against Nuso Esva's agents while she went after the governor's family. If she hadn't done that . . .

She sighed. If she hadn't done that, who could tell what might have happened? Ferrouz's family would probably be dead. The stormtroopers might still be dead.

Mara herself might be dead.

My child?

Mara closed her eyes and stretched out to the Force. *My lord,* she called back.

Is all well?

Mara hesitated, suddenly wanting very badly to tell him of her loss, to feel his strength and to be comforted.

But he was the Emperor. His responsibilities spanned a galaxy. He had no time for the softness of emotion or sorrow.

And she was the Emperor's Hand. Neither did she.

All is well, my lord, she told him. *Governor Ferrouz has been cleared.*

Excellent, the Emperor said. *Return to Imperial Center.*

Yes, my lord, Mara said.

The connection was broken. With a sigh, Mara keyed the panel for engine start-up. She would take the Suwantek out to where they'd left her shuttle, she decided, take it in tow, and head back to Imperial Center. There, she would return the Suwantek to its rightful owners in the ISB.

Or maybe she wouldn't. The ISB didn't know she had it, after all. Maybe she would instead stash it away somewhere in an out-of-the-way system, just in case she ended up needing it someday.

Or in case, somehow, LaRone and the others came back.

The odds were small, she knew. But in this crazy universe, one could never be sure.

Grave's injuries had been severe, and interrupting his bacta treatment hadn't helped matters any.

Fortunately, their current home's medical facilities were far better than the subminiature tank Chewbacca had lugged across Whitestone City from the Suwantek. Grave was out of the tank, dressed, and comparing scars with Quiller when Vaantaar arrived with the news that his master was ready to see them.

Given the name of the ship, and the crewers LaRone had seen during their three days aboard, he wasn't really surprised to learn who that master was.

"Welcome aboard the *Admonitor*," Senior Captain Thrawn greeted them gravely as the stormtroopers filed into his command office. "I'm told your injuries have been successfully treated."

"Very well treated, sir, thank you," LaRone assured him.

"But your curiosity remains," Thrawn continued. "It's very simple, Squad Commander LaRone. I brought you here because Vaantaar tells me you're excellent stormtroopers. I want you in my command."

LaRone felt his mouth go dry. It was a very flattering offer, especially coming from a commander who had so deftly turned certain defeat into a resounding victory.

But if Thrawn put in the request through the proper channels, there would be alarms going off all over Imperial Center. And the minute the ISB got wind of it . . .

Marcross was obviously thinking the same thing. "We appreciate the offer, Captain," he said. "But there are a few problems with our situation that you may not be aware of. Our current position in the fleet—"

"Is that you have no position," Thrawn finished. "Technically, you're deserters. One of you—" His glowing red eyes shifted back to LaRone. "—is technically a murderer."

And with that, LaRone knew, it was finally over. They'd gotten past Jade, and they'd even gotten past Vader.

But now they were caught. And in some ways, it was almost a relief. "It was self-defense, sir," he said, though he wasn't sure why he was even bothering to try. The ISB wouldn't care what the circumstances had been. "As to the desertion, I forced the others to go along with me."

Thrawn raised an eyebrow. "Vaantaar?"

"I spoke to you of their loyalty to one another," the Troukree said. "This is but one more example."

"Indeed," Thrawn said. "But as you may recall, Squad Commander, I said you were only *technically* a murderer and deserter. I've seen the various reports, plus a quiet inquiry that was done by the Emperor's Hand, and I believe I understand what happened."

LaRone looked at Vaantaar in sudden understanding. "Is that why you had Vaantaar kidnap us? So that you could keep all of this off the record?"

"Exactly," Thrawn said, sounding pleased. "You did excellent work on Poln Major. All of you did."

"For whatever good it did," LaRone said ruefully. "From what I saw in the ship's after-action reports, the only reason Nuso Esva wanted to kill Ferrouz was to get you over to the Poln system so he could spring his trap. But the palace went ahead and issued the directive anyway."

"Which I was happy to comply with," Thrawn said. "As for what you accomplished, you helped save the life of a good and valuable man, along with the lives of his family."

"At the cost of another being's life," Brightwater murmured, looking at Vaantaar.

"Which he was more than willing to give," Vaantaar said gravely. "As were we all."

"Beyond that, though, you need to understand the full scope of Nuso Esva's plan," Thrawn continued. "If Governor Ferrouz had been murdered on schedule, his Poln Major squad and their Whisperlike fighter would have been on Poln Minor when the full nest of missile-armed ships were launched. Their presence at the crucial moment might have saved some or all of those ships from destruction. But because you first delayed and then destroyed that particular squad, the other Whisperlikes were in fact destroyed."

He smiled tightly. "But even more important is the fact that with the Poln Major squad destroyed, the Whisperlike you retrieved at the spaceport was abandoned and therefore could be retrieved intact by Vaantaar and his warriors. Studying it will give us vital insights into Nuso Esva's technology and warship philosophy."

"I see," LaRone said, feeling somewhat better. Maybe all their sound and fury hadn't been as useless as he'd been thinking.

"But warships are only part of the equation," Thrawn continued. "Releasing Nuso Esva's slave peoples from his grip will also require ground troops. Not just any troops, but Imperial stormtroopers."

LaRone glanced at the others. They seemed as underwhelmed by the offer as he was feeling. "Once again, we appreciate the offer, sir," he said, looking back at Thrawn. "But we've seen enough action. Possibly more than enough."

Thrawn shook his head. "You misunderstand me, Squad Commander," he said. "I don't want you to fight. I want you to train."

LaRone felt his eyes widen. "To *train*?"

"Specifically, to train people like Vaantaar," Thrawn said, gesturing to the Troukree. "Their world has suffered greatly under Nuso Esva's domination, and the few who escaped have been strong and able allies. That was why I chose them to go to Poln Major in the guise of refugees, to watch and report on the movements and activities of Nuso Esva's agents.

"But while they are excellent soldiers, they and I both agree that they can become better. They can become true Imperial stormtroopers."

The image of the Troukree's sacrifice in the tapcaf cellar floated back to LaRone's mind. "I have no doubt of that, sir," he said. "But surely the *Admonitor* already has its share of capable stormtroopers."

"So it does," Thrawn said. "What it doesn't have is capable stormtroopers who can deal honestly and enthusiastically with the idea of aliens joining their ranks."

And suddenly, it all made sense. LaRone looked at the others again, then turned to Vaantaar. "This is something you want?"

"We do," the Troukree said firmly. "The Empire that Senior Captain Thrawn is carving into the evil that pervades our worlds is not the Empire you chose to leave. His is an Empire of justice and dignity for all beings. His Empire is one we gladly serve." He looked at Thrawn. "One we are willing to die for."

"The choice is of course yours," Thrawn said. "We're still three days from my base. Think on it and discuss it. I will await your decision."

They were following Vaantaar back toward their quarters when Grave broke the thoughtful silence. "I think we should name the new unit the Five-oh-First," he said.

"I thought Vader had that one locked down," Quiller pointed out.

"I somehow doubt Vader will ever know," Grave said. "I'm sure not going to tell him."

"Wise choice," Marcross said. "Any particular reason you want that unit number?"

Grave shrugged. "They're supposed to be the best. If we're going to take this job, we might as well aim high."

"*If* we take the job," LaRone said.

"I don't think we've got a choice," Quiller said soberly. "You read the reports, LaRone—you saw how Nuso Esva operates. Kidnapping children, suborning Imperial officers, threatening to slag entire planets. The guy has to be stopped."

"And if people like Vaantaar are going to fight him anyway, someone has to make sure they're the best fighters they can be," Marcross agreed. "That someone might as well be us."

"Hence, the new Five-oh-First," Grave concluded. "Like I already said."

LaRone looked over at Brightwater. The other was staring at the deck beneath them, his forehead wrinkled with concentration or perhaps regret. "Brightwater, you're being awfully quiet," LaRone said. "You having a problem with any of this?"

"Um?" Brightwater asked, his eyes refocusing on LaRone. "Oh, no, I'm good. I was just wishing we'd had a chance to see Skywalker one last time before we left."

"Skywalker?" LaRone asked, frowning. "Why?"

Brightwater waved a hand. "He's still got my lucky coin."

Rieekan was sitting behind his desk, studying a datapad, when Han arrived at his office. "Leia said you wanted to see me," he said.

"Leia said *you* wanted to see *me*," Rieekan said, laying down the data-pad. "I take it this is about the Poln mission?"

"Yes," Han said, planting himself in front of the desk. "You still want me to be an officer?"

"I've always wanted that," Rieekan said, taking Han's bluntness in typical calm stride. "Especially now." He gestured to the datapad. "I've been reading Colonel Cracken's report. He was very impressed by you, and he doesn't impress easily."

"Yeah, I know," Han said. "So okay. You want me, you've got me."

"Wonderful," Rieekan said, eyeing him closely. "Any reason in particular for this change of heart? Aside from your irritation at being left out of all the fun meetings?"

"You told me leadership brings responsibility," Han reminded him. "It's looking like I'm getting loaded with the responsibility anyway. I might as well get the stupid rank bars, too."

"Okay," Rieekan said. "I'll get the datawork started right away." He held out his hand. "Congratulations, Lieutenant Solo."

Chewie was waiting by the *Falcon*, the ship's torn-apart swivel blaster cannon on the deck at his feet, when Han got back to the hangar. "We're in," Han confirmed, peering up into the cannon's now-empty compartment. "Go ahead and put in for the upgrade. I can sign for it now."

The Wookiee warbled a question.

"I don't know," Han said, nudging the blackened pieces of the old cannon with his toe. "Something by BlasTech—I've always liked their stuff. Maybe a Ground Buzzer, either the Ax-108 or III. Just make sure you get something that isn't going to overheat and burn out the couplings every fifty shots."

A movement from across the hangar caught his eye. He looked up to see Leia walking toward the rows of X-wings, Luke and Wedge with her, both of them smiling as she waved her hands in emphasis to whatever it was she was telling them.

Beside Han, Chewie rumbled.

"Absolutely," Han agreed, watching as the others disappeared behind one of the other ships. "Come on, let's get back to work."

ABOUT THE AUTHOR

Since 1978 TIMOTHY ZAHN has written nearly seventy short stories and novelettes, numerous novels, and three short fiction collections, and won the Hugo Award for best novella. Zahn is best known for his *Star Wars* novels: *Heir to the Empire, Dark Force Rising, The Last Command, Specter of the Past, Vision of the Future, Survivor's Quest, Outbound Flight,* and *Allegiance,* and has more than four million copies of his books in print. His most recent publications have been the science fiction Cobra series and the six-part young adult series Dragonback. Zahn has a B.S. in physics from Michigan State University, and an M.S. in physics from the University of Illinois. He lives with his family on the Oregon coast.

Read on for an excerpt from
Star Wars®
RIPTIDE
by
Paul S. Kemp
The follow-up to *New York Times* bestseller
Star Wars: Crosscurrent
In stores Fall 2011

J ADEN FOUND HIMSELF ON HIS KNEES, THE ROOM SPINNING. BLOOD
leaked from his right temple, spattered the floor in little crimson circles. More blood oozed from the stumps of his fingers. Pain blurred his vision, clouded his thinking. The short, rapid shrieks of an alarm blared in
his ears, rising and falling in time with the dim flashes of overhead backup
lights. Strange lights. Like little starbursts buried deep in the green resin of
the ceiling. A haze of black smoke congealed near the ceiling and darkened air that stank of melted plastoid, rubber, and ozone. He thought he
caught the faint stink of decaying flesh but could not be sure.

Gingerly he placed his unwounded hand to his right temple, felt the
warm, sticky blood, the small hole there. The blood was fresh; the wound
recent.

The rapid flashes of the lights made his movements seem herky-jerky,
not his own, the stop-starts of a marionette in unpracticed hands. His body
ached. He felt as if he'd been beaten. The stumps of the fingers he'd lost
on the frozen moon throbbed, the wounds somehow reopened and seeping pus. His skull felt as if someone had driven a nail through it.

And he had no idea where he was.

He thought he felt eyes on him. He looked around the dark corridor, his eyes unable to focus. He saw no one. The floor vibrated under him, as if coursing with power, the rale of enormous lungs. He found the feeling disquieting. Filaments dangled like entrails from irregular gashes torn in the walls. Black scorch marks bordered the gashes. A control panel, a dark rectangle, hung loose from an aperture in the wall, as if blown out by a power surge.

He found it difficult to focus for long on anything before his field of vision started to spin. His bleary eyes watered from the smoke. The flashing lights and the wail of the siren disoriented him, would not let him gather his thoughts.

The pain in his head simply would not relent. He wanted to scream, to dig his fingers into his brain and root out the agony. He'd never felt anything like it.

What had happened to him?

He could not remember. Worse, he could not think clearly.

And then he felt it: the faint tang of dark-side energy. Its taint suffused the air, greasy on his skin, angry, evil. He swallowed down a dry throat.

Had he been attacked by a Sith?

With an effort of will, he pushed the touch of the dark side away from his core, held it at arm's length. Having an enemy gave him focus. He steeled himself against the pain in his head and stood on weak legs. Each beat of his heart felt like a hammer blow to his skull. Pound. Pound.

He tried to hold his ground but the room began to spin more rapidly, the alarm loud in his ears, the floor growling under him, the ringing, spinning, whirling. He wobbled, swayed. Nausea pushed bile into the back of his throat.

Without warning, the pain in his temple spiked, a white-hot flash of agony that summoned a prolonged scream. His wail rebounded off the walls, carried off into the darkness, and with the scream as a sound track, a flood of memories and images streamed across his consciousness, rapid flashes of colors, faces, a series of half-remembered or half-imagined things. He was unable to focus for long on any of the images, unable to slow them down; they blazed in and out of his awareness like sparks, flashing for a moment, then gone, leaving only a shadowy afterimage.

He squeezed his eyes shut and clamped his mouth closed to cut off the scream. The pain would not stop. His head was going to explode, surely it was going to burst.

He was teetering, his head pounding, his stomach in his throat, his eyes watering.

Unable to keep his feet, he sagged back to the floor. The spinning began to subside. The pain, too, began to fade. He sagged with relief. He would not have been able to bear much more.

Clarity replaced pain, and as his head cleared, images and events refitted themselves into the jigsaw puzzle of his memory, reconstituted him from their fragments. He sank into the Force, found comfort there. He closed his eyes for a time and when he opened them, he looked about with what felt like new eyes.

He sat in the middle of a wide corridor. The dim, intermittent flashes of the strange overhead lights showed little detail. The walls, ceilings, and floors were composed of a substance he'd never seen before, light green, semitranslucent. At first he thought it was some form of plastoid, or hued transparisteel, but no, it was a resin of some kind. For the first time, he realized that the floor was not merely vibrating under him, it was warm, like flesh. Faint lines of light glowed deep within it, barely visible, capillaries of luminescence. The arrangement looked ordered, a matrix of some kind, and the pattern of their flashes was not random, though he could not look at it long without its flashes disorienting him.

He tried to make sense of what he was seeing. The architecture, the technology it implied. . . .

Where was he?

A word leapt to the forefront of his mind, a flash that came and went without explanation.

Rakatan.

He leaned forward, trying to remember, feeling as if he were on the verge of some revelation. He tried to pull the word back, to force it to take on meaning and make sense, but it eluded him.

"Rakatan," he said, and the word sounded strange on his lips. Saying it aloud triggered no more memories.

But more and more memories were clicking into place, connecting names, events, and faces, the backstory of his life being told just below the level of his consciousness. He must have been hit on the head, hit hard. Understanding would come eventually, or so he hoped.

Yet he knew he could not sit still and wait for it. The dark side was all around him. Palpable anger polluted the air, pressed against him. Alarms were wailing. The vibrations in the floor rose and fell like lungs, lurching, not so much like ordinary breathing as a death rale. He had to get away from wherever he was.

An explosion rumbled somewhere in the distance and everything shook.

He was in a ship then, or a station of some kind. He looked for a viewport but saw none.

He crawled over to the wall and used it to help himself stand. The pain in the stumps of his fingers caused him to wince. The smooth surface of the wall pulsed faintly under his touch and he had the sudden, uncomfortable fear that he had awakened in the belly of some nameless pseudomechanical beast, that he'd been swallowed and was now being slowly digested.

Licking his lips, he stood away from the wall. His wounded fingers had left bloody smears on the smooth green surface.

The comforting weight of his lightsaber hung from his belt and he put his hand on its cool hilt. He had made it. . . .

Where had he made it?

On a ship. On *Junker*. He'd made it on *Junker*.

He remembered giving his other blade, the one he'd made as a boy on Coruscant, to Marr.

To Marr.

A face flashed in his memory: tan, weathered, a ruff of hair haloing a towering forehead. The face of a Cerean. Marr.

"Marr?" he called over the sirens, his raw voice bouncing down the corridor. In his mind's eye he saw a lazy eye, a malformed asymmetrical face, and a ready smile, and a name accompanied the image. "Khedryn?"

No response.

He was alone.

He took a moment to evaluate his physical condition, examining his limbs, chest, abdomen. Other than the reopened wounds on his hand and the small hole in his head, he'd suffered no serious visible harm. He had been in a fight, though. His cheek felt sore to the touch; his ribs and his arms had several bruises, as if from blocking blows.

He took inventory of his gear, sifting through pockets, the cases on his belt—nutrition bars, extra power packs for his blaster, liquid rope, a glow lamp. No medpack, though.

He took the glow lamp in his wounded hand and activated it. Its beam put a path of luminescence on the semitranslucent floor, down the corridor. The hair-thin filaments in the floor seemed to glow in response, the photons communicating in a tongue he could not comprehend. He fell in behind the beam of his glow lamp and tried to find a way out.

He felt more himself as he moved. The corridor split repeatedly. Vertical seams in the walls opened wetly at his approach to reveal corridors and rooms beyond. Once more, he marveled at the technology.

The smoke made his eyes leak, turned his throat raw. The blinking patterns of light in the walls and floor drew him on, will-o'-the-wisps tempting him to some fate he did not understand. Distant explosions continued to rock the vessel and he staggered under their onslaught, his legs still weak.

The energy of the dark side thickened. He was closing on its source. Its power alarmed him. He leaned into it, against it, as he might against a rainstorm. He flashed on a memory of Force lightning crackling out of his fingers, energy born of fear or anger. He studied his hands, the one unwounded, the other missing three fingers, and knew that fear and anger no longer held any power over him. Force lightning was not a weapon he would use again.

Ahead he saw a large vertical seam, its size suggestive of a much larger door, a much larger chamber beyond. The lights in the floor and walls made a kaleidoscope of color around him, reds, greens, yellows, beckoning him forward, but he slowed, sensing something awful in the air, some lurking danger that lived in the darkness beyond the door. The hairs on the back of his neck rose. The lights flared more rapidly, more urgently, as if sensing his emotion. He stopped, swallowed. Sweat collected on his flesh.

His glow lamp died, then the lights in the walls and floor, leaving only the dim intermittent flashes of the overhead lights. He stood alone in the corridor, bathed in darkness, in light, in darkness, in light.

A shriek carried from the room beyond the seam and pierced the tension, a prolonged wail of hate only partially human. Its pure, unadulterated rage staggered Jaden. He took a half-step back, his hand on the hilt of his lightsaber. Adrenaline flooded him, turned his senses hyperacute.

The shriek diminished to a savage growl, but he heard the cunning in it. A huge boom sounded from within the chamber, another. Footsteps? Some kind of locomotion, surely. Whatever horror lurked in the chamber was coming toward him.

He fell into the Force and unclipped his lightsaber from his belt, the metal of the hilt cool in his sweat-slicked hand.

"Jaden," said a voice from behind him, a voice that sunk a fishhook into his memory and started reeling recollections to the surface of his consciousness.

He turned, saw furtive figures emerge from the shadows. Had they been following him? How had he missed them?

Jaden recognized them, one with his arm around the throat of the other, but his mind did not put a name to them right away.

"I know you," Jaden said.

And all at once memories flooded him. He remembered where he was, why he had come, what had happened to him. The sudden rush of memory and emotion overwhelmed him. He clutched at his head and groaned.

One of the figures held something in his off hand, a lightsaber hilt. He ignited it and a red line split the darkness.

Another shriek sounded from the chamber behind Jaden. The lights in the wall flared to life in response, brighter than before, and Jaden at last recognized them for what they were—veins coursing with dark-side energy.

He *had* awakened in the belly of a beast.

Another shriek shook the walls.

He ignited his lightsaber, its yellow light his answer to the darkness that surrounded him.